BEST
AFRICAN AMERICAN
FICTION: 2009

BEST
AFRICAN AMERICAN
FICTION: 2009

GERALD EARLY, Series Editor
E. LYNN HARRIS, Guest Editor

BANTAM BOOKS

BEST AFRICAN AMERICAN FICTION: 2009
Bantam hardcover and trade paperback editions / January 2009

Published by Bantam Dell
A Division of Random House, Inc.
New York, New York

Bantam Books and the rooster colophon are registered trademarks of Random House, Inc.

978-0-553-80689-2 (hardcover)
978-0-553-38534-2 (trade paperback)
978-0-553-90605-9 (e-book)

Printed in the United States of America
Published simultaneously in Canada

www.bantamdell.com

10 9 8 7 6 5 4 3 2 1
BVG

ᴐ⸺ CONTENTS ⸺ᴐ

STORIES

NOVEL EXCERPTS

INTRODUCTION

African Americans have a long tradition of writing fiction in the United States, which began even before the Civil War. Among the published novels were William Wells Brown's *Clotel, or the President's Daughter,* which came out in England in 1853; Frank Webb's *The Garies and Their Friends,* which appeared in 1857, also in England; Harriet E. Wilson's *Our Nig, or Sketches from the Life of a Free Black,* brought out by a Boston publishing house in 1859; and Martin R. Delany's *Blake, or the Huts of America,* which appeared serially in the *Anglo-African Magazine* in 1859. (Yes, African Americans published newspapers and magazines before the Civil War, featuring occasional pieces of fiction.) One unpublished black novel has been discovered from this period: *The Bondwoman's Narrative* by Hannah Crafts, written sometime between 1853 and 1861.

Two of the published novels were about free black life in the North, which may seem surprising since ten times as many blacks were enslaved as were free, and abolition was the main subject of concern for most antebellum black writers. But uplifting the race and defeating racism were also general concerns that would mark African American fiction for many years to come.

These early works constituted a modest, even precarious

beginning, but were nonetheless quite an achievement given the circumstances. It must be remembered that before the Civil War slave states made it a crime to teach blacks to read; and often blacks in the North had comparable difficulty acquiring an education, since various combinations of law, custom, and general public sentiment conspired against it—on occasion, violently so. So few black people would have had the ability even to read a novel, let alone write one, even a bad one. Establishing a serious black literature thus required struggling against a number of political, cultural, and social factors.

Where, moreover, was the audience for black fiction? Why would an oppressed people want or need it? And why would white people want to read a novel written by a black person, someone they believed to be socially and intellectually inferior? And if these books had no audience, why would a white publisher publish them, and how could a black publisher ever find the wherewithal to get them into print? Wasn't writing novels, even ones protesting slavery and racism, a frivolous activity? During the antebellum era and even later, many people thought of novel reading much as we now think of television watching—as a waste of time and a destroyer of the mind. More problematic still, whites commonly believed that literate blacks were more likely to cause mischief than those who couldn't read. And couldn't black fiction potentially spread ideas among the blacks that were not in the best interest of the white ruling class?

All these objections notwithstanding, over the course of American literary history African Americans tried many times to read, write, and publish their own books as a sign of cultural independence and racial entrepreneurism. In the end, the act of writing black fiction was both quixotic and heroic. It served black and white readers alike by reminding them that black people wanted to write fiction, for its own sake and because it might empower the race. And it served the nation by reminding everyone that the creation of black literature was an act of freedom. For every new possibility that blacks fulfilled, such as the utterly preposterous one of becoming fiction writers, further possibilities opened for everyone else.

The effort required, however, was surely daunting. So far as we know, none of the black writers mentioned above ever wrote a second novel. Not until after the Civil War would African American writers become sufficiently practiced in the craft of fiction writing to produce more than one novel or enough short stories to be collected in a volume. But those early writers, unpracticed and frequently unoriginal as they may have been, did much to establish a tradition of black literature. While these literary ancestors did not directly influence black writers who came later, one can appreciate them for a variety of reasons, even just for persevering to get what was in their heads on paper, at a time when society was organized to ensure that they had nothing in their heads and no way of putting anything on paper. For later generations filiopiety has limits but also satisfies certain necessities of the mind and heart. As the bassist Charles Mingus once put it so succinctly, "Thank god I've got roots!"

My hope for the *Best African American Fiction* series is that it will show how far African American fiction has come and, more important, how far it extends, from Paul Laurence Dunbar and Charles W. Chesnutt to Jessie Fauset and Nella Larsen, from Langston Hughes and Wallace Thurman to Zora Neale Hurston and Richard Wright, from James Baldwin and Ralph Ellison to John A. Williams and Ann Petry, from Toni Morrison and Alice Walker to John Edgar Wideman and Charles Johnson, from Chester Himes to Virginia Hamilton—and then on to the remarkable writers showcased in these volumes. Writers may not be influenced by all of their ancestors, literary or otherwise, but they may find it useful to remember them, if only to pick and choose their influences.

This annual series of African American fiction is meant to showcase both short stories and excerpts from novels, authored by both well-known writers and new names on the scene. The first volume in the series features adult fiction as well as several pieces of fiction written for adolescent or young adult audiences. My feeling is that this sort of writing gets neglected, as if it were a lesser endeavor than writing for adults. My motto for this new series is that good fiction writing is good fiction writing, no matter the audience for which it is intended.

Each volume will highlight the work of a particular year: this volume focuses on literature published in 2007. It also includes a few pieces from 2006, which both the guest editor and I felt simply had to be included. Moreover, as these volumes continue, something may get overlooked, or one guest editor may value something that another guest editor does not. So including a couple of pieces from 2006 is meant to establish a precedent for future volumes, to give both the guest editors and me a bit of latitude.

The *Best African American Fiction* anthologies are intended to accomplish three goals:

1. to bring to the attention of a wide variety of readers the best fiction published by African Americans in a particular year;
2. to bring to their attention some of the lesser-known sources that feature African American fiction writing; and
3. to offer an organic, ongoing anthology wherein, from year to year, one may observe shifts and changes, trends and innovations, in African American fiction writing.

This series is not trying to define or enshrine African American fiction, to establish the magisterial anthology, the definitive canon, or the quasi-Norton edition. Rather it will attempt to offer writing that has a feeling of immediacy, of urgency, that helps us understand the way we live now. The way we read, the way we engage with literature, is all part of a process of growth and change, mutation and divergence. Over time, by showing us how literature continually redefines itself, both gradually and quickly, these volumes will offer a historical perspective, while being historical in very important ways themselves.

A point of clarification: What is an African American? This question has no obvious or even objective answer. For the purposes of these volumes, I choose a broad definition: an African American is any person of color from anywhere in the recognized African Diaspora who lives in the United States either temporarily or permanently, who writes in English, and who is published by an American-based publisher or in an American-based publication.

I wish to thank guest editor E. Lynn Harris for making most of the selections for this first volume. I added a few more to round it out. Harris is the author of a number of popular novels including *Just Too Good to Be True* (2008) and *I Say a Little Prayer* (2006). It was a pleasure to work with him. I cannot think of any current fiction writer better suited to get this series off the ground. He is, as James Baldwin once aspired to be, an honest man and a good writer.

I wish to extend gratitude and support to Keya Kraft, Jian Leng, and Barbara Liebmann for all the work they did to make this volume possible. I very much appreciate their dedication and support.

Gerald Early

Series Editor

INTRODUCTION

When I was a child growing up in Little Rock, Arkansas, I had a passion for sports, especially football. I used to love watching the older kids running around on the rock-covered vacant lots, throwing the ball, and having a good time. There finally came a point when I wanted to join them, only there was one big problem. I was small in stature and not coordinated enough to handle a ball—any ball. Even at the young age of seven, it was apparent to me that as much as I loved sports, I'd never make the team. And I didn't make the team. But my enthusiasm for football continued regardless, and I became a lifelong fan of college football. A childhood passion protected.

More important than turning me into a fan, however, not making the team led me to another adolescent love: books. With all that time and energy on my hands, I became an avid reader. It started when I was eight years old, when my mother took me to get my library card at the Little Rock Public Library on Center Street. I spent countless Saturdays at that library reading anything I could get my hands on. Sometimes hanging out there most of the day wasn't enough for me. When it came time for the library to close, I grabbed six books—the limit you were allowed to check out—to last me through the week.

Considering the time and place of my Southern upbringing, it ought to come as no surprise that most of the books I encountered were by white authors. The libraries and schools were full of books by no one else. Not for years would I discover James Baldwin's *Go Tell It on the Mountain,* the first book that truly spoke to me—it depicted a world I closely identified with. More than that, it suggested to me for the first time that I might become a writer, that my life as a young African American boy was a story worthy of being written. Up till then I had had no idea that books like that—or that authors like Baldwin—existed, and that sudden awareness was a revelation to me. I devoured everything I could find by him. If that weren't enough, Baldwin's work led me to other African American literary giants like Richard Wright and Maya Angelou. I felt a kinship with Dr. Angelou because she, like me, was an Arkansas native.

Starting out, however, I didn't really care who a book's author was or what he or she looked like. No matter who wrote them, books held the power to carry me off to meet people and visit places outside my shotgun house and my hometown. Books fed my imagination in a way that movies and television never quite did. They became my refuge. I think this is fairly common among African American authors. Some of our best writers—from Phillis Wheatley and Frederick Douglass to Langston Hughes and Alice Walker—had a youthful passion for reading that radically changed, if not literally saved (in the case of slaves), their lives. While I can't claim that reading saved my life, books nevertheless profoundly shaped me. They made my dreams bigger. They served as my stepping-stones to becoming a novelist and to living a life born of those dreams.

I had the good fortune to burst onto the literary scene in 1994, a time when African American fiction was in vogue as never before. In the 1980s Pulitzer Prize–winning novels by Alice Walker and Toni Morrison had opened doors in the publishing industry to dozens of newcomers such as Terry McMillan and myself. Terry's blockbuster third novel *Waiting to Exhale* (1992) followed my own best-selling debut, *Invisible Life,* and together they helped to create a publishing boom in African American fiction that hasn't yet dissipated. Never again will publishing insiders be able to deny the existence of a wealth of African American writing talent and an enthusiastic audience for their work, an audience that includes but is not limited to African American readers.

In fact, so abundant is African American writing now that I have yet to read many of those published in recent years. Once I became a full-time novelist—much to my surprise—I suddenly no longer had time to keep up with the latest books. I was too busy writing and publicizing my own work, and when I wasn't doing that, I was teaching creative writing and African American literature to college students. Somehow I'd assumed all along that I'd go on reading just as I had as a kid, eating up whatever struck my fancy. But with so many books by African American writers suddenly on the market, I easily fell behind. For black authors, of course, that hasn't always been a problem. For generations so few of us were published that it was a breeze to stay abreast of the new writing. But I'm pleased to say that writers of color are now so numerous, and they are making themselves at home in so many different genres, both literary and commercial, that it's virtually impossible to stay up to speed.

Being asked to write the introduction for the inaugural volume of *Best African American Fiction* is therefore a welcome opportunity to me as a reader and an honor to me as an author. It's the perfect chance to get acquainted with some of the best new work by some of the best African American writers being published today. With this volume, whose knockout roster reads like a who's who of contemporary black fiction, it's difficult to know where to begin.

Since I've already mentioned the Pulitzer Prizes awarded to *The Color Purple* and *Beloved*, I'll start with another Pulitzer Prize–winning author, Edward P. Jones, who won it for *The Known World*, a novel that electrified readers in 2003. His story "In the Blink of God's Eye" (taken from his follow-up collection *All Aunt Hagar's Children*) evokes the author's native Washington, D.C., at the turn of the twentieth century, with a supreme craftsman's eye for historical detail. Here we meet a newly married African American couple—the descendants of slaves—attempting to reconcile the past while establishing their future as recent arrivals in the nation's capital. Mat Johnson revisits the past as well in an excerpt from his historical novel *The Great Negro Plot*. (The book's harrowing story is encapsulated nicely by its subtitle: *A Tale of Conspiracy and Murder in Eighteenth-Century New York.*) A courtroom drama that unfolds in the wake of a slave revolt (which is rumored to have actually taken place in Manhattan), it delivers all the intrigue and suspense that the subtitle promises.

I've been an admirer of ZZ Packer ever since *Drinking Coffee Elsewhere* (2003), so I was particularly excited to see her "Pita Delicious" chosen as one of this year's selections—its title comes from the hamburger and falafel joint where the narrator works. She is writing away her life with Gideon, her academic Jewish boyfriend, whose Ph.D. thesis, "Temporal Modes of Discourse and Ekphrasis in Elizabethan Poetry," mystifies not only the narrator but Gideon as well. "Pita Delicious" is simultaneously hilarious and heartbreaking. Another featured writer whose work I've enjoyed over the years is Helen Elaine Lee, and her short story "This Kind of Red" won't disappoint fans of the novels *Serpent's Gift* (1994) and *Water Marked* (2001). Never one to shy away from difficult but urgent subject matter, Lee tackles domestic violence in African American relationships with so much guts, grit, and—surprisingly—poetry that her account of one woman's incarceration following the murder of her abusive husband is a marvel to read.

One particularly refreshing element of this edition of *Best African American Fiction*—and there are many!—is that not all of its stories are set exclusively in the U.S. Indeed, just as African American life plays out beyond American borders, so too do two of my favorite selections. In fact, these stories set in foreign lands almost ask us to rethink what we define as African American writing. Nigeria is the setting of Chimamanda Ngozi Adichie's "Cell One," a fascinating look at one family's struggle to come to terms with a troubled teenaged son and sibling whose gang involvement lands him in jail, despite his protests that he's innocent. Through this intimate family drama, Adichie paints a disturbing portrait of the bigger issues of the random street violence and political corruption that threaten Nigerians from opposite ends of the social spectrum. In Tiphanie Yanique's "The Saving Work," an unnamed island in the Caribbean serves as the almost dream-like backdrop for a story of interracial tensions between two families whose biracial children meet and intend to marry despite their battling white mothers. Yanique's work was among a handful of other stories by writers in this collection new to me, which made this first encounter with her talent that much more enjoyable.

Another unexpected dimension to *Best African American Fiction* is the inclusion of young adult material. Traditionally young adult writing has been relegated to the margins of literature as somehow not sufficiently complex to command respect. I must say that books for young readers have come a long way since I was a kid, as this anthology makes abundantly clear. I've long respected Jacqueline Woodson's gifts as a distinguished young adult writer, so it was a pleasant surprise to find the excerpt from her acclaimed novel *Feathers*. Here an all-black sixth-grade schoolroom circa 1971 is disrupted by the sudden appearance of Jesus Boy, a newly arrived long-haired white student who's jokingly given this nickname owing to his supposed resemblance to Jesus Christ. Here as in so much of her young adult fiction, Woodson is well versed in speaking to young adults, not as children, but as adults who happen to be young. Walter Dean Myers's *Harlem Summer*—a fast-paced period piece for young readers, set in 1925—concerns a sixteen-year-old saxophone musician who, in the hope of playing with jazz legend Fats Waller, gets caught up in a bootlegging operation. What would life have been like for me if books like these two had been available to me back in Little Rock! As my beloved mother would say, "Young folks don't know how good they have it." Reading these excerpts, I'm incredibly heartened to think of all the African American youth who are now able to turn to books to see their lives—and those of their forebears—depicted with so much warmth, dignity, and humor.

Were there the time and space available to me, I could write at length in praise of these works and all the additional, equally outstanding stories not commented on. However, don't let that prevent you from jumping into this extraordinary collection of world-class fiction. You'll encounter many of our best and most familiar black authors publishing today, along with lesser-known but equally accomplished writers who in time are sure to join the ranks of the celebrated. Young people today don't have to wait till they discover *Go Tell It on the Mountain* in order to find inspiration as writers and readers—I hope this anthology will provide for them what Baldwin provided for me all those years ago.

E. Lynn Harris

Guest Editor
Atlanta, Georgia
May 2008

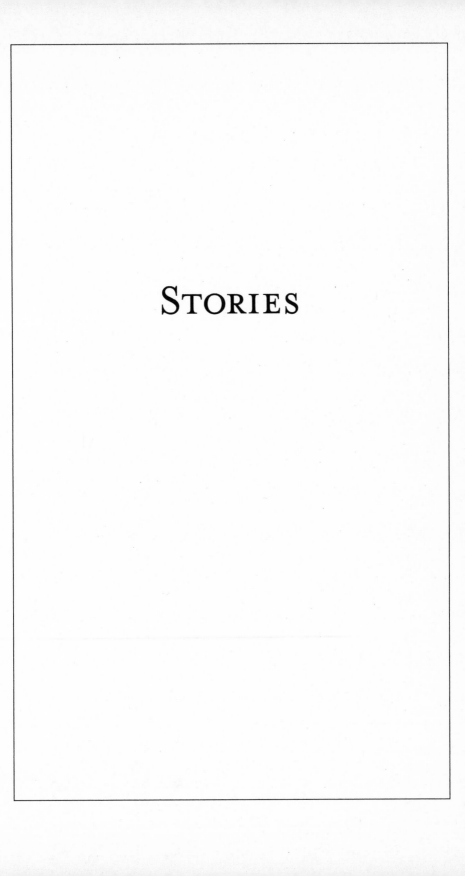

STORIES

Pita Delicious

ZZ Packer

You know what I mean? I was 19 and crazy back then. I'd met this Jewish guy with a really Jewish name: Gideon. He had hair like an Afro wig and a nervous smile that kept unfolding quickly, like origami. He was one of those white guys who had a thing for black women, but he'd apparently been too afraid to ask out anyone until he met me.

That one day, when everything went wrong, Gideon was working on his dissertation, which meant he was in cutoffs in bed with me, the fan whirring over us while he was getting political about something or other. He was always getting political, even though his Ph.D. had nothing to do with politics and was called "Temporal Modes of Discourse and Ekphrasis in Elizabethan Poetry." Even he didn't like his dissertation. He was always opening some musty book, reading for a while, then closing it and saying, "You know what's wrong with these fascist corporations?" No matter how you responded, you'd always be wrong because he'd say, "Exactly!" then go on to tell you his theory, which had nothing to do with anything you'd just said.

He was philosophizing, per usual, all worked up with nervous energy while feeding our crickets. "And you," he said, unscrewing a cricket jar, looking at the cricket but speaking to me, "you think the neoindustrial complex doesn't pertain to you, but it does, because by tacitly participating *blah blah blah* you're engaging in blah blah commodification of workers blah blah blah allowing the neo-Reaganites to blah blah blah, but you can't escape the dialectic."

His thing that summer was crickets—I don't know why. Maybe it was something about the way they formed an orchestra at night. All around our bed with the sky too hot and the torn screen windows, all you could hear were those damn crickets, moving their muscular little thighs and wings to make music. He would stick his nose out the window and smell the air. Sometimes he would go out barefoot with a flashlight and try to catch a cricket. If he was successful, he'd put it in one of those little jars—jars that once held gourmet items like tapenade and aioli. I'd never heard of these things before, but with Gideon, I'd find myself eating tapenade on fancy stale bread one night, and the next night we'd rinse out the jar, and, voila, a cricket would be living in it.

Whenever he'd come back to bed from gathering crickets, he'd try to wedge his cold, skinny body around my fetal position. "Come closer," he'd say. And I'd want to and, then again, I wouldn't want to. He always smelled different after being outside. Like a farm animal or watercress. Plus, he had tons of calluses.

Sometimes I'd stare in the mid-darkness at how white he was. If I pressed his skin, he'd bruise deep fuchsia, and you'd be able to see it even in the dark. I was very dark compared to him. He was so white, it was freaky sometimes. Other times it was kind of cool and beautiful, how his skin would glow against mine, how our bodies together looked like art.

Well, that one day—after he'd railed against the Federal Reserve Board, NAFTA, the gun lobby and the neoindustrial complex—we fed the crickets and went to bed. When I say went to bed, I mean we made love. I used to call it sex, but Gideon said I might as well call it rape. Making love was all about the mind. One time, when we were in a position that would have been beautiful art, he said, "Look at me. Really look at me." I didn't like looking at people when I did it, and when I looked at him, we locked eyes, and I must admit, it did feel different. Like we were—for a moment—part of the same picture.

———

That night we did it again. I couldn't say for sure if the condom broke or not, but it all felt weird, and Gideon said, "The whole condom-breaking-thing is a myth." But we looked at it under the light, the condom looking all dead and slimy, and finally he threw the thing across the room, where it stuck to the wall like a slug, then fell. *"Lifestyles! Who the hell buys Lifestyles?"*

"They're free at the clinic," I said. "What do you want, organic condoms?" We looked it over again, but that didn't stop it from being broke. Gideon made a look that just about sent me over the edge.

I had to think. I went in the bathroom and sat on the toilet. I'd done everything right. I hadn't gotten pregnant or done drugs or hurt anybody. I had a little life, working at Pita Delicious serving up burgers and falafel. Almost everything was awful, but the falafel wasn't half bad. It was at Pita Delicious where I first met Gideon, with his bobbing nosetip and Afro-Jewish hair. The Syrian guys who owned the place always made me go and talk to him, because they didn't like him. The first couple of times he came in, he'd tried talking to them about the Middle East, and even though he was on their side, they still hated him. "Talk to the Jew," they said whenever he came in. Soon we were eating falafel on my break, with Gideon helping me plot out how I was going to go back to school, which was just a figure of speech, because I hadn't entered school in the first place.

When I came back to bed, Gideon was splayed out on top of the blanket, slices of moonlight on his bony body. "All right," he said. "Let's get a pregnancy test."

"Don't you know anything? It's not going to work immediately."

He made a weird face and asked, "Is this the voice of experience talking?"

I looked at him. "Everyone knows," I said, trying to sound calm and condescending, "that it's your first missed period."

He mouthed the word *Okay,* real slowly, like I was the crazy one.

When my period went AWOL, I took the pregnancy test in the bathroom at Pita Delicious. I don't know why. I guess I didn't want Gideon hovering over me. I didn't even tell him when I was going to do it. One pink stripe. Negative. I should have been relieved, relieved to have my lame life back, but the surprising thing was that I wasn't. Then I did something I never thought I'd do, something unlike anything I've ever done before: It was really simple to get a pink marker and take off the plastic cover and draw another little stripe. Two stripes, the test said, means you're pregnant.

———————

When I got back home, I told him the test was positive, and flicked it into his lap: "What do you care?"

I told him that I didn't know what I was going to do—what we were going to do. He paced in front of the crickets for a while. Then he put his arm around me, like I'd just told him I had AIDS and he'd mustered the courage to give me a hug.

"What're we gonna *do?*" I asked. I don't know what I expected—whether I thought I'd catch him in a lie, or have him say something about not wanting the baby, or what—I forgot. All I knew was that something was pressing down on me, drowning me. If he'd said anything, anything at all, I would have been fine. If he'd started talking about the dialectic or about mesothelioma or aioli or how many types of cancer you could get from one little Newport menthol—I'd have been all right. Even if he cursed me out and blamed me and said he didn't want the baby—I'd have understood.

But he didn't say anything. I saw everything he was thinking, though. I saw him thinking about his parents—Sy and Rita—growing worried in their condo's sunny Sarasota kitchen; I saw him never finishing his thesis and going to work for some grubby nonprofit where everyone ate tempeh and couldn't wear leather and almost had a Ph.D.; I saw him hauling the kid around to parks, saying it was the best thing he'd ever done. Really. The best.

I walked out of that room, out of that house he rented with its really nice wood everywhere. I kept walking away, quickly at first, then so fast that the tears were the only thing to keep me from burning myself out like a comet. I wasn't running from Gideon anymore; but even if he was following me, it was too late. Even with no baby, I could see there'd be no day when I'd meet Sy and Rita, no day when I'd quit Pita Delicious before they quit me, no day when I'd hang around a table of students talking about post-post-feminism, no day when Gideon and I would lock hands in front of the house we'd just bought. Anyone could have told him it was too late for that, for us, but Gideon was Gideon, and I could hear him calling after me, hoping the way he always did that the words would do the chasing for him.

Albino Crow

Chris Abani

I am looking for an albatross.

This is no joke. This is no curse. An albatross spread like the span of a hand across the soft white sky of a woman's left buttock. It is a sign, an omen of true love. I have seen it, here in the photo I have tucked into the safety of my wallet. I reach into the soft leather fold and shake it out, wrinkled and faded even behind the soft plastic laminate. A naked woman with blonde hair, on her side, her left rump riding up, lies on tussled sheets that spread away from her in a puddle of crimson, like blood, or maybe paint. Yeah, I decide, more like paint, all clotted and textured. And there, on the side of her left rump, the one riding up in the air, is the albatross, a full hand's span on her buttock. I stare at her face, which is in the shadow of her arm; I imagine she is smiling and her eyes, green, are alive with an expression somewhere between love, lust and awe. I love this woman. I love her in ways that words cannot contain, and I wake up some nights with the ache of her in my bones and I cannot sleep. I have never met her, this woman in the photograph, but I know her like blood.

It is four a.m. in this no-man's land, a twenty-four-hour diner on the lower east side of town. I like it here, at this time, because it be-longs to that strangeness, which is not night and not light, and it is peopled not by the lost, but the purposeful. The lost wander the city aimlessly, pushing carts, begging for change, dying for the shame of others, but we are a different breed, resolute and dedicated to the annihilation of anything safe and wholesome in our lives; we spill out of bars and houses, no matter the specificities, the domicile is usually the bottom of a bottle or some other such desperation, we spill out and into this diner while the rest of the city sleeps or twitches. I say, *this* diner, but I mean, *these* diners: there are many, for we, the driven-night-walkers, are many. We aren't vampires or any such gothic crap, we are scarier than that, we are the driven earnest souls of life and we come here to wait because we believe and we have hope and we stir that heady concoction into swine-swill-coffee and mix it in with eggs over-easy and hash browns, contemplate it in the crunch of crispy bacon. We are so full of shit and therein lies all the possibility.

Returning to the photograph, I trace the outline of the woman's hip as I motion to the waitress for more coffee. I wonder what the name of this town is; I have been through so many, touring as I am with a new jazz band made up of a bunch of balding, early-retired baby boomers. Charlie, the bandleader, is the only real jazz musician among us. I should count myself too except that this is only temporary. And if keeping up with the towns is hard enough, the diners are impossible. My life in diners: forget that. I do this because I am chasing the woman in the photo, I must find her, this albatross-marked figment of my fevered dreams and desires, I live to find her and seduce her and make her love me. Make her love me in the same bone-aching way that I love her, make her love me so much that should she lose me and if, in a heart-crazed-state, she wandered into an AA meeting she would say, my name is Janis, my name is Janis and I am hooked on Clearwater. Yep, Clearwater and Janis. It was the sixties what can I say? At least she didn't name me MoonoverClearwater. That's a girl's name.

Janis left so long ago I can barely remember her, but I burn for her still, burn for her the way I have burned for no other woman and though it has been at least twenty-six years, I haven't found her yet, or again.

"Is that your wife, mister?"

I look up at the waitress and shake my head. She could be Janis,

except she is too old, and too ugly and brunette with a touch of grey.
Her eyes are narrowed from smoke and I ask her:

"Do you sell cigarettes here?"

"No," she says, though the way she shakes her head she doesn't
need to speak. "Do you have one you could spare?"

She looks at me, smiles, and then without speaking takes a packet
of American Spirits out of her apron pocket and passes me one. I
stick it in my mouth and she lights it for me. I blow smoke out lazily.

"No," I say, returning the photo to my wallet, though the question has long since passed. "No, she's my mother."

The waitress gives me an odd look, refills my coffee cup, slams
the check down a little harder than necessary and walks off. The message is clear. I pay and leave, making sure to tip her just enough to
piss her off, to make her want to chase me down the street and throw
my money back at me. I smile and step out into the night. I will find
you Janis, I say to the dark and the noise and the cars stirring up rain
with their wheels. I will.

———

This battered trumpet belonged to my father, who once had preten-
sions of being a jazz musician. I don't know how long he held onto
this dream, but I know that by the time I was ten he wasn't playing
anymore. He would sit on the roof and drink, drink and sob, holding
the trumpet like some talisman against the night, and he would finger
the notes, play whole songs without blowing into it once. I don't
know what he might have sounded like in the days when the dreams
burned intensely in him, but I know this: some of those breathless
songs he played on the roof at night, tears running down his face and
salting the alcohol on his lips, were probably the best things he ever
played. So sad when the loudest and sweetest sound your soul can
make is silence.

Even though I share this with you and even though I sit here myself in the dark, smoking and sipping whiskey that burns like penance
each time it goes down my throat, I am not mournful. I don't miss my
father, I hated that fucker and I am glad he is dead. Of course there
are those who would argue and say these outbursts are themselves
proof of love, but I say screw them.

So, this trumpet belonged to my father and I can play it. I can play the hell out of it. I play solos that bring tears of awe and frustration to the eyes of the other musicians, but although I get paid, I never take it seriously. It is just my revenge against my father. Like when he lay dying and I would play outside his door all night and keep that fucker from rest, from sleep. I made sure he died crying, sobbing his heart out, what little there was left of it. One song, "Hallelujah," played over and over, the way I'd heard Jeff Buckley sing it, live, once in that long ago before night took it all, took Jeff and everything good.

But here I am in a no-name-town by the pool of a no-name-chain-motel, in the dark because they have turned off the floodlights, playing the song that drove my father crazy, that filled his last wordless moments with a torment of sobs and incoherent cries. It is five a.m. and if I am disturbing anyone they say nothing. I can't sleep. I went from a gig to the diner and now back to the motel and this poolside, walking all the way, stopping only to buy a six-pack and a bottle of Jack Daniel's. Jack is the devil you know, the devil and god rolled into one. Ah what the heck, I am a bit of a drama queen, always have been, but then I figure I've earned it. My mother, albatross girl, left when I was seven months old for parts unknown, leaving me behind with her hate-filled husband, and her photo in his wallet. Of course like any self-respecting-but-self-loathing-because-he-never-made-it-jazz-musician my father took to alcohol and more self-loathing which he worked out on me with a belt or a piece of wood, whatever was handy, until the social workers took me away. I won't bore you with the details of my foster home arrangements and I won't say that my foster parents were terrible because they were not, or that I was shipped from home to home, because I wasn't. My foster parents were in fact good and in fact paid for me to have lessons on the battered trumpet I took from under my father's bed the night I left. That's how come I am so good.

And don't feel sad for me because I returned to my father when I was eighteen. Returned to beat the crap out of him now that I figured I was big enough, old enough. But the fucker was sick. Cancer, he said. Doctors found two lumps the size of golf balls in both lungs, he said. I should have left, but there was no one else to take care of him and though I didn't want to, he was my dad. So I stayed with him in that one bedroom apartment, he in the bedroom, me in the living

room, hardly going out, roaming it like some big cat caged and playing my trumpet, his trumpet, endlessly, until the neighbors got tired
of banging on the walls, until the landlord got tired of coming
around. Until. I stayed for the guilt and for hate, which sometimes
can be a deeper love. Stayed and hated him and played.

Just as I see the first hint of light spilling over the water in the
pool, I pack up my horn and stumble to my room. I am well and truly
drunk. I wish I had at least attempted a pass at the old waitress. I
don't want sex though; I just want to be held. I don't know what
I want.

On television the weatherman is announcing a scorcher when I
fall asleep to the soft drone of the air-conditioning. Nina Simone
singing *Here Comes the Sun* is, strangely, my last thought.

Eagle-Eye Cherry is singing some kind of poppy blues on the car
radio. I turn it up and yawn.

"How can you listen to that shit?" Charlie says and makes to turn
it down. I slap away his hand. He curses under his breath but leaves
the radio alone. Charlie is the bass player, the leader/manager of this
band I am touring with now and a sour individual, but I get to ride
with him 'cause I can't drive and no one else wants me. That happens
when you play too well. I look at Charlie and start to say something
but stuff a cigarette into my mouth instead. It is raining as I wind the
window down and blow smoke out into the wet darkness. There is
something romantic about this: the rain, the lonely stretch of road,
two silent men, music on the radio, and a car speeding through it all,
searching for the heart of something that can never exist. Doesn't
stop me from believing though. I pass the cigarette slowly to Charlie
without looking over at him. He takes it, puffs a couple of times and
hands it back. His heart isn't in it. Charlie's heart isn't in the music
either. There is no romance for him in this, no Camelot quest. This
is work, work he does to support three hard-eating kids and a wife
worn to a nag by the constant worry of money, the tiresome inven-
tiveness of cutting corners and the endless nights by herself, waiting
in the dark for a man who is never home long enough; and Charlie,
forty-five, balding and playing bad gigs, squinting through wind-

shields at night as we head for another town. That's why I'm not married. I am looking for my grail, the woman in the photo, my mother.

"Want me to drive?" I ask him. I've been sleeping for hours in the passenger seat and I am awake and ready. He shakes his head, which really means he doesn't trust me to drive the old Volvo with the worn tires and grimy windscreen. Or maybe he knows I can't drive. Maybe I told him. I yawn and stretch, fishing in the bag at my feet for a drink. I am out. I take the Big Gulp out of the cup holder between us and down some soda, Coca-Cola I think. It tastes sweet and cold and alive. I aahh and put it back.

"Hey, get your own fucking drink," Charlie snarls.

"Sure. Just pull over."

"Fuck you."

I shrug. It's been this way since the solo I played last night, my first note cutting into his solo when he was only halfway done, but he was boring the audience. I was doing him a favor, the untalented fuck. Charlie turns the radio off so hard he snaps the button off. I turn slightly and smile into the night, lighting another cigarette.

It is too cloudy to see the North Star.

The "er" of the sign, like an undecided drunk, can't make up its mind: flicker flicker. The parking lot in front of the diner is full, mostly of pick-ups and other trucks. The only thing marking it for Big Sur and not the south is that the trucks have roof racks and surf-boards instead of rifle racks.

"Why are we stopping?" I ask.

"I am hungry and I need to make a phone call," Charlie says, getting out and heading for the diner.

"Hey, why couldn't we stop when I asked?"

"My car, my stops," he says, banging into the place.

"Motherfucker," I swear as I get out and cross the lot. Somewhere in the darkness I can hear the sea. Diners, I mutter under my breath, a dime a dozen, all the same. Damn, I've run out of clichés. Anyway, everyone knows diners make the best hash browns. I slam inside and make my way to the back, waitress trailing me, grumbling about people needing to read the sign and wait to be seated. As my ass polishes two weeks of grease from the cracked vinyl booth, I want to laugh, but the waitress looks old, fifty at least, and though she has the breasts of a sixteen-year-old, I don't like disrespecting my elders.

"Coffee and some eggs and some hash browns," I say, not bothering to take the menu she's holding out to me. She writes my order with a pencil stub, and then pauses. "How would you like your eggs?" she asks, but I can tell from her voice that she couldn't care less. Neither can I.

"Over easy," I say.

When she gets back, Charlie has found his way to the table.

"What do you want?" she asks him as she pours me a coffee, reaches into her apron pocket and fishes out a handful of sweeteners and some cream in the little plastic cups. She spills them on the table in the off-handed-crap-shoot-manner I've seen drug dealers on TV use. Charlie orders the chili. I am tempted to say something about not ordering chili in an unknown diner, but I think, what the heck, the guy is a prick, so I don't. Charlie looks like he is about to cry and as I stir cream into my coffee, I say: "What's up Charlie Brown."

"Fuck you," he says, and the look he gives me tells me this is a sore point or should I say, these are sore points: whatever he is going through plus being called Charlie Brown.

"Anytime baby," I say, and blow him a kiss because I know that Charlie is pretty uptight. He makes a face but says nothing as the waitress sets his coffee down. She says nothing about our orders. I don't want to ask; I am afraid she'll spit in my food.

As we eat, a woman in a red dress sitting at the counter laughing a little too loudly catches my attention. Something about her makes me think of Janis, and I rub my wallet through my clothes, pretending to stroke her face. I would like to take out her photo and compare it to the red-dress-woman, but I don't want Charlie shitting on my dream. The photo is important, not only because it is of Janis, but also because I had to steal it from my father's wallet after he died. That was all he left me, the cheap bastard, and the trumpet of course. Like so many times before, I try to imagine where my parents met, what my father had said to my mother to make her fall in love with him, even if only for a while. I look up. Charlie is staring at me pointedly and I think it is because I am stroking my pocket, but I realize that the check has come and he wants me to pay my share. What kind of cheap fucking manager can't even buy you some hash browns and eggs? I fish for some cash in my back pocket and pay. I follow him out.

———————

Sometimes the only thing that can fill the despair of a night sky bereft of stars is the lone call of an instrument, stark against it all like a bone flayed of skin: bare. There is nothing like a cello rumbling under a railway arch in the rain to unstitch you. Or a muted trumpet; and the player feeling his way along the scales with an urgency so tight it holds him up on each note, like stones across a set of rapids, each one the death rattle of melancholy. Though I haven't said any of this aloud, Charlie turns in the dark car to look at me, his expression in the dim glow of the instrument cluster says: you are so full of shit. I look away and stare out of the window. Sometimes silence can be a heavy blow.

We pull over, the car barely balanced on the dirt edge of the cliff road that falls away into the sea. Charlie gets out to hurl again, his body shaking from the effort. I should have told him not to eat that chili, I think, chuckling under my breath as I light up: we still have a gig to play. I step from the car, feeling the night air coming off the ocean chilly against my skin. I unzip and piss into the edge between the road and night. Shaking more than I need to, I zip up, pull a half bottle of scotch from my back pocket and take a swig. Charlie joins me, reaching wordlessly for the scotch. I pass it. There are tears running down his face. What the fuck is this? I think. It's a lonely stretch of road, one of those places on the Pacific highway where the sky un-rolls from the sea and spreads itself like a meadow across the world and you feel like you are in God's fishbowl. Why did people like Charlie always have breakdowns in beautiful places like this? With strangers like me who don't really give a fuck, but who invariably have to pretend we understand, as though caught in the sensitive sub-plot of a clichéd movie? Drink, I want to say to him, take drugs, play your soul out of your fucking instrument, but don't lay your shit on me. I turn back to the night sky.

I have seen a sky like this only once before. A sempiternal sky so full of sea you feel like you are drowning. Long ago I sat in a Greyhound making my way across the Marfa plateau in Texas, headed for El Paso. It was eerie, haunting, like a place you know something other than man has walked, some higher being. All along that drive I kept hearing Leo Sayer's *Endless Flight* in my head, even though my Walkman was going full blast, spooling out Pink Floyd's *Dark Side of the Moon*. If Charlie were there, or if I told him he would say, why do you listen to that shit? Because my mother left me as a baby, I would say, even though I doubt that your mother leaving you is a credible reason for bad taste in music. The thing is, in spite of it all, in spite of everything, the profound moments of my life, if measured out like beads on a rosary, would be one pop song after the other. In the end, and apologies to Gloria Estefan and The Miami Sound Machine, the schmaltz is going to get you.

I clear my throat. Charlie takes this as a cue to speak.

"It's my wife," he says. "She's leaving me, taking the kids."

I nod. I can't figure why he is crying though. It's not like he sees them anyway. I take the bottle back before he drinks too much and pat him on the back. He smiles as though I have just said something really fucking deep and healing, and then he leans into my palm for a second too long, seeking its open warmth.

As we head off, gravel crunching under wheels like all the little hurts that eventually kill us, I know why he is suffering, how you can love someone with every breath in your body even though they are miles away and you never see them. Have never, in fact, seen them.

Jazz and pain, the perfect bromide; still hurts though. It would be easier if I could be one of those degenerate musicians. A city jazzman. But I don't believe in the jazz of cities. The brooding down-and-out kind of weed growing in allotments abutted by empty-eyed tenements drowning in piss and their own misery kind of jazz. None of that for me. I'm kind of whitey—Pat Metheny out in the endless vastness of a summer night sky and a road unwinding a slow measured beat by a sea crashing like cymbals while the fast car is the horn, lonely, sporadic, and melancholic, yet driving it all forward. That's me. I know what you are going to say, that I have no pedigree, but you lie, you lie, shame is my pedigree.

I focus on the broken white lines in the road reading them as if they were a score.

In perfect time.

It was a short gig, the audience at the Henry Miller Library clearly not keen to stay out too long. I am glad for it. This dark night, there is no moon in sight, and in the low glow of the tree lamps, the small stage in a clearing before the wooden cabin that houses the library looks forlorn. I wonder what Henry would have thought of all this: aging hippies holding early evening jazz concerts here, pretending that he actually lived here, and that somehow this made them cool. I can't help feeling self-pity. I walk the soft path to the back where there is nothing but pine trees rising in dark collaboration like the backdrop of a Hans Christian Andersen story. I wonder if there are wolves here, or ghosts. I light up and suck greedily on the cigarette. Exhaling, I lean against a tree. Somewhere in the darkness I think I hear my father laughing.

"I thought you were masturbating for a minute," a voice says, and startles me as bad as if I were. I drop my cigarette and turn to the voice. It belongs to a woman, although in the shadows that's all I can tell.

"Who the fuck are you?" I ask.

She laughs. It sounds like—I don't know, it sounds good.

"Didn't meant to scare you," she says, "Good playing tonight," she adds.

I don't speak, instead bending for the still glowing cigarette. I taste dirt when I put it back in my mouth. Dirt and time.

"My husband was a trumpet player. My ex-husband," she says. "He gave it up, though. Gave it up and sold insurance," she continues. "Say do you have another one of those cancer sticks?" she adds.

"Sure," I say, more to myself, to the night, to the sea of it, like an anchor, a comma, a placeholder, and part of me wants to make her Janis. Bullshit, I swear in my head. "I know what you mean."

"Really?" she says, pausing in lighting the cigarette. "How?"

"You seem like the kind of woman to be drawn to trumpet

players," I lie smoothly, pointing to my horn case. "Anyway," I say, moving things forward. "Why do you think he gave it up?"

"You mean other than to sell insurance?"

"Yeah."

"Because he was addicted to failure," she says, as though it was the most obvious thing in the world. "Why else?"

Why else.

"So where next?" she asks.

I concentrate on the glowing tip of her cigarette.

"Wherever the road takes me."

"Seems like your band is breaking up."

"Why do you say that?"

"I heard the bass player canceling the rest of your gigs. He was crying."

"Shit. His wife is leaving him."

"Yeah, well. Happens."

"I have to go on, though."

"A one man band?"

"No. I'll join another."

"My, you're driven," she said.

I shrug.

"Are you looking for something?"

"How do you mean?"

"Aren't all jazz musicians in search of the perfect solo?"

"That's some bullshit. But I am searching for something I guess. A lost love, maybe," I say, shrugging in the dark.

"Really? Who?" she asks, and steps forward, her face caught in a sliver of light coming from out front somewhere. Her face is not all at all what I suspect Janis will look like. Her skin is lined, her lips too full, collagen full, and her nose big, Gaelic big; and her eyes, well, they aren't green but black, like nothing. But sometimes melancholy will fuck with you and I am beginning to wonder if this can be Janis. I step back. She laughs and my knees turn to jelly.

"I won't bite. At least not yet," she says, her finger tracing a line down my cheek.

I swallow, loudly.

"So who are you looking for?"

"I don't know," I lie. "I just know that she has a white albatross tattooed on her butt," I say.

"White albatross. That's strange. I have a tattoo too, a strange one. Guess."

"I have no idea."

"An albino crow."

"That's unusual," I say, and my voice sounds as if I am talking with socks in my mouth. "Where is it?"

"You sound parched. Should we go get a drink?" she asks, already turning away. "I'll might tell you later. Let's see what old Johnny Walker thinks."

"Sure."

I begin to follow, but she stops and turns.

"I guess we should introduce ourselves formally," she says. "I know your name."

For a second I think she is onto me. A mother should know her son, right? Instinctively. Even after all this time. But then I realize she is referring to my professional name.

"I'm Janis," she says, putting out her hand to shake. "And don't give me any shit about my name, *Miles.*"

"Of course not," I mumble, feeling like a cretin. It is all so confusing and unsettling. To meet your mother for the first time in the shadows of a pine forest up the side of Big Sur and to plan her seduction in the dark. It's all a little much.

"Janis," I say, and think *mother*, shuddering as our hands touch.

"Boy, you're eager," she says, as she feels me shudder. "Patience. If you are a good boy, I'll show you my tattoo."

"Yes, ma'am," I say.

"Call me Janis. I'm not your mother," she says.

"Janis," I say, and think, *mother.*

"See?" she says. "Sounds good when you say it. Sensual."

I smile, unaccountably happy, but naturally so.

"You don't even know me. Isn't it dangerous picking up strange men in dark woods? Many a cautionary tale about that, I think."

Janis shrugs.

"I've never been one for caution."

I nod though she can't see me in the dark.

"Can I ask you something?"

"Sure. I might not answer it though."

"Do I seem familiar to you?"

She turns to look at me, black eyes piercing. I shift uncomfortably under her gaze.

"What an odd question," she says, finally. Then: "I can only assume you are asking whether I am drawn to you because you remind me of my ex-husband. The trumpet and all." Pause. "Look, let's have a drink, have some fun. For now, I am just Janis and you are Miles."

I nod.

"You like older women?"

"Yes."

"Then say it, say my name," she says, breathing a little harder.

"Janis," I say, and think, *Janis.*

She laughs, softly, back in her throat, and takes my hand.

Orb Weaver

Emily Raboteau

A woman reclined in a yellow Adirondack chair with a back like a tongue depressor, watching the sun go down over the Vermont mountains. Summer was almost done. She looked out across the fields washed in orange light and saw herself in the third person, looking out across the fields washed in orange light. She tried to think of a way to describe the sound of the insects. The writer approached her from the side. She spotted him in her periphery and straightened her posture. Her heart quickened. She had been willing this moment, writing it out in her mind already, so it didn't come as a surprise when he asked her if she'd seen the creek.

She tried to think of a witty way to say no.

—No.

—Let's go, he said, handing her a peach. She bit into the fruit. It was mealy but because she liked the idea of the writer watching her eat it she pretended it was ripe. She wondered with sweet unease if her mouth would taste of peaches, if he had been with a black woman before, if she would appear in one of his stories.

They were at a writing conference in a former ski lodge. Each day was apportioned into a rigid schedule of workshops and readings and master classes on craft. In attendance were famous writers, less famous writers and people who aspired to be writers—people who had paid handsomely to be in the midst of writers. These people wanted to be published with a sickening desperation, and sometimes, when he was drunk enough in the evenings before the fieldstone fireplace in the Barn, the writer told them what he really thought of their work. It was kinder to be cruel, of course, but it wasn't the kindness he enjoyed.

Oh to be bad! To be devilishly bad! When he was a boy he wanted to be a boxer, a bank robber, a bullfighter. Later he wanted to be Hemingway. But now he was fifty and fat in the middle— midlist, midlife. This young woman was half his age and the only black woman there. He noticed her. She had read all of his novels, even the ones that were painfully dated and out of print. She had hunted out his titles in dusty remainder bins. She wanted to be a writer. Not a black writer, but a writer. Not a female writer, but a writer. He told her he understood; he thought her writing was very, very good.

They struck out for the woods across a shaggy field of wasting hay. The hay was blonde and damp and clung to their shoes. He lamented that it would not go to feed any animals.

—So this field was plowed for beauty? she asked.

—Yes, he scoffed.—For the view of the sunset it affords the writers.

—The cicadas sound like a hundred and six tin wind-up toys going all at once, she said.

—You're right, he smiled.—You're exactly right.

They approached the motionless forest, each of them seeing the scene from behind, framed at a great distance. The sunset bled across the top of the picture. They saw themselves as characters about to do something dangerous, but the plot was the writer's design. At the tree line, his voice deepened.

—Hey, beautiful, he said.

She became beautiful. He had that much power. She thought he did, so he did. He touched her cheek. She smiled. She smiled.— "This is the forest primeval," he said.

Hand in hand, they descended the cool dark trail.

She noticed the lichen, the various mosses, and the white fungi sprouting through the rotting leaves of the forest floor. She noticed the trees: maple, birch, ash. She noticed the tracks of a fox in the mud. She noticed the writer's gold wedding band.

—"Two roads diverged in a yellow wood," she said, though there was no fork in the path they were on. It led to the water and stopped.

At the creek, the dying sun was reflecting itself, glinting itself over rocks and dappling through the branches. The creek was clear and swollen with the summer rains. He pulled her to his chest there by the waterside.

—I can feel your beautiful heart beating, he lied.

—I can feel yours, she lied.

Oh, to be bad! She believed she enjoyed being in the writer's arms. When he leaned in to kiss her, she did and didn't want his lips on hers. Her eyes remained open. There was something ridiculous about his face at this perspective. His pores and the gray stubble sticking out of them; the red network of capillaries around his nostrils and his slightly unpleasant breath. She closed her eyes and thought of the author photo on the back flap of his big book—the one that won the Pulitzer, the one about his retarded son. Still, his tongue was unwelcome in her mouth. Not what she expected. A fish. A slab of meat. Disquieted, she bit his lower lip.

—Can I have my lip back? he joked.

—Can I have my dignity back? she joked.

They were both pleased by this dialogue.

—Can we just sit by the water and not say anything? she asked. She was content to stop at the kiss. The kiss was illicit enough to be good material.

The writer's knees cracked as he lowered himself onto the creek bed.—Come here, he said. He pulled her into his lap and slowly undid her braid. She stiffened and watched the water. What did his fingers think of her hair? Didn't he feel her desire to sit in stillness with him? To be still, like a painting? To be silent?

The writer licked her earlobe. He urgently nibbled the back of her neck. She was getting wet, becoming the thing in his arms being kissed. At the same time, she felt entirely detached from the scene. She noticed a box turtle swimming under the surface of the water and had an impulse to smash it with a rock.

The writer cupped her breasts from behind. She noticed a pinecone being carried downstream. The writer pinched her nipples through the cotton of her summer dress.

—Your breathing just changed, he narrated.

Had she quickened her breath to excite him or was she genuinely excited? She didn't know. Whatever the case, a growing wetness spread between her legs. She pondered this.

—Turn around, he told her. She obeyed. He pulled her against his groin. She wrapped her legs around his thick middle and hooked her ankles at the base of his spine. She noticed their long, four-armed shadow working itself over the exposed roots of a fallen tree. He ground into her and groaned deeply, like a bear might groan. Swiftly, he stood, carrying her up with him, his hands supporting her rear. He rocked her from side to side, to prove her lightness.

—Little girl, the writer said. He buried his face in her chest and for a moment she thought he was crying.

Then his back spasmed. A dying pine creaked in the wind. He put her down.

—Are you all right? she asked.

He put his finger to her lips.—Shhhhhhh, he said.

He slid his right hand under the skirt of her dress and up her inner thigh. He cupped the mound of her crotch as if he owned it.

—You're dripping, he whispered.

He snaked his right hand under the elastic of her panties and slowly inserted his first and second fingers. He was skilled at this. He scissor-kicked his fingers and rotated his thumb knuckle over the bud of her clitoris. He did this for a full two minutes, troubling the carpal tunnel syndrome in his wrist. When she moaned and trembled, he fisted her unloosed hair and jerked her head backwards to bare the cords of her long brown throat.

He wanted to watch her face contort when she came.—Come for me, he said, kicking his fingers inside her, faster and faster.

She pretended to, and in pretending halfway did.

A woodpecker castanetted its beak against the trunk of a nearby tree.

—Feel how hard you make me. He grabbed her wrist and placed her hand on his erection.

His penis was smaller than that of other men she'd been with. He pushed her hand down his pants to touch that disappointing bulge of flesh. Repulsed, she pulled back. He undid his belt in a hurry and exposed himself. It couldn't be avoided. She witnessed its violent pink color thrusting from a mass of brown hair and knew he expected her to suck it. It was pointing at her, the color of an earthworm after the rain, with one white drop of pre-come glistening at its tip.

Feeling a little sick, she knelt before the writer. A twig snapped under her knee.

—Say it, he said, withholding it from her mouth. His testicles had given in to gravity.—I want to hear you say it.

He is the cliché of a lecherous man, she thought.

—Say it, he begged.

She did not say anything. She thought, Why should this be a story about a black woman kneeling before a white man in a muddy summer dress?

It was cold for August. His penis began to shrink into itself. She watched it become a snail.

—If you won't say it, I will, he said, gripping her shoulders.—I love you, he lied.

It was a terrible word choice and they both knew it. The young woman pitied him now. She was outside her body, participating in the scene, but not in the first person. She wasn't really there, except that there was a speck of something in her eye. A fleck of dust. She tugged at her eyelid.

He tucked away his penis. It had gone soft.

On the way back she held her elbows. She studied his back, in front of her. How many students had he brought into these woods?

—What kind of animal would you be? she asked, a little meanly.—A wolf?

—An eagle, he spat.

Yes, she thought. An eagle. That is the kind of vision you need to be a writer. It occurred to her that she had walked into some sort of story about the writer's fear of getting old.

He steered her to a yellow cottage, one in a row of quaint yellow cottages. Two aspiring writers swung in a hammock, drinking bourbon from the bottle and examining the porch slats with great attention, as if to make sure they were straight.

—Do you know how ridiculous you look? the writer asked them.

—Come see, they slurred.—The spiders are being born!

The sun's last light played off a cobweb insinuated in the porch railing. Spider hatchlings glinted on the strands of the web, each of them tiny and translucent, with all eight legs perfectly formed. The young woman lowered her face in front of the web. It formed a lace curtain between her and the world she used to inhabit. Something had shifted. Someone on the other side would judge what she had done in the woods as bad. She could smell her own musky odor. It did not please or displease her. She noticed it, was all.

—Come, said the writer, pulling her to his room on the first floor.

One of the aspiring writers pronounced the word *slut* under her breath, but with perfect diction.

The writer carried the young woman over the threshold like a bride.—I'm not finished with you.

His bed was badly made. The untucked sheet hung at a diagonal beneath the light blue blanket. A cardigan hung limp on one of the bedposts. She noticed the geometry of little rosebuds on the wallpaper. She noticed the writer's reading glasses on the bedside table next to a half-eaten roll of antacid tablets, and that the window shade was not completely drawn.

A writer might easily spy him kissing her. She sensed he liked this and she wondered if she liked it too. Here was her chance to excuse herself from the seduction and simply leave. She could have said no. Instead she imagined the picture the two of them made on the other side of the window frame. Better to be a slut than to be boring, she thought. Better to be honest than to lie.

—Why did you choose me? she asked, re-braiding her hair.

—Because I like the way you see, he answered.

—And because you like the way I look.

—Yes.

—Because I'm black.

He traced her eyebrows with his thumbs.—Maybe, he admitted.

She put her palm on his chest.—Because I'm black.

The writer fingered her full lips.—Yes, he whispered.

—Am I really a good writer? she asked.

—You really are.

She lay down on the bed then, lifted her dress and told him to kiss her.

He noticed her musky odor. She smelled like the mason jar of filthy pennies he'd kept beneath his bed as a boy in Duluth, he thought. He catalogued this sentence in his mind as he kissed her inner thighs.

She closed her eyes and saw the spider. It was imprinted in her memory because of the thing she had done in the woods with the writer, and because of what she was about to do. The young woman would remember the spider's swollen abdomen, the way she hung face downward in the complicated architecture of her web, and the bands, like a tiger's stripes, on her elegant legs.

The dinner bell clanged outside the dining room at the Bread Loaf Inn.

She put her hand in the writer's thinning hair.—What kind of spider was that? she asked.—Out on the porch?

He looked up at her and said,—An orb weaver.

Then he rose to stand between the V of her legs and pulled out his erection for the second time. It couldn't be ignored. Just as a gun on the stage of a play must go off before the curtain closes, the woman knew she must put him in her mouth and satisfy his need to be adored. This need was not any more pitiful or less human than her own. She sighed and got on the floor.

The woman watched her reflection sucking the writer in the cloudy mirror above the antique dresser, his hands circling the stem of her neck. This is a story about an orb weaver, she thought. I am going to be a great writer.

—Do you want me to come, baby? he asked. He had heard that somewhere, he had said it before. He liked to say it. It worked for him.

She nodded, working her tongue over the short shaft of his cock.

He closed his eyes.—Do you want to drink my cum? he asked. He pushed against her soft palate, her molars, her uvula.

To stop herself from choking, she spoke to herself in the second person:

Writer! Don't let the "I" get in the way of your seeing. Your task is only this: open your eyes until you forget you have a throat. You are not you. You are an eagle writing the wind. What do you see? Down by the creek, the fox is washing his face. Out in the field of wasting hay the pit of the peach you ate is already reentering the earth. Who you were when you ate the peach doesn't matter. What you are doing doesn't matter, whether you want to or not, whether you kissed him or he kissed you, whether or not it is happening at all.

Far more enchanting is the orb weaver, poised like a diadem in the eye of her web, letting her spiderlings balloon away from her on strands of silk to land in the dark vegetation of Frost's woods.

THE SAVING WORK

Tiphanie Yanique

1.

A church is burning down. On a Caribbean island, in the country-side, up a road that might lead to a saving beach, but does not—a church is burning down. Everyone who is associated with this church will later think "my church has burnt down." But for now there are only two women there to look at the fire, and blame each other.

They are both white American women in the middle of their lives. They and their families are members of this church. They are each married to a local black man, both of whom are skinny and frail of body. These women want to be the strong ones. They have always been the strong ones.

Deirdre Thompson has brought the garlands for the church stairs. She has brought the pew pins and the flowers for the altar. She was the first to arrive and see the bright flames. She is already dressed in her gold silk suit. She saw the smoke from far away in her car, but she imagined some filthy native was burning garbage in his yard. The smoke seemed to disappear as Deirdre drew near the church. This was an illusion.

Her car had lumbered its way along the narrow cut into the land that is the church road. The men of the church laid the road, and, as a result, it dips erratically. The arms of thin trees scraped at the closed windows of Deirdre's car. She wondered why no one had cut them back. She thought, with some worry, about how the limousine would make its way. The road opened into the clearing where the church crackled in the center. Through the windshield Deirdre saw what she thought was just a smallish fire, more smoke than anything. Nothing to alert the people in the nearby houses, some two hundred yards beyond the bushes.

But now Deirdre knows what she's seeing. She's seeing the end.

Deirdre Thompson has always been a negative kind of woman. She has one child because her womb had been stingy. And perhaps also because she left her husband once when their son was two. They did not reunite until the boy was twelve.

Her son is called Thomas—after the island of his birth. Deirdre's husband is an insurance salesman. It is better than it sounds. He owns the business and has other men do the work of selling by foot. He stays in his office downtown and lets his faithful customers come to him. He does well. And his small family does well. But what Mr. Thompson really wants is to be a preacher. He knows he could lead the common folk. He knows he could get better pews for the main room and better robes for the choir.

During the week Deirdre Thompson works as a dental assistant. In the office and outside, as she walks on her lunch break, she wears a white coat and allows patients and passersby to call her Doctor.

On Sundays, when Deirdre teaches the high school religious classes, she does not tell her students that marriage is challenging and a thing to be careful with—like a baby. She tells them instead how much Mr. Thompson loves her and that love saves everything. She tells them that when she met Mr. Thompson she had blond hair down to her ankles and that is why he fell in love with her. She makes them turn the thin Bible pages to Sampson and study the strength that was in his hair. She makes them memorize passages from the Old Testament that demonstrate beauty as a woman's greatest honor. The girl students are mostly of African descent and native to the island. They could never hope for blond hair to their ankles. They look at their teacher with envy or hate or pity—the last because they suspect Deirdre is lying.

Deirdre's son does not attend his mother's Sunday school classes. He was the crossing guard aide in middle school and the student government president in high school. He has always been a ruler of sorts. Thomas is besotted with a girl named Jasmine, the eldest daughter of Violet de Flaubert. He is a year older than the de Flaubert girl but she was skipped ahead, so she and Thomas Thompson are in the same grade. The de Flaubert girl is shy, and Thomas has been in love with her since he was twelve.

Deirdre stands a few safe yards in front of the burning church, watching it creak and break. She hears an engine sputter and knows it must be Violet de Flaubert's car graveling up behind her. Deirdre does not turn to greet her. Now that Violet has arrived she wonders about her own inaction. Wonders about her own ability to simply watch the church crack, and crumble into ashes.

———————

Violet de Flaubert sees the smoke and thinks it must be a campfire. This makes no sense. There are no campgrounds. Then she thinks maybe it's a barbeque, but people don't barbeque much on the island. She thinks on anything but a burning church. She is fighting not to think of a burning church.

Violet has five daughters who are each named after flowers, and with all those girls she somehow still feels virginal. When she teaches middle school religious classes on Sunday, she tells them, truthfully, that she was a virgin when she met Mr. de Flaubert. She makes them turn to passages on the mother of Jesus. She makes them act out the Christmas story. The girl students look at her with respect and adoration, for they are at the age for such things. The boy students look away from her with shame, because they are wishing they were *Mister* de Flaubert. The students don't think Violet is white from America. They assume she is Frenchy and native to the islands because she talks with native inflections and because she's been on the island since before they were born.

Mr. de Flaubert works for the government in the tax system. He is a cog, but he tells his daughters and his wife that he is an accountant. He makes decent money, but with all those girls the money does not last. He, too, wishes he were a preacher. He knows he could give good sermons. He longs to reach out and put his hands on people and speak tongues and see flames of Jesus spark on their heads.

Violet de Flaubert is a teacher in the school where her daughters and Deidre's son are enrolled. She teaches high school because her daughters are in high school. Before that she taught middle school. And before that she was a teacher's aide in the elementary school. She is a teacher because she is a mother. To her they are the same thing.

Two of her daughters are students in her Sunday school class. All five of her girls are strangely beautiful and brilliant. And they all have a saving flaw. One is overly shy, another is overly bookish, another cares only for her violin and practices incessantly, one is prone to fits and the last is a bit of a tart. But even this last one reads science fiction and is friends with the oily-faced girls.

Jasmine is the eldest. She is the shy one. She has a debilitating crush on a boy named Moby. Moby is the shortstop of the baseball team and during football season he is the quarterback and during basketball he is the tall center. Many girls are fond of Moby, and quiet Jasmine does not stand a chance. Though Moby has every now and then complimented her on her outfit during free clothes day or asked her about Calculus, Jasmine hasn't said more than a few sentences to him during their entire middle and high school years together.

Jasmine is unaware of Thomas Thompson's adoration for her. She thinks of him as the brother she never had, and in high school she went to watch his soccer games. But this island is American and soccer isn't yet popular. No one thinks that the soccer players are valiant. Jasmine doesn't understand the game at all and thinks the players look like overgrown squirrels fighting for a nut.

Despite the friendship of their children, Deirdre Thompson and Violet de Flaubert hate each other. They act, of course, as though they are very good friends.

2.

Violet is already crying as she eases out of her rotten station wagon and feels the heat of the fire. She knows what a burning church

means. She was a child in the America of the sixties. She doesn't understand how this hate has followed her. How her father's klanish-
ness has found her on this island of black people. She wonders if
somehow her father has burned down the church. Somehow he has
hunted her down, and this is her punishment for marrying a nigger
and having half-nigger children. Beautiful amber-colored children—
the kind she had hoped for to save her father's sins. Daughters her
father would have adored if they had just been lighter skinned and
straighter haired. But then Violet remembers her father is dead.

Violet thinks of all her daughters as strong. She calls them "tough
as nails." Her girls' shyness or bookishness or violinness is their armor
to face the world. A girl's kind of trick armor. She doesn't know her
daughters very well—there are just so many of them—but she knows
them better than most mothers could.

She doesn't know that their armor is insufficient when battling
the world.

Only four months ago Deirdre's son Thomas and Violet's daughter Jasmine went away to college in America. To the same city, but
not to the same college. Violet didn't think much of this. She thought
maybe the two would meet up for coffee every once in a while.

Deirdre hoped that shy Jasmine, with her slutty name, would disappear into the sewers of the city and from her son's mind. She hoped
the girl would end up on drugs or pregnant, and that her son would
end up married to an Ivy League co-ed with professional ambitions
and cooking skills. That would show Violet—but then Deirdre would
whisk away these devilish thoughts with a little prayer. She does not
wish to be so evil. She was only thinking of her son. Deirdre knows
Thomas wants to be President someday, but she believes that sons are
fragile and in need of their mothers.

What happened with Thomas and Jasmine is common but not simple. They did meet for coffee in a chain café with a French name.
They didn't know any better, coming from a small island, so they
thought the place must be the only one of its kind.

"It's cute in here, Thomas. I like it. I'll be coming back for sticky
buns."

Thomas frowned thinking of Jasmine here without him. This was a public place. There were many people around. He thought that this should be their place now.

"Thomas. Stop making that face and get me some sugar, no. Brown, please."

He got up. He loved that she could barely speak to anyone for her shyness, yet she could order him to get her some sugar. She could demand brown sugar.

While he was gone Jasmine watched the other people, who all seemed pleased with their organic orange juice or chai lattes—things she had never known before. She could hear their private conversations clearly. They spoke carelessly, as though it didn't matter who was listening. Beneath Jasmine's new fall jacket was a silk blouse that Moby had once told her looked nice. She shifted now so she could feel it slide across her shoulders.

Thomas rested half a dozen little brown packets beside her cup. "So," he said. "How's Chemistry?"

"I'm not taking Chemistry."

"It's a joke. You know, like Chem is so hard, so that's all that anyone really cares about." Perhaps this was only a joke on his campus or perhaps just in his dorm among his new friends. "So what are you taking?"

Jasmine chewed a sticky bun and sipped on her coffee. She began her list and leaned across the table so the others wouldn't hear. "Intro to Women's Studies. Intro to Psychology. Race and the Essay. The History of Math."

"Aren't you taking English Comp or like Biology 101 or the regular stuff?"

"Yes, stupidee. Race and Essay—that's a composition class. The psychology is for my science credit."

"The classes sound cool." He thought to make a joke about Women's Studies but then thought against it. "Race and the Essay. What you learning there?"

She sucked her teeth with annoyance. "I don't know. We only been in class for a month or something." She sipped her milky coffee. It was the color of her skin. "Theory and history, mostly. You know...how ethnicity impacts the way we relate to the world and is reflected on the text...and all that. The stuff we didn't learn at St. Mark's."

Thomas sat up straight now and stirred his Earl Grey. He wanted to ask what 'the text' was but he suddenly felt defensive. "St. Mark's was good to us, Jasmine. I mean, I feel it really prepared me for college. Like, I know all about Plato's cave and like no one else in my comp class does. I mean that's education..." but he realized that he was rambling and she wasn't paying any attention. He tried again. "Tell me about your roommate. You get along?"

He watched her face as she talked about her roommate, who had a new college boyfriend already. It seemed Jasmine didn't care for her roommate because the girl had pushed herself onto the dorm committee. Jasmine said this might be a sign that the girl was arrogant. Thomas had to force himself not to watch Jasmine's mouth. He thought to look into her eyes but that often made his own eyes well with tears. So he watched her forehead and her cheeks. She looked out into the street and then back into her cup of coffee.

Though Violet and Thomas are both a combination of white American and black Caribbean, they are different in color. He is a kind of yellow color. Almost like gold. Her color is muted and therefore more mysterious. This is not something that Jasmine thinks. It is what Thomas thought that day in the café as she talked and talked.

———————

From her dorm room phone Jasmine called her mother. "I met with Thomas Thompson today."

"Well, that's nice," Violet said. "How are you doing making new friends?"

"Fine. I mean I haven't made any. My roommate is frigging annoying."

"And a boyfriend?"

"Yeah, she already has a boyfriend. Not even a month of school yet. Can you believe it, Mom?"

"I mean you, baby. Is there a nice smart boy in your science class maybe? Remember, you want a smart man. One with a bright future."

"Oh, Mom. You know you're harassing me. My roommate is so..."

"She's just having fun. Fun is okay."

"Okay, Mom. Okay."

Jasmine hung up. She hadn't spoken to her father, but now she wondered about him. She wondered about her mother's insistence that she search her science class for a boyfriend. She wondered about her father's inadequacies. She felt bad for him and mad at her mother. But Jasmine also felt that her mother had made a mistake in her choice of a husband. It was not a mistake Jasmine would repeat.

3.

"My father killed himself just like this." Violet says this in a screechy voice though she has only meant to think it. It is not something she has said to anyone and now she has said it to the fire and to the figure ahead. She is almost hysterical with tears. There really is a church, her church, burning right in front of her. Right here on this island that was supposed to be brown skin paradise. The suicide is a secret Violet has kept from her husband and her daughters. Her parents are dead. Her children are told honorable stories. They do not seem to mind that they don't know their white cousins, and Violet has been grateful for that indifference.

She sees with disgust that it is Deirdre Thompson there ahead, standing before the church as though just watching is serious work. As though the burning was her own doing. Deirdre who is chubby and unhappy and dangerously insecure. Violet focuses on the back of Deirdre's head, with its short, sharp hair. She cannot help but finger her own rolling curls thankfully, and then feel ashamed for her blessed endowment. Violet cannot remember ever touching Deirdre, even in the peace during church services. But now she thinks that the goodly thing would be to move towards Deirdre, closer to the flames, so they can work this fire out as a team.

Violet says out loud, like an offering, "My mother died in the fire, too. They never said suicide, but it was." And though she is crying, the words are very clear.

But Deirdre does not move at all, and for a second Violet thinks she should step forward and hug the thick woman. Then it comes to her like a pinch that Deirdre is the arsonist. That self-righteous cow would love to see Violet's daughter sullied. She clenches her jaw and takes a breath. Deirdre can burn for all she cares. Instead she asks, employing her slight island accent for strength, "Can you at least fucking tell me if there's anyone inside?"

Deirdre feels her shoulders and neck tighten. What is Violet de Flaubert carrying on about? Her dumb racist roots? And she has the nerve to ask the question that Deirdre herself should have asked. Deirdre hadn't thought about anyone being trapped inside. She hadn't thought about anybody but her son at home waiting, and now Violet is about to do the saving work. But then again, perhaps Violet has just gone mad. Deirdre wonders if this insanity is connected to the fire and why. But Deirdre knows why Violet would want to bring down the church. It is easy to know why. She has always been jealous of my family, Deirdre thinks.

Between Deirdre and Violet there is more than a fire. There is something more destructive. It is something like history and the future converted into flesh. They have children between them. And now they have their similar histories and their common futures like a leash from one to another.

Jasmine's face went hot under her skin when her roommate explained to her that if she ever arrives at their door and sees a hair scrunchy on the doorknob that she should go to the lounge and watch TV for an hour.

But the first time Jasmine saw the pink scrunchy, she sat in front of the door and waited for the animal noises to calm. Then she opened the door with her key and got in her bed—shoes and all. She could hear them in the dark talking about her. Whispering about what to do now, until finally the boy slid out of the door like a thief in the night.

The second time the pink scrunchy was ringed around the doorknob Jasmine sat in front of the door and cried. She sniffled loudly until another girl walked by in a towel and asked if she was okay. Jasmine nodded and buried her head. But the girl wouldn't go. She sat next to Jasmine and put her arm around her. Then she offered to make her some tea. She had a forbidden electric teapot in her room. The two of them sipped green tea until past midnight and the other girl's roommate came home.

The third time Jasmine came home to the scrunchy, she thought about barging in and demanding the boy get out. She thought about calling her roommate a slut. But then Jasmine thought on her own sister. The youngest, who was just 14, and the only one of the sisters who had gone all the way with a boy. Instead of barging in the room again, Jasmine went to the girl with the teapot. But that girl's roommate was in, and Jasmine was too uncomfortable to stay there with them both and drink tea. She asked to use their phone. "You have a great accent," the other roommate said. "Are you from Jamaica?" Jasmine nodded her head to avoid conversation. She was calling Thomas.

The subway station was emptier than usual. The café where she was meeting Thomas was only three stops away but the ride took a long time. Jasmine was a little afraid as she sat on the train and the few people got on and off. She didn't risk even glancing at her books. She held them to her chest and thought about the best ways to use them as a weapon. The train rumbled like a can and creaked to a stop. Her sneakers rubbed and squeaked on the ground of the dark station. She pushed her way through the turnstile and began to run. There was no one around until she burst out of the stairway and into the street. But there was the café and there was Thomas standing at its door. He took her books and held the door open for her.

At their table he laid the brown sugar packets on her saucer without her having to ask.

"Are you okay?"

"Fine."

"So, what's up? I mean, I'm glad you called and all. We haven't talked for a good while and you didn't return my calls, but I was just wondering..." He was doing it again. Rambling on and complaining.

"What are you?" Jasmine asked.

"What?"

"You know. White or black? What do you feel more?" It was a question from her Race and the Essay class. It was a question about passing. About being something you were not or becoming something you were not meant to be. But it was also a question that she and Thomas had been thinking about all their lives.

"It's different." Thomas didn't want to say the wrong thing but he wanted to be honest. He always wanted to be honest with Jasmine.

"How so?"

"At home, I feel mixed. Everyone knows my mother and father. They all know what I am." She nodded her understanding. But he continued. "Here I feel more white, I guess. I mean, I think some people might think I'm all white even. I guess I'm white in America."

This was the wrong answer. "You should take the class I'm taking. You'll think more about the responsibility you have to be true to yourself."

He slapped his spoon clumsily around in his cup. "Well, what do you feel?"

"I feel mixed here." She stared into her tawny coffee. "Everyone asks me what I am and where I'm from. They assume I'm from Jamaica whenever I say anything. Don't you hate that?"

"People say they can't hear my accent at all. I have to pull out my driver's license to prove I'm not from right here." This wasn't right either, so he stopped. "What do you feel like at home? Since you're mixed up here. Do you feel black at home?"

"I just feel like myself at home. I just feel like Jasmine." But as she said it she knew this wasn't all true. Jasmine. What kind of name was that? Her sisters were Rose, Lily, Iris and the youngest, fast one was Daisy. Rose and Lily seemed dignified, Iris seemed sharp and tidy, and Daisy, well, was lighthearted. But Jasmine—what a name. A little, ugly flower that gave off a strong, whorish smell.

Thomas held Jasmine's hand as they walked back to his dorm. He didn't let go even when he had to pull out his school ID to unlock the main entrance and then his keys to open his door. His was a suite with a common room and kitchen. The common room stunk of sweat and corn. Thomas only noticed it now that Jasmine was with him. The TV in this room belonged to one of the suitemates. Its light flashed onto the face of another suitemate, asleep on the university-issued couch. Thomas opened his door and hesitated before turning on the light. They had to wade through his t-shirts and jeans that lay on the floor. His bed was made, thank God. A habit his mother had instilled in him.

He poured Jasmine a Coke that had gone flat and offered her a pair of his cleanest t-shirt and boxers. They had undressed in front of each other only once, but that was in her parents' station wagon at the beach and it had been a claustrophobic, platonic thing. Now he left the room.

In the room alone, Jasmine still felt as though she were being watched. She wanted to take a shower, actually, but she imagined the bathroom might not be very clean. She thought about removing her underwear. She took the panties off but then didn't know where to put them. She hadn't come with a purse. Only her books and her keys that she'd stuffed into her pockets. She put the underwear back on and felt a little dirty, but also less so in another way.

4.

Because Deirdre hasn't moved or even acknowledged her presence, Violet begins to skitter around the church and call out: "Anyone inside? Anyone? Inside!" She knows this is ludicrous. If there were anyone they would be screaming or dead already. Violet cannot even get close. The heat is so heavy now that it seems to burn her. She has been clutching a white pillow and now she waves it like a flag. It's a little satin thing with a hook for the rings.

The church is a small two-story, surrounded on the sides by a wide clearing of gravel for cars to park. Beyond the clearing, endless trees. Behind the church, the edge of the mountain. In front, the small road that leads to the main road. At the main road is the sign: *Christ's Mission Evangelical* with an arrow pointing up the road less traveled. At the end of the road is the church. A simple structure. The bottom floor for worshipping and the second floor, with its outside staircase, for the children's classes. The congregation had planned to add on to it. But now as Violet steps closer, the church makes a screeching noise and seems to implode, as the upstairs crashes down into the first floor. Violet runs back to where Deirdre stands sweating.

The women still do not trust each other. Now they never will.

Because Thomas had his own room he didn't have to signal Jasmine's presence with a scrunchy or a tie. His naked doorknob made her think of their sleeping in the same bed as an innocent act. They lay down in the extra long twin bed and faced each other. She smiled to show him she was grateful, but he only looked at her, trying not to blink, until his eyes teared up. He touched her face. He kissed her forehead. And though that could have been just a brotherly gesture, they were, after all, in a bed together. And though they were fully clothed, though they had known each other for so long, they weren't really siblings after all. And so they kissed, and Thomas, who had kissed a few girls, tried very hard to be sweet and gentle. Tried very hard to not be forceful, but his whole body was in it. To him it was the beginning.

To Jasmine the kiss was kind of nasty, but thrilling. It was her first real kiss. The first with tongue. She let him explore her mouth and press against her body. It was a curious thing to her and she imagined it would stop and then they would go to sleep and then never talk about it. But then he whimpered, "Oh shit," and popped out of bed as though burned. She saw that something milky was seeping through the crotch of his boxers and had smeared on her thighs where they had been rubbing. "Oh shit," he said again and seemed as though he would cry. She looked at him, fascinated and disgusted, as he bit his lip and pressed into a corner of the room.

"I made you do that," she said without thinking. "I mean, I made you do that without us even doing it for real." Thomas didn't nod or address her observation in any way. He grabbed a towel. He turned his back to her when he took his shorts off.

"I'm sorry," he said, when they were back in the bed, new pajama pants on them both. "That's not how I wanted it to be."

It wasn't anything, Jasmine wanted to tell him, but couldn't. For a long time she didn't sleep, but finally her dreams were filled with images of her own feet climbing over walls of water.

Early in the morning, she edged out of the bed. She took her clothes into the common room and dressed there with the sleeping roommate and the blinking TV as an audience. She left and took the train. She felt bold and brave, and other things she had never felt before.

She rode the subway back to her dorm room and packed her small bag. She emailed her teachers to say that she had to go on a trip and would miss class and to please let her know what the homework was. She got on a train and then transferred to a bigger, sleeker train where the seats were soft and personal. She finished a luscious collection of short stories during the three hours the train took to get to the next city. When she arrived she caught a yellow cab. Only then, with the cab slamming through the city streets, did she marvel at herself again. She thought of her fast roommate and her loose sister and then of her own sluttish power over Thomas. "The new me," she said to the audacious skyscrapers around her.

But when she arrived and knocked on the dorm room door, she thought that this was all very crazy. It had taken her more than three hours to get here, but only now did she really consider what she was attempting. She started to run back down the hallway, her one small bag like a hump on her back, but by then Moby had opened the door and called to her, "Jasmine? Jasmine de Flaubert, is that you?" And she had stopped running and turned to him. "Yes, Moby. It's me—Jasmine."

5.

Church ashes are not like any other. When this fire has cooled perhaps Dierdre will return and find a golden chalice that had refused to melt. Or the ruby from the preacher's wife's favorite ring. Dierdre will return and take the ashes in her palm. She might wonder if the New or Old Testament is sifting through her fingers. Perhaps it will be the Christmas story, there on her fingernail. Perhaps it will be Revelations settling on her shoe.

But now, facing the fire, Deirdre has thought of what to do. Finally, now that the church is doomed and her pew pins a certified waste of money, she pulls out her cell phone and calls the police, who connect her to the fire station. They have no idea where on island she is and now the church is shuddering with the growl of an earthquake. It is making such a racket that Deirdre has to walk farther away to give directions to the fire station operator. And now Deirdre notices the trees and wonders if they will catch and she says slowly into the phone that the church is close to Crossroads and to take the road to Fortuna. But they must look for the church sign. They must look... and as Deirdre says it she looks at Violet de Flaubert, who is crying in front of the fire as though she is about to become a sacrifice. Deirdre wonders whether perhaps Violet has pulled down the sign the fire trucks will need in order to find them.

Deirdre leaves the operator on the phone to back away from Violet and run to her car. Violet might be a madwoman, but she's smart. Deirdre knows her. She knows that Violet keeps liquor in her fridge and jokes that Jesus drank wine. She knows that Violet lets her youngest daughter wear short skirts and calls it "finding oneself." She watches as Violet's face grows panicked but smaller as Deirdre reverses her car all the way down the long path to the main road.

Now Violet is there alone. Alone with the maniacal fire. She must pull herself together. Where is her armor? Her mind moves frantically to thoughts of her eldest daughter. She looks down at the sooty lace of the tiny pillow in her hand. It is made of the same material as the dress. And then she is running. Violet runs a wide arc behind the disappearing church. She runs to look for Jasmine.

When Thomas called home to his mother, he said that he had news. Difficult, but wonderful news. Deirdre knew, from the tension in his voice, that the news might be those things for him but a tragedy for her.

"Jasmine and I are getting married."

As Deirdre's hand stiffened around the phone, she noted that her son did not say, "I want to marry..." or even "I have asked to marry..." He said it as though it would happen any minute and without his mother's say. Deirdre's hearing became very sharp as she listened to her son breathe. Finally he said, "It will be okay, Mama. We'll live in her school's married dorms. Neither of us will have to quit college or anything. I mean, Jasmine might have to take a semester off, but..." and then Deirdre began to scream. She poured her Christian obscenities into the cavity of the receiver.

Thomas knew his mother. He knew she would get over this because she was tough. He rested the phone down quietly. He wasn't scared at all about getting married. This was what he had always wanted, and now it had been granted. He couldn't disparage it because it happened differently than he had hoped. It had happened. Now he would fast track their future together.

Jasmine called her mother. She held her breath and listened to Violet say, "Hello. Hello? I'm sorry, I can't hear you. Try again." After a few minutes Jasmine called back and heard the same sweet voice say the same thing. It took the fourth call in a row for her mother to pronounce calmly into the silence, "Look here, you cow, stop calling my fucking house." And finally Jasmine announced into the phone, "Mommy, I'm pregnant."

The wedding was planned for Christmas Break. They were only freshmen in college. He was eighteen and she was still seventeen. The church folk would whisper, but Jasmine wouldn't be much more than two months gone when Thomas made her honest.

With money his father sent him, Thomas bought Jasmine a diamond ring. He told his roommates that he was moving out to be a father and a husband. He told his advisor he was getting married and so would have to speed up his coursework.

Jasmine only wore the ring when Thomas reminded her it was supposed to stay on her hand. She didn't tell her roommate anything. She did not tell Moby anything. She only thought on the way Moby had said her name, Jasmine, again and again in the dusky light, as though it was something holy. The musk of their bodies had made her feel safe when she lay there with him afterwards, but now she could not seem to wash it off. She feared people could smell it on her. That time with Moby was not something to tell a sister or a friend. It was not something to write in a diary. It was something to keep to herself, simply to know she was capable of it.

Thomas bought their tickets home on the same flight. They held hands in the airport as they window-shopped and as they sampled the camouflage of Lancôme and Chanel on her wrists. Jasmine thought, yes, I can do this. I can be this woman. I can love Thomas like a woman would. They still hadn't had sex. But now he kissed her in a way that was all gentle—like he was calm now. And he whispered a little joke as the plane took off: "I can't believe you're so fertile. When we do it for real we'll have to use the rhythm method so you won't get pregnant again too quickly." She gripped his hand as the plane lifted and tried to smile. She wondered if he really believed himself.

At home on the island Jasmine's younger sisters were either embarrassed that their sister was pregnant or eager to ask her questions about sex. The violinist sister didn't seem to care either way. She practiced and filled the house with her music—the same desperate song again and again. It was the song she would play for the wedding.

Jasmine sat on the bed that was still hers in the room she shared with Daisy. She clenched her stomach to see if she could feel something that was more than herself. I'm not ready, she said in her head and hoped the baby could hear. I want you, but not now. Not in seven months either. Come back another time. I'll be good to you then. She lay back and pressed her fingertips into her stomach. Then she made two fists. But Daisy, the youngest, walked in. She sat on the bed at Jasmine's feet.

"So, why didn't you and Thomas use protection?" The violin screeched from the next room, but then resumed its melody.

"I didn't have sex with Thomas."

"Oh." Daisy had been the first sister to do it and so knew a lot despite her age. "Well, then you're the Virgin Mary. And when she got pregnant she got married."

Jasmine touched her stomach with the flat of her hand. "I haven't talked to the other guy since. I just wanted to do it. It was just a one time thing. Just one brave thing that I did. And now it's done. Okay?"

Daisy took Jasmine by the arm. She dragged her to face the bottom drawer of the bureau that they had always shared. Below the holey socks was a string of little square packets. Daisy pressed two condoms into Jasmine's hand. "For the next time you contemplate bravery."

———

The Thompson and de Flaubert houses became places of bustling activity. The wedding colors were purple at first, because that was Violet's name and she was the mother of the bride, but Thomas's mother insisted purple was a funeral color. So Deirdre picked out the pew dressings and the tablecloths and even the official color—a yellow that was almost gold. Deirdre's husband tried to offer that the color might be gaudy, but she wouldn't have it. "My son is a prince," Deirdre spat, as if they hadn't made Thomas together.

Anyone would have thought that Deirdre was the mother of the bride, what with the fuss she was making. The floor of her living room was strewn with invitation samples and yards of tulle. In the kitchen, stray Jordan almonds rolled around like tiny rotten Easter eggs.

Thomas stepped over things and tried to be patient when his mother asked his opinion. "We don't need all this, Mama. The only reason we didn't elope was that Jasmine wanted her mother to be there for the wedding." Sometimes Deirdre would look at her son as though he were a stranger and then go back to her catering menu. Sometimes she would look at him and then pull him close, as though he were just born. Either way, he would leave her shaking his head and marveling at his mother's passionate strength. Then he would call up his beloved to check on her, but often Jasmine was sleeping or out or sick. They had not seen each other since they'd arrived on island and their mothers had taken over.

Violet hit her sewing machine like a calling and made the bridesmaid dresses all in purple, despite Deirdre's choice of gold. The dresses were short and simple because there was so little time. There wasn't time to make a wedding dress at all, so one afternoon Violet and Jasmine went to a boutique. There among the pretty things, Jasmine grew excited despite herself. The dresses were so lovely, she felt like a princess. Maybe she could get married after all. Maybe it wouldn't be so bad. She thought that maybe she would talk to Thomas. Maybe he would say something romantic and her chest would swell with love, instead of the doughy feeling that filled her throat now when she thought of having to consummate their marriage.

The dress they chose was too expensive, but they bought it anyway and put in on Mr. de Flaubert's credit card. With a corset Jasmine's stomach became totally flat and no one would ever have to know. The gown ballooned into the back seat of the car when they drove it home. The skirt of the dress was wide and fluffy, like a ballerina's tutu.

6.

And so it is easy for Violet to find Jasmine behind the church, the smoke curling around her like a lover, standing at the cliff, her tutu of a dress flapping about her as she rips it off and releases the corset and finally her belly. By the time Violet grabs her from the edge, the girl is only in her underthings. The wire of the can-can like a guarding loop around her.

Violet holds her daughter until she herself stops crying and the smoke begins to burn her own eyes. She guides her daughter, can-can and all, to the car. They leave the virginal white dress in pieces behind them. As they are leaving, the fire trucks come screaming. The road is so narrow that Violet has to reverse her vehicle back to the smoldering church—and since they are there, they now have to stay so Violet can answer questions and lie that she has no idea how the church fire began. No idea at all. And she doesn't even pass an incriminating look at her half-naked daughter sitting like a stone in the passenger seat of the car.

The firefighters don't address the almost-bride because they think her devastation is too precious to disturb. But really Jasmine is sitting there feeling the thing in her womb churn like a fist of fire. "Another time," she commands it. And finally the blood burns out of her.

————————

When Deirdre walks into her living room she sees her son and his father ready in their tuxedos. They look at her with their eagerness and excitement, but Deirdre's face gives something away because Thomas stands as though ready to fight the thing that has hurt his mother. "Sit," she says. It comes out dry and smoky. The boy sits slowly. Deirdre looks from the father to the son and sees, only now, that the two look alike. All she has contributed, it seems, is a slight lightness in color, a slight thinness of the lips, a slight narrowing in the nostrils. It is like someone has shown her that she does not really exist.

She gestures for them to make room on the couch. "I have something to say." She takes their hands into her lap. But then all she can say as she looks from one to the other is, "Marriage isn't everything."

The future leader of corporations and civic clubs and maybe even the free world stares at his mother as though she is mad, because there she is crying, and he has never seen his mother cry. "What are you saying, Mama? Pop, what is she saying?" Thomas clutches at his groom's boutonnière until he feels it come loose.

This family has never thrown a Frisbee around together in a sunny park. They have never sat in a circle and told each other stories. They have never prayed together except at church. They have never talked to each other about the divine risks of love.

Dance for Me

Amina Gautier

The girls on Lexington had it the worst. Hated maroon skirts the color of dried blood. Navy blazers complete with gaudy emblem. Goldenrod blouses with Peter Pan collars. And knee socks. Actually, knee socks weren't so bad. Knee socks served their purpose in the winter, keeping sturdy calves warm.

The girls on East End wore gray or navy skirts, plain and not pleated, with a white blouse, sweater optional.

Multiple skirts were another way to go. We had our choice of navy, gray, maroon and an unpleated light blue seersucker meant only for the spring. The choices allowed us to pretend we weren't really wearing a uniform. We merely hoped to be thought eccentric. Girls with fetishes for skirts with panels. But we fooled no one. Our clothing, our talk, our walk, our avid interest in grooming, and normal people's clothing, and daily preoccupation with what we would wear on up-coming field trips when allowed to be out of uniform, filled our time and talk. We had a special way of standing that was part lean, part slouch, as if posture were too much of a bother to consider.

Nameless, faceless on a school trip, we stood out. Solid-colored blouses, pleated skirts, knee socks, loafers, bluchers, or oxfords.

Private school girls. Not to be confused with Catholic school girls. Or reform school girls (how many times did the kids in my neighborhood look at me in condescending pity?). Not to be confused with the girls from *The Facts of Life*. They were boarders. No matter how many times I tried to explain this, the kids in my neighborhood persisted in calling me Tootie.

We attended a second-tier all-girls' school. We weren't as illustrious as the private schools on the Upper East Side, yet not as seedy as the ones in Midtown. We clung to our small but unique differences. For example, having our choice of uniforms made us the envy of the other all-girls' schools. Girls were sure to take it out on us during soccer games. Secondly, there was our partnership with a nearby all-boys' school, our "brother" school two blocks away, which allowed us to have kissing partners whenever we put on a play.

At school, there were the WASPS and the JAPS. And me. Girls with last names for first names. Riley. Taylor. Haley. Morgan. Hayden. Girls whose names are meant for a boy or girl, depending.

I'd never told anyone this, but I always felt naked in my pleated skirt, vulnerable. There was a trick to rolling the skirt that would take several inches off, a way of rolling tightly and minutely that would allow one to hide the extra material beneath a fold of a shirt if one tucked one's shirt in properly, then pulled out just enough material to camouflage the extra skirt. Only I didn't know it. I'd seen it numerous times, jealously watching girls enter the bathroom with skirts that covered their knees and walk back out with skirts that skimmed their thighs, but I still couldn't get it. The lines of my pleats were never quite right, always drooping in the front, making me look slightly off kilter.

———

It was lunchtime and I was in the school's bathroom with my stomach bared to the mirror, trying to roll my skirt, when Taylor and Ashley entered and headed for the stalls, deep in conversation. Neither of them noticed me.

"Well, I wouldn't go with a guy from Buckley, that's for sure."

"I might not get to go at all. We're supposed to go to the

Hamptons and my dad really has his heart set on it. How am I supposed to get out of it?"

"I don't know. I so need a new pair of jeans. Do you want to go to The Gap today after we get out of chorus?"

"Um, yeah. Hey, did you hear Heather's parents let Chase go to Cabo San Lucas with her for spring break?"

"No."

"They even paid his way."

So caught up in eavesdropping on their conversation, I didn't hear the squeal of the bathroom door the second time it opened. Heather walked in alone and went straight to the mirror. She frowned slightly when she heard herself being discussed. Then she went into a stall near theirs.

"Who said that?"

"Heather, that's who."

"I heard she broke up with him."

"For the coxswain? That's like way over."

"What happened?"

"He dumped her for a girl from Chapin."

Two toilets flushed simultaneously. By the time Taylor and Ashley emerged, I'd whipped out my Carmex and pretended to be carefully moisturizing, all thoughts of fixing my skirt gone. They washed their hands and walked out without looking at me. Once they left, Heather came out of her stall.

Moments like these were common. They happened several times during the day—self-reflective moments when girls met between classes, gathering in bathrooms and on stairways to consider the grave issues of the times and their place in the world. Usually the person being discussed wasn't present.

Heather was still standing there. Her eyes met mine in the mirror. "It's not true, you know."

"What?"

"I never went out with that guy. Never even kissed him. He was a total turd."

I shrugged. "Okay."

She scrutinized me. "You're in my class."

I nodded. "Yeah."

"Do you know about the party on West 91st this Friday?"

"At Trinity?"

"Are you going?"

I pretended to give the question some thought. The parties were hosted by coed private day schools that issued invitations to certain schools, which then issued memberships to certain students. She knew I couldn't go. The memberships were a subtle way of excluding the undesirables. The membership lists went out in sixth grade. The scholarship girls who came in through the enrichment programs started in seventh grade. There was no way ever to be included on the lists, unless someone sponsored me, which no one ever did. I had no plans to go to the party this Friday or any other Friday, and she knew it.

"I wasn't planning on it," I said.

"Oh. Do you know how to do that new dance they're doing?" she asked me. "You know the one that goes like this." Heather's gyrations resembled nothing I could identify.

"Um no, I can't say that I know that one," I said. "Sorry."

"Maybe I'm doing it wrong," she said.

"Maybe."

"It's called Running something."

"The Running Man?"

"That's it!" She touched my arm. "Do you know it?"

"Sure."

"Can you show me?"

I looked around. "Here? In the bathroom?"

"Yeah." Heather smiled at me, warm and eager. I really didn't want to. I wasn't a very good dancer and I didn't like to perform. At home, I would only sing in the shower, and I danced at house parties only when the lights were very low. But I danced for her, awkward at first since there was no music, but she didn't seem to notice or mind. Once I started dancing, her eyes never met mine. They were riveted instead to my legs and feet. I had a feeling she wanted to take notes.

"That looks so hard," she said.

"It's not," I huffed. I danced harder, wanting to show off. I was silently repeating the words of a popular song in my head to give myself a beat. I danced harder as I tried to incorporate moves I'd seen on Video Music Box, getting ahead of myself and quickly losing the beat. A video diva I had never been, watching videos only on

Saturdays when my mother was out. I was losing my rhythm and running out of breath when she finally said, "Wow. You're good. Really, really good."

I stopped and took a deep breath. I smiled. "Thanks."

That evening, our phone rang, something it hardly ever did. My mother eyed the phone suspiciously, letting it ring three times before picking up. "Hello?" she answered warily, frowning at the unseen offender who'd interrupted her silence. "Yes, hold on." She held the phone out to me. "It's for you?" I ignored the question in her voice and grabbed it.

"Hi, it's me."

"Hi."

"It's Heather," she said, as if I wouldn't know her voice.

"Hey."

Who is it? my mother mouthed silently.

Heather, I mouthed back. *From school.*

It had been my mother's idea to put me in the enrichment program that had given me a scholarship for the all-girls' school, a decision she'd come to regret in the face of my loneliness and unpopularity. Now, she hovered and tried to listen in, filled with hope.

Heather's excitement came through, giddy and loud. "You're coming! You are so coming," she shrieked into my ear.

"What are you talking about?"

"The party this Friday. Did you forget?"

"No, I remember."

"Well, I got you in. I sponsored you," she said. There was a pause in her voice, as if she were waiting for something.

"Thanks," I said.

"You don't sound excited."

"I am."

"You are going to go, right?"

I didn't answer. I was taking my time to think about it. Although she'd sponsored me, there was still the question of clothing. I had nothing suitable to wear. The dance would also end late and I didn't think my mother would want me riding home from Manhattan to Brooklyn that late at night by myself. "Well—"

"Nadira is going," Heather said, as if it made a difference.

Nadira was the other black girl in our class. She'd been at the school since kindergarten, while I'd come in seventh grade on a scholarship. Although there were a number of affluent black and Asian girls in my school who'd been attending since kindergarten, I was not one of them and we claimed no kinship with one another. If I closed my eyes and listened to them speak, I wouldn't know they weren't white. Though Nadira and I belonged to the same race, she had more in common with the white girls. She and they lived in the same neighborhoods, had the same friends, values, and ideals. They listened to z100 and sang classical in the choir. Like the white girls, she could not dance. I couldn't either, but no one knew that. They all took it for granted that I could.

"I'd like to, but I don't think my mom will let me because it ends so late."

"Tell her that's no problem. I wanted you to stay over. I'm having a little get-together at my house after the dance. You know, an after the party party. Just a couple of girls. A sleepover. Taylor. Maya. Ashley and maybe some others. Ask your mom if it's okay."

I held the receiver to my chest. "Mom? Heather wants to know if it's okay if I sleep over at her house this Friday." Heather lived in a penthouse on 95th and Park. Of course it was okay.

Heather invited me to sit with her at lunch the next day. Four girls smiled at me as I sat, and they continued on with their discussions.

"I have this body suit and I'm going to wear it with my white jeans," Maya said. The other girls nodded their approval.

"You should wear your hair half up and half down," Heather told her.

"I don't have anything to wear. I'm going to need something new," Taylor said.

"Let's go to The Gap after class today and find something," Ashley suggested.

They were all wearing fleeced pullovers in different colors from

L.L. Bean or Patagonia over their collared blouses and heather gray leggings beneath their pleated skirts. None of them had on socks. Their feet were bare in their loafers, docksiders, and bluchers.

I excused myself to go to the bathroom. There, I peeled off my socks. Ashley followed behind me. When I stood up, socks in hand, she said, "Um, do you think you could show me the dance you showed Heather?"

The next day, I was back in the bathroom, showing five new girls. For the next two days, Heather brought girls to me and we took them into the bathroom to teach them the steps. For the next two days, I danced and danced on the cold white tiles while white girls leaned against sinks and stall doors and watched. The dancing, I thought, brought me respect and admiration. Through it, I was redeeming myself in their eyes. I was, after all these years, good for something.

The day before the dance, Heather caught me on my way out to the train station. "I've been meaning to tell you this. About the party on Friday." Hands jammed into her jacket pockets, she stood on one foot, the other snaked around her calf, rubbing the back of her leg with the toe of her shoe.

My stomach tightened. Now she'd tell me it had all been a joke. They'd been teasing me. Making me feel as though I fit in was a prank some upperclasswoman had put them up to. "What about it?"

"Well, I know I told you there were just going to be girls at the party, but I wanted to make sure you'd come. There are going to be a few guys there, too. Don't worry, they're cool. They're guys I know from St. Bernard's, Allen-Stevenson, Buckley, and Collegiate."

"But—"

"They're going to sleep in the den. We'll meet them at the party and they'll come back with us. Is that cool?"

"Yeah," I said, relieved that her groundbreaking news had nothing to do with me.

"Good. Look, the girls and I chipped in on this. We were wondering if you could score us some weed? We want to have some real fun. I hope this is enough," Heather said, pressing crinkly bills into my hand. She patted my arm and stepped off the curb to hail a cab to take her home. I clutched the money in my hand, walked down Lexington to catch the 4 train, and rode home.

———————

When I got home that night, I searched in my mother's sewing basket until I found her seam ripper. I removed the deadly thing and carefully pulled off the stitches surrounding the little horse on the back pocket of my jeans.

I changed into these jeans, a trial run for the real test tomorrow. I was surprised to see myself in regular clothes. I changed shirts and threw on a light jacket. I counted out the money Heather had given me, then folded it neatly and slipped it into my pocket.

"Where are you going?" my mother asked when she saw me at the door.

"Out."

She didn't ask for any further explanation. Something had changed between us ever since the phone call. My blossoming friendships pleased her. My mother was as happy as if the invitation had been extended to her. Just yesterday, she'd put her hand on my shoulder while I was washing dishes. "I just want you to be happy," she'd said, her guilt now assuaged.

There was a store two blocks away that I knew was just a front. I'd gone in once to buy snacks and everything they sold me was expired, stale. I pushed through the door and walked in. One teenager hunched over an arcade game and two lounged against the corners of the wall. Twenty-five cent bags of popcorn, potato chips, and cheese curls, ten cent lollipops and five cent Peanut Chews and Super Bubbles were behind a counter covered in Plexiglas.

I walked up to the counter.

"Can I buy some weed here?"

I could feel everyone look at me. The man behind the counter squinted. He cleared his throat. He took a long time before he spoke. "We got soda and chips. What you see, that's what we got."

"But I want to buy some weed," I said. "I have money."

"We sell candy, soda, and chips," he said. "You wanna buy some candy?"

I didn't know what else do to. I was frustrated, wanting to argue. He knew it was a weed spot; I knew it was a weed spot. Was there some magic word I needed to say, some secret code that would let him know I meant business?

I pulled my money out and held it up to the Plexiglas. "Open sesame," I said.

He shook his head. I walked out.

A minute later, I felt someone behind me. I turned. I recognized him from the store; he'd been playing Pac-Man. "What was you doing in there? You crazy or something?"

I walked faster. "Leave me alone."

"That was real stupid. What, you not from around here?"

"I live here," I told him.

He didn't believe me. "Where?"

"Miller and Pitkin."

"I live on that block and I never seen you."

"Well, I go to school," I said.

His lips curled up then. They were full, made brown from smoking. His eyes were large, round, sleepy. He was older. Beautiful. I felt my mistake. "I didn't mean it like that."

He walked by my side. "So why you wanna buy weed?"

"Just to try it," I said. "For fun."

"You ever smoke a blunt before?"

"I didn't want a blunt. I wanted a joint."

He looked at me like I was stupid. "I was going to buy it for my friends," I said. "They asked me to get it for a party."

"So, you still want it?"

"Five dollars for a nickel bag, right?"

"You been watching too much TV," he said.

He refused to give it to me out on the street.

"Let's take a walk." We walked past my block and past the intermediate school to the park.

He stopped when we got to the swings. He sat down on one and backpedaled with his feet. "Come here."

I stood between his legs; we were eye to eye.

"What's your name?" he asked.

"You don't need to know."

He nodded. "So, you like white boys."

"No," I said.

"Black guys?"

"Nope."

"Girls?" he asked, his voice filled with disbelief and excitement.

"I don't like anybody," I said.

He pulled me towards him and kissed me. The faint sweet scent of smoke clung to his chin and I knew that I would smell of him. I had a feeling as if I were waiting in the subway for my train just before it pulls in and it was rushing down the track, blowing its dirty hot wind underneath my skirt, caressing the bare skin between pleats and socks. I tried to pull away but felt his hands on me cupping my butt, felt him slip the bag of weed into my back pocket. He turned me away from him, adjusting me so that I sat on his front thighs. Pretending to put his arms around me, he slipped his hands into my front pockets, seeking until he found my folded cash. Slick, I thought. Smooth. To anyone passing by, we looked like two fools making out in the park.

———————

The party, because I had longed for it, was a disappointment. The DJ could not mix one song into another. The lights never got very low. We stood in a papered gymnasium, in jeans, stretchy shirts, and too many coats of mascara. Girls from different schools divided themselves accordingly. Even without their uniforms, I could pick out the girls from Brearley, Chapin, and Spence. The boys Heather knew didn't show up until the end of the party. The only people I really knew were Heather, Taylor, Maya, and Ashley, and every time I saw them, they were all dancing, proudly showing off the moves I'd taught them. I ran into Nadira once that night when we were both getting sodas, but she didn't speak to me. I held up the wall all night. No one asked me to dance. I held my plastic cup of soda and thought of my mother at home, sleeping blissfully, happy and proud.

I only had one chance to talk to Heather at the dance. She came over to where I stood on the wall, her face flushed from dancing. "Did I do okay?" she asked me.

"You look good," I said.

"How do you like it?"

I shrugged. "It's okay."

"Aren't you dancing?"

"Nobody asked me."

"They probably don't want you to embarrass them," Heather said. I didn't bother to tell her that the dance I'd shown her was the only one I knew. "Don't worry," she said. "The real party starts when we get to my house."

At Heather's house, we had carte blanche. Her parents were asleep. Heather brought out the alcohol, I pulled out the small bag of weed, and we wasted no time getting drunk and high. A boy Heather had introduced as Gabe wanted to play a version of Spin the Bottle.

I was the first victim. Gabe and I looked at each other across the thin neck of the bottle, unsure.

"He's never made it with a black girl before," Taylor said.

"So?"

"Go in the closet with him," Heather suggested. "Show him how it's done." She clapped me on the arm and gave me a push. Gabe held out his hand and I got up, unsteadily taking it. I wasn't sure that I wanted to go, but I went.

We sat in the deep closet; the hems of Heather's jackets grazed the tops of our heads. I decided I couldn't, wouldn't do it. Gabe slid a finger up my arm and I shivered, backing away. "Wow, this closet is really big, huh?"

"It's cool," he said. "We don't have to, you know, I mean unless you want..." He looked hopeful even in the dark.

"I can't," I said.

"Maybe if you touch it." He took my hand and rubbed it against his denim crotch, his hand over mine.

"I'm going to be sick," I said.

"Whoa, wait a minute," he said. "Okay."

"Sick sick sick," I said.

He leaned back, but in a minute he asked, "Can I touch your breasts?"

"I don't think so."

"Just once?" He reached under my shirt. My bra was lace, one of my mother's castoffs. My underwear did not match, but I knew he would never know that.

"Hey," he said, feeling the lace cups of my bra. "Whoa. Hey."

"Whoa. Hey," I said, mocking him, feeling suddenly warm.

His hand closed over my breast and squeezed. It made me think of the old-fashioned cars in a Bugs Bunny cartoon. "Beep beep," I said, then burst out laughing. He laughed too and then the two of us couldn't stop laughing. We fell against each other, laughing. Then he pulled me through the jackets and across his lap, pushing his tongue into my mouth, banging his teeth against mine, kissing me wet and sloppy. I tasted the strong flavor of weed on his tongue and thought of the boy who'd sold it to me, how beautiful he'd been, how though we lived just a few blocks apart, we were strangers. Like the boy pressing himself against me, we were from two different worlds. They were both from the real world, their own distinct ones, but I was somewhere in limbo. Set apart, I didn't know how to let either of them in.

I knew Gabe's hands were tugging my shirt down, that in a minute they'd be working the latch of my bra, but I didn't stop him. In the dark of Heather's closet, I tried to see what Gabe saw. I pictured an image of myself that was Heather's body and face, only it was black and it was me. I saw how much of me would change; I saw the girl I would become. And I decided to go ahead and miss myself right now, knowing that the girl I would become wouldn't know how to appreciate me at all.

CELL ONE

Chimamanda Ngozi Adichie

The first time our house was robbed, it was our neighbor Osita who climbed in through the dining-room window and stole our TV and VCR, and the *Purple Rain* and *Thriller* videotapes that my father had brought back from America. The second time our house was robbed, it was my brother Nnamabia, who faked a break-in and stole my mother's jewelry. It happened on a Sunday. My parents had travelled to their home town to visit our grandparents, so Nnamabia and I went to church alone. He drove my mother's green Peugeot 504. We sat together in church as we usually did, but we did not have time to nudge each other and stifle giggles about somebody's ugly hat or threadbare caftan, because Nnamabia left without a word after ten minutes. He came back just before the priest said, "The Mass is ended, go in peace." I was a little piqued. I imagined that he had gone off to smoke or to see some girl, since he had the car to himself for once; but he could at least have told me. We drove home in silence, and when he parked in our long driveway I stayed back to pick some ixora flowers while Nnamabia unlocked the front door. I went inside to find him standing in the middle of the parlor.

"We've been robbed!" he said.

It took me a moment to take in the room. Even then, I felt that there was a theatrical quality to the way the drawers had been flung open. Or perhaps it was simply that I knew my brother too well. Later, when my parents had come home and neighbors began to troop in to say *ndo*—sorry—and to snap their fingers and heave their shoulders up and down, I sat alone in my room upstairs and realized what the queasiness in my gut was: Nnamabia had done it, I knew. My father knew, too. He pointed out that the window louvres had been slipped out from the inside, rather than from the outside (Nnamabia was usually smarter than that—perhaps he had been in a hurry to get back to church before Mass ended), and that the robber knew exactly where my mother's jewelry was: in the back left corner of her metal trunk. Nnamabia stared at my father with wounded eyes and said that he may have done horrible things in the past, things that had caused my parents pain, but that he had done nothing in this case. He walked out the back door and did not come home that night. Or the next night. Or the night after. Two weeks later, he came home gaunt, smelling of beer, crying, saying he was sorry, that he had pawned the jewelry to the Hausa traders in Enugu, and that all the money was gone.

"How much did they give you for my gold?" our mother asked him. And when he told her she placed both hands on her head and cried, "Oh! Oh! *Chi m egbuo m!* My God has killed me!" I wanted to slap her. My father asked Nnamabia to write a report: how he had pawned the jewelry, what he had spent the money on, with whom he had spent it. I didn't think that Nnamabia would tell the truth, and I don't think that my father thought he would, but he liked reports, my professor father, he liked to have things written down and nicely documented. Besides, Nnamabia was seventeen, with a carefully tended beard. He was already between secondary school and university, and was too old for caning. What else could my father have done? After Nnamabia had written the report, my father filed it in the steel cabinet in his study where he kept our school papers.

"That he could hurt his mother like that!" was the last thing my father said on the subject.

But Nnamabia hadn't set out to hurt her. He had done it because my mother's jewelry was the only thing of any value in the house: a lifetime's accumulation of solid-gold pieces. He had done it, too, because other sons of professors were doing it. This was the season of thefts on our serene campus. Boys who had grown up watching *Sesame Street*, reading Enid Blyton, eating cornflakes for breakfast, and attending the university staff primary school in polished brown sandals were now cutting through the mosquito netting of their neighbors' windows, sliding out glass louvres, and climbing in to steal TVs and VCRs. We knew the thieves. Still, when the professors saw one another at the staff club or at church or at a faculty meeting, they were careful to moan about the riffraff from town coming onto their sacred campus to steal.

The thieving boys were the popular ones. They drove their parents' cars in the evening, their seats pushed back and their arms stretched out to reach the steering wheel. Osita, our neighbor who had stolen our TV only weeks before Nnamabia's theft, was lithe and handsome in a brooding sort of way, and walked with the grace of a cat. His shirts were always crisply ironed, and I used to watch him across the hedge, then close my eyes and imagine that he was walking toward me, coming to claim me as his. He never noticed me. When he stole from us, my parents did not go over to Professor Ebube's house to ask for our things back. But they knew it was Osita. Osita was two years older than Nnamabia; most of the thieving boys were a little older than Nnamabia, and maybe that was why Nnamabia had not stolen from another person's house. Perhaps he did not feel old enough, qualified enough, for anything more serious than my mother's jewelry.

Nnamabia looked just like my mother—he had her fair complexion and large eyes, and a generous mouth that curved perfectly. When my mother took us to the market, traders would call out, "Hey! Madam, why did you waste your fair skin on a boy and leave the girl so dark? What is a boy doing with all this beauty?" And my mother would chuckle, as though she took a mischievous and joyful responsibility for Nnamabia's looks. When, at eleven, Nnamabia broke the window of his classroom with a stone, my mother gave him the money to replace it and didn't tell my father. When, a few years later, he took the key to my father's car and pressed it into a bar of soap that my father found before Nnamabia could take it to a locksmith, she made vague sounds about how he was just experimenting and it didn't mean anything. When he stole the exam questions from the study and sold them to my father's students, she yelled at him, but then told my father that Nnamabia was sixteen, after all, and really should be given more pocket money.

I don't know whether Nnamabia felt remorse for stealing her jewelry. I could not always tell from my brother's gracious, smiling face what he really felt. He and I did not talk about it, and neither did my parents. Even though my mother's sisters sent her their gold earrings, even though she bought a new gold chain from Mrs. Mozie—the glamorous woman who imported gold from Italy—and began to drive to Mrs. Mozie's house once a month to pay in installments, we never talked about what had happened to her jewelry. It was as if by pretending that Nnamabia had not done the things he had done we could give him the opportunity to start afresh. The robbery might never have been mentioned again if Nnamabia had not been arrested two years later, in his second year of university.

By then, it was the season of cults on the Nsukka campus, when signs all over the university read in bold letters, "SAY NO TO CULTS." The Black Axe, the Buccaneers, and the Pirates were the best known. They had once been benign fraternities, but they had evolved, and now eighteen-year-olds who had mastered the swagger of American rap videos were undergoing secret initiations that sometimes left one or two of them dead on Odim Hill. Guns and tortured loyalties became common. A boy would leer at a girl who turned out to be the girlfriend of the Capone of the Black Axe, and that boy, as he walked to a kiosk later to buy a cigarette, would be stabbed in the thigh. He would turn out to be a Buccaneer, and so one of his fellow-Buccaneers would go to a beer parlor and shoot the nearest Black Axe in the leg, and then the next day another Buccaneer would be shot dead in the refectory, his body falling onto aluminum plates of *garri*, and that evening a Black Axe—a professor's son—would be hacked to death in his room, his CD player splattered with blood. It was inane. It was so abnormal that it quickly became normal. Girls stayed in their rooms after classes, and lecturers quivered, and when a fly buzzed too loudly people jumped. So the police were called in. They sped across campus in their rickety blue Peugeot 505 and glowered at the students, their rusty guns poking out of the car windows.

Nnamabia came home from his lectures laughing. He thought that the police would have to do better than that; everyone knew the cult boys had newer guns.

My parents watched Nnamabia with silent concern, and I knew that they, too, were wondering if he was in a cult. Cult boys were popular, and Nnamabia was very popular. Boys yelled out his nickname—"The Funk!"—and shook his hand whenever he passed by, and girls, especially the popular ones, hugged him for too long when they said hello. He went to all the parties, the tame ones on campus and the wilder ones in town, and he was the kind of ladies' man who was also a guy's guy, the kind who smoked a packet of Rothmans a day and was reputed to be able to finish a case of Star beer in a single sitting. But it seemed more his style to befriend all the cult boys and yet not be one himself. And I was not entirely sure, either, that my brother had whatever it took—guts or diffidence—to join a cult.

The only time I asked him if he was in a cult, he looked at me with surprise, as if I should have known better than to ask, before replying, "Of course not." I believed him. My dad believed him, too, when he asked. But our believing him made little difference, because he had already been arrested for belonging to a cult.

This is how it happened. On a humid Monday, four cult members waited at the campus gate and waylaid a professor driving a red Mercedes. They pressed a gun to her head, shoved her out of the car, and drove it to the Faculty of Engineering, where they shot three boys who were coming out of the building. It was noon. I was in a class nearby, and when we heard the shots our lecturer was the first to run out the door. There was loud screaming, and suddenly the stairwells were packed with scrambling students unsure where to run. Outside, the bodies lay on the lawn. The Mercedes had already screeched away. Many students hastily packed their bags, and *okada* drivers charged twice the usual fare to take them to the motor park to get on a bus. The vice-chancellor announced that all evening classes would be cancelled and everyone had to stay indoors after 9 P.M. This did not make much sense to me, since the shooting had happened in sparkling daylight, and perhaps it did not make sense to Nnamabia, either, because the first night of the curfew he didn't come home. I assumed that he had spent the night at a friend's; he did not always come home anyway. But the next morning a security man came to tell my parents that Nnamabia had been arrested at a bar with some cult boys and was at the police station. My mother screamed, *"Ekwuzikwana!* Don't say that!" My father calmly thanked the security man. We drove to the police station in town, and there a constable chewing on the tip of a dirty pen said, "You mean those cult boys arrested last night? They have been taken to Enugu. Very serious case! We must stop this cult business once and for all!"

We got back into the car, and a new fear gripped us all. Nsukka, which was made up of our slow, insular campus and the slower, more insular town, was manageable; my father knew the police superintendent. But Enugu was anonymous. There the police could do what they were famous for doing when under pressure to produce results: kill people.

––––––––––

The Enugu police station was in a sprawling, sandy compound. My mother bribed the policemen at the desk with money, and with jollof rice and meat, and they allowed Nnamabia to come out of his cell and sit on a bench under a mango tree with us. Nobody asked why he had stayed out the night before. Nobody said that the police were wrong to walk into a bar and arrest all the boys drinking there, including the barman. Instead, we listened to Nnamabia talk.

"If we ran Nigeria like this cell," he said, "we would have no problems. Things are so organized. Our cell has a chief and he has a second-in-command, and when you come in you are expected to give them some money. If you don't, you're in trouble."

"And did you have any money?" my mother asked.

Nnamabia smiled, his face more beautiful than ever, despite the new pimple-like insect bite on his forehead, and said that he had slipped his money into his anus shortly after the arrest. He knew the policemen would take it if he didn't hide it, and he knew that he would need it to buy his peace in the cell. My parents said nothing for a while. I imagined Nnamabia rolling hundred-naira notes into a thin cigarette shape and then reaching into the back of his trousers to slip them into himself. Later, as we drove back to Nsukka, my father said, "This is what I should have done when he stole your jewelry. I should have had him locked up in a cell."

My mother stared out the window.

"Why?" I asked.

"Because this has shaken him. Couldn't you see?" my father asked with a smile. I couldn't see it. Nnamabia had seemed fine to me, slipping his money into his anus and all.

Nnamabia's first shock was seeing a Buccaneer sobbing. The boy was tall and tough, rumored to have carried out one of the killings and likely to become Capone next semester, and yet there he was in the cell, cowering and sobbing after the chief gave him a light slap on the back of the head. Nnamabia told me this in a voice lined with both disgust and disappointment; it was as if he had suddenly been made to see that the Incredible Hulk was really just painted green. His second shock was learning about the cell farthest away from his, Cell One. He had never seen it, but every day two policemen carried a dead man out of Cell One, stopping by Nnamabia's cell to make sure that the corpse was seen by all.

Those in the cell who could afford to buy old plastic paint cans of water bathed every other morning. When they were let out into the yard, the policemen watched them and often shouted, "Stop that or you are going to Cell One now!" Nnamabia could not imagine a place worse than his cell, which was so crowded that he often stood pressed against the wall. The wall had cracks where tiny *kwalikwata* lived; their bites were fierce and sharp, and when he yelped his cellmates mocked him. The biting was worse during the night, when they all slept on their sides, head to foot, to make room for one another, except the chief, who slept with his whole back lavishly on the floor. It was also the chief who divided up the two plates of rice that were pushed into the cell every day. Each person got two mouthfuls.

Nnamabia told us this during the first week. As he spoke, I wondered if the bugs in the wall had bitten his face or if the bumps spreading across his forehead were due to an infection. Some of them were tipped with cream-colored pus. Once in a while, he scratched at them. I wanted him to stop talking. He seemed to enjoy his new role as the sufferer of indignities, and he did not understand how lucky he was that the policemen allowed him to come out and eat our food, or how stupid he'd been to stay out drinking that night, and how uncertain his chances were of being released.

We visited him every day for the first week. We took my father's old Volvo, because my mother's Peugeot was unsafe for trips outside Nsukka. By the end of the week, I noticed that my parents were acting differently—subtly so, but differently. My father no longer gave a monologue, as soon as we were waved through the police checkpoints, on how illiterate and corrupt the police were. He did not bring up the day when they had delayed us for an hour because he'd refused to bribe them, or how they had stopped a bus in which my beautiful cousin Ogechi was travelling and singled her out and called her a whore because she had two cell phones, and asked her for so much money that she had knelt on the ground in the rain begging them to let her go. My mother did not mumble that the policemen were symptoms of a larger malaise. Instead, my parents remained silent. It was as if by refusing to criticize the police they would somehow make Nnamabia's freedom more likely. "Delicate" was the word the superintendent at Nsukka had used. To get Nnamabia out anytime soon would be delicate, especially with the police commissioner in Enugu giving gloating, preening interviews about the arrest of the cultists. The cult problem was serious. Big Men in Abuja were following events. Everybody wanted to seem as if he were doing something.

The second week, I told my parents that we were not going to visit Nnamabia. We did not know how long this would last, and petrol was too expensive for us to drive three hours every day. Besides, it would not hurt Nnamabia to fend for himself for one day.

My mother said that nobody was begging me to come—I could sit there and do nothing while my innocent brother suffered. She started walking toward the car, and I ran after her. When I got outside, I was not sure what to do, so I picked up a stone near the ixora bush and hurled it at the windshield of the Volvo. I heard the brittle sound and saw the tiny lines spreading like rays on the glass before I turned and dashed upstairs and locked myself in my room. I heard my mother shouting. I heard my father's voice. Finally, there was silence. Nobody went to see Nnamabia that day. It surprised me, this little victory.

We visited him the next day. We said nothing about the windshield, although the cracks had spread out like ripples on a frozen stream. The policeman at the desk, the pleasant dark-skinned one, asked why we had not come the day before—he had missed my mother's jollof rice. I expected Nnamabia to ask, too, even to be upset, but he looked oddly sober. He did not eat all of his rice.

"What is wrong?" my mother said, and Nnamabia began to speak almost immediately, as if he had been waiting to be asked. An old man had been pushed into his cell the day before—a man perhaps in his mid-seventies, white-haired, skin finely wrinkled, with an old-fashioned dignity about him. His son was wanted for armed robbery, and when the police had not been able to find his son they had decided to lock up the father.

"The man did nothing," Nnamabia said.

"But you did nothing, either," my mother said.

Nnamabia shook his head as if our mother did not understand. The following days, he was more subdued. He spoke less, and mostly about the old man: how he could not afford bathing water, how the others made fun of him or accused him of hiding his son, how the chief ignored him, how he looked frightened and so terribly small.

"Does he know where his son is?" my mother asked.

"He has not seen his son in four months," Nnamabia said.

"Of course it is wrong," my mother said. "But this is what the police do all the time. If they do not find the person they are looking for, they lock up his relative."

"The man is ill," Nnamabia said. "His hands shake, even when he's asleep."

He closed the container of rice and turned to my father. "I want to give him some of this, but if I bring it into the cell the chief will take it."

My father went over and asked the policeman at the desk if we could be allowed to see the old man in Nnamabia's cell for a few minutes. The policeman was the light-skinned acerbic one who never said thank you when my mother handed over the rice-and-money bribe, and now he sneered in my father's face and said that he could well lose his job for letting even Nnamabia out and yet now we were asking for another person? Did we think this was visiting day at a boarding school? My father came back and sat down with a sigh, and Nnamabia silently scratched at his bumpy face.

The next day, Nnamabia barely touched his rice. He said that the policemen had splashed soapy water on the floor and walls of the cell, as they usually did, and that the old man, who had not bathed in a week, had yanked his shirt off and rubbed his frail back against the wet floor. The policemen started to laugh when they saw him do this, and then they asked him to take all his clothes off and parade in the corridor outside the cell; as he did, they laughed louder and asked whether his son the thief knew that Papa's buttocks were so shrivelled. Nnamabia was staring at his yellow-orange rice as he spoke, and when he looked up his eyes were filled with tears, my worldly brother, and I felt a tenderness for him that I would not have been able to describe if I had been asked to.

There was another attack on campus—a boy hacked another boy with an axe—two days later.

"This is good," my mother said. "Now they cannot say that they have arrested all the cult boys." We did not go to Enugu that day; instead my parents went to see the local police superintendent, and they came back with good news. Nnamabia and the barman were to be released immediately. One of the cult boys, under questioning, had insisted that Nnamabia was not a member. The next day, we left earlier than usual, without jollof rice. My mother was always nervous when we drove, saying to my father, *"Nekwa ya!* Watch out!," as if he could not see the cars making dangerous turns in the other lane, but this time she did it so often that my father pulled over before we got to Ninth Mile and snapped, "Just who is driving this car?"

Two policemen were flogging a man with *koboko* as we drove into the police station. At first, I thought it was Nnamabia, and then I thought it was the old man from his cell. It was neither. I knew the boy on the ground, who was writhing and shouting with each lash. He was called Aboy and had the grave ugly face of a hound; he drove a Lexus around campus and was said to be a Buccaneer. I tried not to look at him as we walked inside. The policeman on duty, the one with tribal marks on his cheeks who always said "God bless you" when he took his bribe, looked away when he saw us, and I knew that something was wrong. My parents gave him the note from the superintendent. The policeman did not even glance at it. He knew about the release order, he told my father, the barman had already been released, but there was a complication with the boy. My mother began to shout, "What do you mean? Where is my son?"

The policeman got up. "I will call my senior to explain to you."

My mother rushed at him and pulled on his shirt. "Where is my son? Where is my son?" My father pried her away, and the policeman brushed at his chest, as if she had left some dirt there, before he turned to walk away.

"Where is our son?" my father asked in a voice so quiet, so steely, that the policeman stopped.

"They took him away, sir," he said.

"They took him away? What are you saying?" my mother was yelling. "Have you killed my son? Have you killed my son?"

"Where is our son?" my father asked again.

"My senior said I should call him when you came," the policeman said, and this time he hurried through a door.

It was after he left that I felt suddenly chilled by fear; I wanted to run after him and, like my mother, pull at his shirt until he produced Nnamabia. The senior policeman came out, and I searched his blank face for clues.

"Good day, sir," he said to my father.

"Where is our son?" my father asked. My mother breathed noisily.

"No problem, sir. It is just that we transferred him. I will take you there right away." There was something nervous about the policeman; his face remained blank, but he did not meet my father's eyes.

"Transferred him?"

"We got the order this morning. I would have sent somebody for him, but we don't have petrol, so I was waiting for you to come so that we could go together."

"Why was he transferred?"

"I was not here, sir. They said that he misbehaved yesterday and they took him to Cell One, and then yesterday evening there was a transfer of all the people in Cell One to another site."

"He misbehaved? What do you mean?"

"I was not here, sir."

My mother spoke in a broken voice: "Take me to my son! Take me to my son right now!"

I sat in the back with the policeman, who smelled of the kind of old camphor that seemed to last forever in my mother's trunk. No one spoke except for the policeman when he gave my father directions. We arrived about fifteen minutes later, my father driving inordinately fast. The small, walled compound looked neglected, with patches of overgrown grass strewn with old bottles and plastic bags. The policeman hardly waited for my father to stop the car before he opened the door and hurried out, and again I felt chilled. We were in a godforsaken part of town, and there was no sign that said "Police Station." There was a strange deserted feeling in the air. But the policeman soon emerged with Nnamabia. There he was, my handsome brother, walking toward us, seemingly unchanged, until he came close enough for my mother to hug him, and I saw him wince and back away—his arm was covered in soft-looking welts. There was dried blood around his nose.

"Why did they beat you like this?" my mother asked him. She turned to the policeman. "Why did you people do this to my son? Why?"

The man shrugged. There was a new insolence to his demeanor; it was as if he had been uncertain about Nnamabia's well-being but now, reassured, could let himself talk. "You cannot raise your children properly—all of you people who feel important because you work at the university—and when your children misbehave you think they should not be punished. You are lucky they released him."

My father said, "Let's go."

He opened the door and Nnamabia climbed in, and we drove home. My father did not stop at any of the police checkpoints on the road, and, once, a policeman gestured threateningly with his gun as we sped past. The only time my mother opened her mouth on the drive home was to ask Nnamabia if he wanted us to stop and buy some *okpa*. Nnamabia said no. We had arrived in Nsukka before he finally spoke.

"Yesterday, the policemen asked the old man if he wanted a free half bucket of water. He said yes. So they told him to take his clothes off and parade the corridor. Most of my cellmates were laughing. Some of them said it was wrong to treat an old man like that." Nnamabia paused. "I shouted at the policeman. I told him the old man was innocent and ill, and if they kept him here it wouldn't help them find his son, because the man did not even know where his son was. They said that I should shut up immediately, that they would take me to Cell One. I didn't care. I didn't shut up. So they pulled me out and slapped me and took me to Cell One."

Nnamabia stopped there, and we asked him nothing else. Instead, I imagined him calling the policeman a stupid idiot, a spineless coward, a sadist, a bastard, and I imagined the shock of the policemen—the chief staring openmouthed, the other cellmates stunned at the audacity of the boy from the university. And I imagined the old man himself looking on with surprised pride and quietly refusing to undress. Nnamabia did not say what had happened to him in Cell One, or what happened at the new site. It would have been so easy for him, my charming brother, to make a sleek drama of his story, but he did not.

In the Blink of God's Eye

FROM

ALL AUNT HAGAR'S CHILDREN

Edward P. Jones

That 1901 winter when the wife and her husband were still new to Washington, there came to the wife like a scent carried on the wind some word that wolves roamed the streets and roads of the city after sundown. The wife, Ruth Patterson, knew what wolves could do: she had an uncle who went to Alaska in 1895 to hunt for gold, an uncle who was devoured by wolves not long after he slept under his first Alaskan moon. Still, the night, even in godforsaken Washington, sometimes had that old song that could pull Ruth up and out of her bed, the way it did when she was a girl across the Potomac River in Virginia where all was safe and all was family. Her husband, Aubrey, always slept the sleep of a man not long out of boyhood and never woke. Hearing the song call her from her new bed in Washington, Ruth, ever mindful of the wolves, would take up their knife and pistol and kiss Aubrey's still-hairless face and descend to the porch. She was well past seventeen, and he was edging toward eighteen, a couple not even seven whole months married. The house—and its twin next door—was always quiet, for those city houses were populated mostly by country people used to going to bed with the chickens. On the porch, only a few paces from the corner of 3rd and L Streets, N.W., she would stare at the gaslight on the corner and smell the smoke from the hearth of someone's dying fire, listening to the song and remembering the world around Arlington, Virginia.

That night in late January she watched a drunken woman across 3rd Street make her way down 3rd to K Street, where she fell, silently, her dress settling down about her once her body had come to rest. The drunken woman was one more thing to hold against Washington. The woman might have been the same one from two weeks ago, the same one from five weeks ago. The woman lay there for a long time, and Ruth pulled her coat tight around her neck, wondering if she should venture out into the cold of no-man's-land to help her. Then the woman pulled herself up slowly on all four limbs and at last made her stumbling way down K toward 4th Street. She must know, Ruth thought, surely she must know about the wolves. Ruth pulled her eyes back to the gaslight, and as she did, she noticed for the first time the bundle suspended from the tree in the yard, hanging from the apple tree that hadn't borne fruit in more than ten years.

Ruth fell back a step, as if she had been struck. She raised the pistol in her right hand, but the hand refused to steady itself, and so she dropped the knife and held the pistol with both hands, waiting for something terrible and canine to burst from the bundle. An invisible hand locked about her mouth and halted the cry she wanted to give the world. A wind came up and played with her coat, her nightgown, tapped her ankles and hands, then went over and nudged the bundle so that it moved an inch or so to the left, an inch or so to the right. The rope creaked with the brittleness of age. And then the wind came back and gave her breath again.

A kitten's whine rose feebly from the bundle, a cry of innocence she at first refused to believe. Blinking the tears from her eyes, she reached down and took up the knife with her left hand, holding both weapons out in front of her. She waited. What a friend that drunken woman could be now. She looked at the gaslight, and the dancing yellow spirit in the dirty glass box took her down the two steps and walked her out into the yard until she was two feet from the bundle. She poked it twice with the knife, and in response, like some reward, the bundle offered a short whine, a whine it took her a moment or two to recognize.

So this was Washington, she thought as she reached up on her tiptoes and cut the two pieces of rope that held the bundle to the tree's branch and unwrapped first one blanket and then another. So this was the Washington her Aubrey had brought her across the Potomac River to—a city where they hung babies in night trees.

When Aubrey Patterson was three years old, his father took the family to Kansas where some of the father's people were prospering. The sky goes all the way up to God napping on his throne, the father's brother had written from Kansas, and you can get much before he wakes up. The father borrowed money from family and friends for train tickets and a few new clothes, thinking, knowing, he would be able to pay them back with Kansas money before a year or so had gone by. Pay them all back, son, Aubrey's father said moments before he died, some twelve years after the family had boarded the train from Kansas and returned to Virginia with not much more to their names than bile. And with the clarity of a mind seeing death, his father, Miles, reeled off the names of all those he owed money to, commencing with the man to whom he owed the most.

Aubrey's two older sisters married not long after the family returned to Virginia and moved with their husbands to other farms in Arlington County. They—Miles, the mother, Essie, and Aubrey—lived mostly from hand to mouth, but they did not go without. Aubrey's sisters and their husbands were generous, and the three of them, in their little house on their little piece of land with a garden and chickens and two cows, were surrounded by country people just as generous who had known the family when they had had a brighter sun.

A little bit before Aubrey turned thirteen, it came to be that his mother took to going off down the road most evenings. "Goin to set with Miss Sally a piece," she would say of the old woman a half mile or so away. But her son learned that way before Miss Sally's cabin there lived a man in a shack with a busted door, and that was often where she stopped. If his father, a consumptive, knew, he never said. At first, before he closed his heart to her, Aubrey would stand on the porch and watch her go off, one of the yellow dogs following her until she turned and threw a stone at her. The other dog rarely moved from under the house. Aubrey would watch the road even after she had disappeared. "Whatcha you doin, son?" his father would ask from inside. "Come read me a few verses, maybe some chapters." His mother had taught him to read in Kansas when he was four. Her people were all book people.

They grew closer, the father and the son, in a way that had not been possible in Kansas, where each day's new catastrophe had a claim on their hearts. His father encouraged him to attend church. "It's but a little bit outa your whole life, son," Miles said, remembering how angry God must have been after he had awakened from his nap when the family was in Kansas. "And God has a long memory." His son was nearing fourteen then. So each Sunday morning, the boy, alone, would set off down the road, opposite the way to Miss Sally's, carrying the Bible inherited from his maternal grandfather, the same book he read from to his father about the trials and tribulations of the Jews thousands of years before the first black slave set foot in America.

Now Ruth Hawkins, whom Aubrey would one day marry, had four brothers born on one side of her and four brothers born on the other side, so men were no mystery to her, and they were not gods. She and Aubrey had played together as little bitty babies, though they had not remembered. But the old women all around Arlington remembered, and they liked to recite the short history of the two after Aubrey returned from Kansas. The old women would mingle after church, only steps away from the Praying Rock Baptist Church graveyard, leaning on walking sticks and on grandchildren anxious as colts to be out and away. "Come here, little bit," they would say to Ruth and Aubrey, seeing down the line that the two had a future together. "You member that time...," and they would go on with a story about two playing infants that seemed to have no end.

At first, Ruth and Aubrey had nothing to say to each other after church, after the old women's talk had turned to something else and the two were free to go. He was always desperate to get back to his father, and she had a whole world of people and things to occupy all the moments of her days. Even her dreams were crowded, she told a friend. Then, in late August of 1899, Mrs. Halley Stafford, who, people said, had given her name to the comet, decided she had had enough and died in the bed she was conceived and born in. Representing her own family at the funeral, Ruth stepped up to the open grave with a handful of dirt and dust and let it sprinkle on Mrs. Stafford's coffin as it was lowered down into its resting place. The new preacher, with less than a hundred shaves to his name, kept repeating, "Dust to dust...Ashes to ashes..." The dirt flowed ever so slowly out of Ruth's hand, and in the slowness of the moments she began to feel as though she could count each grain as it all fell from her. She turned from the grave and looked at her mother, at her father, at her brothers, at everyone assembled about her, and all the while the dirt and dust kept flowing. After the funeral, she came up to Aubrey along the path that led to the road that would take him home. He stopped, and she walked a half circle or so around him, and he took off his hat and held it midway up his chest, hoping it would not be long off his head. Over her shoulders he could see departing people and buggies and wagons and horses and mules, stirring up heaps of dust. The sun behind her flowed soft yellow through the threads of her summer bonnet. "When you gonna ask my daddy when you and your daddy can take supper with us?" she said. He blinked. "I reckon...I reckon next week," he said, flinging out any words he thought would satisfy her. This was their longest conversation up to that moment. "Could be the fire next time, come next week," Ruth said. He thought of his father carrying him at four years old on his shoulders along the flat roads of Kansas. In his bed that night, he realized that she had made that half circle so the sun would be out of her face and full on his.

Whenever they were together after that, her youngest brother, Harold, eight years old, accompanied them. More and more of the toys that had once belonged to his brothers were coming his way, so he was mostly a happy boy. Armies of wooden men, still vital after all those years of playing hands, were now his to command as he had always dreamed. In October and early November, before the cold

came upon them, he would carry a platoon of soldiers in a small
burlap sack as he walked several steps behind Ruth and Aubrey when
they strolled a foot apart, hands to themselves, down to the creek.
Harold would stamp down the grass and position the soldiers about
the ground as the couple, giggling, skipped stones into the quiet water, or sat on what passed for a bank and saw who could kick up the
biggest splash with their bare feet. The boy would lie back and tap
the soldiers' heads against the face of the sun, putting fighting
words in their mouths. In late February, after the cold took an early
parting, his father told Harold it would be fine if the couple walked
hand in hand, and the boy, on his own, increased the distance between himself and them by three paces and stopped singing the song
he sang when he thought they were too close. Into March, into April,
well beyond the planting season, he rested a squad of men in his lap
while he played checkers with Aubrey's father in the front room that
now doubled as the man's bedroom. And when he could not hear the
mumble of the couple's conversation from the porch, the boy would
excuse himself to Miles and go to the door, soldiers in both his hands.
When he was satisfied that all was proper, he would go back to the
game. He had already given names to all his men in the first days of
his sister's courting, but in the time it took Ruth and Aubrey to grow
comfortable with each other and then to move into love, Harold had
more than enough time to rename them, enough time to promote a
sergeant to colonel for saving a motherless kitten about to drown, to
send a one-arm captain home to his family for sassing him.

Aubrey Patterson would go only twice down to the shack his mother
shared with the man she had taken up with. She was an outcast to all
the world, even more so than the man. Not even the postman went
there.

The dawn he found his father dead, Aubrey first called him and
waited. When he knew at last, he kissed his father's lips and his
hands. Then, as he had done most mornings, he washed his father's
face, combed his hair, and shaved him with the pearl-handled razor
Miles's grandfather had purchased from a whore in Annapolis. He
took off his father's nightclothes and put on the best clothes the man

had owned, just as he would have if they were expecting company. Finally, he sat in a chair beside the man's bed and read a chapter of Genesis and two chapters of Psalms. Then he went down the road to the shack. "Case you wanna know, case you care...," he began after he had shouted for his mother from the yard. All the way down there, he thought of his father, and all the way back, he thought of Ruth.

The second time he went to the shack, it was to tell his mother he was getting married. He and Ruth were in the wagon his father had left him. Ruth stayed in her seat as Aubrey got out and shouted for his mother as he had done the day his father died. In a few minutes they were gone, his mother this time not coming to the door. Essie Patterson, living in sin, disappeared out of his life. His oldest sister sent word to him when she died. "We gotta go to her," Ruth told him, two weeks after they started life in Washington. "We gotta go to her. She the only mother you ever had," which was something she would not be able to say about the baby in the night tree.

They spent the first weeks of their marriage in his house. In between the lovemaking, they told each other things they had not been able, for any manner of reason, to say when they were courting. That third night ended with his confessing that he had once stolen a chicken. He had not started out to do it, he told her, but he was walking by Mr. Johnson's place and the chicken followed him down the road, and no matter what he did, the chicken would not go back home. Then God began to whisper to him, and those whisperings, along with his failing father at home, convinced him that Mr. Johnson could stand the loss of one chicken, a tough thing to eat as it turned out. She found it endearing that he could not tell the difference between God's counsel and the why-the-heck-not advice of the Devil.

About two in the morning that eighth night, Ruth, hearing that old night song, sat on the side of the bed and reached down in the dark for the slippers he had presented her. They were not where she thought she had put them and she settled for his boots. Outside in the warm, she let the flow of the song lead her about the place, lit by a moon that commanded a sky with not even one cloud. She walked all about, even near the dark of the night woods, for there was no cautionary story about wolves roaming in Virginia. An owl hooted and flew up, wings as wide as the arms of a scarecrow. It disappeared in the woods and Ruth turned back to the house. She would miss this little piece of a farm, but Aubrey's aunt, Joan Hardesty, had assured her that Washington was a good place to be. Joan had taken him aside in the moments after his father's funeral and told him there was always a place for him with her if he didn't think Virginia was good enough to give him a future. He had grown up knowing her as a dainty thing, famous for separating the different foods on her plate with toothpicks. Ruth, nearing the house, paused to admire the moon that had started out dusty orange at the horizon and had gotten whiter and whiter the more it rose. Paul Hardesty had married Joan not two months after first meeting her, and they had gone across the Potomac River to Washington, and the city had put some muscle on her. On the day of Aubrey's father's funeral, Joan had been a widow for more than a year, Paul having been killed by one of the first automobiles ever to go down the streets of Washington. The story of death by an automobile was such a novel one that white men told it in their newspapers. The white newspapers never mentioned that Paul was unable to run from the automobile because one of his legs was near useless, having been twisted and turned as the midwife pulled him from the womb.

"It grows on you," Ruth, at the funeral, remembered Joan saying of Washington, like a woman talking about a lover whose shortcomings she would just have to live with. "You just let it grow on you." In Washington Joan had found a special plate with compartments, and so never had to use toothpicks again to separate her food.

Ruth now came around the side of the house, stopped at the well, and pulled up the bucket and drank deeply. A married woman could dispense with the drinking cup. Aubrey's father was dead, and his mother less than a whore, so there was nothing much for him in Virginia anymore. He smiled when he said Ruth's name, and he smiled when he told people he was going to live in Washington, D.C. Ruth had no feeling for Washington. She had generations of family in Virginia, but she was a married woman and had pledged to cling to her husband. And God had the baby in the tree and the story of the wolves in the roads waiting for her.

"Ruth, honey?" Aubrey stood in the doorway. "Sweetheart, you hurtin or somethin?" The bucket had been returned and she had been watching the moon. "You all right, honey?" After your parents, Miles had advised Aubrey, nothing stands between you and unhappiness and death but your own true wife.

She turned from the path that led out to the road. "I'm fine as Sunday," she said. "I get this way sometimes. Specially when I'm happy." He came to her and she came to him.

"Thought maybe you was sleepwalkin. Knew a nice woman in Kansas who did that, useta go out and try to milk her cows till one of em kicked her one night."

"Not me. I'm wide awake. See my eyes." He laughed and put his arms around her. His arms were not trembling the way they had been the very first times. They stood there for a long time, time enough for the moon to hop from one tree across the road to another. The moon shone silver through all the trees, which the wife first noted to herself, then pointed to places on the ground for her husband to see—a shimmering silver all the more precious because it could be enjoyed but not contained. The moon was most generous with the silver where it fell, and even the places where it had not shone had a grayness pleasant and almost anticipatory, as if the moon were saying, I'll be over to you as soon as I can. "I'm gonna miss Virginia," Ruth said and yawned. Aubrey said, "I'll make it up to you. Sides, we be just cross the river. In a lotta places we can stand on the river and see Virginia." Sleep had escaped him now, but it was gaining on her, and at last he had to pick her up and carry her to bed. They were the children of once-upon-a-time slaves, born into a kind of freedom, but they had traveled down through the wombs with what all their kind had been born with—the knowledge that God had promised next week to everyone but themselves.

The feeling that the baby's mother might never come back started coming to Ruth three mornings after she had cut him down from the tree when she alone witnessed his umbilical cord dropping off. She held the blackened thing in the palm of her hand, a thing that was already turning to dust, and she realized her own mother must have done the same thing over and over again, with the children who would live and the ones who died before their first year. Fourteen days after she cut the infant down, she named him Miles, after Aubrey's father, who had treated her like a grown-up who always knew right from wrong. She did not consult Aubrey about calling the baby by his father's name—she just woke up that morning thinking it was a bit of bad luck for a child to be in the world and not be known by anything but "him" on a good day and "it" on a bad day. Aubrey said not a word when he heard her calling the baby Miles; they both had always known that was what they were to call their first son. It would not be untrue to say that it was a very long time before Aubrey stopped thinking that the baby's mother was returning, and for months and months he went all about Washington, even into Virginia, asking who might have lost a baby boy. He came from a land where human beings had a past as tangible as dirt, where even children with no parents or grandparents had laps they could cry into. But while his wife knew this, she also knew a body's world was held up only by a dime-store thread: Playing with three of her youngest brothers one day, she saw a brown bundle fall from the sky and hit the August corn with a *crack!* The children waited in the awful quiet after the fall, and after many seconds, a brown puppy poked most of its trembling body out of the cornfield, looked left, then right, like a well-taught child about to cross a road of danger. The puppy was clearly teetering between alive and dead, tattooed with the bloody marks of a hawk's talons on both haunches. Finally, satisfied it might now be safe, it wobbled its way in the direction of Harold.

Ruth and Aubrey had been two and a half months in Washington when the baby appeared, paid helpers in the various businesses Joan Hardesty ran out of the two-story houses at 1011 and 1013 3rd Street, N.W. She ran a little hotel at the 1011 address for colored people who were forbidden in the city's white hotels. She did laundry out back, and at the 1013 house people could buy supper five days a week and sit at the big table and enjoy their meal. The chickens in the back provided her with eggs, which had just gone up to three cents a dozen when the newlyweds arrived. People could also buy freshly killed chickens, though most of her customers preferred to take them home and wring the birds' necks themselves. There was a little blacksmith business, also in the back, but it had been failing since her husband was killed.

Ruth Patterson's first friend in Washington was forty-seven-year-old Sailor Willie, who rented a room from Joan at the 1013 address, where she herself lived, the place where she gave the big upstairs front room to Ruth and Aubrey. Joan had moved from that big room, where she had spent most of her married life, to the smaller upstairs one in the back after Paul was killed. Sailor Willie, Paul's second cousin, lived in the middle room, which was not big and not small and which looked out at the 1011 house. The view had never mattered to a man who had been all over the world, and it was mattering even less by the time Ruth and Aubrey arrived because his eyes were failing him. He was slowly becoming known as Blind Willie. He had made his living first as a merchant seaman and then as a whaler, and having spent so many years among men who smelled of the rotting flesh of whales, he loved to smell sweet all the day long. Before he came home from the sea for the last time, he had bought many bottles of a man's "evening water" in London, and he patted that on his face almost as soon as he was out of bed in the morning. He had had women all over Washington, before and after he retired from the sea, but as his sight failed, these women began to see a chance to twist the heart of a man who had often twisted theirs, and they turned their backs on him. "Sailor Willie," they mocked, "want a nurse now that he turnin into Blind Willie. He sweet as sugar now, but I don't want none of that in my coffee." In the days before Ruth arrived, he had been going about the city to see some of the women, telling those who would open the door that he just wanted "to pay my respects." He actually wanted to say he was sorry, but the sea had not given him words for that, and what few meetings there were turned out badly. Two women he especially wanted to see had been avoiding him. One of them, Vi Sanchez, was dead, but he didn't know that, and the other, Melinda Barclay, had just been trying to hold on to what life she had left after Sailor Willie went away the second and last time.

In the days before she cut the baby from the tree, Ruth and Aubrey's time on 3rd Street was pleasantly exhausting. Joan was not a slave driver, but she wanted her money's worth from any who worked for her. Whenever the couple happened to meet up in some quiet corner in one of the houses, or in the barn out back, they clung to each other, kissing until they heard a noise. At night in their big front room, they would giggle and tickle each other, waiting until they heard the roar of Willie's snoring in the middle room. Then they made love, and when they were done, he would lick the sweat from her face, her chest. He was desperate to have a child, a son he could name for his father, who was with him always.

No one ever came to claim the baby, and before long Aubrey, no longer blessed with guiltless sleep because of the baby crying in the night, went the other way when he heard Ruth approaching those quiet corners. He began to devote even more time to trying to find who might have "lost" a baby boy. By February he was even knocking on the back doors of white people to find out, as he put it, if they had heard tell of someone who was in the family way and now was not but had no baby to show for it. By February, too, he was resenting Ruth for having so easily made a home for the baby with them in that big front room. From that first night she had put the baby in the wooden crib one of her older brothers had created, a small thing of absolute beauty with cherubs carved on the sides, cherubs doing everything from throwing balls to jumping rope to sitting on tree limbs. A cherub with closed eyes and upraised arms and wings unfurled sat with his fat crossed ankles on the crib's headboard. The crib had always been intended for their own first child, but now day after day Aubrey could see the orphan sleeping in it, his arms spread without a care in the world, his belly fat with milk Aubrey himself had taken from the humpbacked cow Joan rented to make the butter she sold.

It was in late April that he began to think that Ruth was not getting pregnant because her heart was too much with the orphan. ("Don't call him Miles," he had finally told her in March. "Don't call him nothin. Whoever come to get him will wanna give him back his real name, and the boy'll just haveta get used to bein called somethin else." Ruth had sighed, the same way she did in the old days when she was about to fall asleep.) And it was in April that he began to seek her out during the workday to take her wherever he found her alone. The force and frequency of his seed would overpower her heart's fondness for the tree baby. A guest came upon them in one of the upstairs rooms in the 1011 house and complained to Joan. "What kinda damn place yall think I'm runnin here?" she demanded of Ruth and Aubrey. "You can take that mess back to Virginia." All the while she spoke, she seemed about to cry, as if their doing it in broad open daylight like that was only a small part of what was troubling her.

When Aubrey took Ruth at night in their bed, he no longer waited to hear Blind Willie start to snore. In early May she screamed for the first time with the brutality of it. "I won't let you touch me no more if you keep hurtin me," she said one morning as she fed the orphan, the baby's eyes blinking sleepily, one hand raised to touch her mouth. "I'll do it right from now on," Aubrey said quietly, but his word lasted only three days. By the time Ruth got word in late May that her mother was ailing, she had not let him touch her in more than a week. They had quarreled all that week, mostly at night, and though Aubrey tried to contain his shouting, Blind Willie could hear them. He would knock on the wall. "Yall be good to one nother in there, you hear? Ain't no call for yall not bein good to one nother."

She took the orphan when she went to see about her mother, ignoring Aubrey when he asked what he should do when the baby's mother came back to get the child. In Virginia she found peace again, found she could shake off the unsettling way Washington had insinuated itself in her nerves, something that had happened long before she cut the baby down. She helped her father and brothers with the crops. Once her mother improved, the two took the orphan in the buggy and went all about Arlington, visiting people Ruth had not seen in many months. The world in Virignia kept telling her that marriage and Washington had been good for her. Ruth said yes, yes they had. She learned to tell people right away that Miles was not hers, that she had found him in a tree. Then people, the same people who said Washington had been good to her, would tsk-tsk and say what could anyone expect of a city with a president who was so mean to colored people. She slept with the orphan in the bed she had slept in before her marriage. The baby slept holding tightly to her nightgown. May became June, and then before she could turn around, it was July.

Aubrey sent her a letter:

My dear Wife,
*   I write with all hope that your dear Mother is taking well once again. I have prayed for Her. I have prayed for You and I have*

prayed for the Life We have tried to make for ourselves here in the City.

I do not sleep because You are not beside me. I work but I am not happy because I know that I cannot find You quick as I could before You left for your sick Mother and Virginia. I want more than living tomorrow to come to get You before the second day of August, 1902. Please know that I write these words with my Heart true in every word. I will come out to get You.

To my loving Wife Mrs. Ruth Patterson
From Your true and one Husband
Mr. Aubrey Patterson

She read the letter a dozen times the day she received it. That night, after the house was quiet and the baby fast asleep, she went outside, not so much because of the song—though it played on still—but because standing in the yard might bring Aubrey quicker than the second of August.

He came and stayed with her and her family for three days. For some reason he seemed surprised to see the baby, as if he had expected it to have simply disappeared over time. He thought the baby twice as large as he had been before leaving Washington. The same size might have been the most he could ever hope for, but to have blossomed, to appear twice its size, was a blow to the heart. But he said nothing.

———————

While Ruth was away, Joan had increased Aubrey's pay to $2.50 a week. Had he been asked the day he held the new pay in his hand, he would have said that he was now a Washingtonian. Virginia was way over there somewhere in the past. He would not have returned to Virginia to be a man for anything in the world except the resurrection of his father. The only thing that could make his living perfect was Ruth's return. There was a terrible part of him that resented her for being absent for so long, though he could understand about her mother. A woman on I Street owed Joan some money, and she sent Aubrey to collect it. The woman opened her door to invite him in, and he sensed that she wanted to give more than the money. He hesitated, looked all the way up and down I Street, where no one knew him or his business. His father had said once that even if he were ten thousand miles from any human being, he must still sit and eat at his table with a knife and fork and use his eating manners the way he had been taught. So he told the woman that if she didn't have the money that day, he would just tell his aunt. And he banked his pay, every penny except that used to buy sweets, which he could not live without.

Also while Ruth was away, Joan hired Earl Austin, a man only four months up from Georgia. Suffering headaches in Georgia, Earl had gone to a root doctor, and the woman, after having Earl spit on a plate painted black, had diagnosed, "Your wife ain't your wife no more." Free of headaches but with a heart sliced up, he fled the state after catching his wife in their marriage bed with a man still in his hat and socks and then beating the man for nearly an hour and leaving him for dead in his wife's spring garden. He knew how to blacksmith, he had told Joan when seeking a job, and he could even sew and crochet if that would put food in his belly. He did not say that he had seen her one day walking down K Street and had followed her all the way back to 3rd Street. He did not say that he was quitting a good porter job at the Ebbitt House just to be near her, that he had been seized that day on K Street by an emotion that overwhelmed and confused him. He did not say that he would have worked for free or that he knew that even in a thousand years he had no hope of reaching the heart of a woman like her, one with money and property.

Ruth and Miles came back.

Aubrey thought that if he made his wife's life as easy as possible in Washington, her body would consent, and she would at last become pregnant. With Earl around and the baby needing to be watched as he began to explore more and more of his world, Ruth had about a third less work than before she went home to Virginia. And so she took Aubrey to her at night, eager, happy to be back, and he returned to her body, a man in love, in awe, in fear. Washington survived the blazes of August. September was warm, quite acceptable to Joan's guests not from the South. Much of October was fiercely cold, but November was like September all over again.

Like a thick window shade being pulled down in the brightness of day, the world was darkening for Blind Willie. By Ruth's return, he was accepting his new nickname, but he joked it was unfair to be called blind even before he was fully so. "I think I should be just Half-Blind Willie. Next thing you know," he said to Ruth one evening as everyone lingered after a pork chop supper, "they'll wanna put me in the ground when I'm only half dead."

He and Ruth, with Miles, went about the city in the afternoons of November in a wagon pulled by a mule that was good for short trips about the city but would have died, or simply refused, if forced to try anything longer. Born and raised in Washington, Willie told Ruth he wanted to show her the places of his childhood before his eyes took the places away. The truth is that he needed a companion as he went about trying "to pay his respects" to the women he had known. He saw his blindness as a kind of death. By November he had learned that Vi Sanchez was dead, but Melinda Barclay was still managing to avoid him. Her neighbors kept telling him she was off on a trip around the world. Ruth enjoyed being with him. She believed that Miles was going to grow up in Washington, so he may as well learn about it early. And Willie had an endless amount of stories, about the sea, about whales, about foreign countries, about love in Africa and Brazil. That all of Washington seemed to know him reminded her of how well known she was in Virginia. The old people in Washington called him William, for that, they would say, was the name his mother gave him, and it should be good enough for everybody else. With plenty of rest for the mule along the way, he and Ruth would go as far as Georgetown some days, picnicking and fishing at the river's edge.

At last, after months and months, two days before the end of November, Melinda opened the door to her home at 8 Pierce Street, N.W. Her face said nothing when she saw Willie. Indeed, she looked over his shoulders and around him, as if she had been expecting someone who had never caused her pain. She sighed with disappointment. Willie was surprised at how happy he was to find her, and he thought right away of the letter—only the third one of his life—he had written her that last time two years before, a letter labored over only days before he decided to retire from the sea. He wrote in the letter that he would miss her cooking, that it was the hardest thing in the world to go back to the ship's food. He had started the letter in the middle of the Atlantic Ocean and finished it before the ship saw

England, but he had not mailed it. He wrote in the letter that he knew
a dressmaker in Paris and he would have her make Melinda something out of this world.

"Oh, Melinda," Willie said now in the doorway, "you don't
know how happy I am to find you at home."

"Willie."

"I been lookin for you, Melinda."

"I been away, Willie. Way away. Didn't folks tell you?" She had
now stepped back. Her hair was made up quite prettily, as if for some
party. "I heard bout whas happenin to you and it's a shame. To be
blind."

Willie looked around at Ruth and Miles in the wagon.

"You should get back to em," Melinda said and made to close the
door. He saw the darkening figure of the door and raised his hand
to stop it from closing. "Please, Melinda. Please, darlin." She stopped
the closing and sighed once more. "Thas Ruth and little Miles. She my
landlady's niece. Her...her niece-in-law." He turned around to look
at Ruth as if to make certain he had gotten right her relationship to
Joan. There had been a woman in Brazil who had understood very little English and who just nodded at everything he said, even when he
told her he was coming back with a ring that would weigh her hand
down.

"I have somewhere to go, Willie," Melinda said. "You might have
to come back some other time."

Ruth could not hear their words from the wagon, but she sensed
the distress in Willie, in the way his head hung a little bit. Miles was in
her lap, playing with the reins.

"Now, Melinda, please wait a little bit," Willie said. His head was
turned slightly to the side, for there out of the corners of his eyes was
where most of the last of his sight resided. A stranger walking by
would have seen him talking to the side of Melinda's house.

She did a dismissal with her teeth. "You promised me a letter,
Willie. Just some plain letter that a child could manage. Just a plain old
letter."

"I know I did, Melinda."

"And you know what else," she said, opening the door just an
inch or so more. "That damn necklace fell apart on me, do you know
that? But I can understand fallin apart. Everything does that. It

woulda been nice to know it was gonna happen. It woulda been nice to know that it never come from the king of Haiti. I didn't mind the fallin apart. Just the lyin."

"I know," Willie said, not even remembering the necklace. "I shouldna said that. There ain't been no king in Haiti for a lotta years."

"It ain't the necklace. I got all the necklaces I could ever need."

"I'll get you something else, and I mean that," Willie said.

They did not speak for a time, until Miles squealed when he dropped one of the reins.

"Yall may as well come in," Melinda said. "Yall may as well do that. You make my house look poor standin out there like that."

On the morning of the third night Willie was with Melinda, he felt someone tap him lightly on the left side of his head. He woke and found it curious because Melinda was sleeping on his right side. In the half-darkened room he sat on the side of the bed and waited for his eyes to adjust. Finally, he held his hand before his face, moved it back and forth. Melinda was sleeping quietly, like a little girl, the way she had always done. He put his hand in his lap. "Oh, shoot," he said at last. "I'm all the way blind." He said it with no more emotion than a man might say he was late for something of little consequence after seeing his clock had stopped. He had hoped for a few months more.

He dressed with as little noise as possible and went down and out her door. He closed the door behind him and stood in his first morning hearing the sound of the closing door echo in his head. He went out the gate, making sure to shut it tight behind him. A neighbor's smelly dog liked to come in her yard and sleep under the porch. Willie took three tentative steps away from Melinda's house. A rooster crowed and Willie was emboldened. He put his right hand out in front of him, and the left hand he held out to the side where the homes were. He remembered that once he had come out of a woman's house in Northeast on just such a crisp morning and had gone three blocks in the wrong direction before he realized just what woman he had been with. He reached the end of Pierce Street and went down 1st. The slight dip was a surprise, something that had certainly not been there in all the years he had had eyes. He made his way home, to 3rd Street, and with all his steps he spelled out her name. William had never been a good speller in school, and Sailor Willie had been even worse, so Blind Willie made his way to Joan's repeating M-I-L-I-N-D-A.

———————

Late the next day Ruth got word that her mother was again ill. Aubrey sulked all the rest of the day, slept on the edge of their bed that night, and twisted and turned as loudly as he could. He sulked most of the next day as well, until Ruth left with Miles. She was gone nearly two weeks, until days before Christmas. He did not touch her again until well after Christmas. He stopped while inside her, dropped all his weight on her, and then, after she began complaining, rolled away.

One day in early January, he saw her talking to Earl in the kitchen of the 1013 house and suspected something. How, he wondered, as he stepped between them to get to the coffeepot, could he trust any child out of her to be his? He poured his coffee and before taking the first sip told Earl to go tidy up the chicken coop.

"You didn't have to say that to him like that," Ruth said to her husband after Earl left.

"Say it what way?" her husband said, holding his cup in both hands.

"Mean like that. He a good man. Earl don't trouble nobody less they trouble him." With winter, there were fewer guests in the 1011 house and Joan had allowed Earl to stay in the back room upstairs. "Ain't no call for bein mean like that, Aubrey." One morning Earl had raised his shade and saw Joan across the way in 1013, her back to him, looking in her mirror as she fixed her hair. He thought his heart would run away from him.

"Why you takin up for somebody against your own legal husband?" Aubrey knew as soon as he had said them that the words made no sense, but once they were out there in the kitchen where two pots were cooking supper, he could do no more than support them. "Ain't no call for you to do that, thas what I say." Joan had turned from the mirror and saw Earl watching her that morning.

"You could be nicer to everybody, Aubrey, thas all I'm sayin.

Earl, Willie, you could be nicer." As Earl watched Joan, he saw himself exiled back to Georgia, but rather than turning away, Joan had stepped to the window and stuck the second hatpin down through her hat and into her hair and never took her eyes from him. Earl lowered his head until his eyes fell on his shoes. He raised his hand Good Morning and left the window.

"I'm as nice as I need be," Aubrey said, wanting no more of the coffee. "Seem to me that the crime round here is you bein too nice. If I ain't bein nice, you sure makin it all up for me."

What he was saying finally came to her, and it pounded into her heart. "It don't cost one penny to be nice to people, Aubrey. It don't hurt a soul one bit." She wanted to cry, but the baby was asleep upstairs, and it would not have done for him to awaken and find her in distress. The orphan cried at the least little thing. Ruth stepped away to go upstairs.

There came to be nothing to talk about between them. He often pointed to something when he wanted her to do anything. At the dining table, with Joan and Willie and Earl and any guests, they sat as far from each other as they could. Willie was usually the life of the table, with a story about any subject someone could name. Say "speck of sand," for example, and he would regale with a story about an Abyssinian pirate who was caught at his lair near the sea and died wiggling with the hangman's rope around his neck, wiggling with the pain of the rope and the discomfort of the sand that had blown into his eyes. The pirate had lived most of his time on the sea, but he had detested sand all his days. Ruth liked everything Willie said, but her pleasure would dissolve when she would look across the table and find an unsmiling Aubrey staring hard at her, his arms folded.

One day she came into the room after hearing the baby whimpering on the pallet she had made for him. He was now too big for the crib and she had put it out in the barn. Aubrey was kneeling down, holding one of the baby's legs. "What he want?" she said. "I don't know," Aubrey said. "I didn't ask him and he didn't tell me."

He released the leg after she knelt down to the baby. He stood up and left. The child was wet, as it turned out. He was smiling. As she changed him, she kept hearing the sound of his whimpering before she had entered the room. Had the child been quiet or asleep when she found Aubrey over him, it would not have mattered. But the whimpering said so much to her, becoming as she stood up with him in her arms not even whimpering anymore but a long and painful cry.

She did not let Miles out of her sight after that. She carried him about in her arms. Or, when there were jobs that required both hands, she toted him on her back, having fashioned a pouch out of a blanket that he could lie in comfortably. She made the pallet beside the bed bigger and slept there with Miles. That was mid-January.

———

Willie woke in the night toward the end of January and remembered once again that he had promised Melinda to make up for the necklace from the king of Haiti. There had been nothing between them since the morning he went blind and left her asleep in bed. He felt he had enough money saved up from the sea to provide for his room and board at Joan's for the rest of his days. He would not trouble anyone else. He had at first thought that he and Ruth would pick out something for Melinda in some Washington store that would treat colored customers with respect. He would have Ruth or someone else take the jewelry to Melinda, for he would not want her to think he wanted something by taking it himself.

He got up that January night and opened the trunk that had been all around the world with him, a trunk big enough to be a man's coffin. In one corner there was a brooch, wrapped in two handkerchiefs, a brooch that he had not thought about for a long time. It was a cameo of a long-necked woman looking to the left. He had bought it in Marseilles, from a man with only nubs for hands. Intending it as a present for his mother. Twelve American silver dollars. But when he returned home he found that his mother had been dead a little more than two weeks, and he had put the brooch away, vowing not to think about it again. But he owed Melinda something wonderful.

Melinda said nothing when Ruth took the brooch to her. She invited her in. The baby, in a wooden carriage Earl had found in an alley and made over, had fallen asleep. It was early afternoon, a Saturday. Ruth declined to go in, saying she best get back, and Melinda walked her to the corner, to 1st Street. Ruth said, "He told me to tell you to enjoy every time you wear it. He wants you to be happy with it." The next morning Melinda was standing outside their home as the group at

1011 and 1013 prepared to go off to church. They came through the gates of the houses and Melinda touched Blind Willie's shoulder. He could tell it was not one of the people he had come out of the house with.

"Who?" he asked.

"Me," she said. She unwrapped the fingers of one of his hands and placed the brooch, now in one of her own handkerchiefs, in the center of the hand. He knew right off what it was.

"I want you to have it," he said. "I honestly did." Everyone else walked away a piece, up toward L Street.

"Why you treat me like this? What bad thing did I do you, William?"

"Nothin, you know that."

"If I done nothin, then good. Then your and my books been set straight if I never done nothin bad to you. I never want your things. Not a one." He heard her walk away.

"Melinda, please..." He took a step, fearful now of falling, holding the fence as best he could with the hand she had put the brooch in. "Melinda, please please, darlin. Please, darlin." He held his hand out to her, but he began to cry and so had to take that hand and cover his eyes. Ruth, with Miles in his carriage, considered going to him. Willie said, "I meant you no bad thing. Only my kind of love, such as it is." Melinda looked at Ruth, at Miles's hands and feet rising and falling in the carriage, and then she slowly turned around. Everyone in the group going to church started to walk away and they did not stop. It was not very cold considering it was January, but for days there had been talk of snow.

That Sunday the preacher gave his first sermon since returning from South Carolina from burying his mother, who died two days short of her seventy-ninth birthday. He had buried his father three years before, he reminded his congregation, and now "the whole fortress" between him and death was gone because he was their oldest child.

"On that long train ride back here, back to what's gotta be called home now cause Mama and Papa made my home down there and that home ain't really home no more, all the way back up here I kept thinkin how afraid I shoulda been. But I wasn't. I didn't have a crumb's bit of fear," he said, and his people said, "Amen."

"I'm next in that long death line that started with our Daddy Adam. And with Mama Eve. O Mama Eve, we forgive you for pickin that fruit and bitin into it with not a care for all of us what was to come after you and face death. Yes, we forgive you. We forgive, Mama Eve." And his people said, "Yes, we forgive." In that church row Ruth sat at one end with Miles on her lap, and Joan was at the other end. Aubrey sat next to Ruth and Earl sat next to him. Between Earl and Joan there were two guests from 1011, a medical doctor and his wife up from North Carolina. The wife had not even finished the North Carolina Normal School for Colored Girls, but her husband insisted on calling her "Doctor," at times in a very endearing way, punctuated with a touch of his fingers on her wrist. Before their visit to Washington had ended, everyone else was addressing her as "Doctor" as well.

"I tell ya," the preacher said. "I wanna tell yall that the wind was blowin the day we buried my mother down in South Carolina and I looked over at all the empty spaces that was to the right of where they laid her, all the empty spaces all the way to that little baby iron fence, and I said to myself, 'What's the use of goin back to Washington? What's the use? Why not go back to that little house you was raised in and sit on the porch and wait on Papa Death?'"

"Oh, Jesus," the people said. "Oh, my Jesus."

"I tell ya I just stood there watchin the wind rock that baby iron fence of that cemetery and I musta stood there too long, cause my own baby girl pulled on my arm and said, 'Daddy? Daddy?' Her little boy had hold of her frock and the wind stopped and they was fillin in the place where they put my mama. I blinked right then and there. I just blinked and I could see that day I first held her little baby boy and the way he squirmed like I wasn't holdin him right and all that hair on his head like he was a full-grown boy and I could see me again blowin on all that hair till he stopped squirmin and got to knowin I didn't mean him a pip's worth of injury. I tell ya I just blinked and God asked me what was I afraid of." The people said, "I know He did." "And the wind started back and God asked me the same question and I didn't have an answer. Cause there ain't no answer when you get down to the marrow of the marrow, and He knowed that when He asked me. God does that to us, you know?" "He does that," the people said. "I blinked again and I could see myself goin home on that train, goin home to Washington and havin yall tell me I was home. And I wasn't afraid comin out that churchyard where every tombstone had a name I could tell you a hundred stories about and I wasn't afraid goin back to that little baby house and hearin people say what a good and steady woman my mama was, through rain and sunshine and any bad weather she was a good human bein my mama was, and how heaven was lucky to have her and I wasn't afraid comin back home, comin back to yall in Washington. I tell ya I just blinked and it was all laid out to me."

Miles had fallen asleep in Ruth's lap. She was crying as she listened to the preacher. Aubrey had placed a hand on the baby's leg. Ruth picked up Miles and rested his head on her shoulder and Ruth's husband's hand fell away. It was far less cruel to do it that way than remove Aubrey's hand.

"So we forgive you, Mama Eve. God did that for you, so how can we do less? I stand next in the long death line under that eternal gaze of a just and fair God who just blinked, just blinked a few times, I tell ya, and in that little bit of blinkin my mama had lived her seventy-nine good years. Just a blink in God's eye. But O what a wondrous blink!"

Ruth thought to tell her husband that her mother was ill once more, but she was old enough now to know that God would not be pleased with such a lie and might well punish her by hurting her mother and others she loved. So she told her husband simply that she was going home. Aubrey himself took it to mean sickness in the family and said nothing to her.

Earl took her back to Virginia. The weather was cold, the baby wrapped in three blankets. The week before, Earl had seen the man he had beaten in Georgia walking without a care in the world up New Jersey Avenue toward New York Avenue. He lost sight of the man and figured he had been a ghost. He and Ruth and Miles reached

Georgetown about noon. Just before they touched the Aqueduct Bridge to Arlington, Earl asked Ruth, "You think if a man does a great sin, he has a right to any happiness after that?"

She had been home a week when Aubrey decided to go out to Virginia, having awakened one morning and heard only the sound of a solitary heartbeat in their bedroom. He borrowed a sorrel mare from a friend with a large stable on I Street. He left two hours after breakfast and about eleven was a little more than a mile from the place where he and Ruth had spent their first married days. A light snow began, and he apologized to the horse. He did not know why, but he got off the horse less than half a mile before his father's house, where he had been told two days before she was living. He tied the horse to a magnolia tree and walked the rest of the way. There was a handful of trees just before the path that led down to his father's place, and he stopped at the edge of those trees and looked down at Ruth. She could have seen him if she had looked up, but something told Aubrey that she would not. Farther down the road, where his mother's lover had lived, all the land now belonged to Ruth's brothers.

Miles was strapped to her back, his arms flailing as he played with cherubs only he could see. Aubrey looked down at his boots, at the way the wind dusted the snowflakes over them. He did not remember what snow there had been last winter, so this could well be the baby's first snow. He recalled the dimples on the back of the baby's hand when it was outstretched over the green blanket. The dimples Ruth loved to kiss.

Ruth was chopping wood. She cut pieces and threw them around to a pile just behind her. She was accompanied by two massive dogs, as large as wolves, descendants of the brown dog that had fallen from the sky into the August corn. She had taught one of the dogs to take wood up to the porch, where it dropped it in an untidy pile and returned for more. The other dog took pieces from the porch pile into the house. After some minutes, the first dog stopped and looked up at Aubrey. It waited for Aubrey to make some gesture to signal his intent. It turned once or twice as if to make certain that the other dog saw Ruth's husband as well. Finally, the first dog went back to work. The day Earl took Ruth to this place, she had answered his question, "Every last one of us is a sinner, Earl, but we all got some right to peace and happiness till the day we die."

The snow stopped. Aubrey saw the gray smoke rising from the chimney with great energy, and it was, at last, the smoke, the fury and promise of it, the hope and exuberance of it, that took him back down to the horse.

———————

In his mind, Ruth's husband shrugged. He was learning to put the events of his young life on a list according to where they stood with his father's death, which was at the top. He had at first put his mother's death at number ten, even though numbers five to nine were blank. But over the months, as he had remembered her touch, her mama words, he put her dying at number two. He did not know where to put the end with his wife.

The snow came up again and he turned onto the main road that would lead all the way down through Arlington to the bridge. Ruth's husband patted the horse's neck to reassure her that she was capable of the snow journey, that the snow would not amount to much. The horse's mane was in a tangle, and as he made his way through the new snow, he busied himself with trying to untangle it. But it was a hopeless task, and he patted the neck again, told the horse he would do a proper job with a soft brush before he returned her to her owner. The dank smell of the horse rose up and held fast like a stalled cloud before his face. Ruth's husband smiled and told the horse he forgave her.

In less than a mile, the snow came up fierce and he considered stopping for the night at the Landrys. But within sight of their place, the snow returned to a gentle falling, and he passed the Landrys and their hearth and its promise and continued on. He and the horse were alone on the road, and it occurred to him that all the world might know something about the weather to come that he should know, something that maybe he, no more a country boy, had learned and forgotten. In another mile, the snow took a turn toward bad again. Ruth's husband stopped and tied his scarf around his head and pulled the hat tight on top of that. They went on. They came through a small forest virtually empty of snow and he pulled the coat tighter, and as they emerged from the forest, Washington appeared before him, a long grayness shimmering between the snowflakes across the Aqueduct Bridge, across the quiet Potomac.

He halted at the mouth of the bridge, the land of Washington, D.C., spread out forever and ever before him. He ran his hand over his meager mustache and the beginnings of a beard. He wiped the snow from them and thought what a wasted effort it was since there was more snow to come. The horse raised her head high, then a bit higher, perhaps knowing something the man did not. Ruth's husband could hear voices now, and he shuddered. He turned in the saddle to see the southern road so many would travel on to reach that land just across the river. He saw nothing but the horse tracks in the snow, growing fainter with each second as more and more snow covered them. The voices hushed. His boots touched the horse's sides ever so gently. The horse stepped onto the bridge to Washington, her white breath shooting forward to become one with the white of the snow. Ruth's husband patted her neck. The top button on his coat came loose again and he rebuttoned it, thankful that his hand had not yet stiffened up. His heart was pained, and it was pain enough to overwhelm a city of men.

This Kind of Red

Helen Elaine Lee

Think of the good things, Avis," the caseworker tells me. Keep alive that way.

So I close my eyes and try to remember colors.

My head used to be filled with counting things out and checking them off, with keeping track of all my time and all my chores. I made supermarket lists for just how much I could wheel home in my basket, when I was not allowed to drive. What all needed cleaning and cooking. And lists of homework and laundry and what the kids needed. New tennis shoes and leotards and backpacks and decent socks, and how much every thing cost, so I could ask Jerrell for the right money. Lists of what all I was supposed to do, and how many minutes I had to get all of it done right, to keep the peace. How much time before he got home.

But what's the point of keeping track in here? Every day is that very same last one.

I try to think of colors, but not too many or too much. I try to do one at a time.

I knew green, but I think it has forgotten me.

Green is hard, but I try and remember July grass. And the just-coming leaves on the bushes at the edge of our corner lot, yellow-green and the size of your baby fingernail, the itty bitty fringe opening out from the bare dark of winter twigs.

And red. Red is easy.

There's the red of the bricks of our building, growing up. There's red and yellow trees way out there in the distance, it being October, so they say, it's all the same to me. And there's the sun, coming up and going down red, though I can't see neither from my cell. And purple-red, like communion wine. Dark, but letting you see almost through.

And there's blood, which they say is blue inside you and only red when it hits the air. It comes each month, or used to anyways, mocking with the reminder that you can still make life. But the good things. The good things. There's the red of fresh tomatoes, pulling heavy on the vine, and the meat of strawberries bitten through.

I remember a cardinal I saw once, from the corner of my eye. Pay attention, Avis, it seemed to whisper, this can happen, this kind of red. It was gone so fast, and the flash of it, so surprising, so beautiful, it kind of hurt.

Red makes me think of Uncle Rush. He made it home after getting stabbed and layed there bleeding on his living room couch. He must have called for help, and then died in the middle of waiting for it to come. After trying to scrub it clean, Granny had that couch taken to the dump, stained as it was and reminding her of what she wanted to forget. Now that's a bad story, and they say you got to stay positive to make it through your time. But I gotta say, I don't picture much that's good. My kids' faces and little things, I guess you'd call them, that just plain are.

And mostly, in my mind, there's angry-red, strong and thick. And I think that's a clotted red, staining everything, turning to black at the middle and no way to see through.

His red words ring out in the night, telling me he's still alive: *fat bitch ho fuck-up selfish stupid cunt.* And they're mixed with his *sorry's* that follow, and the love talk that came out less and less: *sexy fine adore mine promise baby forever.* That last one was the truth.

What's bad remembers me. And I try to keep these things from getting out of hand. I can't keep them away, but I keep them small. And it's funny how a certain little thing won't disappear.

Feet pointing up from the foot of the bed, I can see that plain as day. Feet I kissed and licked once, even, in our early, passion days. His feet. And him laying there, proud and satisfied in his victory, rubbing his knuckles. He wants me to minister to his hands, which are sore from hitting on me. "Go get the witch hazel, Avis," he says again and again, and I just remember watching his mouth opening and closing with those words, without being able to hear a sound coming out until I realize what he was wanting. He looks silly, childish, even, but scary, too. And those feet pointing up, feet I had recognized and trusted, turned enemy as they kicked at my ribs and back while I curled, like a round beetle does when you take it from the dark safety of a stone or log. I look from his no-sound mouth down to his feet, look the length of him and then at the heels and toes without the hard leather and buried steel of his work boots from the plant, his feet soft and naked now, but still sinister and yet, too, they are still the feet I know and love. And I can't take my eyes off them until I catch his smile, and then the hard-on, another traitor in our tumbled-up, twisted, broke-down love.

In the glance from feet, to face, to dick, and back again, I know I have to make him stop.

As I said, what's bad comes back to me without the asking, and that's one piece of the story of me and Jerrell that I never can forget. Those feet. And all his words. *forever sorry fat bitch ho selfish stupid cunt sexy fine adore mine promise baby sorry fuck-up.* I try, Lord knows I work at forgetting, and think of other things instead.

Like green. I knew green.

Green I try to get ahold of, but it fades and red's as clear as yesterday, as this day, whatever, they're all the same.

And I wish I could say I didn't, but I do, I do know the rusty, red taste of blood.

Before I stood and looked him over head to toe while he layed there on the bed, he had beat my face to a swollen mess, and was working on my chest. He had me pinned down on the floor, my lips swollen and bleeding as he sat across me, and he reached over and scooped the meal I had made, mashed potatoes and corn it was, which was so bad, so "unacceptable," so "wrong," as to be the reason for my beating, scooped a pile of it off the floor, and shoved it in my torn mouth, mixing it with my blood. "Eat it, bitch. There'll be more later, but see what your failure tastes like." All I could think, while I gagged on food and blood, was how long before my kids get home? How long before they see their mama like this? How long will they be safe? "Eat it, bitch," he said, and forced it down my throat.

So I went where I usually did, making myself small as possible and fast-forward to what would come later. The apologizing and taking-it-back. To the I-adore-you-baby and the that's-why-you-get-to-me-so-bad.

Some way, he stopped, and staggered into the bedroom with the rest of his six-pack. And called for me to bring him the witch hazel, which I did. And while I got myself and the kitchen put back together, he forgot about his hard-on and passed out on the bed. Later, as he begins to stir, I check on my face and the clock and his gun. I need to know just where everything is, in case he isn't finished with me yet. I tiptoe to the door and check on him. And there they are, those feet.

Who knew that would be Jerrell's last day on this earth? Well that's the way it started, and while I didn't know how it would end, I knew things would be mighty bad.

sorry fat bitch ho fuck-up selfish stupid cunt forever sexy fine adore mine promise baby sorry

I used to be careful over every little thing, knowing just what time it was and what was supposed to happen, what was expected of me. I was real good at planning and timing and counting.

In here at Oak Hills, you got to make sure you keep the right company and mind the rules, still. I keep to myself. And you don't have to wonder what's coming next or what to do. They sound a buzzer and tell you what to do. And I sure don't need a calendar, like Keisha and Ranita, for crossing off the days. They got reasons to count. My sentence has no ending. I got "Natural Life."

I'm done with counting, but I try to keep things tight enough to fit in this coffin of a cell. Not wanting or missing too hard. I try to manage, and then the caseworker comes talking about imagine. Imagine the good things.

Are we still alive? Can a pulse tell you that? I take my meds and try to say that Yes, I am alive in here. I will make a blanket, and type in the codes and numbers on the keyboard for my work detail. And a little bit at a time, I'll try to imagine the good things. But I'm afraid this is the afterlife Granny was always talking on and on about, and it's not the just reward she thought.

These walls are haunted, and not just by the ones still serving time. By everyone who came before.

But some folks do keep on living hard behind these walls, still fighting and getting degrees and writing poetry and letters, training in food prep and cosmetology, learning to garden, falling in love and hoping and praying. And some are just hibernating, waiting til their out dates to come alive again. I've heard of big old *men* men hooking up with queens inside, and I've heard of men who married women from the free world, even though they'll never get released. Most folks, I guess, their hearts do keep on beating.

Some in here still get to having sex, but it seems like that part of me's just dried up. Even my monthly's stopped coming regular. I guess it's The Change. You got to work hard around the rules against touching, but even so, sometimes I can hear Gwen and Ilene going at it in their cell. They're married, or might as well be, and they act just as crazy jealous and silly as you would not believe. I done it a couple of times in here, or let myself get done. It's as good as anything else, I guess. If you can get it, love's the thing to have. I layed there while Gwen did me, and it was like I could hear her moaning from a long ways off while I was disappearing, and it didn't really matter in the end. That part of me is all spent up; the bank is empty. With my husband, now that was something... that was some love that rocked me. It nearly killed me, do you hear what I'm saying? I've had enough of marriage to last me forever. Any way you cut it, somebody's always on top.

I work on this, where someone with a crochet hook can be supervised. "Occupational therapy," I guess they call it, and it gets bigger and bigger. That's how I know time is passing, after all.

I never thought I could make anything this big, and I never can seem to decide to finish it off. I work on it in the morning in the recreation room. People watch the stories, mostly, and long ago there was fighting over which ones they'd follow. I don't go in for them, myself. They never let any of the characters stay together. You can watch and watch and watch to see a reunion, and before you know it, they're broken up again. Well I guess nothing lasts, even in real life, but it seems like just another addiction to me. Some of the folks in here need a twelve-step program for the stories, but I guess it does make you feel like you're living in something that keeps keeping on.

This blanket is ten feet long and all a kind of nothing-dirt-red brown. The color in the crayon box that no one ever uses, the one that's always sharp. I wanted other yarn, that rainbow kind that turns a different color every foot or so. But I was lucky to get this, from the charity craft shop.

There's not much that's bright in here but there's no white, neither. Just the ugly that happens when you mix all your colors together. And gray, like our sheets, and the waist-high panties that never will look bright and fresh. Every kind of dirty and faded you could ever find. Nothing is yours, alone. Everywhere in here, someone else has been. I can picture those white sheets Granny used to boil and bleach and stretch out on the clothesline, so that even if nothing we had was new or extra nice, where we slept and what we put on our behinds was spotless. Nothing in here will ever be clean again.

There's the browns of most of our faces, and the brown of shit and dirt.

I see yellow in my eyes when I can't avoid the infirmary mirror. I see the yellow of my pee.

Orange is the loud cry of the jumpsuits the new ones wear.

It's the eight-box of crayons in here. You can find a little of something, a little blue, but it's one, single thing. Yellow, too. You know that 64-box is out there somewhere, in another child's hands.

Yeah, we have the things we tape up on the wall, photos and pages from magazines and posters. Flat color, trapped on a page, or pictures on a T.V. screen, looking like they're beamed in here from Mars.

That card Lamar made me I only had half of, and I kept that torn piece folded against the binding of my Bible. That CO Roberts took it in the shakedown my second year in, but then I got it back, torn, it's true, only to lose it again last week. Oh, I miss the robin's egg blue he used on that card, even if his little sky was just a sliver above a rooftop on the ragged edge, like this. How DID I lose it, practically the only thing I had from him? Must be reckless missing that's to blame.

I haven't seen my kids since Mama got too sick to bring them, and they haven't written in so long. Maybe it's best that they forget me, now that they're with my cousins, all the way across the state. Maybe, in their minds, I'm the bad that won't stop surfacing.

fat bitch ho fuck-up selfish stupid cunt sexy fine adore mine promise baby sorry forever sorry

Mama died three years ago, while trying to get my kids from childhood to adulthood. And here I was, not able to help. Not able to see her and tell her a last little thing.

They let me go to the wake and see her, after everyone else was done saying goodbye, in shackles and waist chains. I just did what I was good at: shrink and fast-forward once again.

I guess they thought I'd get away. But I know there's more to getting free than most folks know.

Yes, plenty of bad things remember me. His fists and all the backhands I get for "disobedience." The phone torn from the wall and smashed with a hammer, its wiry guts spilling out. The ringing of his phone calls every twenty minutes, while I'm still allowed to work. Seeing his car as he waits just outside the school to make sure I come right home.

Jerrell always did say I kept a sloppy house. Said I put my job ahead of him and my kids. I had worked so hard for that teaching certificate, studying in the bathroom late at night after everyone else had gone to bed, scraping together the money for each class, that I held on to it as long as I could. What about your own kids, he would say, when I was getting ready for school or working on my lesson plan. I had wanted to be a teacher ever since I was ten years old, and I used to sit the neighborhood kids down in a row and play like I had a school.

It didn't last long, though. He called in mid-semester and told the principal I had to quit. I wasn't well, he said, and that was true. There's that feeling, right here, inside, of knowing that me teaching school was over. There's the taste of my blood and the taste of a gun in my mouth, too, and the way our little house seems to get further and further away from everyone and smaller and smaller, so that I can barely see myself.

Me, locked inside with the safe where he keeps the alternator he took off the car, the money and the checkbook and even my ID, safe from the world and safe from me. The way he pounds and drives himself into me when he has a notion to take the sex he thinks is his, and how it turns to hitting when the beer and vodka make him limp. The faces of my kids as they are watching while I yell for them to go to their room and lock the door. And in-between it all, my sorry's.

And there was a day I realized, just by his tone of voice, that he was turning on Lamar, that he was next. He could go for him in the night time, and in the morning, say that he was sorry and be proud.

Proud of his desk and his starched white shirt. Don't let no one dis him or ignore him when he was plant manager, working evenings. I hope, I hope, Lord, please let him meet his quota today. Always checking in the mirror that his clothes, his hair, his shave was right.

The only good thing about the piece of stainless steel that fills in for a mirror is that I don't have to hide from my body, and the sad, sad story it tells. The soft stomach and stretch marks from being pregnant and the saggy breasts that I swear still ache sometimes from the babies lost to me now. The fat I carry now from the starchy food in here and from being penned, and the healing my skin has done. Faded marks where his cigarettes burned the softest, hidden flesh, and the torn places that did their best to close. Who cares about it anyways? No one sees me and this body's just a shell that never did belong to me.

forever fat bitch ho fuck-up selfish stupid cunt sorry sexy fine adore sorry promise baby mine

Last night? Was it the night before? Whatever, I was lying on my bunk, trying to block out the noise enough to picture my kids' faces the last time I saw them. It was all fuzzy and bleached, but I could see Lavonne with that missing tooth in front and her clumsy eight-year-old smile tries to hide it. Rhonda with her fuzzy hair that just refuses to stay plaited or ponytailed. And Jerrell, Junior, who I call by his middle name, Lamar. My baby, who can't stay still long enough for me to kiss his dimples and talks in whole sentences, even though he's only just turned three.

I know they're all different, because time just keeps moving on, or so they say. For me, they're still just like the last time I saw them, four years ago, just before Mama died. And I try not to miss them too, too much.

Anyhow, they came and told me Mama was gone. Her pressure had been spiking, and the stroke just came. Lord knows, re-mothering three kids didn't help to keep her calm. She was getting ready for church when the stroke hit. Had her stockings and shoes on, but she hadn't finished buttoning up her dress. I know that would have irked her, because she was particular and thorough about everything she did. It must worry on her that she didn't finish with her very last task.

Mama was in the middle of raising my kids, and in the middle of doing her buttons, and when she died, I was in the middle of a life-long apology for wrong loving and wrong choices. For dropping out of school and marrying Jerrell against her warnings that he would lead to trouble, by and by. For leaving all of them behind. Now I'll never get my sorry's finished. I'll never get them said.

People don't die in-between things. Even if they know death's coming for them, they're in the middle of something when they go.

Iva Jean, from Cellblock A, she was in the middle of watching her story, waiting to see if Tad and Dixie ever would get back together and stay. She had complained for days about the pain in her side, but the CO's said she was faking, and she never did get to see the doc. No telling how long she watched that story to see what would happen, and she never did find out.

We knew Granddaddy was passing on, and we were collected all around his big carved, mahogany bed, trying to see him off. He was peaceful, whispering things none of us could understand. I guess he died in the middle of loving us.

Uncle Rush, like I told you, was waiting for help. And Cece was just about to finish school. Planning and hoping for better things to come.

Most of the folks locked up in here, they just keep on hoping. Maybe I'll get a commutation. Maybe a judge will see it a different way. Maybe I'll get numbers 'stead of alphabets. Maybe I'll get free.

I've stopped counting and let go of all my maybes. But I go over and over what I did in little bits and pieces, trying to see how I could have stopped him. Trying to reassure myself that I really did.

Every day is that day, and I am right there, stuck, no matter what colors and good things I try to think about. His last day and mine.

I'll never finish killing him. He's after me, still and yet. It will never be done.

mine sorry fat bitch ho fuck-up selfish stupid cunt sexy fine adore promise baby sorry forever

I see his feet point up and I am ready, knowing just what the clock says, and where the gun is, and waiting to see what will be. Folding the clothes I've ironed, then stacking them, I am counting it all out. Ten minutes before Mama brings Lavonne and Rhonda home and Lamar's still sleeping, but I've locked him in his room in case. In case...in case. Nine minutes until they get here. One step to reach the gun.

The starch is working good and I will do it perfect, just right, no wrinkles, no creases, no buttons that are burned or chipped, I have almost got the collar, almost got it, and there's only three in the basket left to do.

And I hear him rising from the bed like thunder, coming through the doorway with his fists in the air, like the picture of some vengeful god I've seen in books, and I can tell he isn't finished, not yet. Eight minutes and my babies will be here, and if he comes for me I will reach it, I'm deciding with my body, with my arms and hands and stomach, I will save myself I will help myself I will get free I will live. And he does come, like always, like I knew, he comes with thunder in his hands that he has somehow gotten in a flash, the iron in his raised right hand, its cord whipping like a snake, the steam hissing and bubbling where he has yanked it from the wall, and I have six minutes and I'm still close enough to reach and stop this, stop this storm.

I reach for it. I reach for the gun and shoot. And he is down and there is blood and burning metal and too many sounds to sort, and the red, red blood has ruined the perfect white, starched and ironed shirts, and I know that I will get a beating for this. I shoot him, not even seeing where but just trying to stop it and to live, and then, who knows how much later, Mama gets here, who knows how much later because I have stopped counting and I am working on disappearing now. It must have been only minutes because the kids are due from school, and she says that when she gets here with Lavonne and Rhonda, when she sees him and the red, red blood, she tells the kids to wait, wait, just you wait now on the porch, and she breaks a window with a brick to get inside, cursing Jerrell that he refused to let her have a key. And she finds him dead and the gun right there on the floor, and me in the closet with Lamar, screaming that he is coming and the shirts are ruined and he will never let me go.

I keep getting up and washing my face, and tying my shoes, and putting on my clothes, and then doing it all in reverse. First on. Then off. Beginning and ending the very same day. This is the routine of my hours and my days. On and off and on again.

I stopped counting how long since I've had a visitor, and the last one was my brother, Will, who could barely look me in the eye and seemed like he came to keep a promise to Mama he had made. People say life goes on, but is it true?

Seems like it goes and goes until it stops, right in the middle of one thing or another.

When Aunt Irene died, she was cutting coupons from the Sunday paper, talking about what she was gonna buy. Mama said her hands grabbed the table and sent the coupons flying up, and then they drifted down all around her like fanfare, like confetti flags.

And my cousin, Mamie? She was in the middle of talking trash when she went. "You just wait until..." she said, and fell over. We were running a Boston, and I never did enjoy a game of bid whist since.

My first cellie died in the middle of getting herself together, as soon as she wrapped up. Got some dope that was too good a promise to turn down. She was on her fourth step.

Even if you got it all in order: bills paid, house cleaned, dinner ready, kids bathed. You're showered and combed and dressed. Even if everything's taken care of, no loose ends, you're still doing something, you're not in-between things. You're breathing, hoping, waiting. Something's going on.

When Jerrell died, there I was, trying to save my own life.

Who else was going to do it? The police, who took him outside and told him to calm down before they sent him back in to beat me worse? Mama, in one of the only visits he allowed me, who told me to try not to set him off, and then to just leave?

Leave, I thought, is that what you did? Maybe she's wiped her memory of my own daddy clean. Or she hasn't seen my bruises, or heard a word I say. Maybe she doesn't realize I haven't worked in two years and I got these kids and a baby still in arms. That I don't even have a house key, that I got no money or driver's license, or way to start over again. She doesn't know that things could change if I can just get a handle on them and not make him mad, or that I know it's true what he says about me being a *stupid fuck-up* and no one else will ever love me like he does. Maybe Mama doesn't remember how he tracked me across three states when it was just Lavonne and Rhonda, and he swore to hell he'd kill me if I left again. Maybe she doesn't realize that I'm far too much like her.

She brought the kids to see me and tried to provide for them. She was with me, through the jail part and the court part, too.

The booking and the trial, they're all a blur that just gets further and further away. I could barely hold myself together, either shaking in fear, pleading for my children, or numb from the meds they had me on. I was so jumpy I expected him to come thundering through the doorway to the courtroom, not finished, not finished with me yet.

That's the way it went for me, six years ago, when they locked me up. I lost everything except my sometime memories, my today that's just the same as yesterday. He took it all. I may not have saved my life, though I was trying. But I saved my kids from Jerrell, and now they've got to raise themselves. I try to keep from wishing I could see Lavonne's full set of grown-up teeth and whatever Rhonda's done about that rebel hair. And Lamar, whoever he's become. Wishing hurts too much. And I wish I could see Jerrell again, in a good minute, when he was happy with me and his words were the good kind.

But there are his feet, again and again, and the blood in my mouth, and the spitting iron and his ruined shirts, and the safety of the closet, Lamar in my arms and me making us smaller and smaller until Mama opens that door.

I kill him every night, and I am sorry. But like I told you, I was in the middle of trying to save my life.

No need to hold a funeral, or a wake for me. Who would come, anyways? No need to cry for me, for what I caused to happen and what all I'll never see or do.

This is how my story ended. And after all, everyone dies in the middle of something.

NOVEL EXCERPTS

DARK REFLECTIONS

Samuel R. Delany

In 1987's rainy October, when squirrels stopped, stared, then sprinted along the bench-backs away from the kids with the earrings, combat boots, and dog collars, who for more than fifteen years now had been hanging out in Tompkins Square Park, Arnold's sixth book of poems, *Beleaguered Fields,* won the Alfred Proctor Prize—an award given once every three years that concerned a small circle of New York poets and men and women of letters.

In the late afternoon of the day he'd received the news, as he walked home through the park, a wind gusted among the wet leaves, for moments making a rising roar, like the cheer of thousands. Because so few folks were out that day, Arnold smiled—and dropped his head to the left, then to the right, acknowledging playfully the world's recognition. Leaves quieted . . . and fifty-one-year-old Arnold Hawley left the park at Avenue B.

It was the year after he had stopped working for the City Employment Administration and had taken the teaching job out at Staten Island State University—with its three-thousand-dollar-a-year drop in salary and its hour and three quarters travel time, including the trip back and forth on the ferry, for that extra Monday in which to do his own work.

The prize had been a blessing.

Inconsequential as the Alfred Proctor Prize was in the greater scheme, the award carried a three-thousand-six-hundred-dollar stipend, paid out annually over three years.

It would be nice to get twelve-hundred-dollars a year—for three years.

No, it wouldn't support Arnold, the first African American poet to win, over any significant period, not even living on East Ninth Street in '87. But, from '87 to '89, it would mean for a couple or three weeks not having to buy day-old bread; it would mean walking into St. Mark's Bookshop and actually purchasing that paperback he'd wanted to read; it would mean going to a movie the evening the idea struck him, or seeing a play within the brick-and-glass walls of the Theater for the New City even if he didn't know one of the actors who could get him a comp to this or that performance space inside the converted market building. The Proctor Prize would mean—at least now and then—paying his $396.83 a month rent on time for his third-floor rear apartment, one of three rent-stabilized apartments left in the building.

(The 15 percent raise every two years—the legal limit—more than doubled his rent each decade.)

Its annual certainty?

Its perfect gratuity?

Materially they fortified Arnold.

Spiritually they liberated him.

For a month or two out of the year—out of *three* years, actually—Arnold could believe he was a little better off than he'd been, and, what's more, the reason was poetry.

Arnold pushed through the glass doors of his building, opened the mailbox briefly—just some flyers and a blue envelope of coupons that he could throw out tomorrow—and started upstairs. A bit later, in his kitchen, he heated up last night's leftover lentil soup. Sitting at the table, covered with books and papers, typewriter pushed to the side and steaming soup plate before him, Arnold thought: What a pleasant ending to a pleasant day. (I should have brought a celebratory bottle of white wine...well, next time.) Spooning lentils, celery, and carrots carefully away from himself, he pondered: *Next* time, I must put in some sausage. No matter what Aunt Bea says about what Mrs. Polk says

(Aunt Bea had sent the recipe), really, I'm not a vegetarian at heart. And neither is Bea.

Edena Proctor had lived and died on the south side of Gramercy Park, looking out on the black metal gate around its central garden, to which residents had keys—a square a half an hour's stroll to the north, and of a different size, feel, history, and economy from Tompkins. She'd divided her millions between the Poetry Society of America and Yaddo, where, in 1947, she'd spent a pleasant April trying to finish a novel. It had never appeared. In 1975, the year of her death, she had set up an eight-hundred-thousand-dollar trust to sponsor the Alfred Proctor Prize for Poetry, named after her father, who'd encouraged his only daughter's love of opera, Spain, and the arts.

What other educational projects the Proctor Trust engaged in, if there were any, Arnold was never clear on.

They threw some very nice parties.

Even without the Proctor, *Beleaguered Fields* had been Arnold's first book to appear in both hardcover and trade paperback: for both he'd received a nine-hundred-dollar advance. It was his second from what he considered a real publisher: Lark & Dove Books, owned by Sid Lark, with an office in TriBeCa and six editors.

In the converted industrial building's ground-floor space—the whole back seemed to be glass and black girders—Lark & Dove had been one of the scrappier businesses to surface among the early '80s catastrophic publishing mergers.

Leaving her job in publicity at Random House for a downtown editorship, twenty-six-year-old Vikki LaSalle, Arnold's editor, had done three things, one, as far as Arnold was concerned, brilliant, and the other two so wackily idiotic that, really, they were, well... wonderful!

The brilliant one was to send a set of bound galleys for *Beleaguered Fields* to the Proctor competition. (At a Proctor event she'd met someone connected with the Trust.) A week after the book won, Vikki had these circular gold stickers done up—because the cover had already been printed—which said in raised letters around the rim: "Winner of the Proctor Prize for Poetry," with an embossed seven-pointed star in the center.

Perhaps once a year someone called it the Alfred Proctor Prize.

That Tuesday, with her carroty braids curled on the sides of her head, Vikki—with Arnold—had taken the Short Line Bus and the taped-up carton of gilded peel-offs south along the drizzly turnpike to Lark & Dove's second-floor Jersey warehouse space.

Years later Arnold decided the intensity of her belief in him *must* have had something sexual to it—people just didn't carry on the way Vikki did about books of poetry, any book of poetry.

At Vikki's insistence they wasted forty minutes finding someplace where they could buy six containers of coffee and a dozen donuts. "For the warehouse workers," Vikki explained. "Just like Jackie Suzanne. Really, it *does* help." At the coffee stand they wouldn't take Vikki's credit card and she only had a five in her pocketbook. So Arnold paid the nine dollars and eighty-six cents out of his wallet. "Oh, it isn't fair!" Vikki insisted. "Believe me, I'll see you get that back."

"Don't worry." Arnold chuckled. "It is my book, after all."

Then, over three hours, toward the back of the unpainted loft, frigid with air-conditioning, they peeled loose bright circles and hand pasted them to 852 books—what remained to be distributed of the thousand-copy first printing—piled on the slatted skid.

Downstairs, on the counter in front of a guard-booth window in an orange wall with two asbestos pipes across it and lots of ribbed electric cable looping from the ceiling, they left the carrier carton of coffees and the donuts with the single Russian loader in jeans and denim shirt who'd let them in.

As she handed him the donut bag, Vikki said, "This is Arnold Hawley, one of the truly important African American poets, who cares about language, cares about literature, and cares about the truth!"

The Russian had not shaved that day. *"Ty mnogo zarabatyvaesh' stishkami?"* He frowned into the brown paper, translucent in spots with grease.

Arnold's three terms of Russian were the only courses he'd gotten A's in at Brown. *"Niskol'ko."* Arnold had on the dark blue suit and the dark green tie he wore for his students on Staten Island.

The loader nodded. *"V shtatakh chego eshcho oʒhidat'."*

"Nu da..." Arnold said to end what was beginning to feel uncomfortable, and turned away.

Vikki called, "Thank you again!" as they walked out to begin the twenty-minute hike to the bus stop, now and then glancing at Arnold in monolingual awe. As once more it began to sprinkle, Vikki asked: "What was that about?"

"He wanted to know if poets made a lot of money in America."

That evening Arnold realized he didn't have quite enough left in his wallet for house-special egg foo young at Wo Hop's, six blocks south on Second Avenue. Though they knew him there and would surely trust him for the final dollar seventy and the tip, he made himself scrambled eggs for supper. Eating them from a bread-and-butter plate beside the typewriter on the kitchen table, Arnold reflected again: A three-thousand-dollar-a-year drop in salary actually *meant* something about how you lived your life. He had to relegate even cheap Chinese and *comidas criollas* to luxuries, and start cooking in more regularly—a fact which, while he'd known it more than a year, the Proctor had allowed him, for a few weeks, to forget.

And the wacky and wonderful ones?

Shortly, Vikki had convinced cigarillo-gnawing Sid Lark to write out a check for three hundred dollars to finance *Beleaguered Fields'* entrance for the coming year's Drew-Phalen Award, a prize presented annually in fiction, drama, nonfiction, and poetry, which had been around since the '20s, so that most literate folk knew of it. Usually its February announcement made page two of the daily *Times* and, for the last fifteen years, page one of the Sunday *Arts & Leisure* section—on the lower half, with a picture of the dramatist: Fierstein, MacNally, Sondheim....

Then, four months later, when 178 hardcovers still remained in Jersey, Vikki had ordered another printing of three *thousand* hardcover copies, with a new jacket, identical to the old, except that, in white letters, along a green band slanting across the bottom third, it read: "WINNER OF THE PROCTOR PRIZE FOR POETRY" and, in gold letters below that: "Nominated for the DREW-PHALEN AWARD in poetry."

That Thursday she phoned Arnold to come in and see the new cover proof.

Craning around the corner of Vikki's desk, Arnold asked, "Shouldn't that be 'winner of the *Alfred* Proctor Prize'?"

Vikki flattened both her hands on the blue blotter. "Oh, dear!" Sucking her teeth, she grimaced. "I forgot again." With her coiled bright braids, Vikki's head appeared wide and heavy with the knowledge of the young. On her office wall hung a large abstract...thing, all aluminum and clear plastic dowels. Only on his third visit to the office had Arnold realized it was a barometer, not a clock.

That Friday, Sid fired Vikki.

When a confusing Monday morning phone call finally netted from the receptionist—the third time Arnold had been transferred back to her—that Ms. LaSalle no longer worked at Lark & Dove—indeed, she'd left before the weekend—Arnold decided quietly, as for the second time he was switched over to James Farthwell's assistant (only now did Arnold understand that Farthwell had taken over Vikki's writers), he might as well forget the photo his Aunt Bea had taken of him on her last trip to New York, seven years before, as he'd stood at Avenue B by Tompkins Square's broad brick newel. (Bea had come once almost every ten years, to take in an opera or two at Lincoln Center—and always one at the Amatto—to visit museums, to go to a play, staying a week in Arnold's back room and stoically not complaining about the clutter.) When Vikki had asked him for an author's picture for the book's back, he'd found it in the kitchen drawer and sent it in.

Then, without comment, they hadn't used it.

Arnold had gone through paranoid kippages about their not wanting to put a black man's image on the cover. ("Who let the coon in?"—Wallace Stevens' inquiry at the 1950 Drew-Phalen Awards banquet, when that year's recipient, Gwendolyn Brooks, had entered the hall—replayed regularly up from the kerygma of black literary history, a-broil in memory and imagination, even after forty years.) The picture *was* seven years old.

Perhaps it had looked ridiculously young for a poet now over fifty.

Vikki had said it was a slipup. But she'd said it quickly. Nor had she apologized—

Interrupting Arnold's thoughts, the assistant said, "Oh! Mr.

Farthwell just got back to his desk, from Mr. Lark's. Hold on a moment. I'll transfer you."

Then Mr. Farthwell said he would ask in production if anyone had seen the photo; and phoned Arnold a week later to invite him to lunch. "I guess it's a gesture of compensation for the fact that—really, it's embarrassing—we seem to have lost your picture. Basically, though, since you're one of *my* authors now, I'd like to take you out and say hello."

"I'd love to go to lunch!" Wasn't the reason Arnold had worked so hard to get the teaching job at Staten Island State (with its free Mondays), so that when such invitations came up, he could accept them?

The photo had gone with Vikki.

Sexual, yes. But had the object of her desire been the poet, or—as Arnold suspected—poetry?

The second Arnold understood—and shared.

James turned out to be a callow twenty-eight-year-old (white), with wildly bitten nails, who had inherited Vikki's job, Vikki's office, and Vikki's fifty-one-year-old black poet, Arnold Hawley. Going out with Farthwell was fun.

Apparently the barometer had been Vikki's, too. On one taupe wall of James's office—on the floor of which five times the number of manuscripts leaned by the baseboard as had ever stood there during Vikki's tenure—its outline remained near the window, like the line inside a cardboard coffee container, after you'd poured its second-day contents into the sink.

There was no way, when someone was taking him to a seventy- or eighty-dollar lunch, Arnold could ask for a $9.86 reimbursement. Twice, though, he came close.

Some months later, during a third lunch with James, as they sat in a restaurant with a girdered web under the ceiling beside the black columns before some dim tapestry, James leaned forward and smiled: "You know, I'm not supposed to tell you this, Arnold. But the second printing of *Beleaguered Fields* has already half sold out. Borders has just given it front-of-the-store display. And B&N actually called up to find out if Sid wanted to fork over the cash to have it put on the Local Authors table at the Union Square and Astor Place outlets. For twice that, they'll triple their order and put it in the front of all their A-stores associated with universities. Sid's thinking of doing it."

Arnold laughed. "I guess you're not supposed to tell me because they don't want all this attention going to my already very big head—right?" So far his book had gotten all of five reviews, one of which was a pale purple hectographed (!) throwaway from an extracurricular reading club at a Minneapolis community college, surely written by an undergraduate: *The poems in this book are really very interesting. . . .* At the bottom of what school supply closet, today, could you *find* a squishy, hectograph gelatin tray?

James looked uncomfortable. "I'm not supposed to tell you because you're what got my predecessor canned."

"I did?" Arnold frowned. Till then it had never occurred to Arnold that Vikki's dismissal had had anything to do with him. "But what did I—?"

"The reason you see so few books advertised as 'nominated for the Drew-Phalen' is because, Arnold, nomination is just a matter of paying three hundred dollars and sending in six copies. That's all. All publishers nominate their own books. Sure, it's a gamble. But it's a gamble based on a belief in the book's quality. The publisher just has to think what he's entering has a shot. Vikki convinced Sid that yours did. But the nomination fee hasn't gone up in fifty years. The Drew-Phalen Award is an institution drenched—even drowned—in tradition. Fifty years ago, three hundred dollars was more like three thousand. Hell, today three hundred is a fancy lunch for the publisher, editor, and any writer on the bestseller list in town for the afternoon."

Since neither of them had ordered an appetizer, the waiter set before Arnold a broad pink plate on which a square of salmon the size of a new plastic floppy disk had been placed on some plantains, in turn piled on some lentils, atop which, edges reddened with turmeric and red pepper, three shrimp curved around a mint sprig and flaked crabmeat—a low-leaning tower, drizzled about with scallions and cilantro puréed in heavy cream. "He fired her," Arnold said, "even *before* the Drew-Phalen was announced?"

James was having the hamburger. "Sid has a strong sense of...
tradition—and, as much of a go-getter as everybody tells me Vikki
was, Sid felt she wasn't showing the proper—I don't know—respect.
Whatever." (That February, the Drew-Phalen in poetry had gone to
Richard Howard, a poet whose command of intellectual history and
literary minutiae, years before, had delighted Arnold. He'd been ec-
static at the selection, even though he was sure it had really been
awarded for Howard's electric fifth and sixth volumes—knockouts
both—and not last year's *No Traveler* named. *That* had been merely
wonderful.) "Anyway, that's why advertising a Drew-Phalen nomination isn't done. It looks bad to the rest of the book community.
That's why Sid sacked Ms. LaSalle—though the rumor is they had
some sort of wager that if your book *didn't* win, she'd resign."

"Wow." Then Arnold added, *"Mmm.* And he didn't even wait to
see if it *had."*

"Sid said—or at least someone *told* me he said—he was losing
patience with her. She had some sort of plan to prove to him you
could be successful publishing a book of poems."

Arnold grinned. "But even though it *didn't* win, my book has
taken off like hotcakes—right?"

"I wouldn't call it 'hotcakes.' But you've sold twenty-five hundred hardcover copies of a book Sid expected to do about one tenth
of that."

"Two-*hundred*-fifty? Even *with* the Proctor—and the possibility
of the Drew-Phalen?"

"Even with the Proctor." James nodded somberly. Then, from
the old-fashioned fluted sundae glass, he pulled up a tongue of Melba
toast. "And you didn't *get* the Drew-Phalen." Frowning at it, he
pushed it back. "It's not like it's the Pulitzer." Toast crackled among
the other tongues. By the flowers, crumbs fell to the cloth.

"Oh...!" Arnold said.

A memory flickered from the '60s: checking that year's Drew-
Phalen had practically been a Groundhog Day tradition with Arnold
and his friend Bobby Horner. Both had always arrived the same
week—twice when it had been snowing. They'd bring the Sunday
Times and have brunch at that Second Street bar—the only bar back
then that *had* a brunch. God, he hadn't seen Bobby in years. Things
had changed so....

At their fifth lunch on James Farthwell's Lark & Dove expense account, it struck Arnold that this plodding youngster *liked* him—or liked going to lunch with a "successful" poet. Even by someone as stolid and slow as James, Arnold liked being liked.

———————

One Tuesday (this term, flouting their earlier promise, Tuesday—rather than Monday or Friday—was his nonteaching day), in the Graduate Center high above Forty-second Street, where he had gone to talk to a CUNY graduate poetry workshop, Arnold was waiting in the cafeteria for the young woman who was supposed to meet and guide him through the gray and green halls to the seminar room. Sitting at one of the broad cafeteria tables, he picked up and opened a copy of *Grants, Awards, and Prizes* left there aslant on the tabletop. Absently he began paging through.

Under "Alfred Proctor Prize," the index directed him to a West Walton Street address in Chicago as the place to send all entries.... Arnold frowned.

Sixty West Walton Street, Chicago, Illinois, sounded *awfully* familiar.

Then it hit. It was the address of *Poetry*'s Chicago offices: he'd submitted enough poems to them fifteen or twenty years back. When, in '73, they'd accepted two and Arnold had been doing a three-day residency at the University of Illinois, he'd stopped in to visit and discovered that the place was (one) much smaller than he'd assumed and (two) they were not particularly happy to have poets dropping by unannounced, even when that venerable magazine *had* published you.

Rain chittered on the eighteenth-floor window, obscuring the sumptuous city view, and Arnold wondered: What was *Poetry*'s address doing under the Proctor Prize?

The Alfred Proctor Prize was *so* New York.

———————

The next morning, back on Ninth Street, Arnold keyed open his scratched-up mailbox. Inside, an invitation from the Proctor Trust for one of their seasonal to-do's leaned on the tarnished wall.

That afternoon Arnold called James and asked him if, next Thursday, he'd like to go to a Proctor wine-and-cheese party at Writers' House, up on West Twenty-sixth. "You've been so generous with all these lunches, I thought it might be nice to, well ... return a little of the favor. I mean, if you wouldn't mind my company."

"Why—that would be great, Arnold!" James was free that evening. "Sure."

They'd gone.

Arnold recognized—perhaps—half the people milling beneath the ceiling's stamped green tin. Most he'd met at the awards ceremony, largely a memory of gladiolas in a crystal vase, half-obscuring a microphone. At a subsequent reception he'd been reintroduced. But, by now, the only one whose name he actually recalled was Jesse Kolodney—certainly because something about her reminded him of Judy Haindel (Arnold's wife, however briefly, fourteen years ago). Arnold had started a conversation with Jesse, a tall woman (unlike Judy) with a short platinum brush (Judy's hair had been tangled and a dark auburn), a black minidress, black combat boots, and an early piercing through her lower lip. Her second-from-the-top desk drawer at her job at Museum of Modern Art Publications was, Arnold knew—with all these people it seemed a running joke—the closest thing the Proctor Trust had to an office: "Hi, Jesse. I've got a question—it's something you should know the answer to. Is the Proctor connected with *Poetry* (Chicago)?" Once Arnold had wondered how to pronounce parentheses. Years ago he'd given up and now said them as if the first were a hyphen and the second not there.

Jesse swallowed a lot from her plastic cup and stepped back, shaking a hand now sloshed with grape-dark spots. "Oh, my God! *Poetry!* They were supposed to correct that two *years* ago! *Three* years, at least, Oh, my God! It was a perfectly *stupid* slip-up. Believe me, it wasn't *my* fault! Really. They told me they'd fix it in the next edition. My God! That's *terrible!* I called them about *that* one myself—*Grants, Awards, and Prizes*, right? Oh, my God—maybe you were looking at an *old* issue...?" (It was something in her speech....) Jesse stepped forward again, hopeful. "I *know* I called them about that...*four* years—!"

"I saw it the other afternoon," Arnold explained, "up at SUNY.

I'm sure it was the current edition. In fact I checked the date on the masthead just to make sure." He had, too. It had been dated '88.

"My *God . . . !*"

Just then, in tweed jacket and open-necked shirt, James strode forward, grinning widely, a coral glow in each ear, his eyes alcoholically sheened. "Arnold, this is just . . . *great!* This is great, man! I feel like a *real* editor—for the first *time!* All these literary people. *This* is what I came to New York for . . . to be an *editor* for. To meet people like *this*. Thank you. Thank you *so* much! This is just wonderful. I mean—" He turned to explain himself to Jesse—"I've already met three people here whose articles I've actually *read*. And Nathan Corner—he's over there—is wonderfully sharp. I mean, I'm kind of a literary type. That's why I went into editing in the *first* place!"

"You're an *editor?*" Lifting her plastic cup beneath her chin, Jesse smiled her smile for nice kids who'd drunk too much. (Was it the smile . . . ?) "So am *I!*"

Arnold did not say, *Well, it didn't take a* lot, *did it?* He enjoyed James's enthusiasm, even if it was only from a plastic glass or two of plonk out of the crystal decanter over at the green-covered table on the room's second level, up the carpeted steps. Arnold looked around. It was amazing what free wine, a little Brie, some Ritz crackers, and grapes could bring out in people. Who *was* here tonight, anyway?

Beleaguered Fields' third printing sold out six weeks later and, after another eighteen months—and a fourth—went into trade paperback.

In '90, Lark & Dove rejected Arnold's seventh book of poems—*Dashes*. Three and a half months later—after a three-year, ten-month tenure—James Farthwell resigned.

Attenuated by tape hiss: "Hi, Arnold. I'm calling to let you know I am no longer on the staff at Lark and Dove. . . ."

From his shared office, out at Staten Island State, where he'd gotten the blunt message on his voice mail, Arnold phoned James, then rushed back across the sound. Beneath scumbled clouds, Arnold gripped the black wooden rail looking over gray water. Ferries didn't really *rush* anywhere....He got to Union Square on time, only to wait twenty minutes on a cold bench as the winter evening darkened and myriad shoppers passed down to and hurried up from Fourteenth Street. Meeting James, taking him to another Proctor Trust to-do (which happened to be that night), was basically to make the kid feel better.

"Well," James told him, when they were finally on their way, "it could be worse."

"James, I'm *really*—"

"Oh, no! We're celebrating, Arnold," James declaimed with stolid earnestness. "You've made *two* editors lose their jobs at Lark and Dove, now—"

"James! Really—Really, I didn't *mean* to do any—"

"No."

For all his protestations of sympathy, Arnold felt pretty good. Rejection aside, the day before he'd received a $685 royalty check from Lark & Dove. (It was his only book *ever* to earn royalties!) Earlier the same day, out at school, in the voice mail before James's, he'd learned that Copper Canyon Press had accepted *Dashes,* and while they weren't Lark & Dove, they had a lot more presence in the poetry world. He'd submitted it only seven weeks ago, just enough time to let it drop out of mind.

Both James and Arnold were bundled against January, cold enough to make Arnold's shoulders, at any rate, feel chilly under the black cashmere overcoat Aunt Bea had brought him after his cousin Harold died in Appleton. James wore a bulky parka with the hood thrown back. Leaving Union Square, Arnold followed James into the narrow lobby of the converted loft building, to wait for the elevator that would take them up to the fourteenth floor, where Poets & Writers had their long, bright, blond wood offices.

"No," James repeated. "I wasn't the editor for Sid. And Sid *certainly* wasn't the publisher for me! He's too inconsistent, Arnold. You noticed he *kept* the bits about both the Proctor *and* the Drew-Phalen on the cover for your trade paperback? Then, when I presented your new book at our Wednesday editorial, he had the gall to say he didn't feel we could go on supporting a poet whose work had been sold under false pretenses. Now I *remember* the meeting where Sid approved that cover—for the *Beleaguered Fields* trade paperback,

I mean. There's nothing 'false' about the Proctor. And the Drew-Phalen thing, he could have had it taken off then. If he'd had any *real* objections, it's a little late to voice them now. It's not *your* fault. You're a fine poet, Arnold. A *very* fine poet. *I* think so. Everybody involved with the Proctor thinks so. With anybody I meet who reads poetry seriously, I can have a pretty good discussion of your work. Frankly, I don't think Sid's read a line of it, since they accepted your first book." (My sixth, Arnold thought, automatically.) "My father always says the reason you can't work with hypocrites is not because they think they're fooling you, but because they're always trying to fool themselves: *That's* why Sid's so untrustworthy.

"When we were leaving that meeting, Arnold, three months ago, I told Sid, '*You* don't want to have anything to do with publishing poetry at *all*, do you?' Well, he looked at me. Then he said, 'What sane publisher would?' I knew I was going to do this. I've spent ten weeks trying to get the three cookbook writers I'm actually fond of settled so that nothing awful happens to their books once I'm gone—imagine, giving poetry and cookbooks to the *same* editor!—and this morning I went in and told him I was resigning. He did his usual, 'Then have your office vacated by two o'clock.' Bastard! But I *don't* want to work for a publisher who doesn't do *any* poetry—and that's what Sid's become. You're the only poet on his list! You were a *success*, too! And because he's afraid he won't be able to do it again, Sid wouldn't let me take *The Dashes.*" He sighed. (Drink always made James slip "the" into the title, Arnold had noted.) The gray elevator door pulled loudly back. "Between three hardcover printings and a trade paperback, eight and a half thousand copies is nothing to sneeze at, even for a novel—much less a book of poems. Arnold, I feel more like a real editor, a real member of a literary community, when I'm hanging out with you, or the people in your circle, the people I've met through you, than I do when I'm in sales meetings or marketing conferences. And *that's* why I...well, quit." They stepped forward and turned as, clashing and coughing, the industrial elevator door closed them in.

James pressed a button.

Arnold had always thought his "circle" distressingly narrow—if he had one. But when, on fourteen, they left the gray, gray elevator car and walked down the gray, gray hall to push through the gray, gray fire doors into the...yellow wood, polyurethaned, aluminum, and glass opulence of Poets & Writers' not-for-profit offices, Arnold realized he knew the names of perhaps three people there and the faces of another five. While he was trying to decide how to tell James that such idealism, however admirable, was not wise, James strode forward with a hello here and a handshake there. By now, stolid, slightly drunken James (he'd stopped at a bar between leaving Lark & Dove and joining Arnold) knew *every one* of the thirty-five people in that chain of three blond wood rooms!

———————————

About a third of '89's Proctor stipend (Arnold's last, which he had put away for ten months now, for the purpose) went into the first airplane flight Arnold ever paid for himself (rather than some university flying him in for a reading), out to Cleveland for five days with Aunt Bea over the Christmas holiday—because if he didn't do it this year, he might never be able to do it at all.

He'd taken her to Coventry for a steak dinner at the Hyde Park Grill, where they sat like two happy blackbirds amidst a covey of (basically) sedate doves. Bea was the one who'd taught him to be comfortable in such places. "Oh, Arnold, this is *so* good. But if I ever told Mrs. Polk, she'd never let me hear the end of it!" They left through a glow of red neon to attend a Cleveland Orchestra concert in Severance Hall: the Berg Violin Concerto (fingers perched primly on her black pocketbook, beside him in her orchestra seat, Bea muttered: "Imagine—dead of a bee sting, the day before Christmas, at fifty." She'd said it, years before, when they'd gone to hear *Wozzeck* in Lenox. Back then, of course, fifty had been thirty or more years ahead of Arnold; not three years behind) and a David Diamond symphony. While her mind was wonderfully clear, Bea moved around more slowly than he'd remembered.

As the rain stopped and the plane settled into LaGuardia, in the December sun, ribbons of water over the tarmac were gunmetal or scarlet. As Arnold looked out the little window, for moments the plane appeared to tear through webs of crimson and black. He sagged forward, as they slowed to a bumping roll. A minute later, three of Arnold's students he hadn't realized were on the plane crowded past his seat, lugging backpacks. "Oh, gosh! *Hi,* Professor Hawley! Were you in Cleveland, too? ... See you in class Wednesday!" so that Arnold returned home on the narrow-aisled bus in a haze of holiday belonging, with the realization—for the first time, actually—that what the Proctor's three years of moneys, now done with, had meant was that he could settle more easily into true poverty.

———————

Years and years ago, in 1968, between the April his book *Air Tangle* had been accepted and the October it had appeared, something had happened that explained why Arnold never moved from East Ninth Street. A lanky actor, Noel, and another plump fellow, the singer and actor Lamar Alford (where *had* he first met them? At this point, Arnold really didn't remember), used to hang out with Arnold, now at the Annex, now at Stanley's, sometimes at the Stonewall over in the Village— Arnold's favorite because there were the most Negroes—sometimes at the Ninth Circle, or even up at Max's. One day both of them, with their third, Bobby—all were black; all were gay—dropped in on Arnold's third-floor-rear apartment one Saturday morning, when nobody had quite enough to go for one of Speedie's breakfasts (they weren't even *calling* them brunches, yet) at the Old Reliable—*that* had been the name of the place!—on Second Street. "What we're gonna *do*," Noel explained, "on Monday night, is a whole bunch of us—after closing— we're going to hide, in fourteen different branches of the public library, all over New York. Me and Lamar will take the Tompkins Square branch. Bobby here is with some other people up at—"

Sitting on the other end of the gold couch (arrived from Pittsfield that week), Bobby said, "Hey, man—you're not supposed to *tell* anybody who isn't part of it, now!"

"Oh, Arnold's okay," Noel said from the recliner. "We're going to hide in over a dozen branch libraries, and after they close up we're going to take the signs off the shelves that say 'Negro literature' and put up signs that say 'black literature'—like Dr. Du Bois wanted it called, more than fifty years ago. I mean, what's with this 'Negro' crap, like a race is a *real* thing and you got to put a capital letter on it? Don't nobody ever put a capital letter on 'white'!"

"The day they do," Lamar said, standing by the couch's end, "I'm *leavin'* this country!" For a heavy man, Lamar had so much energy. He rarely sat.

"It's a social fact, yes," Noel said. "A cultural reality—but it's not some biological thing."

"Yeah," Bobby said from the couch, "but there are days you look pretty biological to *me*!" They all laughed, as it sometimes seemed they'd done so much, back then.

The fact was, Arnold wasn't paying lots of attention. But, a week later, first in the *East Village Other* that, outside Gem's Spa, he'd reached in among some clustering tourists to pick up from the paper stand's outside counter, then in a *Village Voice* someone had left on a bench in Tompkins Square, he'd read an article about the "vandalism" in libraries the past weekend throughout all five boroughs. At the same time, the Panthers were pushing the slogan "black is beautiful." Three months later, over the shoulder of a woman sitting beside him on the subway, in the letters column of the *New York Times,* he read his first printed reference to "black people" and "blacks," where, only weeks before, certainly they would have written "Negro." It gave him an astonishing sense of... what? Pride, privilege, power? While it hadn't been planned *in* Arnold's living room, those plans had run *through* his living room.

Who, he wondered, had masterminded it?

Bea phoned him that night. "We had such an argument over it—my ladies in the Reading Club. Arnold, you wouldn't have believed it. When I was a lot younger than you, I fought real hard for 'colored' and campaigned against 'Negro' for all I was worth—that capital 'N' sticks in my craw to this day. It's supposed to have something to do with respect? Well, it never meant respect for *me*! It meant white men could call us with another fancy-sounding word that put another mark of scientific alienation against us, this time—like a species of animal in a zoo."

"Oh, Bea," Arnold said, "you *have* to call it—"

"Now don't 'Oh, Bea!' me, honey!"

"—to call it 'black literature'—I mean, because..." Though most of the reason was because of what had happened there in Arnold's apartment.

And people all over the country were *talking* about it!

Somewhere in Cleveland, Bea said, "Well, our librarian, Mrs. Polk, she said it was some schoolchildren in New York, who broke into a library—"

"They *weren't* children!" Arnold said. "I... *know* some of them.

They were highly thinking men . . . and women." The only ones Arnold knew for sure were the three black gay fellows, though he couldn't imagine that—somewhere—there weren't women and even . . . well, *probably* straight black men involved. "And it was *fourteen* libraries! You make sure you tell your group *that*!"

"Mrs. Polk said, as far as she was concerned, they could call it whatever they wanted, as long as it made the young people come in and read it."

"*There!*" Arnold said. "You see?"

Somehow, he saw Noel only a few times after that, but Lamar went on and got a part in a Broadway musical called *Godspell*—and years later Arnold heard he was teaching in Atlanta.

By the bookshelf, in the dark, netted in the myriad physical unpleasantnesses that were his pudgy, fifty-four-year-old body, Arnold stood, a long-nailed forefinger poised on the back of a book. He pulled it free from the shelf, and turned to open it. Before him, he could just see a white field on which he could make out no single word. Is this death, Arnold thought, standing in a dark hall, holding a book you could barely see, opened to a page you could not read?

It was just after three in the morning.

Arnold smiled in the dark—then went to the bathroom. And turned on the light—and looked at the sudden and surprisingly familiar cover of *Air Tangle*. Whenever he'd dedicated a book to Bea (as were all but one of his six books—*Dark Reflections*, which bore no dedication at all), how much she'd enjoyed it! He'd get five phone calls over the next month, telling him what this one and that one had said when she'd showed it off.

Six weeks after *Beleaguered Fields* received its Proctor, the Black Women's Reading Group of Cleveland (a hundred years ago the Colored Women's Reading Group) had sent him a long, gleaming box, in which much green tissue rustled about a dozen long-stemmed white roses. In with them was a congratulatory card:

"*A token of our Great Pleasure at your having won a much deserved prize!*"

Though, from Mrs. Polk on, all the members had crowded their signatures onto the back, the handwriting on the front was Bea's—

indeed, it was all Bea's doing, at once wonderfully sweet, even as it verged on the annoying.

Arnold returned to his sweat-dampened bed, edging toward the far side of the mattress, slipping toward sleep, despite New York's July night heat, an arm wrapping his pillow.

———

Six months after James Farthwell left Lark & Dove, Arnold got a phone call: James was starting his own small publishing company. "I'm calling it Phoenix Press, Arnold—do you like it?"

"You are?" Arnold asked. "How are you doing that?"

"I have a little money," James said, "from my father."

"Oh...!" Arnold thought: Had there been any mention of a father before? Is that what it took to be a cockeyed idealist, these days—money from your father?

Then, with the concern of someone who really cared, James asked again: "Do you *like* the name Phoenix Press?"

"Oh," Arnold said. "Yes. It's...*very* nice!" He wanted to sound sincere. Probably he sounded snide. James had always been a *little* slow. But Arnold had not realized James was a complete fool. What were you supposed to say, though, when, purely because of inflation, only that year you'd become a fifty-five-year-old man who'd gone from never following scrambled eggs with scrambled eggs or oatmeal with oatmeal for supper, to never following scrambled eggs with scrambled eggs or oatmeal with oatmeal more than three nights in a row?

Of course James was also an *idealistic* fool, Arnold was thinking half an hour later, as he stood at the sink washing dishes, below the doorless cabinets. Of such fools poets should make heroes. Phoenix Press? If James did half of what he wanted, he'd have the entire American art scene bursting up, reborn, from its ashes. And he *was* a nice kid—though he'd only broken thirty a year or so back.

———

Copper Canyon, who had almost a two-year lead time, released *Dashes* at the beginning of '92—a week before Arnold's March 15 birthday. So he was still fifty-five. The critical reaction (its three

intelligent reviews) produced five invitations to read and two in-
quiries from magazine editors. In turn, that gave Arnold another encounter with *Grants, Awards, and Prizes*—this one in Nathan Corner's
maroon-carpeted office. Corner was a lawyer, who, retired at fifty,
now edited and published the journal *Spectacle*. (Fifty seemed rather
young to retire. Hell, fifty—to Arnold—seemed pretty young, period.) *Spectacle*'s offices had once been Nathan's law firm's library.
Shelves were still full of multivolume book sets in tan and scarlet,
gold-leaf letters on their matched spines.

Their acquaintanceship went back to the Proctor Prize days.

Grants, Awards, and Prizes lay on the dark desk. It was the current
'92 issue. A flip through the oversized paperback, and Arnold saw
that the Alfred Proctor Prize *still* had the incorrect West Walton
Street address in Chicago. Shaking his head, Arnold put the fat volume back on the desk's edge.

"What...?" Nathan looked from the shelf where he'd been taking down an art book to show Arnold some collages of which they
were planning to do a color portfolio in the next issue. "I thought you
said something."

"Nothing," Arnold said. "It's nothing."

But while he looked at the artist's bits of string, mirror, and
wood, lovingly glued to the impasto pigments, photographed, and
reprinted in what must have been at least a twelve-color plate,
Arnold was imagining someone at Chicago's Walton Street, taking
mailbags full of misaddressed entries out into the back alley to toss
them, with their gray canvas sacks, into some dented Dumpster. How
would those folks have even *heard* of the Alfred Proctor Prize?

Probably, from the cover of his own *Beleaguered Fields*!

Whereupon they'd all rushed out to look it up in...

Under "Alfred Proctor Prize" alone was no address at all.

October light fell through the arched institutional windows by the
crowded bookshelves, through the wrought-iron inner balcony rail,
down on the broad wood table. I wonder (Arnold glanced up and
thought as he always did when he came here) if *that's* where they
hid?

As he sat, two chairs away someone rose, leaving a book closed, and, with something of a grunt, moved to the checkout desk, leaning on her cane.

The book's yellow cover framed a photo of the backs of small children, as if in a sports huddle. Smiling, Arnold pulled the volume over to see the title: *Boys Like Us.*

It was the subtitle, though, that raised Arnold's eyebrows: *Gay Writers Tell Their Coming-Out Stories.* Automatically, Arnold moved his hand back to the table edge. Equally mechanically, he sat back in his own chair. He glanced about. Nobody was looking. But why should they?

Not quite smiling, Arnold thought about how many times in his childhood, now in one library, now in another, he had looked up this volume or that because he'd heard it had some reference to homosexuality. But it had always been a secretive search, with glances over his shoulder, or sitting in a seat to read it far from everyone else: somehow pre-Stonewall fear of discovery had been replaced by a post-Stonewall sense of vulgarity in all this public discussion of what, after all, surely should be private. Which one, Arnold wondered, was finally more effective in keeping people off—though, just as he would have done as a teenager, Arnold had already opened the cover and started reading the editor's introduction (somebody named Merla) so that—at least—no one would recognize the cover.

He didn't read it very closely. But it ended with a memorial roster of writers who had died of AIDS. Arnold ran his eyes down the column.

David Frechette... was that the heavyset young journalist Arnold had talked to a few times after one or another St. Mark's reading a few years back? Oh, dear...

Lamar Alford.

Arnold stopped.

He looked up from the book.

But Lamar had been an actor, not a writer....

Though, of course, he'd been a teacher, too. Perhaps, like Frechette, he had written some articles.

The advent of AIDS in the '80s had been among the factors bringing Arnold's own tentative sexual experiments to an end. Arnold slid his chair back and stood, picked up his briefcase crammed with student papers, and, leaving the book on the table, walked out of the library and down its steps, onto Second Avenue, along the half block to the corner of St. Mark's Place, thick with kids, before, across from Gem's Spa, he turned east.

For several days, Arnold actually thought about writing Lamar an elegy. *They told me, Heraclitus; they told me you were dead....* A lament for the makers... the makers of Arnold's own delicate vision of the world. But no one *had* told him. It was just another thing that had—almost—slipped by.

———————

One mid-April day, as he was walking down Eleventh Street, Arnold Hawley stopped and removed his glasses, because the aging phenomenon by which elderly farsightedness corrects congenital nearsightedness had for more than a year now been apparent—at least in his right eye, though not so much in his left. But Arnold was struck all over with the unfamiliar sharpness of the milled striations on the garbage pails beside the stoop, the granulation of the mortar between the red bricks, between the tan bricks rising by them, the dogwood blossoms hanging above the streets. Just then, as a breeze stirred those fallen over the sidewalk, Arnold realized Eleventh Street was awash in dogwood petals, which, at once, swirled—thousands of them!—into the air. They scarved and unscarved the street, the lamppost's base, the trees, the metal post of a no-parking sign that tried to throw its shadow futilely to the sidewalk's sand-colored paving. They coiled in ribbons, uncoiled in streamers. As Arnold looked about, he saw other trees, days before denuded by winter, touched now with spring's greeny ghosts.

Thicker than bubbles in soda water, petals were above him and around him. (Odd, that year he'd not yet seen a single spear of forsythia, but he hadn't been up to Central Park or Van Courtland, or yet out of the city.) Through a sunlight patch on the pavement beside him, a *thousand* shadows rushed under petals whipping above! Even as so many white flakes seemed to fall, slantwise, they lifted Arnold's eyes. They tickled the backs of his hands, hit his ears and eyelids, so that he thought he'd better put his glasses back on; and did—a petal caught in the frame against his nose, to struggle like a moth. Arnold laughed.

It tugged free, and Arnold walked on in whirls of white, while sunlight winked and glimmered, catching flicks of yellow and pink. From petal-washed pavement, to window frames behind the passing rage of blossoms, to the trees with up-thrust branches—Champagne flutes overspilling silver wines—and above the cornices to the aluminum clouds, immobile and deflecting enough sunlight to keep it from blinding all, urban blue and urban beauty (Arnold thought) lift the eye. Arnold lifted not only his eyes but his hands.

Dozens of poems had choired such states. *My heart leaps up when I behold*—but there was no rainbow. Did it matter when the air was full of flowers? *The earth stands out on either side, no wider than the heart*—a nineteen-year-old girl had written, not all that far from where Arnold had been born, and for the length of her life had remained famous for it. But here were no long mountains, no wood to reinforce the feelings. Only the fabulous day, the beautiful street— to rival Patchin Place or Pomander Walk—that, with the number eleven alone to name it, still spilled raptures.

About him, men and women, boys and girls, black and Hispanic, were swirled around with ivory. They looked up and turned their heads. Now and again one looked at Arnold. Petals billowing between, they gave one another awed smiles.

Arnold dropped his hands and, head still high, wandered, happy enough for the hour, toward what awaited in evening.

Yes, *Dashes* had come out from Copper Canyon back in the spring of '92, and over the next year and a half had garnered eleven reviews, ten of them good and three actually intelligent. For a while, Arnold had thought, Why do I *need* to go on writing? But now that, too, was something to remember tranquilly and smile over.

In '96, three weeks after his sixtieth birthday, Arnold stood in the shadowed hallway of his apartment, looking at his books.

There beside *Dashes*—

Beleaguered Fields (1987), by Arnold Hawley, his Alfred Proctor Prize–winning volume:

Four hardcover and four trade paperback copies stood on his "brag shelf," across from his bathroom. Arnold didn't remember which writer friend had first used the phrase to him, or how many years ago. (*Had* it been Bobby, who'd hung out with all those people who wrote mysteries and pornography and westerns and actually published them, all of which rather terrified Arnold?) Arnold worked a copy half loose, till he realized the cover was cushioned on one of the Cleveland roses, dried inside.

Cleveland—land of cliffs...

Arnold pushed it back. No sense damaging that last flower. (If Aunt Bea ever visited again, he'd show it to her.) To the right stood eight copies of *Dashes,* one of the fifty that Copper Canyon had had bound in hardcover, and seven of the handsome paperbacks, which had received general trade release—and which, after four years, had sold about nine hundred copies, till it had been remaindered. (Pretty paltry compared to *Beleaguered Fields.)* Before the *Fields'* eruption of relative accessibility, there was his fifth book:

High-Toned Homilies with Their Gunwales All Submerged (1984), with its subtitle (his *only* book with a subtitle): *Meditations on George Jones, Giovanni da Palestrina, and Bonnie Tyler*—the single volume put out by the brief-lived Croaton Press.

Yes, his Fifth Book: five had always seemed to Arnold an important number. A single book-length prose poem, it had received only two reviews, neither good ("...unreadable..." "...tedious..."), neither intelligent ("...makes you wonder why somebody would even..." "...finally art-as-ordeal is just dull and, anyway, who..."), with a promise of a third ("...next month I'll be discussing Arnold Hawley's impressive new work, though obviously it's one you have to live with awhile..."). The promise had not been kept. The California reviewer had never gotten around to it. Or hadn't lived with it enough.

Or, perhaps, she simply hadn't liked it.

For Arnold there'd been ways in which *High-Toned Homilies with Their Gunwales All Submerged* was the work he himself had learned most from. Robert Graves had declared all true poems to be about love, death, or the changing of the seasons. Well, this was the poem of Arnold's that he most doubted *was* a poem, since it was about music—music that lived in language, and what instruments might wring from it. It was the work which taught Arnold that, while sexual love, however unrequited, might flog him toward poetry, for him it could never be the topic of the poem. As a boy he had lived too long and closely with Aunt Bea, and, more, had loved her too deeply.

Even more than *Dark Reflections,* it was Arnold's most painful book.

One hundred eighteen pages of solid print, arranged to correspond only to the pages' margins, his greatest formal *coup,* unrelieved by period or paragraph indentation, *High-Toned Homilies with Their Gunwales All Submerged* was also his most difficult. For a month in the midst of writing it, Arnold had walked about, mumbling, "Come on! This makes *When the Sun Tries to Go On* chopped liver! Hey, Koch! 'The New Spirit' and 'The Recital' have nothing on me, Ashbery! Move over, Caliban. *I've* got the audience, now!" Personally Arnold was convinced it contained passages as gorgeous as anything in Tolson's *Gallery* or Johnson's *Ark.* But had any reader other than himself ever burrowed through to them?

The spine and the cover were black. The lettering was silver foil—Croaton's attempt to make it look elegant. In a very, very few readings (two? one...?) just after *High-Toned Homilies* appeared, Arnold had included a number of selections. But when, afterward, the third person came up to say, "It sounds so nice when you hear it out loud. It's just so hard to read. On the page, I mean. Maybe you should sell it with a cassette...?" (CDs were just coming in.) Well, Arnold's rising anger meant he had never read from the book again. All public pleasure in it had been leached.

Croaton had distributed 140 of the 500 printed before they went out of business—though Arnold only learned of it four years later, when a belated wrap-up letter arrived. How few of those 140 had actually sold, Arnold would simply *not* flay himself by imagining.

(Twelve? Fifteen? Six?)

In what cellar—or Dumpster—the other 360 had ended up was anyone's guess. They hadn't even offered him copies. But there it was.

His major work, in his hallway—Arnold did *not* take down one of the seven—and otherwise unknown.

The sixteen Lark & Dove volumes, hardcover and paperback, still looked nice—even if they were a bit overpowered, as was everything else on the shelf, by the red spines of the seven copies of *Pewter Pan* (number four) from Yellow Star, back in '79.

After eighteen years, three cartons of *Pewter Pan* still sat under the kitchen table, up against the refrigerator. Though that was the one he had the most of, he only kept seven out. It had actually sold about four hundred—not bad....

Through overenthusiastic gift giving or friends who'd sworn they'd return it next week—then decamped for Sweden or Bogotá—*Dark Reflections* (number three: 1974) was down to a singleton. An old Harper Torchbook, it had appeared only in paperback. The title should have been *Pretenses*. But the editor, Sam, had insisted Arnold change it. It told the story, as much of it as he'd dared, of Arnold's catastrophic marriage to the insane Haindel girl.

As a delayed response to that marriage, once it was a year or so behind him, Arnold had finally gone to bed with—well, had sex with—a man. Three men, actually, and, all when he was between thirty-eight and forty: first Eddy, then, ten months later, Tony, who'd turned up again, and finally, a year and a half after that, Big Ukrainian Mike. He'd paid each twenty dollars—and had found none much fun or interesting. He'd run into the last one, the very drunken Mike, with his single eye and the sleeves torn off his sweat-drenched flannel, that Indian summer, at two in the morning in Tompkins Square, coming unsteadily from his job at the Odessa's kitchen, where, apparently, at that hour, they didn't mind if he kept a flask in his jeans. Rarely was the park deserted—but that night it was empty. After they'd talked for five minutes, practically using force, which, oddly, Arnold had neither liked nor disliked, Mike had made him do it up against the gate beside the comfort station's side wall. Mike hadn't *asked* for money, but, after managing to stand up, Arnold had handed it to him. Mike took it, turned, lunged forward, nearly tripping over his own feet, and sprinted west. Even drunk as he was, only Big Mike had come—which, yes, had been what Arnold had hoped the others would do.

But they hadn't.

Arnold walked east, back to his apartment, holding Mike's semen in his mouth, thinking he ought to spit it out. He didn't particularly like the taste. But it was *so* close to something he had fantasized about so many times before, he couldn't. By the time he reached home, it seemed to have become a slightly bitter part of him, something he'd grown one with, words in a poem he might keep or discard. Diluted with so much of his own saliva, by now it felt like—if it did not taste like—his own waters. Aware he would probably never do *that* again, Arnold swallowed, pushed opened the glass door, and went upstairs. . . .

He had to get a *few* more copies of *Dark Reflections*, even if he had to pay rare-book prices. He'd been telling himself that for more than a decade. Would a rare-book dealer have it, after all these years?

Though officially his second volume, *Air Tangle* (1968) had been Arnold's first *real* book. Old Stone Press. What had *happened* to those people? Without turning on the hall light, Arnold pulled one free—to heft it on his fingertips. He still felt it was the best looking, with its enameled ivory cover, its pale picture of a sunrise over farmland, its black deco lettering: eighty-four pages and, like the others (except *Dark Reflections*), dedicated to Aunt Bea: "For Beatrice Carmentha Hawley."

For years Arnold had wondered what misappropriation of "Carmen" had produced "Carmentha." Aunt Bea knew only that it had been the name of a woman friend of her own mother's—not Sara Alice. (Aunt Bea was his father's *half* sister.) But because he'd grown up with the name, it had never really struck Arnold as odd until he'd finished college and moved away from home.

Nice as it looked, the book did seem oddly old-fashioned. It hadn't when it was published. How had *that* happened?

And number one?

That was his chapbook, *Waters*—done while he'd been at school in Boston, in '63.

In public Arnold considered *Air Tangle* his first.

Alone in front of his brag shelf, at night, *Air Tangle* was his second.

Hadn't there been six copies of *Waters*? But he could feel only four spines. . . . Where *were* the other two? Somewhere in the apartment, he hoped.

Waters—he slipped one pamphlet out and opened the cover—was still the one he returned to most, with its epigraph from Xenophanes. In darkness, Arnold recited it:

". . . For not without great oceans would there come to be in clouds the force of wind blowing out from within, nor the streams of rivers nor rain water from the upper sky . . ."

At Boston University (when Brown hadn't really...worked out), Arnold had found the quotation in a book someone had left on a bench in a library carrel. He'd picked it up, read it almost by accident, and decided that it would be perfect. At twenty-five, Arnold had had no idea who Xenophanes was—some little-known but impressive Greek. The day he'd copied the passage into his notebook, he'd read neither the entire page it had occurred on, nor even the paragraph the writer had quoted it in. Nor, indeed, who the writer citing it was. Three days later, he could not have told you the larger book's title. It had been green—and old. The print on the cover and spine had been gold leaf.

That, Arnold remembered, even today.

A month after *Waters* appeared, Professor Cohen, who taught history, had said he'd read it—and that he'd liked it. And that he was surprised he had. Professor Cohen had a short beard and spoke Greek, Latin, and Hebrew, as well as Italian, German, French, and Aramaic, with his Brooklyn twang and his dark neckties. He also said something to Arnold about "given your interest in the presocratics..." so that it occurred to Arnold to look Xenophanes up—in the eleventh edition of the *Britannica*, suggested a helpful librarian: that was the last one that still had all the classical articles.

Thus, months after the chapbook had come out, Arnold discovered that Xenophanes was a presocratic poet-and-philosopher (apparently the distinction between them hadn't settled into place until Plato), born on the Ionian coast about 570 BC, whose dates had him overlapping with the early Milesian trio, Thales, Anaximander, and Anaximanes—not to mention Heraclitus, whom one ancient claimed Xenophanes had taught. Actually he'd outlived the Obscure Philosopher by a decade. As well, Xenophanes had survived the devastating invasion of the Persians under General Harpagus, left Asia Minor, and probably gone to Elea in Italy, where he may have been an early instructor of Parmenides, who, along with Empedocles (*he* dressed superbly, claimed himself immortal, and had or had not ended his days by leaping into Etna's lavid cone), was another poet-philosopher.

It had started Arnold on a year of reading.

Anaximanes was pretty soon Arnold's favorite of those early thinkers, because the least was known about him. Still, imagine the conceptual jump, the historical upheaval, discovering for the first time that *air* was a *thing* and not a *nothing*, a *being* rather than a *nonbeing*—Anaximanes's contribution to that combination of science and abstract thought that was philosophy before Plato—that there could be more of it, less of it, that it could be thinner, thicker, and that, invisible as it was, it moved about, and could, in itself, be cold or hot.... (It's why he'd named *Air Tangle* "Air Tangle.") Wasn't that the first *real* vault into the unseen world Parmenides had later pictured and that had produced modernity, unto radio waves, electricity, and atomic energy? Anaximanes had first discovered the fundamentalness of the medium they moved through.

During the months when he was despairing of *Air Tangle*'s ever actually getting accepted, Arnold had written his one extended prose work, that embarrassing gay pornographic novel about the adventures of some Sicilian youth in the reign of the emperor Hadrian. It had been Bobby Horner's idea.

Horner had outlined the thing, all fifty-one chapters. Then, sitting at his kitchen table from September through December, working at his portable electric typewriter, Arnold had strained his imagination—and his sense of prose—to fill up the pages. Eventually, taking a break to sit on the living room couch, the only way he'd managed to get through it was to divide Bobby's absurd and abhorrent outline still further into lists of separate paragraphs, each with its narrative task.

Back in his kitchen, one after the other, rhapsodically Arnold had written them out.

It had been supposed to take him three weeks. He took four months, spending the last one lapped in sweaters because the heat had gone out.

Three weeks after Thanksgiving—that year no one, including Bobby, had invited him over; though Arnold hadn't noticed because he'd been too busy writing—when Arnold completed and delivered the thing, Bobby asked: "Come on, Arnold—didn't you have fun writing that? It reads as if you did."

"Good Lord," Arnold (who was, by then, an atheist, though occasionally during the writing he'd found himself in honest fear of hell) answered honestly, "who could have 'fun' writing *that*? I just turned my mind off and *did* it!"

"I think"—and Horner had laughed—"the reason your sex scenes are so passionate is because you're a virgin."

"Oh, *please!*" Arnold had protested. "Spare me!" But, for the first time, it occurred to Arnold that possibly Horner had actually thought there was something *to* the incomprehensible narrative—that, indeed, Arnold's friend had considered it meaningful and not just something nasty whose only excuse was, in the air of legal laxness pervading the decade, penury.

Arnold's single copy—it had arrived with a check from Bobby Arnold took six weeks to cash—was hidden behind the magazines that stuffed the upper of the four magazine shelves. How Bobby had figured out how to divide the $750 they had gotten for the whole horrible thing, Arnold didn't know and wouldn't ask. He was honestly surprised he'd gotten more than half.

Once, after owning the published copy over a year, Arnold took it from behind the magazines, wiped the dust from the cover with the heel of his hand, sat, and read twenty pages. Appalled and finally unable to go on, he stood and put it back.

For years the possibility that Aunt Bea might discover he was gay needled at Arnold, till finally he'd realized she probably knew—at least she knew he was different. But by now he also knew she'd never bring it up—because, till now, she . . . hadn't.

Indeed, it was the center of the trust between them, Arnold thought, "coming out" be damned. You didn't change your central trust with the most important person in your life, even for a nationwide political movement, at least not if you'd survived with it till you were over forty, fifty, sixty. . . .

Or did you?

That Bea might learn about his part in the porn book, however, was an actual nightmare that had shattered his sleep at least five times, when Arnold had been particularly worried or stressed.

Relatively complete, his magazine publications on the shelves below the books ran back to Arnold's first published poem in '58 (because, when he'd come down from Pittsfield with some other college friends, he'd met the editor at a party: an extremely mature white kid named Peter, who'd worn a sports jacket and must have been at the time an elderly nineteen or, who knows, even twenty . . .) on the City College's *Promethean* staff: a cascade of morbid quatrains about a dead dog, never reprinted.

"Roxbury Leaves," "Loud Children," "Moritat," "Paradise

Hill"—the first of his intermittent Vision-of-Hell poems; Arnold had written one practically every decade—"Pittsfield," "Blackmailers"— still his favorite from the chapbook: its twelve stanzas began respectively with B, L, A, C, K, M, A ... each an impressionistic evocation of a different Roxbury house. The one thing it was *not* about was blackmail!—"Clouds" ... After paging through *Waters* for the thousandth time in forty years Arnold closed the blue cover with its etching in white of a seaside. Back in '89, the second year of his Proctor stipend, he'd added two names to the dedication, in case it should ever be reprinted, though he seldom thought about them today. With its flaking corners and edges, he returned it to the shelf.

Because of these, and these alone (sixty-year-old Arnold Hawley thought in the narrow dark), I exist.

THE GREAT NEGRO PLOT

A TALE OF CONSPIRACY AND MURDER
IN EIGHTEENTH-CENTURY NEW YORK

Mat Johnson

NOT CUTE ENOUGH

To be poor in England in the eighteenth century was not simply a shame, it was a crime. English poor laws had been in effect since the fourteenth century, but while far from a new phenomenon, poverty had a special meaning as the empire became global. Before expansion into the new lands, the dirty and impoverished were something that the English elite simply had to endure. No matter how harsh the penalties for poverty and indolence, no matter how many perished from starvation or disease, there were always more to replace the unwashed masses. Now, with the discovered countries, England could unburden itself of its human refuse, recycling its undesirables as fodder for the construction of the empire. In America, in exchange for years of free labor, the cost of relocating the poor, the convicted, the indigent was covered by the landowner who would make use of them. At the end of their service, the indentured servant would at least have the chance to start a new life in the land of opportunity, usually with some sort of severance to usher him or her along. Often indentured servants finished their terms with a trade learned or parcel of land gained, the fruit of their time in captivity.

Unlike in the Chesapeake colonies or those English outposts to the north, the New York colony had few indentured servants, and those they did attract were seldom "transports," or convicts, but "freewillers," free immigrants who chose on their own to enter a period of bond. That there was such a difference in culture between colonies of the same flag can be attributed to the fact that the city of New York, whether under Dutch, English, or later American control, has always been about money, as opposed to religious freedom or creating a utopia. New York means business, is business. This alone informs every aspect of New York's character, from conception forward.

Slavery was about business. As far as economic value to the employer, slavery just couldn't be beat. It was a steal—literally. For the slaveholders, it was impossible to get a better deal than the one-time payment slavery demanded. For the immigrating European working class, slavery was impossible to compete against. Unlike in the other regions where slaves were largely utilized for unskilled, manual labor, the slaves of Manhattan Island were often skilled artisans, trained in the crafts and trades of their masters, or retained specifically for their skill to serve as craftsmen for households. By training slaves for such specified labor, slaveholders could also hire out their captives for additional profits when demand arose—something particularly convenient in what was largely a port town, with ships arriving regularly in need of various forms of labor. Slavery also (and this was no small thing) alleviated the constant risk of having former apprentices leave to branch out on their own, going from an artisan's much needed assistant to his much unwanted competitor. Because of this, tensions between poor workers struggling to make a living and wageless slaves would begin early in New York, and find several eruption points along the line long before the hideous Draft Riots of the Civil War would spark one of the city's greatest atrocities.

In New York, apprenticeship among whites was a willfully neglected practice. In 1737, lieutenant governor George Clarke warned that "the artificers complain and with too much reason of the pernicious custom of breeding slaves to trades whereby the honest and industrious tradesmen are reduced to poverty for want of employ, and many of them forced to leave us to seek their living in other countries." White flight, the old-fashioned way. In an attempt to make indentured servitude more attractive to employers, in 1711 the term of indentured service was lengthened from four to eleven years. This helped a bit, but with only 203 apprentices indentured in the colony between 1718 and 1727, it in no way took care of the massive demand of an expanding city. In 1734, colonial governor William Cosby echoed the fears of white Manhattan when he said, "I see with concern that whilst the neighboring Provinces are filled with honest, useful and labourious [*sic*] white people, the truest riches and surest strength of country, this Province seems regardless of...the disadvantages that attend the too great importation of negroes and convicts."

Without enough white workers to go around, New York became a city that was carried by black, skilled hands. Still, there were some advantages for adventurous Brits to become indentured servants here. As one of the few and prized, for instance, you were likely to encounter better treatment and status than in colonies overrun with the indentured. And of course, damn near anything was an improvement over the chances for the lower class in overcrowded, class-obsessed England.

Perhaps this is what motivated young Mary Burton to choose to lease herself to John Hughson as a house servant, as opposed to any of the other options available to her. Perhaps, as it was later insinuated (by a less than objective party), it was that Mary had arrived at the Hughsons' as damaged goods after she'd left the house of her last employ pregnant with the master's child. Inflammatory, certainly speculative accusations—Mary Burton was only sixteen years old. Still, how else would a young girl end up in servitude to such a disreputable house such as the Hughsons', unless it was that she had nowhere else to go? Much was said of Mary Burton. Most deserved. Very little complimentary.

Who would think that such a humble girl could do so much damage, could, in just a few months, cause the deaths of scores and the terror of thousands? The following day after the under-sheriff, Mills, and his constables had searched Hughson's home a final time, Mary Burton entered the house of a neighbor, James Kannady, one of the constables whom Mary had just witnessed doing the searching. Mary came under the guise of borrowing a pound of candles, but it was just an excuse to get in the door and hear the latest gossip on the Hogg burglary. If Sarah Hughson had known her little disobedient, loose-lipped servant girl had snuck off to Kannady's she would have surely taken the switch to her, but it was worth it.

Mary didn't even have to broach the subject; Mrs. Kannady seized the opportunity.

"Listen, girl," Mrs. Kannady prodded her young neighbor. "If you know anything, you'd do best to discover it now, lest you yourself should be brought into trouble."

"Madam, I...I can't," Mary dodged coyly. "Begging your pardon, it's not my place to say."

"Love, you're forced to work in that house of sin but no one begrudges you for it. You're young, you don't want to spoil your life over that lot. If you know anything, you tell me, and my husband will see to it that you're freed from your master."

Mary Burton pulled away from Mrs. Kannady, candles in hand. The thoughts of freedom were intoxicating, the temptation overwhelming. The only problem: She actually had no information to offer.

Still that did not stop her. "I've things to say, madam," Mary told her, "but my mistress will be waiting. Tomorrow, though, I will come with news for you."

"By the morrow my husband will have already found the stolen goods by himself," Mrs. Kannady pushed. "Now is your chance, girl," she persisted, sensing that Mary Burton was ever eager to say more.

However, Mary just shrugged and giggled her response back at her. "He's not cute enough," she said in a near whisper, "for he has already trod upon them."

Not cute enough? Not sufficiently shrewd? The words haunted Mrs. Kannady long after Mary Burton had left her door. That night, when her husband came home from work, Mrs. Kannady retold her story with passion and insistence, inspiring the off-duty officer to tackle the issue at hand that very evening. Gathering together in a small posse consisting of the Kannadys, Under-Sheriff Mills and his wife, the victimized shop owners Mr. and Mrs. Hogg, as well as several more constables, they stormed the Hughsons' tavern in search of answers.

This search was an act of dedication, not simply an act of service. Both sheriffs and constables worked in their roles only part-time. They were less keepers of the peace than citizen officers of the court. Colonial New York's sheriff functioned primarily as a representative of the judicial system, relegated to retrieving the accused in order to be brought before the bar. The constables were appointed by the court on a yearly basis, again, worked only part-time, and were paid per assignment. While it might be thought that the Kannadys were ever eager because of the commission they would receive, the salary was paltry, little more than a token. Few constables stayed on after their year's appointment. The job paid next to nothing, and, invariably, put them at odds with their neighbors.

These were jobs done strictly out of civic duty.

At the tavern front, it was Mrs. Mills's wish that she and her husband go in first and retrieve young Mary Burton from this den of iniquity. Once out on the road, Mrs. Kannady could then continue interrogation of the girl.

So the Millses went in with that simple plan. The door closed behind them, and then...nothing. The others waited behind them, staring at the door, their apprehension peaking as the moments ticked. "Any minute now" never came, and, patience and decorum abandoning her, Mrs. Kannady gave up, and stormed the tavern. As the door swung open, to her surprise she saw Mr. and Mrs. Mills were just sitting there in the parlor as Mary Burton, standing in front of them, offered up her complete innocence.

"I don't know what she's talking about. I never said no such thing," Mary was protesting. "The Hughsons are decent people, wrongly persecuted. They had nothing to do with—"

"Stop the lies!" Mrs. Kannady interrupted, walking straight up to the girl and grabbing her by the wrists.

For a few moments, in the face of confusion, Mary Burton considered she might slough off her earlier indiscretion as nothing more than a misunderstanding, delusion, even a lie. With Mrs. Kannady before her, however, whatever illusion Mary held that this older woman would simply let the issue go was abandoned. Hushed, nervous, anxious, the servant girl changed her tactic altogether.

Leaning forward, her eyes full of true fear, Mary whispered, "It was them, not me. The black scoundrels in this wretched place will surely kill me. Have mercy."

Together, the Kannadys and Millses yanked Mary Burton out of the tavern, onto the street, and into the Manhattan evening. Hughson's drinking establishment was situated along the island's southwestern edge, near where the World Trade Center would briefly sit centuries later. With the village transitioning into farmland not far beyond, the pub was close to the edge of town, but it was still a well-populated area with citizens strolling around the streets. Workers, free and enslaved, traveled to and from the neighboring piers where ships were serviced before they sailed up the Hudson or out into the Atlantic bound for distant ports and faraway continents. Once she felt herself securely out of range from any prying eyes that might be watching her from the tavern, with a little prodding, Mary Burton loosened again.

"Now speak, girl," Mrs. Kannady pushed her. "Tell us all that you know and you will still be spared. Is Hughson involved in Hogg's theft?"

Mary didn't respond with words at first. Reaching a hand into her pocket, she pulled out one Spanish silver coin. Cold hard evidence, undeniable.

"Mrs. Hogg," she said, offering up the coin, "I think this belongs to you."

Mrs. Hogg jumped forward, snatching the silver out of the girl's hand. "Where did you get this?" she demanded.

"The Negroes," was Mary's solemn reply.

The group was excited, satisfied—finally, evidence of what they all knew must be true. So aroused were they by this substantiation of their hard felt suspicions, that no one bothered to question *why* Mary might have been given the coin in the first place. They were too busy celebrating their assurance that justice was served to question the motives or reliability of their new witness.

To resolve the situation, Mary Burton was taken to Alderman Bancker, governor of the district, with Mrs. Kannady further declaring in front of the official her promise that the indentured servant, Burton, would be freed from her master in payment for testifying.

"They will murder me," Mary beseeched them. "The Hughsons or the Negroes will surely poison me if I'm discovered," she insisted.

"Nonsense, dear," comforted the alderman. "You will go into Mr. Mills's custody; he shall protect you. As for Hughson, I will have him standing before me within the hour."

For his part, John Hughson had known it was trouble as soon as Mary Burton had been dragged out from his place. "That nasty little wench," he thought to himself as the constables arrived for him. He'd known it was trouble as soon as she was dragged out of the tavern, no matter how much he had bribed her. Surely it was she, Mary Burton, the little girl with the big mouth, and now he was in bigger trouble.

———————

Unforseen and to his credit, Alderman Bancker did not presume Hughson's guilt in the matter at all. Bancker studied the tavern owner as he made his protestations of innocence, coming to the conclusion, despite the man's obvious nervousness, that Hughson's denials were truthful in nature.

Still it was surely evident Hughson's tavern was clearly of the lowest, nuisance sort. Rowdy, to say the least. And given this, the alderman said to him, "In light of this evidence, Mr. Hughson, you must assist the constables in their efforts at last and help reveal the stolen goods and those guilty of acquiring them."

"Certainly, sir." Hughson smiled, showing his rough teeth back at the alderman. "Why, they have but to ask and I shall be there, assisting and such. I shall give it my full attention, and prove to you, sir, my innocence in the matter."

See, things weren't so bad, Hughson judged. Just got to give a little. Just got to get to the bottom of this theft (of which he continued to contend he knew nothing) and, by so cooperating, clear his name. A good plan, considering the circumstances, and if played intelligently it could be to his advantage and see him to the end of this fiasco.

Unfortunately, while John Hughson could fairly be called many things, none of them would be "intelligent." Instead of reappearing with some incidental trace evidence that might lead the authorities away from his own culpability, the taverner took it one step further and returned instead with *all* the stolen goods in question, silver coins, speckled linen, everything. The constables looked at the loot in disbelief, then peered back at the beaming Hughson. There he stood, so happy and relieved to have the whole thing up and done with. Completely unconscious of the fact that he'd just given proof that he was in direct possession of the stash the whole time, substantiating definitively his own utter guilt in the matter.

Ah, the genius of John Hughson!

"MARY BURTON, OF THE CITY OF NEW-YORK, SPINSTER"

There may have been worse colonies than New York in which to find yourself standing accused before the court in the eighteenth century, other places where mere accusation alone seemed to be counted as evidence of wrongdoing. In nearby New Haven, for instance, 90 percent of defendants brought to trial were found guilty. In New York, at least, nearly half of the accused on trial were given the chance to prove their innocence (or feign it). And considering that the Hogg crime involved theft of personal property that amounted to a small fortune, it was somewhat to John Hughson's advantage that the trial was being held on the American continent altogether, for this was a time of even harsher punishment for thievery back in fair England, where intolerance for such sins had resulted in frequent capital sentences. While the hangman's noose was offered for the crime of thievery in the new land as well, that option was rarely selected. Even if convicted, with any luck, Hughson might be sentenced to a good flogging, or at worst a pillorying, both of which it was, theoretically, possible to live through.

Colonial justice was made more complicated for its defendants by its simplicity: The justice of the case served not only as a "judge" in the modern sense, but also played the role of prosecutor. Judges were responsible for choosing to go to trial, gathering the incriminating evidence, securing the prosecuting witnesses, as well as interrogating both them and the suspects. It was an arrangement that made impartiality, at best, difficult; a power dynamic that made any trial without an impartial judge no more than a formality to sentencing. To make matters worse, most judges in the colonies had no qualifications for the job other than that they were wealthy landowners with enough political clout to wrangle these influential, though part-time, appointments. A census taken two decades after the events of 1741 found that only 41 percent of New York's judges had any proper legal training or experience before taking the mantle. As prominent New Yorker, and former legal apprentice, William Livingston would put it in 1745, "There is perhaps no Set of men that bear so ill a Character in the Estimation of the Vulgar, as the Gentlemen of the Long Robe."

Standing before the court to hear the charges, John Hughson was joined by his wife, Sarah, per the court's order, along with their lodger, Margaret Sorubiero.

Margaret Sorubiero, also known as Margaret Salingburgh, was better known as Peggy Kerry. What could be said of a common Irish woman who lived above this tavern known to be populated by lowly whites and Negroes? That she was a prostitute, of course; it was unproven but there was no need (there were hundreds of such women in the area around the fort). That her board and lodging were paid for by Caesar, the primary Negro in question, was proof enough. The reason for this latest addition to the alderman's request list was made clear when the Hughsons and Peggy laid eyes on the court's first witness.

"Mary Burton, of the city of New York, spinster, aged about sixteen years, being sworn, deposed," the clerk called, and the slight peasant girl took center stage in the drama. Avoiding the penetrating glances of her former housemates, Mary nervously began:

"Must have been two o'clock in the morning I'd seen him, that Negro, Caesar, the one what also goes by the name John Gwin (or is it Quin?), sneaking in through the window of Miss Peggy. Yes, Peggy Kerry, this white woman. The Negro slipped right into her bedroom window in the dark of night, he did. What's more, he often made her bed his own, made a habit of it. God's truth."

The stage-whispered curses of the accused beside her threatened to cut Mary Burton's narrative short, but the mortified gasps from the rest of the room pushed her on, fed her with attention, giving her the strength to continue.

"The following morn, the speckled linen, it was right there," Mary went on. "I seen the stolen fabric," she told them, but what went unsaid was that Caesar had seen Mary see it, her eyes grow wide at the sight of the fine cloth. Mary failed to mention that Caesar had thrown her two pieces of silver to shut her up, or that Peggy cut an apron from the material to give to her to ensure her silence. Mary was not on trial here. She was simply an innocent corrupted.

So much money in his hand as Caesar sat that morning in the tavern, gloating. So much more than he could have ever earned honestly, far more intoxicating to him than any liquor he could buy. Mary couldn't tell them that, because she couldn't imagine the feeling, but she could tell other things.

"Caesar was all casual-like, too, the cat with a mouse, he was. Bought a pair of proper white stockings for his Peggy right then from my master, added two mugs of punch on top to get his silver's worth. The master and the mistress both seen the speckled linen that morning as well, as sure as I did."

As Mary spoke, the Hughsons sat in terror and disbelief. As they listened they blustered with indignation at such betrayal from this hypocritical and scandalous girl!

"After Under-Sheriff Mills done arrived the first time in search of this soldier, Gwin, Mrs. Hughson hid the linen in the garret. Then she took it out again after the first search to hide it under the stairs. She's real clever-like, so when the constables came back they missed it. Then later that night, I seen the mistress carrying it to her mother's house."

John Hughson leaped to his feet, interrupting. "She is a vile, good-for-nothing girl!" he shouted. "She had been got with child by her former master!"

Hughson hoped that his outburst might distract the court, but his bit of rumor was not the morsel in which this room was interested.

"Who else, young Burton?" the court demanded. "Who else took part in this nefarious plot? You are reminded, you are before a court of law, and your pardon depends on a complete testimony."

"Well, just yesterday morning I was sweeping the porch and I heard the Dutchman John Romme saying to my master, 'If you will be true to me, then I will be true to you.' To this my master replied, 'I will, and I will never betray you.' Which I found odd and suspicious, as such."

With this added revelation, examining the room and pondering his own situation, Hughson belatedly came to the realization that he was screwed, and it suddenly dawned on him how he had just managed to hurt his cause not only with the room but also with the one person who had the power to stop this madness. In a typical John Hughson style adjustment of strategy, before the entire audience to whom he had just defamed young Mary, Hughson instantly tried the opposite tactic of compliment and flattery.

"She was a very good girl," he cried, assuring those who were still bothering to listen. "Why, in hard weather last winter, she used to dress herself in me own clothes, put on boots, and go out with me in my sleigh in the deep snows into the commons to help me fetch firewood for my family. Love her like one of my own, really."

In response, the crowd stared back at Hughson, largely quiet. The ones that were making a sound giggled at his ineptitude.

"Silence, man!" the deputy town clerk ordered him. "Continue. Speak the truth."

"I hardly dare speak," Mary cringed back dramatically. "I am so much afraid I will be murdered by them!"

Hughson and the other accused were doomed and they knew it. If there was any doubt, the testimony that came next from John Vaarck, the baker—Caesar's owner—took that away as well. After demonstratively apologizing for the fact that he was too busy with work to enslave his Negro properly, Vaarck told a story that would further cement the fate of the accused.

That very afternoon, he said, his younger slave, Bastian, had met his master's growing anxiety about this recent trouble with a look of guilt of his own. "What do you know, boy?" the baker insisted he pressed him. They stood in the kitchen, where the slave boy slept on a mat in the corner.

" 'Nothing sir,' " the baker said Bastian had offered sheepishly. " 'I don't know nothing.' "

"This is no time for nonsense. Have it out now, boy, before that black bastard, Caesar, has us all marched to the gallows."

Bastian thought that an excellent point. After apparently allowing the thought to settle, the boy pointed down to the floor below them.

"What? Something wrong with your bloody foot? Stop the riddles!"

"Look underneath the floor, sir. There's something down there."

Vaarck did indeed look down there. As far as he could tell, there was no trapdoor, no loose floorboard. In order to look underneath his kitchen, Vaarck had to walk out his house, climb through his neighbor's yard, then come alongside to stare into the small dark crevice beneath his home. Huffing, on his knees, Vaarck looked up at where Bastian stood behind him.

"And you just happened to come across this little hiding space, did you?"

Bastian shrugged back at his pink owner.

Reaching into the darkness, hoping not to find a handful of skunk or porcupine for his efforts, Vaarck's hand came on the texture of rough fabric atop the dry soil. As he pulled out the heavy bag, the contents clinked as they rubbed together. Plates, stolen linen, filled it.

That bastard Caesar, Vaarck said he thought. He'd spent good money on that darky, gave him damn near free rein, and this was how Caesar had repaid him.

What interested the court as much as the booty, which was brought out now for the three judges to see, was the location itself.

When questioned Vaarck told them, "The only way you can get down there is through the yard of John Romme." That neighbor whose yard the house and its kitchen adjoined was the very John Romme whom Mary Burton had just described as being in cahoots with John Hughson. The area was only accessible through Romme's small yard, Vaarck insisted. The implication: that even if his own slave had strayed, there were whites guilty of more than just loose management, to be discovered in this affair. John Romme was married into the Dutch upper class of the colony, but this allegation and implication of guilt was too much to ignore. Despite his high-up connections, John Romme was sent for immediately.

Not even adding another white suspect, this one a member of the old Dutch gentry, would be able to move John Hughson from the focus of the judicial eye. Considering the social relations and possible ramifications of prosecuting one of their own class for such a petty crime, if anything, an arrest of John Romme would make it more likely the Hughsons would be made the scapegoats, that the burden of blame could be carried by them completely. Fate dictated this to be the case, as the constables sent to retrieve Romme returned with the news that the gentleman had already absconded. Still, too much of a political bother, really, when you had a perfectly good (and perfectly guilty) white man to take the burden right in front of you. So it turned out that John Hughson was good for something after all.

Seeing his predicament, Hughson thought confession his best alternative, and proved to have much to offer to the conversation. He confided that Peggy had given him goods, and told him that they had been left by Caesar, a stash, Hughson admitted, he later delivered to his mother-in-law. He added that he proceeded to hide the silver coins through repeated visits to confound the investigation. He further went on to say that it was Peggy that gave him the remainder of the bundle, which he delivered that morning to the authorities.

The court scribe struggled to keep up with Hughson's guilty revelation, making sure the language was correct to ensure its legal worth. Finishing up the last words, the document was turned back to Hughson for his approval.

"Sign your confession, John Hughson. Your testimony will be noted," the court clerk told him on completion. Hughson just stared at the lengthy page, its ink still wet.

But now he declined to put his signature to the document.

"What? What are you on about?" the court demanded. "It's your confession, man. You agreed to give your confession; you've already told the room of your part in this matter, what is the point of resistance now? Don't be daft, sign the paper."

Hughson continued to stare at the words on the page, considering the matter. Then, coming to a decision, he shook his head at the whole thing. "No, I don't think I shall. No, not at all. Thank you anyway, gentlemen."

"Are you quite mad? Sign the paper!"

"There is no occasion for me to sign it," Hughson insisted.

The court was aghast at the insolence of this rascal. They were so busy voicing the outrage over this affront to the court that they didn't bother to discern that the reason John Hughson wouldn't sign the confession was in fact fairly practical. The old fool couldn't read even the simplest words on the page, even if he could have managed more than an X to add to them. He was illiterate.

Regardless, both John and Sarah were remitted right then and there, with the understanding that they would be brought back in front of the Supreme Court on the very first day of the next term.

The last white on trial, Peggy Kerry, had more fight to offer. Despite the wealth of witnesses against her and the detailed confessions, Peggy stood on the witness stand unmoved, and unmoving.

"Do you, Peggy Kerry, admit to having had possession of the stolen property from Hogg's store?"

"I do not," the redhead resisted, her back straight despite the societal shame engendered in that room and foisted down upon her.

"You do not even admit to the repeated attempts to conceal the evidence from the rightful authorities, as already laid out by the confession of your landlord, John Hughson?"

"I most certainly do not." Peggy stood strong, ignoring the rumbling of the onlooking crowd.

"Will you admit, then," the court continued, "as it has already been revealed here this day, that you willingly have shared your bed with a Negro property of Vaarck, the baker, this notorious black called Caesar, that now stands bound in this courtroom?"

"I deny that as well," Peggy said to them, ignoring the motion off to her right when Caesar's shocked gaze snapped in her direction.

Focused on Peggy's eyes, Caesar silently begged a response as his lover forcibly tried to ignore him.

"You what?" the court continued. "Oh, I see you are being quite the villainess this day, miss. Then, may I ask, what fact is it that you would be willing to testify to this day?"

"Only to the goodness of my landlords, John and Sarah Hughson," Peggy told the room. "They are honorable, decent people and I am fortunate to board with them," she said, looking over to where the Hughsons sat, making sure they heard her every recommendation. The stolen property was not the only treasure that had been removed from John Hughson's tavern to his mother-in-law's. Unknown to the court that day, Peggy's young son was waiting for her with the old woman as well. Her only son, in the hands of the people she was being asked to incriminate. Some said the boy was as white as any colonist's child, others that he had the African blood in him as sure as any other mulatto. Either way, Peggy knew her only chance of protecting him would be to hold her tongue as concerned the family that now had him.

After listening to his alleged sins revealed, his guilt reasserted, when called to testify, Caesar, too, denied all that involved him in the crime of the stolen property of Mr. and Mrs. Hogg. Not that his denial would mean much; any hope either he or Peggy held for being released on bail was now far gone. But when it came time to address the issue of his relationship with Miss Kerry, Caesar, his pride evidently still intact, and despite the sure knowledge of persecution such revelation would beg, was more forthcoming.

"Mary Burton told the truth, in that regard," Caesar told the room as Peggy took her turn to stare downcast.

He looked directly at her as he spoke, nonetheless. "I have been sleeping in the room of Peggy Kerry and I will not deny that," he said.

It was an admission that could surely cause his destruction, but Caesar stood proudly behind the pronouncement. Displaying the very defiance, stubbornness, and nihilism that soon would be revealed as archetypal of his brown brethren in response to their enslavement in New York City.

The Brief Wondrous Life of Oscar Wao

Junot Díaz

GhettoNerd at the End of the World
1974–1987

THE GOLDEN AGE

Our hero was not one of those Dominican cats everybody's always going on about—he wasn't no home-run hitter or a fly bachatero, not a playboy with a million hots on his jock.

And except for one period early in his life, dude never had much luck with the females (how *very* un-Dominican of him).

He was seven then.

In those blessed days of his youth, Oscar was something of a Casanova. One of those preschool loverboys who was always trying to kiss the girls, always coming up behind them during a merengue and giving them the pelvic pump, the first nigger to learn the perrito and the one who danced it any chance he got. Because in those days he was (still) a "normal" Dominican boy raised in a "typical" Dominican family, his nascent pimp-liness was encouraged by blood and friends alike. During parties—and there were many many parties in those long-ago seventies days, before Washington Heights was Washington Heights, before the Bergenline became a straight shot of Spanish for almost a hundred blocks—some drunk relative inevitably pushed Oscar onto some little girl and then everyone would howl as boy and girl approximated the hip-motism of the adults.

You should have seen him, his mother sighed in her Last Days. He was our little Porfirio Rubirosa.*

All the other boys his age avoided the girls like they were a bad case of Captain Trips. Not Oscar. The little guy loved himself the females, had "girlfriends" galore. (He was a stout kid, heading straight to fat, but his mother kept him nice in haircuts and clothes, and before the proportions of his head changed he'd had these lovely flashing eyes and these cute-ass cheeks, visible in all his pictures.) The girls—his sister Lola's friends, his mother's friends, even their neighbor, Mari Colón, a thirtysomething postal employee who wore red on her lips and walked like she had a bell for an ass—all purportedly fell for him. Ese muchacho está bueno! (Did it hurt that he was earnest and clearly attention-deprived? Not at all!) In the DR during summer visits to his family digs in Baní he was the worst, would stand in front of Nena Inca's house and call out to passing women—Tú eres guapa! Tú eres guapa!—until a Seventh-day Adventist complained to his grandmother and she shut down the hit parade lickety-split. Muchacho del diablo! This is not a cabaret!

It truly was a Golden Age for Oscar, one that reached its apotheosis in the fall of his seventh year, when he had two little girlfriends

---

*In the forties and fifties, Porfirio Rubirosa—or Rubi, as he was known in the papers—was the third-most-famous Dominican in the world (first came the Failed Cattle Thief, and then the Cobra Woman herself, María Montez). A tall, debonair prettyboy whose "enormous phallus created havoc in Europe and North America," Rubirosa was the quintessential jet-setting car-racing polo-obsessed playboy, the Trujillato's "happy side" (for he was indeed one of Trujillo's best-known minions). A part-time former model and dashing man-about-town, Rubirosa famously married Trujillo's daughter Flor de Oro in 1932, and even though they were divorced five years later, in the Year of the Haitian Genocide, homeboy managed to remain in El Jefe's good graces throughout the regime's long run. Unlike his ex-brother-in-law Ramfis (to whom he was frequently connected), Rubirosa seemed incapable of carrying out many murders; in 1935 he traveled to New York to deliver El Jefe's death sentence against the exile leader Angel Morales but fled before the botched assassination could take place. Rubi was the original Dominican Player, fucked all sorts of women—Barbara Hutton, Doris Duke (who happened to be the richest woman in the world), the French actress Danielle Darrieux, and Zsa Zsa Gabor—to name but a few. Like his pal Ramfis, Porfirio died in a car crash, in 1965, his twelve-cylinder Ferrari skidding off a road in the Bois de Boulogne. (Hard to overstate the role cars play in our narrative.)

at the same time, his first and only ménage à trois. With Maritza
Chacón and Olga Polanco.

Maritza was Lola's friend. Long-haired and prissy and so pretty
she could have played young Dejah Thoris. Olga, on the other hand,
was no friend of the family. She lived in the house at the end of the
block that his mother complained about because it was filled with puer-
toricans who were always hanging out on their porch drinking beer.
(What, they couldn't have done that in Cuamo? Oscar's mom asked
crossly.) Olga had like ninety cousins, all who seemed to be named
Hector or Luis or Wanda. And since her mother was una maldita bor-
racha (to quote Oscar's mom), Olga smelled on some days of ass,
which is why the kids took to calling her Mrs. Peabody.

Mrs. Peabody or not, Oscar liked how quiet she was, how she let
him throw her to the ground and wrestle with her, the interest she
showed in his *Star Trek* dolls. Maritza was just plain beautiful, no
need for motivation there, always around too, and it was just a stroke
of pure genius that convinced him to kick it to them both at once. At
first he pretended that it was his number-one hero, Shazam, who
wanted to date them. But after they agreed he dropped all pretense. It
wasn't Shazam—it was Oscar.

Those were more innocent days, so their relationship amounted
to standing close to each other at the bus stop, some undercover
hand-holding, and twice kissing on the cheeks very seriously, first
Maritza, then Olga, while they were hidden from the street by some
bushes. (Look at that little macho, his mother's friends said. Que
hombre.)

The threesome only lasted a single beautiful week. One day after
school Maritza cornered Oscar behind the swing set and laid down
the law, It's either her or *me*! Oscar held Maritza's hand and talked seriously and at great length about his love for her and reminded her
that they had agreed to *share*, but Maritza wasn't having any of it.
She had three older sisters, knew everything she needed to know
about the possibilities of *sharing*. Don't talk to me no more unless
you get rid of her! Maritza, with her chocolate skin and narrow eyes,
already expressing the Ogún energy that she would chop at everybody with for the rest of her life. Oscar went home morose to his
pre–Korean-sweatshop-era cartoons—to the *Herculoids* and *Space*

Ghost. What's wrong with you? his mother asked. She was getting ready to go to her second job, the eczema on her hands looking like a messy meal that had set. When Oscar whimpered, Girls, Moms de León nearly exploded. Tú ta llorando por una muchacha? She hauled Oscar to his feet by his ear.

Mami, stop it, his sister cried, stop it!

She threw him to the floor. Dale un galletazo, she panted, then see if the little puta respects you.

If he'd been a different nigger he might have considered the galletazo. It wasn't just that he didn't have no kind of father to show him the masculine ropes, he simply lacked all aggressive and martial tendencies. (Unlike his sister, who fought boys and packs of morena girls who hated her thin nose and straightish hair.) Oscar had like a zero combat rating; even Olga and her toothpick arms could have stomped him silly. Aggression and intimidation out of the question. So he thought it over. Didn't take him long to decide. After all, Maritza was beautiful and Olga was not; Olga sometimes smelled like pee and Maritza did not. Maritza was allowed over their house and Olga was not. (A puertorican over here? his mother scoffed. Jamás!) His logic as close to the yes/no math of insects as a nigger could get. He broke up with Olga the following day on the playground, Maritza at his side, and how Olga had cried! Shaking like a rag in her hand-me-downs and in the shoes that were four sizes too big! Snots pouring out her nose and everything!

In later years, after he and Olga had both turned into overweight freaks, Oscar could not resist feeling the occasional flash of guilt when he saw Olga loping across a street or staring blankly out near the New York bus stop, couldn't stop himself from wondering how much his cold-as-balls breakup had contributed to her present fucked-upness. (Breaking up with her, he would remember, hadn't felt like anything; even when she started crying, he hadn't been moved. He'd said, No be a baby.)

What *had* hurt, however, was when Maritza dumped *him*. Monday after he'd fed Olga to the dogs he arrived at the bus stop with his beloved *Planet of the Apes* lunch box only to discover beautiful Maritza holding hands with butt-ugly Nelson Pardo. Nelson Pardo who looked like Chaka from *Land of the Lost*! Nelson Pardo who was so stupid he thought the moon was a stain that God had forgotten to clean. (He'll get to it soon, he assured his whole class.) Nelson Pardo who would become the neighborhood B&E expert before joining the Marines and losing eight toes in the First Gulf War. At first Oscar thought it a mistake; the sun was in his eyes, he'd not slept enough the night before. He stood next to them and admired his lunch box, how realistic and diabolical Dr. Zaius looked. But Maritza wouldn't even *smile* at him! Pretended he wasn't there. We should get married, she said to Nelson, and Nelson grinned moronically, turning up the street to look for the bus. Oscar had been too hurt to speak; he sat down on the curb and felt something overwhelming surge up from his chest, scared the shit out of him, and before he knew it he was crying; when his sister, Lola, walked over and asked him what was the matter he'd shaken his head. Look at the mariconcito, somebody snickered. Somebody else kicked his beloved lunch box and scratched it right across General Urko's face. When he got on the bus, still crying, the driver, a famously reformed PCP addict, had said, Christ, don't be a fucking *baby*.

How had the breakup affected Olga? What he really was asking was: How had the breakup affected Oscar?

It seemed to Oscar that from the moment Maritza dumped him—Shazam!—his life started going down the tubes. Over the next couple of years he grew fatter and fatter. Early adolescence hit him especially hard, scrambling his face into nothing you could call cute, splotching his skin with zits, making him self-conscious; and his interest—in Genres!—which nobody had said boo about before, suddenly became synonymous with being a loser with a capital L. Couldn't make friends for the life of him, too dorky, too shy, and (if the kids from his neighborhood are to be believed) too *weird* (had a habit of using big words he had memorized only the day before). He no longer went anywhere near the girls because at best they ignored him, at worst they shrieked and called him gordo asqueroso! He forgot the perrito, forgot the pride he felt when the women in the family had called him hombre. Did not kiss another girl for a long *long* time. As though almost everything he had in the girl department had burned up that one fucking week.

Not that his "girlfriends" fared much better. It seemed that whatever bad no-love karma hit Oscar hit them too. By seventh grade Olga had grown huge and scary, a troll gene in her somewhere, started drinking 151 straight out the bottle and was finally taken out of school because she had a habit of screaming *NATAS!* in the middle of homeroom. Even her breasts, when they finally emerged, were floppy and terrifying. Once on the bus Olga had called Oscar a *cake eater,* and he'd almost said, Look who's talking, puerca, but he was afraid that she would rear back and trample him; his cool-index, already low, couldn't have survived that kind of paliza, would have put him on par with the handicapped kids and with Joe Locorotundo, who was famous for masturbating in public.

And the lovely Maritza Chacón? The hypotenuse of our triangle, how had she fared? Well, before you could say *Oh Mighty Isis,* Maritza blew up into the flyest guapa in Paterson, one of the Queens of New Peru. Since they stayed neighbors, Oscar saw her plenty, a ghetto Mary Jane, hair as black and lush as a thunderhead, probably the only Peruvian girl on the planet with pelo curlier than his sister's (he hadn't heard of Afro-Peruvians yet, or of a town called Chincha), body fine enough to make old men forget their infirmities, and from the sixth grade on dating men two, three times her age. (Maritza might not have been good at much—not sports, not school, not work—but she was good at men.) Did that mean she had avoided the curse—that she was happier than Oscar or Olga? That was doubtful. From what Oscar could see, Maritza was a girl who seemed to delight in getting slapped around by her boyfriends. Since it happened to her *all the time.* If a boy hit *me,* Lola said cockily, I would bite his *face.*

See Maritza: French-kissing on the front stoop of her house, getting in or out of some roughneck's ride, being pushed down onto the sidewalk. Oscar would watch the French-kissing, the getting in and out, the pushing, all through his cheerless, sexless adolescence. What else could he do? His bedroom window looked out over the front of her house, and so he always peeped her while he was painting his D&D miniatures or reading the latest Stephen King. The only things that changed in those years were the models of the cars, the size of Maritza's ass, and the kind of music volting out the cars' speakers. First freestyle, then Ill Will–era hiphop, and, right at the very end, for just a little while, Héctor Lavoe and the boys.

He said hi to her almost every day, all upbeat and faux-happy, and she said hi back, indifferently, but that was it. He didn't imagine that she remembered their kissing—but of course he could not forget.

THE MORONIC INFERNO

High school was Don Bosco Tech, and since Don Bosco Tech was an urban all-boys Catholic school packed to the strakes with a couple hundred insecure hyperactive adolescents, it was, for a fat sci-fi–reading nerd like Oscar, a source of endless anguish. For Oscar, high school was the equivalent of a medieval spectacle, like being put in the stocks and forced to endure the peltings and outrages of a mob of deranged half-wits, an experience from which he supposed he should have emerged a better person, but that's not really what happened—and if there were any lessons to be gleaned from the ordeal of those years he never quite figured out what they were. He walked into school every day like the fat lonely nerdy kid he was, and all he could think about was the day of his manumission, when he would at last be set free from its unending horror. *Hey, Oscar, are there faggots on Mars?*—*Hey, Kazoo, catch this.* The first time he heard the term *moronic inferno* he knew exactly where it was located and who were its inhabitants.

Sophomore year Oscar found himself weighing in at a whopping 245 (260 when he was depressed, which was often) and it had become clear to everybody, especially his family, that he'd become the neighborhood parigüayo.* Had none of the Higher Powers of your typical Dominican male, couldn't have pulled a girl if his life depended on it. Couldn't play sports for shit, or dominoes, was beyond uncoordinated, threw a ball like a girl. Had no knack for music or business or dance, no hustle, no rap, no G. And most damning of all: no looks.

*The pejorative *parigüayo*, Watchers agree, is a corruption of the English neologism "party watcher." The word came into common usage during the First American Occupation of the DR, which ran from 1916 to 1924. (You didn't know we were occupied twice in the twentieth century? Don't worry, when you have kids they won't know the U.S. occupied Iraq either.) During the First Occupation it was reported that members of the American Occupying Forces would often attend Dominican parties but instead of joining in the fun the Outlanders would simply stand at the edge of dances and *watch*. Which of course must have seemed like the craziest thing in the world. Who goes to a party to *watch*? Thereafter, the Marines were parigüayos—a word that in contemporary usage describes anybody who stands outside and watches while other people scoop up the girls. The kid who don't dance, who ain't got game, who lets people clown him—he's the parigüayo.

If you looked in the Dictionary of Dominican Things, the entry for parigüayo would include a wood carving of Oscar. It is a name that would haunt him for the rest of his life and that would lead him to another Watcher, the one who lamps on the Blue Side of the Moon.

He wore his semikink hair in a Puerto Rican afro, rocked enormous Section 8 glasses—his "anti-pussy devices," Al and Miggs, his only friends, called them—sported an unappealing trace of mustache on his upper lip and possessed a pair of close-set eyes that made him look somewhat retarded. The Eyes of Mingus. (A comparison he made himself one day going through his mother's record collection; she was the only old-school dominicana he knew who had dated a moreno until Oscar's father put an end to that particular chapter of the All-African World Party.) You have the same eyes as your abuelo, his Nena Inca had told him on one of his visits to the DR, which should have been some comfort—who doesn't like resembling an ancestor?—except this particular ancestor had ended his days in prison.

Oscar had always been a young nerd—the kind of kid who read Tom Swift, who loved comic books and watched *Ultraman*—but by high school his commitment to the Genres had become absolute. Back when the rest of us were learning to play wallball and pitch quarters and drive our older brothers' cars and sneak dead soldiers from under our parents' eyes, he was gorging himself on a steady stream of Lovecraft, Wells, Burroughs, Howard, Alexander, Herbert, Asimov, Bova, and Heinlein, and even the Old Ones who were already beginning to fade—E.E. "Doc" Smith, Stapledon, and the guy who wrote all the Doc Savage books—moving hungrily from book to book, author to author, age to age. (It was his good fortune that the libraries of Paterson were so underfunded that they still kept a lot of the previous generation's nerdery in circulation.) You couldn't have torn him away from any movie or TV show or cartoon where there were monsters or spaceships or mutants or doomsday devices or'destinies or magic or evil villains. In these pursuits alone Oscar showed the genius his grandmother insisted was part of the family patrimony. Could write in Elvish, could speak Chakobsa, could differentiate between a Slan, a Dorsai, and a Lensman in acute detail, knew more about the Marvel Universe than Stan Lee, and was a role-playing game fanatic. (If only he'd been good at videogames it would have been a slam dunk but despite owning an Atari and an Intellivision he didn't have the reflexes for it.) Perhaps if like me he'd been able to hide his otakuness maybe shit would have been easier for him, but he couldn't. Dude wore his nerdiness like a Jedi wore his light saber or a Lensman her lens. Couldn't have passed for Normal if he'd wanted to.*

Oscar was a social introvert who trembled with fear during gym class and watched nerd British shows like *Doctor Who* and *Blake's 7*, and could tell you the difference between a Veritech fighter and a Zentraedi walker, and he used a lot of huge-sounding nerd words like *indefatigable* and *ubiquitous* when talking to niggers who would barely graduate from high school. One of those nerds who was always hiding out in the library, who adored Tolkien and later the Margaret Weis and Tracy Hickman novels (his favorite character was of course Raistlin), and who, as the eighties marched on, developed a growing obsession with the End of the World. (No apocalyptic movie or book or game existed that he had not seen or read or played—Wyndham and Christopher and Gamma World were his absolute favorites.) You get the picture. His adolescent nerdliness vaporizing any iota of a chance he had for young love. Everybody else

---

*Where this outsized love of genre jumped off from no one quite seems to know. It might have been a consequence of being Antillean (who more sci-fi than us?) or of living in the DR for the first couple of years of his life and then abruptly wrenchingly relocating to New Jersey—a single green card shifting not only worlds (from Third to First) but centuries (from almost no TV or electricity to plenty of both). After a transition like that I'm guessing only the most extreme scenarios could have satisfied. Maybe it was that in the DR he had watched too much *Spider-Man*, been taken to too many Run Run Shaw kung fu movies, listened to too many of his abuela's spooky stories about el Cuco and la Ciguapa? Maybe it was his first librarian in the U.S., who hooked him on reading, the electricity he felt when he touched that first Danny Dunn book? Maybe it was just the zeitgeist (were not the early seventies the dawn of the Nerd Age?) or the fact that for most of his childhood he had absolutely no friends? Or was it something deeper, something ancestral?

   Who can say?

   What is clear is that being a reader/fanboy (for lack of a better term) helped him get through the rough days of his youth, but it also made him stick out in the mean streets of Paterson even more than he already did. Victimized by the other boys—punches and pushes and wedgies and broken glasses and brand-new books from Scholastic, at a cost of fifty cents each, torn in half before his very eyes. You like books? Now you got two! Har-har! No one, alas, more oppressive than the oppressed. Even his own mother found his preoccupations nutty. Go outside and play! she commanded at least once a day. Pórtate como un muchacho normal.

   (Only his sister, a reader too, supporting him. Bringing him books from her own school, which had a better library.)

   You really want to know what being an X-Man feels like? Just be a smart bookish boy of color in a contemporary U.S. ghetto. Mamma mia! Like having bat wings or a pair of tentacles growing out of your chest.

   Pa' 'fuera! his mother roared. And out he would go, like a boy condemned, to spend a few hours being tormented by the other boys—Please, I want to stay, he would beg his mother, but she shoved him out—You ain't a woman to be staying in the house—one hour, two, until finally he could slip back inside unnoticed, hiding himself in the upstairs closet, where he'd read by the slat of light that razored in from the cracked door. Eventually, his mother rooting him out again: What in carajo is the matter with you?

   (And already on scraps of paper, in his composition books, on the backs of his hands, he was beginning to scribble, nothing serious for now, just rough facsimiles of his favorite stories, no sign yet that these half-assed pastiches were to be his Destiny.)

going through the terror and joy of their first crushes, their first dates, their first kisses while Oscar sat in the back of the class, behind his DM's screen, and watched his adolescence stream by. Sucks to be left out of adolescence, sort of like getting locked in the closet on Venus when the sun appears for the first time in a hundred years. It would have been one thing if like some of the nerdboys I'd grown up with he hadn't cared about girls, but alas he was still the passionate enamorao who fell in love easily and deeply. He had secret loves all over town, the kind of curly-haired big-bodied girls who wouldn't have said boo to a loser like him but about whom he could not stop dreaming. His affection—that gravitational mass of love, fear, longing, desire, and lust that he directed at any and every girl in the vicinity without regard to looks, age, or availability—broke his heart each and every day. Despite the fact that he considered it this huge sputtering force, it was actually most like a ghost because no girl ever really seemed to notice it. Occasionally they might shudder or cross their arms when he walked near, but that was about it. He cried often for his love of some girl or another. Cried in the bathroom, where nobody could hear him.

Anywhere else his triple-zero batting average with the ladies might have passed without comment, but this is a Dominican kid we're talking about, in a Dominican family: dude was supposed to have Atomic Level G, was supposed to be pulling in the bitches with both hands. Everybody noticed his lack of game and because they were Dominican everybody talked about it. His tío Rudolfo (only recently released from his last and final bid in the Justice and now living in their house on Main Street) was especially generous in his tutelage. Listen, palomo: you have to grab a muchacha, y metéselo! That will take care of *everything*. Start with a fea. Coje that fea y metéselo! Tío Rudolfo had four kids with three different women so the nigger was without doubt the family's resident metéselo expert.

His mother's only comment? You need to worry about your grades. And in more introspective moments: Just be glad you didn't get my luck, hijo.

What luck? his tío snorted.

Exactly, she said.

His friends Al and Miggs? Dude, you're kinda way fat, you know.

His abuela, La Inca? Hijo, you're the most buenmoso man I know!

Oscar's sister, Lola, was a lot more practical. Now that her crazy years were over—what Dominican girl doesn't have those?—she'd turned into one of those tough Jersey dominicanas, a long-distance runner who drove her own car, had her own car, had her own check-book, called men bitches, and would eat fat cat in front of you without a speck of vüenza. When she was in fourth grade she'd been attacked by an older acquaintance, and this was common knowledge through-out the family (and by extension a sizable section of Paterson, Union City, and Teaneck), and surviving that urikán of pain, judgment, and bochinche had made her tougher than adamantine. Recently she'd cut her hair short—flipping out her mother yet again—partially I think because when she'd been little her family had let it grow down past her ass, a source of pride, something I'm sure her attacker noticed and admired.

Oscar, Lola warned repeatedly, you're going to die a virgin un-less you start *changing*.

Don't you think I know that? Another five years of this and I'll bet you somebody tries to name a church after me.

Cut the hair, lose the glasses, exercise. And get rid of those porn magazines. They're disgusting, they bother Mami, and they'll never get you a date.

Sound counsel that in the end he did not adopt. He tried a couple of times to exercise, leg lifts, sit-ups, walks around the block in the early morning, that sort of thing, but he would notice how every-body else had a girl but him and would despair, plunging right back into eating, *Penthouses*, designing dungeons, and self-pity.

I seem to be allergic to diligence, and Lola said, Ha. What you're allergic to is *trying*.

It wouldn't have been half bad if Paterson and its surrounding precincts had been like Don Bosco or those seventies feminist sci-fi novels he sometimes read—an all-male-exclusion zone. Paterson, however, was girls the way NYC was girls, Paterson was girls the way Santo Domingo was girls. Paterson had mad girls, and if that wasn't guapas enough for you, well, motherfucker, then roll south and there'd be Newark, Elizabeth, Jersey City, the Oranges, Union City, West New York, Weehawken, Perth Amboy—an urban swath known to niggers everywhere as Negrapolis One. So in effect he saw girls—Hispanophone Caribbean girls—everywhere.

He wasn't safe even in his own house, his sister's girlfriends were always hanging out, permanent guests. When they were around he didn't need no *Penthouses*. Her girls were not too smart but they were fine as shit: the sort of hot-as-balls Latinas who only dated weight-lifting morenos or Latino cats with guns in their cribs. They were all on the volleyball team together and tall and fit as colts and when they went for runs it was what the track team might have looked like in ter-rorist heaven. Bergen County's very own cigüapas: la primera was Gladys, who complained endlessly about her chest being too big, that maybe she'd find normal boyfriends if she'd had a smaller pair; Marisol, who'd end up at MIT and *hated* Oscar but whom Oscar liked most of all; Leticia, just off the boat, half Haitian half Dominican, that special blend the Dominican government swears *no existe*, who spoke with the deepest accent, a girl so good she refused to sleep with *three consecutive boyfriends!* It wouldn't have been so bad if these chickies hadn't treated Oscar like some deaf-mute harem guard, ordering him around, having him run their errands, making fun of his games and his looks; to make shit even worse, they blithely went on about the particulars of their sex lives with no re-gard for him, while he sat in the kitchen, clutching the latest issue of *Dragon*. Hey, he would yell, in case you're wondering there's a male unit in here.

Where? Marisol would say blandly. I don't see one.

And when they talked about how all the Latin guys only seemed to want to date whitegirls, he would offer, *I* like Spanish girls, to which Marisol responded with wide condescension. That's great, Oscar. Only problem is no Spanish girl would date you.

Leave him alone, Leticia said. I think you're cute, Oscar.

Yeah, right, Marisol laughed, rolling her eyes. Now he'll proba-bly write a book about you.

These were Oscar's furies, his personal pantheon, the girls he most dreamed about and most beat off to and who eventually found their way into his little stories. In his dreams he was either saving them from aliens or he was returning to the neighborhood, rich and famous—It's him! The Dominican Stephen King!—and then

Marisol would appear, carrying one each of his books for him to sign. Please, Oscar, marry me. Oscar, drolly: I'm sorry, Marisol, I don't marry ignorant bitches. (But then of course he would.) Maritza he still watched from afar, convinced that one day, when the nuclear bombs fell (or the plague broke out or the Tripods invaded) and civilization was wiped out he would end up saving her from a pack of irradiated ghouls and together they'd set out across a ravaged America in search of a better tomorrow. In these apocalyptic daydreams he was always some kind of plátano Doc Savage, a supergenius who combined world-class martial artistry with deadly firearms proficiency. Not bad for a nigger who'd never even shot an air rifle, thrown a punch, or scored higher than a thousand on his SATs.

OSCAR IS BRAVE

Senior year found him bloated, dyspeptic, and, most cruelly, alone in his lack of girlfriend. His two nerdboys, Al and Miggs, had, in the craziest twist of fortune, both succeeded in landing themselves girls that year. Nothing special, skanks really, but girls nonetheless. Al had met his at Menlo Park. She'd come onto *him*, he bragged, and when she informed him, after she sucked his dick of course, that she had a girlfriend *desperate* to meet somebody, Al had dragged Miggs away from his Atari and out to a movie and the rest was, as they say, history. By the end of the week Miggs was getting his too, and only then did Oscar find out about any of it. While they were in his room setting up for another "hair-raising" Champions adventure against the Death-Dealing Destroyers. (Oscar had to retire his famous Aftermath! campaign because nobody else but him was hankering to play in the postapocalyptic ruins of virus-wracked America.) At first, after hearing about the double-bootie coup, Oscar didn't say nothing much. He just rolled his d10's over and over. Said, You guys sure got lucky. It killed him that they hadn't thought to include him in their girl heists; he hated Al for inviting Miggs instead of him and he hated Miggs for getting a girl, period. Al getting a girl Oscar could comprehend; Al (real name Alok) was one of those tall Indian prettyboys who would never have been pegged by anyone as a role-playing nerd. It was Miggs's girl-getting he could not fathom, that astounded him and left him sick with jealousy. Oscar had always considered Miggs to be an even bigger freak than he was. Acne galore and a retard's laugh and gray fucking teeth from having been given some medicine too young. So is your girlfriend cute? he asked Miggs. He said, Dude, you should see her, she's beautiful. Big fucking tits, Al seconded. That day what little faith Oscar had in the world took an SS-N-17 snipe to the head. When finally he couldn't take it no more he asked, pathetically, What, these girls don't have any other friends?

Al and Miggs traded glances over their character sheets. I don't think so, dude.

And right there he learned something about his friends he'd never known (or at least never admitted to himself). Right there he had an epiphany that echoed through his fat self. He realized his fucked-up comic-book-reading, role-playing-game-loving, no-sports-playing friends were embarrassed by *him*.

Knocked the architecture right out of his legs. He closed the game early, the Exterminators found the Destroyers' hideout right away—That was bogus, Al groused. After he showed them out he locked himself in his room, lay in bed for a couple of stunned hours, then got up, undressed in the bathroom he no longer had to share because his sister was at Rutgers, and examined himself in the mirror. The fat! The miles of stretch marks! The tumescent horribleness of his proportions! He looked straight out of a Daniel Clowes comic book. Or like the fat blackish kid in Beto Hernández's Palomar.

Jesus Christ, he whispered. I'm a Morlock.

The next day at breakfast he asked his mother: Am I ugly?

She sighed. Well, hijo, you certainly don't take after me.

Dominican parents! You got to love them!

Spent a week looking at himself in the mirror, turning every which way, taking stock, not flinching, and decided at last to be like Roberto Durán: No más. That Sunday he went to Chucho's and had the barber shave his Puerto Rican 'fro off. (Wait a minute, Chucho's partner said. *You're* Dominican?) Oscar lost the mustache next, then the glasses, bought contacts with the money he was making at the lumberyard and tried to polish up what remained of his Dominicanness, tried to be more like his cursing swaggering cousins, if only because he had started to suspect that in their Latin hyper-maleness there might be an answer. But he was really too far gone for quick fixes. The next time Al and Miggs saw him he'd been starving himself for three days straight. Miggs said, Dude, what's the matter with *you*?

Changes, Oscar said pseudo-cryptically.

What, are you some album cover now?

He shook his head solemnly. I'm embarking on a new cycle of my life.

Listen to the guy. He already sounds like he's in college.

That summer his mother sent him and his sister to Santo Domingo, and this time he didn't fight it like he had in the recent past. It's not like he had much in the States keeping him. He arrived in Baní with a stack of notebooks and a plan to fill them all up. Since he could no longer be a gamemaster he decided to try his hand at being a writer. The trip turned out to be something of a turning point for him. Instead of discouraging his writing, chasing him out of the house like his mother used to, his abuela, Nena Inca, let him be. Allowed him to sit in the back of the house as long as he wanted, didn't insist that he should be "out in the world." (She had always been overprotective of him and his sister. Too much bad luck in this family, she sniffed.) Kept the music off and brought him his meals at exactly the same time every day. His sister ran around with her hot Island friends, always jumping out of the house in a bikini and going off to different parts of the Island for overnight trips, but he stayed put. When any family members came looking for him his abuela chased them off with a single imperial sweep of her hand. Can't you see the muchacho's working? What's he doing? his cousins asked, confused. He's being a genius is what, La Inca replied haughtily. Now váyanse. (Later when he thought about it he realized that these very cousins could probably have gotten him laid if only he'd bothered to hang out with them. But you can't regret the life you didn't lead.) In the afternoons, when he couldn't write another word, he'd sit out in front of the house with his abuela and watch the street scene, listen to the raucous exchanges between the neighbors. One evening, at the end of his trip, his abuela confided: Your mother could have been a doctor just like your grandfather was.

What happened?

La Inca shook her head. She was looking at her favorite picture of his mother on her first day at private school, one of those typical serious DR shots. What always happens. Un maldito hombre.

He wrote two books that summer about a young man fighting mutants at the end of the world (neither of them survive). Took crazy amounts of field notes, too, names of things he intended to later adapt for science-fictional and fantastic purposes. (Heard about the family curse for like the thousandth time but strangely enough didn't think it worth incorporating into his fiction—I mean, shit, what Latino family doesn't think it's cursed?) When it was time for him and his sister to return to Paterson he was almost sad. Almost. His abuela placed her hand on his head in blessing. Cuidate mucho, mi hijo. Know that in this world there's somebody who will always love you.

At JFK, almost not being recognized by his uncle. Great his tío said, looking askance at his complexion, now you look Haitian.

After his return he hung out with Miggs and Al, saw movies with them, talked Los Brothers Hernández, Frank Miller, and Alan Moore with them but overall they never regained the friendship they had before Santo Domingo. Oscar listened to their messages on the machine and resisted the urge to run over to their places. Didn't see them but once, twice a week. Focused on his writing. Those were some fucking lonely weeks when all he had were his games, his books, and his words. So now I have a hermit for a son, his mother complained bitterly. At night, unable to sleep, he watched a lot of bad TV, became obsessed with two movies in particular: *Zardoz* (which he'd seen with his uncle before they put him away for the second time) and *Virus* (the Japanese end-of-the-world movie with the hot chick from *Romeo and Juliet*). *Virus* especially he could not watch to the end without crying, the Japanese hero arriving at the South Pole base, having walked from Washington, D.C., down the whole spine of the Andes, for the woman of his dreams. I've been working on my fifth novel, he told the boys when they asked about his absences. It's *amazing*.

See? What did I tell you? Mr. Collegeboy.

In the old days when his so-called friends would hurt him or drag his trust through the mud he always crawled voluntarily back into the abuse, out of fear and loneliness, something he'd always hated himself for, but not this time. If there existed in his high school years any one moment he took pride in it was clearly this one. Even told his sister about it during her next visit. She said, Way to go, O! He'd finally showed some backbone, hence some pride, and although it hurt, it also felt motherfucking *good*.

OSCAR COMES CLOSE

In October, after all his college applications were in (Fairleigh Dickinson, Montclair, Rutgers, Drew, Glassboro State, William Paterson; he also sent an app to NYU, a one-in-a-million shot, and they rejected him so fast he was amazed the shit hadn't come back Pony Express) and winter was settling its pale miserable ass across northern New Jersey, Oscar fell in love with a girl in his SAT prep class. The class was being conducted in one of those "Learning Centers" not far from where he lived, less than a mile, so he'd been walking, a healthy way to lose weight, he thought. He hadn't been expecting to meet anyone, but then he'd seen the beauty in the back row and felt his senses fly out of him. Her name was Ana Obregón, a pretty, loudmouthed gordita who read Henry Miller while she should have been learning to wrestle logic problems. On about their fifth class he noticed her reading *Sexus* and she noticed him noticing, and, leaning over, she showed him a passage and he got an erection like a motherfucker.

You must think I'm weird, right? she said during the break.

You ain't weird, he said. Believe me—I'm the top expert in the state.

Ana was a talker, had beautiful Caribbean-girl eyes, pure anthracite, and was the sort of heavy that almost every Island nigger dug, a body that you just knew would look good in and out of clothes; wasn't shy about her weight, either; she wore tight black stirrup pants like every other girl in the neighborhood and the sexiest underwear she could afford and was a meticulous putter-on of makeup, an intricate bit of multitasking for which Oscar never lost his fascination. She was this peculiar combination of badmash and little girl—even before he'd visited her house he knew she'd have a whole collection of stuffed animals avalanched on her bed—and there was something in the seamlessness with which she switched between these aspects that convinced him that both were masks, that there existed a third Ana, a hidden Ana who determined what mask to throw up for what occasion but who was otherwise obscure and impossible to know. She'd gotten into Miller because her ex-boyfriend, Manny, had given her the books before he joined the army. He used to read passages to her all the time: That made me *so* hot. She'd been thirteen when they started dating, he was twenty-four, a recovering coke addict—Ana talking about these things like they weren't nothing at all.

You were thirteen and your mother *allowed* you to date a septuagenarian?

My parents *loved* Manny, she said. My mom used to cook dinner for him all the time.

He said, That seems highly unorthodox, and later at home he asked his sister, back on winter break, For the sake of argument, would you allow your pubescent daughter to have relations with a twenty-four-old-male?

I'd kill him first.

He was amazed how relieved he felt to hear that.

Let me guess: You know somebody who's doing this?

He nodded. She sits next to me in SAT class. I think she's orchidaceous.

Lola considered him with her tiger-colored irises. She'd been back a week and it was clear that college-level track was kicking her ass, the sclera in her normally wide manga-eyes were shot through with blood vessels. You know, she said finally, we colored folks talk plenty of shit about loving our children but we really don't. She exhaled. We don't, we don't, we don't.

He tried to put a hand on his sister's shoulder but she shrugged it off. You better go bust some crunches, Mister.

That's what she called him whenever she was feeling tender or wronged. Mister. Later she'd want to put that on his gravestone but no one would let her, not even me.

Stupid.

AMOR DE PENDEJO

He and Ana in SAT class, he and Ana in the parking lot afterward, he and Ana at the McDonald's, he and Ana become friends. Each day Oscar expected her to be adiós, each day she was still there. They got into the habit of talking on the phone a couple times a week, about nothing really, spinning words out of their everyday; the first time she called *him*, offering him a ride to SAT class; a week later he called her, just to try it. His heart beating so hard he thought he would die but all she did when she picked him up was say, Oscar, listen to the *bullshit* my sister pulled, and off they'd gone, building another one of their word-scrapers. By the fifth time he called he no longer expected the Big Blow-off. She was the only girl outside his family who admitted to having a period, who actually said to him, I'm bleeding like a *hog*, an astounding confidence he turned over and over in his head, sure it meant something, and when he thought about the way she laughed, as though she owned the air around her, his heart thudded inside his chest, a lonely rada. Ana Obregón, unlike every other girl in his secret cosmology, he actually fell for *as* they were getting to know each other. Because her appearance in his life was sudden, because she'd come in under his radar, he didn't have time to raise his usual wall of nonsense or level some wild-ass expectations her way. Maybe he was plain tired after four years of not getting ass, or maybe he'd finally found his zone. Incredibly enough, instead of making an idiot out of himself as one might have expected, given the hard fact that this was the first girl he'd ever had a conversation with, he actually took it a day at a time. He spoke to her plainly and without effort and discovered that his constant self-deprecation pleased her immensely. It was amazing how it was between them; he would say something obvious and uninspired, and she'd say, Oscar, you're really fucking smart. When she said, I *love* men's hands, he spread both of his across his face and said, faux-casual-like, Oh, *really?* It cracked her up.

She never talked about what they were; she only said, Man, I'm glad I got to know you.

And he said, I'm glad I'm me knowing you.

One night while he was listening to New Order and trying to chug through *Clay's Ark*, his sister knocked on his door.

You got a visitor.

I do?

Yup. Lola leaned against his door frame. She'd shaved her head down to the bone, Sinéad-style, and now everybody, including their mother, was convinced she'd turned into a lesbiana.

You might want to clean up a little. She touched his face gently. Shave those pussy hairs.

It was Ana. Standing in his foyer, wearing a full-length leather, her trigueña skin blood-charged from the cold, her face gorgeous with eyeliner, mascara, foundation, lipstick, and blush.

Freezing out, she said. She had her gloves in one hand like a crumpled bouquet.

Hey, was all he managed to say. He could hear his sister upstairs, listening.

What you doing? Ana asked.

Like nothing.

Like let's go to a movie, then.

Like OK, he said.

Upstairs his sister was jumping up and down on his bed, low-screaming, It's a date, it's a date, and then she jumped on his back and nearly toppled them clean through the bedroom window.

So is this some kind of date? he said as he slipped into her car.

She smiled wanly. You could call it that.

Ana drove a Cressida, and instead of taking them to the local theater she headed down to the Amboy Multiplex.

I love this place, she said as she was wrangling for a parking space. My father used to take us here when it was still a drive-in. Did you ever come here back then?

He shook his head. Though I heard they steal plenty of cars here now.

Nobody's stealing *this* baby.

It was so hard to believe what was happening that Oscar really couldn't take it seriously. The whole time the movie—*Manhunter*—was on, he kept expecting niggers to jump out with cameras and scream, Surprise! Boy, he said, trying to remain on her map, this is some movie. Ana nodded; she smelled of some perfume he could not name, and when she pressed close the heat off her body was *vertiginous*.

On the ride home Ana complained about having a headache and they didn't speak for a long time. He tried to turn on the radio but she said, No, my head's really killing me. He joked, Would you like some crack? No, Oscar. So he sat back and watched the Hess Building and the rest of Woodbridge slide past through a snarl of overpasses. He was suddenly aware of how tired he was; the nervousness that had raged through him the entire night had exhausted his ass. The longer they went without speaking the more morose he became. It's just a movie, he told himself. It's not like it's a date.

Ana seemed unaccountably sad and she chewed her bottom lip, a real bembe, until most of her lipstick was on her teeth. He was going to make a comment about it but decided not to.

You reading anything good?

Nope, she said. You?

I'm reading *Dune*.

She nodded. I *hate* that book.

They reached the Elizabeth exit, which is what New Jersey is *really* known for, industrial wastes on both sides of the turnpike. He had started holding his breath against those horrible fumes when Ana let loose a scream that threw him into his passenger door. Elizabeth! she shrieked. Close your fucking legs!

Then she looked over at him, tipped back her head, and laughed.

When he returned to the house his sister said, Well?

Well what?

Did you *fuck* her?

Jesus, Lola, he said, blushing.

Don't lie to me.

I do not move so precipitously. He paused and then sighed. In other words, I didn't even get her scarf off.

Sounds a little suspicious. I know you Dominican men. She held up her hands and flexed the fingers in playful menace. Son pulpos.

The next day he woke up feeling like he'd been unshackled from his fat, like he'd been washed clean of his misery, and for a long time he couldn't remember why he felt this way, and then he said her name.

OSCAR IN LOVE

And so now every week they headed out to either a movie or the mall. They talked. He learned that her ex-boyfriend, Manny, used to smack the shit out of her, which was a problem, she confessed, because she liked it when guys were a little rough with her in bed; he learned that her father had died in a car accident when she was a young girl in Macorís, and that her new stepfather didn't care two shits about her but that it didn't matter because once she got into Penn State she didn't ever intend to come back home. In turn he showed her some of his writings and told her about the time he'd gotten struck by a car and put in the hospital and about how his tío used to smack the shit out of him in the old days; he even told her about the crush he had on Maritza Chacón and she screamed, Maritza Chacón? I know that cuero! Oh my God, Oscar, I think even my stepfather slept with her!

Oh, they got close all right, but did they ever kiss in her car? Did he ever put his hands up her skirt? Did he ever thumb her clit? Did she ever push up against him and say his name in a throaty voice? Did he ever stroke her hair while she sucked him off? Did they ever fuck?

Poor Oscar. Without even realizing it he'd fallen into one of those Let's-Be-Friends Vortexes, the bane of nerdboys everywhere. These relationships were love's version of a stay in the stocks, in you go, plenty of misery guaranteed and what you got out of it besides bitterness and heartbreak nobody knows. Perhaps some knowledge of self and of women.

Perhaps.

In April he got his second set of SAT scores back (1020 under the old system) and a week later he learned he was heading to Rutgers New Brunswick. Well, you did it, hijo, his mother said, looking more relieved than was polite. No more selling pencils for me, he agreed. You'll love it, his sister promised him. I know I will. I was meant for college. As for Ana, she was on her way to Penn State, honors program, full ride. And now my stepfather can kiss my ass! It was also in April that her ex-boyfriend, Manny, returned from the army—Ana told him during one of their trips to the Yaohan Mall. His sudden appearance, and Ana's joy over it, shattered the hopes Oscar had cultivated. He's back, Oscar asked, like forever? Ana nodded. Apparently Manny had gotten into trouble again, drugs, but this time, Ana insisted, he'd been set up by these three cocolos, a word he'd never heard her use before, so he figured she'd gotten it from Manny. Poor Manny, she said.

Yeah, poor Manny, Oscar muttered under his breath.

Poor Manny, poor Ana, poor Oscar. Things changed quickly. First off, Ana stopped being home all the time, and Oscar found himself stacking messages on her machine: This is Oscar, a bear is chewing my legs off, please call me; This is Oscar, they want a million dollars or it's over, please call me; This is Oscar, I've just spotted a strange meteorite and I'm going out to investigate. She always got back to him after a couple of days, and was pleasant about it, but still. Then she canceled three Fridays in a row and he had to settle for the clearly reduced berth of Sunday after church. She'd pick him up and they'd drive out to Boulevard East and park and together they'd stare out over the Manhattan skyline. It wasn't an ocean, or a mountain range; it was, at least to Oscar, better, and it inspired their best conversations.

It was during one of those little chats that Ana let slip, God, I'd forgotten how big Manny's cock was.

Like I really need to hear that, he snapped.

I'm sorry, she said hesitantly. I thought we could talk about everything.

Well, it wouldn't be bad if you actually kept Manny's anatomical enormity to yourself.

So we can't talk about everything?

He didn't even bother answering her.

With Manny and his *big cock* around, Oscar was back to dreaming about nuclear annihilation, how through some miraculous accident he'd hear about the attack first and without pausing he'd steal his tío's car, drive it to the stores, stock it full of supplies (maybe shoot a couple of looters en route), and then fetch Ana. What about Manny? she'd wail. There's no time! he'd insist, peeling out, shoot a couple more looters (now slightly mutated), and then repair to the sweaty love den where Ana would quickly succumb to his take-charge genius and his by-then ectomorphic physique. When he was in a better mood he let Ana find Manny hanging from a light fixture in his apartment, his tongue a swollen purple bladder in his mouth, his pants around his ankles. The news of the imminent attack on the TV, a half-literate note pinned to his chest. *I koona taek it.* And then Oscar would comfort Ana with the terse insight, He was too weak for his Hard New World.

So she has a boyfriend? Lola asked him suddenly.

Yes, he said.

You should back off for a little while.

Did he listen? Of course he didn't. Available any time she needed to kvetch. And he even got—joy of joys!—the opportunity to meet the famous Manny, which was about as fun as being called a fag during a school assembly (which had happened). (Twice.) Met him outside Ana's house. He was this intense emaciated guy with marathon-runner limbs and voracious eyes; when they shook hands Oscar was sure the nigger was going to smack him, he acted so surly. Manny was muy bald and completely shaved his head to hide it, had a hoop in each ear and this leathery out-in-the-sun buzzardy look of an old cat straining for youth.

So you're Ana's little friend, Manny said.

That's me, Oscar said in a voice so full of cheerful innocuousness that he could have shot himself for it.

Oscar is a brilliant writer, Ana offered. Even though she had never once asked to read anything he wrote.

He snorted. What would you have to write about?

I'm into the more speculative genres. He knew how absurd he sounded.

The more speculative genres. Manny looked ready to cut a steak off him. You sound mad corny, guy, you know that?

Oscar smiled, hoping somehow an earthquake would demolish all of Paterson.

I just hope you ain't trying to chisel in on my girl, guy.

Oscar said, Ha-ha. Ana flushed red, looked at the ground.

A joy.

With Manny around, he was exposed to an entirely new side of Ana. All they talked about now, the little they saw each other, was Manny and the terrible things he did to her. Manny smacked her, Manny kicked her, Manny called her a fat twat, Manny cheated on her, she was sure, with this Cuban chickie from the middle school. So that explains why I couldn't get a date in those days; it was Manny,

Oscar joked, but Ana didn't laugh. They couldn't talk ten minutes without Manny beeping her and her having to call him back and assure him she wasn't with anybody else. And one day she arrived at Oscar's house with a bruise on her face and with her blouse torn, and his mother had said: I don't want any trouble here!

What am I going to do? she asked over and over and Oscar always found himself holding her awkwardly and telling her, Well, I think if he's this bad to you, you should break up with him, but she shook her head and said, I know I should, but I can't. I *love* him.

Love. Oscar knew he should have checked out right then. He liked to kid himself that it was only cold anthropological interest that kept him around to see how it would all end, but the truth was he couldn't extricate himself. He was totally and irrevocably in love with Ana. What he used to feel for those girls he'd never really known was nothing compared to the amor he was carrying in his heart for Ana. It had the density of a dwarf-motherfucking-star and at times he was a hundred percent sure it would drive him mad. The only thing that came close was how he felt about his books; only the combined love he had for everything he'd read and everything he hoped to write came even close.

Every Dominican family has stories about crazy loves, about niggers who take love too far, and Oscar's family was no different.

His abuelo, the dead one, had been unyielding about one thing or another (no one ever exactly said) and ended up in prison, first mad, then dead; his abuela Nena Inca had lost her husband six months after they got married. He had drowned on Semana Santa and she never remarried, never touched another man. We'll be together soon enough, Oscar had heard her say.

Your mother, his tía Rubelka had once whispered, was a loca when it came to love. It almost killed her.

And now it seemed that it was Oscar's turn. *Welcome to the family,* his sister said in a dream. *The real family.*

It was obvious what was happening, but what could he do? There was no denying what he felt. Did he lose sleep? Yes. Did he lose important hours of concentration? Yes. Did he stop reading his Andre Norton books and even lose interest in the final issues of *Watchmen,* which were unfolding in the illest way? Yes. Did he start borrowing his tío's car for long rides to the Shore, parking at Sandy Hook, where his mom used to take them before she got sick, back when Oscar hadn't been too fat, before she stopped going to the beach altogether? Yes. Did his youthful unrequited love cause him to lose weight? Unfortunately, this alone it did not provide, and for the life of him he couldn't understand why. When Lola had broken up with the Golden Gloves she'd lost almost twenty pounds. What kind of genetic discrimination was this, handed down by what kind of scrub God?

Miraculous things started happening. Once he blacked out while crossing an intersection and woke up with a rugby team gathered around him. Another time Miggs was goofing on him, talking smack about his aspirations to write role-playing games—complicated story, the company Oscar had been hoping to write for, Fantasy Games Unlimited, and which was considering one of his modules for PsiWorld, had recently closed, scuttling all of Oscar's hopes and dreams that he was about to turn into the next Gary Gygax. Well, Miggs said, it looks like *that* didn't work out, and for the first time ever in their relationship Oscar lost his temper and without a word swung on Miggs, connected so hard that homeboy's mouth spouted blood. Jesus Christ, Al said. Calm down! I didn't mean to do it, he said unconvincingly. It was an accident. Mudafuffer, Miggs said. Mudafuffer! He got so bad that one desperate night, after listening to Ana sobbing to him on the phone about Manny's latest bullshit, he said, I have to go to church now, and put down the phone, went to his tío's room (Rudolfo was out at the titty bar), and stole his antique Virginia Dragoon, that oh-so-famous First Nation–exterminating Colt .44, heavier than bad luck and twice as ugly. Stuck its impressive snout down the front of his pants and proceeded to stand in front of Manny's building almost the entire night. Got real friendly with the aluminum siding. Come on, motherfucker, he said calmly. I got a nice eleven-year-old girl for you. He didn't care that he would more than likely be put away forever, or that niggers like him got ass *and* mouth raped in jail, or that if the cops picked him up and found the gun they'd send his tío's ass up the river for parole violation. He didn't care about nada that night. His head contained zero, a perfect vacuum. He saw his entire writing future flash before his eyes; he'd only written one novel worth a damn, about an Australian hunger spirit preying on a group of small-town friends, wouldn't get a chance to write anything better—career over. Luckily for the future of American Letters, Manny did not come home that night.

It was hard to explain. It wasn't just that he thought Ana was his last fucking chance for happiness—this was clearly on his mind—it was also that he'd never ever in all his miserable eighteen years of life experienced anything like he'd felt when he was around that girl. I've waited forever to be in love, he wrote his sister. How many times I thought *this is never going to happen to me.* (When in his second-favorite anime of all time, *Robotech Macross,* Rich Hunter finally hooked up with Lisa, he broke down in front of the TV and cried. Don't tell me they shot the president, his tío called from the back room, where he was quietly snorting you-know-what.) It's like I swallowed a piece of heaven, he wrote to his sister in a letter. You can't imagine how it feels.

Two days later he broke down and confessed to his sister about the gun stuff and she, back on a short laundry visit, flipped out. She got them both on their knees in front of the altar she'd built to their dead abuelo and had him swear on their mother's living soul that he'd never pull anything like that again as long as he lived. She even cried, she was so worried about him.

You need to stop this, Mister.

I know I do, he said. But I don't know if I'm even here, you know?

That night he and his sister both fell asleep on the couch, she first. Lola had just broken up with her boyfriend for like the tenth time, but even Oscar, in his condition, knew they would be back together in no time at all. Sometime before dawn he dreamt about all the girlfriends he'd never had, row upon row upon row upon row, like the extra bodies that the Miraclepeople had in Alan Moore's *Miracleman. You can do it,* they said.

He awoke, cold, with a dry throat.

––––––––

They met at the Japanese mall on Edgewater Road, Yaohan, which he had discovered one day on his long I'm-bored drives and which he now considered part of their landscape, something to tell their children about. It was where he came for his anime tapes and his mecha models. Ordered them both chicken katsu curries and then sat in the large cafeteria with the view of Manhattan, the only gaijin in the whole joint.

You have beautiful breasts, he said as an opener.

Confusion, alarm. Oscar. What's the matter with you?

He looked out through the glass at Manhattan's western flank, looked out like he was some deep nigger. Then he told her.

There were no surprises. Her eyes went soft, she put a hand on his hand, her chair scraped closer, there was a strand of yellow in her teeth. Oscar, she said gently, I *have* a boyfriend.

She drove him home; at the house he thanked her for her time, walked inside, lay in bed.

In June he graduated from Don Bosco. See them at graduation: his mother starting to look thin (the cancer would grab her soon enough), Rudolfo high as shit, only Lola looking her best, beaming, happy. You did it, Mister. You did it. He heard in passing that of everybody in their section of P-town only he and Olga—poor fucked-up Olga—had not attended even one prom. Dude, Miggs joked, maybe you should have asked *her* out.

In September he headed to Rutgers New Brunswick, his mother gave him a hundred dollars and his first kiss in five years, his tío a box of condoms: Use them all, he said, and then added: On girls. There was the initial euphoria of finding himself alone at college, free of everything, completely on his fucking own, and with an optimism that here among these thousands of young people he would find someone like him. That, alas, didn't happen. The white kids looked at his black skin and his afro and treated him with inhuman cheeriness. The kids of color, upon hearing him speak and seeing him move his body, shook their heads. You're not Dominican. And he said, over and over again, But I am. Soy dominicano. Dominicano soy. After a spate of parties that led to nothing but being threatened by some drunk whiteboys, and dozens of classes where not a single girl looked at him, he felt the optimism wane, and before he even realized what had happened he had buried himself in what amounted to the college version of what he'd majored in all throughout high school: getting no ass. His happiest moments were genre moments, like when *Akira* was released (1988). Pretty sad. Twice a week he and his sister would dine at the Douglass dining hall; she was a Big Woman on Campus and knew just about everybody with any pigment, had her hand on every protest and every march, but that didn't help his situation any. During their get-togethers she would give him advice and he would nod quietly and afterward would sit at the E bus stop and stare at all the pretty Douglass girls and wonder where he'd gone wrong in his life. He wanted to blame the books, the sci-fi, but he couldn't—he loved them too much. Despite swearing early on to change his nerdly ways, he continued to eat, continued not to exercise, continued to use flash words, and after a couple semesters without any friends but his sister, he joined the university's resident geek organization, RU Gamers, which met in the classrooms beneath Frelinghuysen and boasted an entirely male membership. He had thought college would be better, as far as girls were concerned, but those first years it wasn't.

Man Gone Down

⤵︎

Michael Thomas

THE LOSER

1.

I know I'm not doing well. I have an emotional relationship with a fish—Thomas Strawberry. My oldest son, C, named him, and that name was given weight because a six-year-old voiced it as though he'd had an epiphany: *"He looks like a strawberry."* The three adults in the room had nodded in agreement.

"I only gave you one," his godfather, Jack, the marine biologist, told him. "If you have more than one, they kill each other." Jack laughed. He doesn't have kids. He doesn't know that one's not supposed to speak of death in front of them and cackle. One speaks of death in hushed, sober tones—the way one speaks of alcoholism, race, or secret bubble gum a younger sibling can't have. Jack figured it out on some level from the way both C and X looked at him blankly and then stared into the small aquarium, perhaps envisioning a battle royal between a bowlful of savage little fish, or the empty space left behind. We left the boys in their bedroom and took

the baby with us. *"They don't live very long,"* he whispered to us. *"About six weeks."* That was C's birthday in February. It's August, and he's not dead.

He's with me on the desk, next to my stack of books and legal pads. I left my laptop at my mother-in-law's for C to use. She'd raised an eyebrow as I started to the door. Allegedly, my magnum opus was on that hard drive—the book that would launch my career and provide me with the financial independence she desired. *"I write better if the first draft is longhand."* She hadn't believed me. It had been a Christmas gift from Claire. I remember opening it and being genuinely surprised. All three children had stopped to see what was in the box.

"Merry Christmas, honey," she'd cooed in my ear. She then took me by the chin and gently turned my face to meet hers. *"This is your year."* She kissed me—too long—and the children, in unison, looked away. The computer was sleek and gray and brimming with the potential to organize my thoughts, my work, my time. It would help extract that last portion of whatever it was that I was working on and buff it with the requisite polish to make it salable. *"This is our year."* Her eyes looked glazed, as though she had been intoxicated by the machine's power, the early hour, and the spirit of the season. It had been bought, I was sure, with her mother's money. And I knew Edith had never believed me to have any literary talent, but she'd wanted to make her daughter feel supported and loved—although she probably had expected it to end like this. C had seemed happy when I left, though, sitting on the floor with his legs stretched under the coffee table, the glow from the screen washing out his copper skin.

"Bye, C."

"By-ye." He'd made it two syllables. He hadn't looked up.

———

Marco walks up the stairs and stops outside his kid's study, where I'm working. He knocks at the door. I don't know whether to be thankful or annoyed, but the door's open and it's his house. I try to be as friendly as I can.

"Yo!"

"Yo! What's up?" He walks in. I turn halfway and throw him a wave. He comes to the desk and looks down at the stack of legal pads.

"Damn, you're cranking it out, man."

"I'm writing for my life." He laughs. I don't. I wonder if he notices.

"Is it a novel?"

I can't explain to him that three pads are one novel and seven are another, but what I'm working on is a short story. I can't tell him that each hour I have what I believe to be an epiphany, and I must begin again—thinking about my life.

"Want to eat something?"

"No thanks, man, I have to finish this part."

I turn around on the stool. I'm being rude. He's moved back to the doorway, leaning. His tie's loose. He holds his leather bag in one hand and a fresh beer in the other. He's dark haired, olive skinned, and long nosed. He's five-ten and in weekend racquetball shape. He stands there, framed by a clear, solid maple jamb. Next to him is more millwork—a solid maple bookcase, wonderfully spare, with books and photos of his son's trophies. There's a picture of his boy with C. They were on the same peewee soccer team. They're grinning, holding trophies in front of what I believe to be my leg. Marco clicks his wedding band on the bottle. I stare at him. I've forgotten what we were talking about. I hope he'll pick me up.

"Want me to bring you something back?"

"No, man. Thanks, I'm good."

I'm broke, but I can't tell him this because while his family's away on Long Island for the summer, I'm sleeping in his kid's bed and he earns daily what I, at my best, earn in a month, because he has a beautiful home, because in spite of all this, I like him. I believe he's a decent man.

"All right, man." He goes to take a sip, then stops. He's probably learned of my drinking problem through the neighborhood gossip channels, but he's never confirmed any of it with me.

"Call me on the cell if you change your mind."

He leaves. In the margins, I tally our monthly costs. *"We need to make $140,000 a year,"* Claire told me last week. I compute that I'll have to teach twenty-two freshman comp sections a semester as well as pick up full-time work as a carpenter. Thomas Strawberry swims across his bowl to face me.

"I fed you," I say to him as though he's my dog. He floats, puckering his lips. Thomas, at one time, had the whole family copying his pucker face, but the boys got tired of it. The little one, my girl, kept doing it—the fish, the only animal she'd recognize. *"What does the cow say?"* I'd ask. *"What does the cat say?"* She'd stare at me, blankly, giving me the deadeye that only children can give—a glimpse of her indecipherable consciousness. *"What does the fish say?"* She'd pucker, the same way as when I'd ask her for a kiss—the fish face and a forehead to the cheekbone.

I packed my wife and kids into my mother-in-law's enormous Mercedes-Benz at 7:45 p.m. on Friday, June 26. It was essential for both Claire and her mother to leave Brooklyn by eight with the kids fed and washed and ready for sleep for the three-and-a-half-hour drive to Massachusetts. Claire, I suppose, had learned the trick of planning long drives around sleeping schedules from her mother. Road trips required careful planning and the exact execution of those plans. I'd have to park in the bus stop on Atlantic Avenue in front of our building then run the bags, toys, books, and snacks down the stairs, trying to beat the thieves and meter maids. Then I'd signal for Claire to bring the kids down, and we'd strap them into their seats, equipping them with juice and crackers and their special toys. Then, in her mind, she'd make one last sweep of the house, while I'd calculate the purchasing of whatever toiletries I knew I'd left behind.

After the last bathroom check and the last seatbelt check, we'd be off. We'd sing. We'd tell stories. We'd play I Spy. Then one kid would drop off and we'd shush the other two until Jersey or Connecticut and continue to shush until the last one dropped. There's something about children sleeping in cars, perhaps something felt by parents, and perhaps only by the parents of multiple children—their heads tilted, their mouths open, eyes closed. The stillness and the quiet that had vanished from your life returns, but you must be quiet—respect their stillness, their silence. You must also make the most of it. It's when you speak about important things that you don't want them to hear: money, time, death—we'd almost whisper. We'd honor their breath, their silence, knowing that their faces would be changed each time they awoke, one nap older, that less easily lulled to sleep. Before we had children, we joked, we played music loud, we talked about a future with children. *"What do you think they'll be like?"* she'd ask. But I knew I could never voice the image in my head and make it real for her—our child; my broad head, her sharp nose, blond afro, and freckles—the cacophony phenotype alone caused. I would shake my head. She'd smile and whine, *"What?"* playfully, as though I was flirting with or teasing her, but in actuality, I was reeling from the picture of the imagined face, the noise inside her dichotomized mind, and the ache of his broken mongrel heart.

X was already beginning to fade when Edith turned on the engine. The sun was setting over the East River. The corrugated metal warehouses, the giant dinosaur-like cranes, and the silver chassis of the car were swept with a mix of rosy light and shadow. I used to drive on a hill in a park outside of Boston with my best friend, Gavin. He'd gotten too drunk at too many high school parties and he wasn't welcome at them anymore, so we drank by ourselves outside. We'd say nothing and watch the sun set. And when the light was gone from the sky, one of us would try to articulate whatever was troubling us that day.

"Okay, honey." Claire was buckling up. "We're all in." Edith tried to smile at me and mouthed, *"Bye."* She took a hand off the wheel and gave a short wave. I closed C's door and looked in at him to wave good-bye, but he was watching the dome light slowly fade from halogen white through orange to umber—soft and warm enough through its transitions to temporarily calm the brassiness of Edith's hair. I saw him say, *"Cool,"* as it dulled, suspended on the ceiling, emberlike. Perhaps it reminded him of a fire he'd once seen in its dying stages, or a sunset. I watched him until it went off, and there was more light outside the car than in and he was partially obscured by my reflection.

C said something to his grandmother and his window lowered. He unbuckled himself and got up on his knees. Edith put the car in gear.

"Sit down and buckle up, hon." C didn't acknowledge her and stuck his hand out the window.

"Say good-bye to your dad."

"Bye, Daddy."

There was something about *daddy* versus *dad*. Something that made it seem as though it was the last good-bye he'd say to me as a little boy. X's eyes were closed. My girl yawned, shook her head, searched for and then found her bottle in her lap. C was still waving. Edith rolled up all the windows. Claire turned to tell him to sit, and they pulled away.

Thomas Strawberry's bowl looks cloudy. There's bright green algae growing on the sides, leftover food and what I imagine to be fish poop on the bottom—charcoal-green balls that list back and forth, betraying an underwater current. Cleaning his bowl is always difficult for me because the risk of killing him seems so high. I don't know how much trauma a little fish can handle. So I hold off cleaning until his habitat resembles something like a bayou backwater—more suitable for a catfish than for Thomas. He has bright orange markings and elaborate fins. He looks flimsy—effete. I can't imagine him fighting anything, especially one of his own.

I tap the glass and remember aquarium visits and classroom fish tanks. There was always a sign or a person in charge warning not to touch the glass. Thomas swims over to me, and while he examines my fingertip, I sneak the net in behind him. I scoop him out of the water. He wriggles and then goes limp. He does this every time, and every time I think I've killed him. I let him out into his temporary lodgings. He darts out of the net, back to life, and swims around the much smaller confines of the cereal bowl. I clean his bowl in the bathroom sink and refill it with the tepid water I believe he likes. I go back to the desk. He's stopped circling. I slowly pour him back in. I wonder if his stillness in the net is because of shock or if he's playing possum. The latter of the two ideas suggests the possibility of a fishy consciousness. Since school begins for the boys in two weeks and I haven't found an apartment, a job, or paid tuition, I let it go.

I wonder if I'm too damaged. Baldwin somewhere once wrote about someone who had *"a wound that he would never recover from,"* but I don't remember where. He also wrote about a missing member that was lost but still aching. Maybe something inside of me was no longer intact. Perhaps something had been cut off or broken down—collateral damage of the diaspora. Marco seems to be intact. Perhaps he was damaged, too. Perhaps whatever he'd had was completely lost, or never there. I wonder if I'm too damaged. Thomas Strawberry puckers at me. I tap the glass. He swims away.

I had a girlfriend in high school named Sally, and one day I told her everything. How at the age of six I'd been treed by an angry mob of adults who hadn't liked the idea of Boston busing. They threw rocks up at me, yelling, *"Nigger go home!"* And how the policeman who rescued me called me *"Sammy."* How I'd been sodomized in the bathroom of the Brighton Boys Club when I was seven, and how later that year, my mother, divorced and broke, began telling me that she should've flushed me down the toilet when she'd had the chance. I told Sally that from the day we met, I'd been writing poems about it all, for her, which I then gave to her. She held the book of words like it was a cold brick, with a glassy film, not tears, forming in front of her eyes. I fear, perhaps, that I'm too damaged. In the margins of the yellow pad I write down titles for the story—unholy trinities: *Drunk, Black, and Stupid. Black, Broke, and Stupid. Drunk, Black, and Blue.* The last seems the best—the most melodic, the least concrete. Whether or not it was a mystery remained to be seen.

The phone rings. It's Claire.

"Happy almost birthday."

"Thanks."

It's been three weeks since I've seen my family. Three weeks of over-the-phone progress reports. We've used up all the platitudes we know. Neither of us can stand it.

"Are you coming?"

"Yeah."

"How?"

It's a setup. She knows I can't afford the fare.

"Do you have something lined up for tomorrow?"

"Yeah," I answer. As of now it's a lie, but it's nine. I have till Labor Day to come up with several thousand dollars for a new apartment and long overdue bills, plus an extra fifty for the bus. It's unlikely, but not unreasonable.

"Did you get the security check from Marta?" she asks, excited for a moment that someone owes us money.

"No."

"Fuck." She breathes. Claire's never been convincing when she curses. She sighs purposefully into the receiver. "Do you have a plan?"

"I'll make a plan."

"Will you let me know?"

"I'll let you know."

"I dropped my mother at the airport this morning."

"It's her house. I like your mother." It's a lie, but I've never, in the twelve years we've been together, shown any evidence of my contempt.

"I think C wants a Ronaldo shirt." She stops. "Not the club team. He wants a Brazil one." Silence again. "Is that possible?"

"I'll try." More silence. "How's your nose?"

"It's fine." She sighs. She waits. I can tell she's crunching numbers in her head. She turns her voice up to sound excited. "We'd all love to see you," then turns it back down—soft, caring, to pad the directive. "Make a plan."

2.

The last time I saw them was late July at Edith's. The boys and I were in the kitchen. X was naked and broad-jumping tiles, trying to clear at least three at once. C had stopped stirring his potion, put down his makeshift magic wand and was pumping up a soccer ball. I was sipping coffee, watching them. We were listening to the Beatles. C was mouthing the words, X was singing aloud while in the air. As he jumped, he alternated between the lyrics and dinosaur names: Thump. "Dilophosaurus." Jump. *"She's got a ticket to ride..."* Thump. "Parasaurolophus." His muscles flexed and elongated—too much mass and too well defined for a boy, even a man-boy, especially one with such a tiny, lispy voice. He vaulted up onto the round table. It rocked. I braced it. He stood up and flashed a toothy smile.

"Sorry, Daddy."

X looks exactly like me. Not me at three years old, me as a man. He has a man's body and a man's head, square jawed, no fat or softness. He has everything except the stubble, scars, and age lines. X looks exactly like me except he's white. He has bright blue-gray eyes that at times fade to green. They're the only part of him that at times looks young, wild, and unfocused, looking at you but spinning everywhere. In the summer he's blond and bronze—colored. He looks like a tan elf on steroids. It would seem fitting to tie a sword to his waist and strap a shield on his back.

X could pass. It was too soon to tell about his sister, but it was obvious that C could not. I sometimes see the arcs of each boy's life based solely on the reactions from strangers, friends, and family— the reaction to their colors. They've already assigned my boys qualities: C is quiet and moody. X is eccentric. X, who from the age of two has believed he is a carnivorous dinosaur, who leaps, claws, and bites, who speaks to no one outside his immediate family, who regards interlopers with a cool, reptilian smirk, is charming. His blue eyes somehow signify a grace and virtue and respect that needn't be earned—privilege—something that his brother will never possess, even if he puts down the paintbrush, the soccer ball, and smiles at people in the same impish way. But they are my boys. They both call me Daddy in the same soft way; C with his husky snarl, X with his baby lisp. What will it take to make them not brothers?

X was poised on the table as though he was waiting in ambush. C had finished pumping and was testing the ball against one of the four-by-four wooden mullions for the picture window that looked out on the back lawn. Claire came in, holding the girl, and turned the music down.

"Honey, get down, please." X remained poised, unlistening, as though acknowledging that his mother would ruin his chance of making a successful kill.

"He's a raptor," said his brother without looking up.

"Get down." She didn't wait. She put down the girl, who shrieked in protest, grabbed X, who squawked like a bird, and put him down on the floor. He bolted as soon as his feet touched the ground and disappeared around the corner, growling as he ran.

"They'll be here soon," said Claire. "Can everyone be ready?"

"Who'll be here?" mumbled C. His rasp made him sound like a junior bluesman.

"The Whites." His shot missed the post and smacked into the glass. Claire inhaled sharply.

"Put that ball outside."

C looked at me. I pointed to the door. He ran out.

"No," Claire called after him. "Just the ball." The girl screeched and pulled on her mother's legs, begging to be picked up. Claire obliged, then looked to me.

"*'Look what the new world hath wrought,'*" I said.

She looked at the table, the ring from my coffee cup, the slop in the bowl C had been mixing, and the gooey, discarded wand.

I shrugged my shoulders. "To fight evil?"

"Just go get him and get dressed. I'll deal with the other two."

I put my cup down and stood up at attention. "The Whites are coming. The Whites are coming!" When we moved out of Boston to the near suburbs, my cousins had helped. I'd ridden in the back of their pickup with Frankie, who had just gotten out of Concord Correctional. We'd sat on a couch speeding through the new town, following the trail of white flight with Frankie shouting, *"The niggers are coming! The niggers are coming!"*

I snapped off a salute. My girl, happy to be in her mother's arms, giggled. I blew her a kiss. She reciprocated. I saluted again. The Whites were some long-lost Brahmin family friends of Edith's. As a girl Claire had been paired with the daughter. They were of Boston and Newport but had gone west some time ago. They were coming to stay for the week. I was to go back to Brooklyn the next day and continue my search for a place to work and live. "The Whites are coming." Claire wasn't amused. She rolled her eyes like a teenager, flipped me the bird, and headed for the bedroom.

I went outside. It was cool for July and gray, no good for the beach. We'd be stuck entertaining them in the house all day. C was under the branches of a ring of cedars. He was working on step-overs, foxing imaginary defenders in his homemade Ronaldo shirt. We'd made it the summer before—yellow dye, stenciled, green indelible marker. I'd done the letters, he'd done the number nine. It was a bit off center and tilted because we'd aligned the form a bit a-whack. It hadn't been a problem at first because the shirt had been so baggy that you couldn't detect the error, but he'd grown so much over the year, and filled it out, that it looked somewhat ridiculous.

He passed the ball to me. I trapped it and looked up. He was standing about ten yards away, arms spread, palms turned up, and mouth agape.

"Hello."

"The Whites are coming."

"So."

"So you need to change."

"Why?"

"Because your mother said so."

"I haven't even gotten to do anything."

"What is it that you need to do?"

He scrunched up his face, making his big eyes slits. Then he raised one eyebrow, signaling that it was a stupid question. And with a voice like mine but two octaves higher said, *"Pass the ball."* Slowly, as though he was speaking to a child. *"Pass the ball."* As if he were flipping some lesson back at me. *"Pass the ball."* Then he smiled, crooked and wide mouthed like his mother. He softened his voice—*"Pass, Dad."*

Almost everyone—friends, family, strangers—has at some time tried to place the origins of my children's body parts—this person's nose, that one's legs. C is a split between Claire and me, so in a sense, he looks like no one—a compromise between the two lines. He has light brown skin, which in the summer turns copper. He has long wavy hair, which is a blend. Hers is laser straight. I have curls. C's hair is red-brown, which makes one realize that Claire and I have the same color hair. *"Look what the new world hath wrought."* A boy who looks like neither mommy nor daddy but has a face all his own. No schema or box for him to fit in.

"Dad, pass." I led him with the ball toward the trees, which served as goalposts. He struck it, one time, *"Goooaaaal!"* He ran in a slight arc away from the trees with his right index finger in the air as his hero would've. *"Goal! Ronaldo! Gooooaaal!"* He blew a kiss to the imaginary crowd.

Claire knocked on the window. I turned. She was holding the naked girl in one arm. The other arm was extended, just as C's had been. X came sprinting into the kitchen and leapt at her, legs and arms extended, toes and fingers spread like raptor claws. He crashed into his mother's hip and wrapped his limbs around her waist all at once. She stumbled from the impact, then regained her balance. She peeled him off her waist and barked something at him. He stood looking up at her, his eyes melting down at the corners, his lip quivering, ready to cry. She bent down to his level, kissed him on his forehead, and said something that made him smile. He roared, spun, and bounded off. Her shoulders sagged. She turned back to me, shot a thumb over her shoulder, and mouthed, "Get ready!" She sat on the floor and laid the girl down on her back.

C was still celebrating his goal—or perhaps a new one I'd missed. He was on his knees, appealing to the gray July morning sky.

"Yo!" I yelled to him, breaking his trance. "Inside."

"In a minute."

"Cecil, now!" He snapped his head around and stood up like a little soldier. C had been named Cecil, but when he was four, he asked us to call him C. He, in some ways, had always been an easy child. As a toddler you could trust him to be alone in a room. We could give him markers and paper, and he would take care of himself. He was difficult, though, in that he's always been such a private boy who so rarely asks for anything that we've always given him what he wants. *"I want you to call me C."* Cecil had been Claire's father's and grandfather's name, but she swallowed her disappointment and coughed out an okay. I'd shrugged my shoulders. It had been a given that our first child would be named after them.

I thought, when he was born, that his eyes would be closed. I didn't know if he'd be sleeping or screaming, but that his eyes would be closed. They weren't. They were big, almond shaped, and copper— almost like mine. He stared at me. I gave him a knuckle and he gummed it—still staring. He saw everything about me: the chicken pox scar on my forehead, the keloid scar beside it, the absent-minded boozy cigarette burn my father had given me on my stomach. Insults and epithets that had been thrown like bricks out of car windows or spat like poison darts from junior high locker rows. Words and threats, which at the time they'd been uttered, hadn't seemed to cause me any injury because they'd not been strong enough or because they'd simply missed. But holding him, the long skinny boy with the shock of dark hair and the dusky newborn skin, I realized that I had been hit by all of them and that they still hurt. My boy was silent, but I shushed him anyway— long and soft—and I promised him that I would never let them do to him what had been done to me. He would be safe with me.

Claire was still on the floor wrestling the girl into a diaper. She turned just in time to see X leave his feet. His forehead smashed into her nose, flattening it, sending her down. C shot past me and ran into the house, past the accident scene and around the corner. The girl sat up and X, unsure of what it was that he'd done, smiled nervously. He looked down at his mother, who was lying motionless on the floor, staring blankly at the ceiling. Then her eyes closed. Then the blood came. It ran from her nostrils as though something inside her head had suddenly burst. Claire has a very long mouth and what she calls a bird lip. The top and bottom come together in the middle in a point, slightly off center—crooked— creating a deep valley between her mouth and her long, Anglican nose. So the blood flowed down her cheeks, over and into her ears, into her hair, down the sides of her neck, and onto the white granite floor.

C came running back in with the first aid kit and a washcloth. He opened it, got out the rubbing alcohol, and soaked the washcloth. He stood above his mother, looking at her stained face, the stained floor, contemplating where to begin. He knelt beside her and started wiping her cheeks. The smell of the alcohol brought her back, and she pushed his hand from her face. C backed away. She raised her arm into the air and began waving, as though she was offering up her surrender.

I came inside. I took the kit from C, dampened a gauze pad with saline, and began to clean her up. She still hadn't said anything, but she began weeping. Our children stood around us in silence.

"It's going to be okay," I told them. "It looks a lot worse than it is." X began to cry. C tried to hug him, but he wriggled loose and started backing out of the kitchen.

"It's okay, buddy." He stopped crying, wanting to believe me. "It's not your fault." I activated the chemical ice pack and gently placed it on her nose.

"Don't leave me," she whispered. Her lips barely moved. I wondered, if it hadn't yet lapsed, if our insurance covered reconstructive surgery. Her chest started heaving.

"Hey, guys. Take your sister in the back and put on a video." They wouldn't budge. "C," I pointed in the direction of the TV room. "Go on." Claire was about to burst. "Go."

They left and Claire let out a low, wounded moan, stopped, took a quick breath and moaned again. Then she let out a high whine that was the same pitch as the noise from something electrical somewhere in the house. *My wife is white,* I thought, as though I hadn't considered it before. Her blood contrasted against the granite as it did on her face. *I married a white woman.* She stopped her whine, looked at me, and tried to manage a smile.

"*Look what the new world hath wrought.*"

Her face went blank; then she stared at me as though she hadn't heard what I said, or hadn't believed what I said. I should've said something soothing to make her nose stop throbbing or to halt the darkening purple rings that were forming under her eyes. I shifted the ice pack. Her nose was already twice its normal size. She closed her eyes. I slid my arms under her neck and knees and lifted.

"No."

"No what?"

"Leave me."

"I'm going to put you to bed."

"Leave me."

"I'm not going to leave you."

Although she'd been through three cesarean sections, Claire can't take much pain. She was still crying, but only tears and the occasional snuffle. Her nose was clogged with blood. She wasn't going to be able to get up. Claire has always been athletic. She has muscular legs and injury-free joints. It seemed ridiculous that I should need to carry her—my brown arm wrapped around her white legs—I knew there was a lynch mob forming somewhere. I laid her down on the bed. She turned on her side away from me. There was little light in the room. The air was as cool and gray inside as it was out. I left her alone.

C was waiting for me outside the door. He was shirtless, trying to ready himself to face the Whites.

"Dad, is Mom gonna be okay?"

"She'll be fine." He didn't believe me. He tried another tack.

"Is it broken?"

"Yeah."

"Is that bad?"

"She'll be fine." I patted his head and left my hand there. C has never been an openly affectionate boy, but he does like to be touched. I'd forgotten that until he rolled his eyes up and, against his wishes, smiled. I steered him by his head into the bathroom and began to prepare for a shower and shave.

"Have I ever broken my nose?" he asked, fiddling with the shaving cream.

"No."

"Have you ever broken your nose?"

"Yes."

He put the can down, stroked the imaginary whiskers on his chin, and looked at my face. I have a thick beard—red and brown and blond and gray. It makes no sense. The rest of my body is hairless. I could see him trying to connect the hair, the scars, the nose.

"Did you cry?"

"No."

"Really?"

"Really."

"Did you break your nose more than once?"

"Yeah."

"And you never cried?"

"Never."

"What happened?" I had taken off my shirt and shorts, and he was scanning what he could see of my body, an athlete's body, not like the bodies of other men my age he'd seen on the beach. He looked at my underwear, perhaps wondering why I'd stopped at them.

He grinned. "You're naked."

"No, I'm not," I said sternly.

He tried mimicking my tone. "Yes, you are."

"What are these?" I gestured to my boxers.

"The emperor has no clothes," he sang.

"I'm not the emperor."

C stopped grinning, sensing he shouldn't take it any further.

"What happened?"

"When?"

"When you broke your nose."

"What do you mean?"

"How did you break your nose all those times?"

"Sports and stuff."

"What stuff?"

"Sports."

He squinted at me and curled his lips in. He fingered the shaving cream can again. His face went blank, as it always seemed to when he questioned and got no answer. I hid things from him. I always had. Perhaps I was a coward. C already seemed to know what was going to happen to him. Just as I had been watching him, he'd been watching me, making the calculations, extrapolating, charting the map of the territory that lay between us—little brown boy to big brown man.

He was already sick of it. He was sick of his extended family. He was sick of his private-school mates. He seemed world weary before the age of seven. His little friends had already made it clear to him that he was brown like poop or brown like dirt and that his father was ugly because he was brown. He was only four the first time he'd heard it and he kept silent as long as he could, but his mother had found him alone weeping. He'd begged us not to say anything to his teachers or the other children's parents—they were his friends, he'd said. Claire wanted blood spilt. There were meetings and protests and petitions and apologies. People had gotten angry at the kids who'd ganged up on the little brown boy. One mother had dragged her wailing son to me, demanding that he apologize, and seemed perplexed when I noogied his head and told him it was okay. Other parents were even more perplexed when I refused to sign the petitions that would broaden the curriculum. Claire had been surprised.

"Why don't you want to sign?"

"What good would it do?"

"What do you mean?"

"No institutional legislation can change the hearts of bigots and chickenshits."

Bigots and chickenshits, my boy was surrounded by them, and no one would come clean and say it, not even me. They would all betray him at some point, some because they actually were the sons and daughters of bigots and would become so themselves, some because they would never stand by his side—unswervable. Which little chickenshit would stand up for him when they chanted, *"Brown like poop, brown like dirt"*? They would all be afraid to be his friend.

Even at this age they knew what it was to go down with him—my little brown boy.

The Whites were coming. I had to be ready.

"Get ready," I said. I sent my little brown boy out and took a shower.

As soon as I finished, C knocked on the door. It was as if he'd been waiting right outside.

"Yeah?"

"Can I come in?"

"No."

"Why?"

"Wait."

Noah had appeared naked before his son Ham, and Ham's line was cursed forever. I didn't want to start that mess again. I dressed quickly. I opened the door. My three children stood there: the brown boy, the white boy, and the girl of indeterminate race. They wore the confused look of children who'd just finished watching TV.

"She's got a poop," C said, pointing at his sister's bottom, holding his nose.

"Yeah, poop," said X.

"No poopoo," said the girl. I scooped her up and smelled, then I peeked into her diaper.

"No poop."

I got them dressed and presentable and lined up near the front door. I could hear Claire in the bathroom, fiddling with her mother's makeup. She seldom wore anything besides lipstick. We heard the car pull onto the gravel driveway. C leaned toward the kitchen.

"Let's go."

"Wait until you've said hello." Claire emerged from the bathroom. It looked as though the kids had shoved a golf ball up her nose and then set upon her sinus area with dark magic markers. Her children looked at her in horror, as though their mother had been replaced by some well-mannered pug.

C pulled on my arm. *"Please."* He sounded desperate. He was looking at the door as though something evil was about to enter. The screen door whined and the knob turned and he bolted to the back. Edith walked in, saw her daughter, and gasped. She remembered she had company with her and turned to welcome them in.

The Whites were here: the grandmother, the daughter, the grand-children, and the son-in-law. Edith held him by the wrist, squeezing it as though to reassure him. I don't think Edith had ever touched me, other than by mistake—both reaching for the marmalade jar, both pulling back. Edith is still very beautiful. I think she's a natural blonde. She has blue eyes, not lasers like X's, but firm, giving strength to her diminutive self. Her skin is beach worn, permanently tanned from walks in the wind and sand. High cheekboned, long nosed, as if she was trying to assume the face of some long dead Peqout or Wampanoag. *Massachusetts.* I thought about the word, like a name, *Massasoit,* as though I was he, welcoming a visiting tribe from the south, the Narragansett.

The prelude to the introduction was taking too long. I offered my hand to my alleged peer. I'm six-three and have the hands of some-one a foot taller. They are hard and marked by the miscues of a decade and a half of absentminded carpentry. His hand disappeared in mine, but he didn't flinch. He did his best to meet me.

"Good to see you." He let go, stepped back. The two women had joined Edith, staring at Claire's nose.

"Hello," said Claire to the elder, trying to break the spell. They stopped staring, but they couldn't move. Claire hugged both of them, kissing the sides of their faces as well.

"It's been so long," she said to the younger. Claire is truly beau-tiful—in visage, in tone, in manner. She's always had the ability, at least in the world she's from, to make everything seem all right, to make people feel that things are in their proper place and all is well. It wasn't working. As she held the younger's hand, the elder surveyed the wreckage of miscegenation: the battered Brahmin jewel, the afro blonde in her arms, the brown man. What was there to say other than hello and good-bye? The elder looked from Edith to Claire to the girl to me. Her eyes darted faster and faster. For a moment I wanted to explain, begin the narrative simply because I believed I could and I knew she couldn't: *Milton Brown of Georgia raped the slave girl Minette. That boy-child escaped and was taken in by the Cherokee peoples on their forced march to Oklahoma.*

Claire knelt to address the children—two boys, perhaps three and five. They were both hiding behind their mother's legs. The younger bent down and pushed her sons in front of her. They couldn't look at Claire. They buried their faces into their mother's skirt.

"And who is this?" asked the younger, looking at X. "Oh, my goodness—those eyes!" She gasped, forgetting herself, forgetting her children. It was as if X really was reptilian and she'd fallen under his hypnotic spell. The White children, against their better judgment, turned as well. They looked as though they'd been bled, particularly next to X, who seemed ready to jump, howl, or sprint. He stared back at them, not with the fear and wonder with which they regarded him, but in an equally inappropriate way, as though he was a boy looking at cupcakes, or a carnivore looking at flesh—child-eyed, man-jawed. If there was to be a battle, it was obvious who would be left when everything shook down. The new world regarded the old world. The old world clung to its mother's legs.

The younger tried to snap out of it. "You're such a big boy."

"I'm not a boy," said X in his lisp-growl. "I'm a Tyrannosaurus rex."

"Oh my," she said, summoning courage for her and her brood. The other Whites tittered nervously. The elder joined in.

"You must be Michael."

X kept staring at the children as though they were tasty meat bits.

"I'm not Michael! I'm X!"

The younger pressed on.

"These are my boys, James and George." The smaller of the two leaned his head forward and smiled.

"Hi."

The Whites and Edith smiled, and then cooed in unison, *"Oh."*

Edith leaned into X. "Michael, can you say hello?"

"I'm not Michael. I'm X."

"Hello," said the older child.

The bastard half-breed son of Milton and Minette was a schizophrenic. He married a Cherokee woman and they had two children. He disappeared, and she and her children were considered outcasts on the reservation. One day she left with them and headed east.

"I'm brown," said X.

"No, you're not," said the older child. "You're white."

"I'm brown!" he growled. "I'm the tyrant lizard king!" He snorted at them. The boys took a step back. X widened his nostrils and sniffed at them in an exaggerated way. He opened his eyes wide so that they were almost circles and smiled, coolly, making sure to show his teeth. He leaned forward and sniffed again.

She met the traveling preacher-salesman Gabriel Lloyd, settled in central Virginia, and had one child with him. Then she and Lloyd died.

"I eat you."

———————

As she tells it, once an acquaintance of Claire's who knew nothing of me had asked her upon seeing C for the first time, "How *did* you get such a brown baby?" Claire had shot back, "Brown *man*." I went outside to find C. Like his younger brother, he can smell fear. It makes X attack. The same fear causes C to withdraw—to keep his distance. He was standing in the middle of the yard with his back to the window and his ball under one arm.

"Yo, C-dawg." He turned and saw me, smiled weakly, walked over and took me by the hand. We turned toward the kitchen. The adults had entered and Edith and Claire were handing out drinks. My boy, big-eyed, vulnerable, brown, looked in at the white people. They looked out at him. The White boys ran into the room. The older one was crying. His father scooped him up and shushed him. The younger hid behind his mother. X came in, arms bent, mouth open. He was stomping instead of sprinting. He roared at everyone and stomped out.

"Do you have to go?"

"Yeah."

He let go of my hand.

"He's definitely a T. rex now." C turned and punted the ball across the yard into a patch of hostas. He watched it for a while as though he expected the plants to protest. He turned back to me, squinting his eyes, I thought, to keep from crying.

3.

*In the midst of the ocean
there grows a green tree
and I will be true
to the girl who loves me*

for I'll eat when I'm hungry
and drink when I'm dry
and if nobody kills me
I'll live 'til I die.

Claire's grandfather wanted to sing that song at our wedding, but he'd stopped taking his Thorazine the week leading up to it and "flipped his gizzard." So he'd sat quietly next to his nurse, cane between his legs, freshly dosed, staring into the void above the wedding party.

My father tried to assume the role of patriarch. In the clearing, between the woods and the sea, under the big tent, he'd stepped up on the bandstand. Hopped up on draft beer and with ill-fitting dentures, he'd taken the microphone. "May you and your love be *evah-gween.*" He'd been unable to roll the *r*'s. The drink and the teeth had undermined his once perfect diction. He raised his glass to tepid cheers.

———————

Ray Charles is singing "America the Beautiful." It's a bad idea to put on music while trying to make a plan. It may be that I need to stop listening altogether. Dylan makes me feel alienated and old; hip-hop, militant. Otis Redding is too gritty and makes me think about dying young. Robert Johnson makes me feel like catching the next thing smoking and Satan. Marley makes me feel like Jesus. I thought for some reason that listening to Ray in the background would be good, or at least better than the others. He's not. I'm confused. I never know what he's singing about in his prelude. It makes no sense. A blind, black, R & B junkie gone country, singing an also-ran anthem—dragging it back through the tunnel of his experience, coloring it with his growl, his rough falsetto. The gospel organ pulse, the backing voices, not from Nashville, not from Harlem, Mississippi, or Chicago—they float somewhere in the mix, evoking pearly gates and elevators going to the mall's upper mezzanine, *"America, America . . ."* It falls apart. I remember back in my school when people used to co-opt philosophy. They'd say that they were going to *deconstruct* something. I thought, one can't do that; one can only watch it happen. Only in America could someone try to make the musings of a whacked-out Frenchman utile. Anyway, the song falls apart. Perhaps even that's incorrect; I hear it for its many parts. It's not like a bad song, which disappears. In this, the multiplicity sings. *"America..."* Democracy's din made dulcet via the scratchy bark of a native son. *"God shed his grace on thee..."* Things fall apart, coalesce, then fall apart again. Like at the beach—fish schools, light rays. It's like being a drunk teen again, waiting for Gavin in the freight yard under the turnpike. The whistle blows. I see him appear from behind a car, bottle held aloft in the sunset. Things fall apart, come together, and sometimes I feel fortunate to bear witness. The timpanis boom. *"Amen..."* I have to hear that song again.

I don't. I turn it off. I go into the kiddie bedroom, turn the light off, and lie down in the kiddie bed. I need to make a plan, which means I need to make a list of the things I need to do. I need to get our security deposit back from our old landlady. I need to call the English Departments I'm still welcome in to see if there are any classes to be had. I need to call more contractors and foremen I know to see if there's any construction work. I need to call the boys' school to see if I can pay their tuition in installments. I need an installment. I try to make a complete list of things in my head. It doesn't work. I open my eyes and try to picture it in the darkness. Claire has always been good at making lists—to do lists, grocery lists, gift lists, wish lists, packing lists. They have dashes and arrows to coordinate disparate tasks and do the work of synthesis— laundry to pasta, pasta to rent check, rent check to a flower or animal doodle in the margin, depicting perhaps the world that exists beyond the documented tasks or between them: of fish minds and baby talk and sibling-to-sibling, child-to-parent metalanguage or microcode; the green tree that grows in the middle of the ocean; the space in which the song exists.

From downstairs Marco's clock chimes out the half hour. Outside, around the corner, the busted church bell sounds its metal gag. I'll be thirty-five at midnight. The phone rings. It's Gavin.

"Mush, what's up?" His speaking voice, accent, and tone are always in flux. It's never contingent on whom he's speaking to, but on what it is that he's saying. Now he uses a thick Boston accent. Not the bizarre Kennedy-speak that movie stars believe is real outside that family. *R*s don't exist and only the *o* and *u* vowel sounds are extended: *Loser* becomes *loo-sah*. It's a speak that sounds like it needs a six-pack or two to make it flow, to make it sing. He sounds happy, full of coffee, still inside, yet to be struck by the day.

"S'up?"

"Nothin', mush."

"All right."

"Happy birthday, mush. I'm a couple of days late."

"You're a couple of hours early."

"Sorry." He switches to another speaking voice, closer perhaps, to what his must be—a smoker's voice, in which you can hear both Harvard and Cavan County, Ireland. Gavin spent much of his adolescence with his father in jazz bars and can sound like the combination of a stoned horn player and a Jesuit priest.

"It's all right." I've been told that my accent's too neutral for me to be from Boston.

"You don't sound so good, man."

I almost tell him why—more out of resentment than camaraderie. He owes me at least four hundred dollars: a credit card payment, or a couple of weeks of groceries.

"I'm fine."

"What's the matter, white man gettin' you down?"

"You're the white man."

"No, baby, I'm the Black Irish."

"No. I'm the Black Irish."

"Whatever, man. You drinking?"

"No."

I had three friends in high school: Shaky—née Donovan—Brian, and Gavin. Brian had to become a Buddhist monk to sober up, went missing for a decade in the Burmese jungle, disrobed, became a stockbroker, and died in the Twin Towers attack. Shaky, who in high school and college had been named Shake because of basketball prowess, had moved with Gavin and me to the East Village, where he had a schizophrenic break. He was now roaming the streets of Lower Manhattan and south Brooklyn. Privately, between Gavin and myself, his name had evolved to Shaky. Gavin fluctuated between poems, paintings, and biannual death-defying benders, losing apartments, jobs, and potential girlfriends along the way.

When I moved out of the place I shared with him and in with Claire, he'd come to visit and use her mugs for his tobacco spit. We'd drink pots of coffee and cackle about institutions and heebie-jeebies and never ever succeeding. Gavin never dated much. Never *settled down*. He rarely had a telephone and was reachable only when he wanted to be. *"He checked out,"* Claire once said in such a way as if to be asking me if I'd done the same. She liked him, perhaps even loved him, but she was scared of him and he felt this. By the time C was a toddler she'd unconsciously pushed Gavin out of our lives— to the point where I didn't even think about him in her presence. But after a while, when Claire could see that I'd had enough of the gen- trifying neighborhood and private-school mixers, she tracked him down and invited him to a party at our place. He'd had a good five years clean and had managed to start over again in Boston and get himself a Harvard degree. "He's too smart and cute to be single," she'd said, looking at a commencement photo. When he returned to New York, she'd thought it would be a good idea for us to escort him back into the mainstream.

It was this past spring and he looked well—tall, dark haired, blue eyed, strangely russet skinned, as though some of his many freckles had leaked; the Black Irish. He'd made the transition, despite a good decade of delirium tremens and shelters, from handsome boy to handsome man. His lined face and graying hair made him look rugged and weary, but his freckles and eyes still flashed innocent. He'd just had a poem rejected by some literary rag, but on arriving, he seemed fine. We sat around the table. My girl was in my lap play- ing with my food. There were three other couples besides us, a single writer friend of Claire's, and Gavin. The woman, his alleged date, asked him what kind of poems he wrote.

"Sonnets."

"Sonnets?"

"Petrarchan sonnets."

She giggled. "How quaint."

"Quaint, hmm."

He emptied his water glass, refilled it with wine, and swallowed it in one gulp. Claire looked at me, concerned. He drank another glass, excused himself, and stood to leave. I caught him in the hallway.

"Where are you going with this?" I asked.

"Down, I suppose."

Three days later he showed up, beat up and already detoxing. Claire used to try to swap stories with us, about drunken uncles and acquaintances that had hit it too hard. She's never seen me drunk. I never had a fall as an adult. I never suffered Gavin's blood pressure spikes, seizures, or bat-winged dive bombers—only some lost years, insomnia, and psychosomatic heart failure. But she watched Gavin convulse on her couch while her babies played in the next room. She realized that the stories we told had actually happened to us and not to someone we used to know. The damage was real and lasting. And more stories were just an ignorant dinner comment away.

"How are you, Gav?" I ask. It sounds empty.

"I'm all right, I guess. My bell's still a'ringing a bit." He pauses for me to ask where he's calling from, how the last jag went down, but I don't. He covers for me. "You bustin' out for the weekend, or are you staying around?"

"I'm supposed to go."

"So you're going to be away Friday?"

"I suppose."

"Kids making you a cake?"

"Yeah. Probably."

"Hey, man?"

"Yeah."

"Your kids start giving you Old Spice yet?"

"No."

"What's going to happen?"

"C's going to count to thirty-five, and even though he knows the answer, will then ask me how old I'll be when he's thirty-five."

He snorts a laugh. "Children—a paradox." He shifts to MidAtlantic speak, the accent of one who hailed from an island between high-born Boston and London. "I have no wife. I have no children."

"Yes."

"I'm calling from a pay phone in a detox."

"Yes."

"I went on a twelve-week drunk because a girl didn't like my poems."

I should say something to him—that I'll come visit with a carton of cigarettes, or pick him up, like I always used to—but Claire's list opens up in my head like a computer file and I stay silent.

"Mush." He switches back. "Do something. Get your head out of your ass. Go get a coffee." More silence. "Happy birthday."

I go downstairs. It's dark. Out of respect for my host I leave the lights off. I go into the kitchen. It's posh and industrial, clad in stainless steel, maple, and absolute black granite. I open the oversized refrigerator. There's a Diet Coke and a doggie bag. Butter. Marco is a good bachelor. The house seems far too big for the three of them. I close the door and wonder if it's better to have an empty large refrigerator or a full one. There's a white ceramic bowl on the center island full of change. I pick through it, taking the nickels and dimes, leaving the quarters, as though big-change larceny would be too great a crime.

There's a big window in the back of the house. It's double height. It rises up through a void in the ceiling above. The mullions are aluminum, glazed with large panes of tempered glass. The curtain-wall spans the width of the building with one centered glass door. It's a structure unto itself. Like everything else in the house, it's unadorned. It looks out on the backyard, which isn't much, gravel, an unused sandbox, two soccer goals, and the neighbors' tall cedar fences on all three sides. There's no ocean, river, woods, or great lawn to look upon—functionless modernism. It may well have been a mirror—two stories tall, twenty-five feet wide—the giant mirror of Brooklyn. People could come from far and wee to look at themselves in it. *I could run the whole thing for you, Marco. I'll only take 20 percent. It'll pay off whatever it cost you to put it in within the first year.* I realize I don't know how much it cost, how much the whole house cost to buy and renovate and furnish. I don't have any way to price the glass, the metal, the labor, the markup. Marco had asked me my opinion on the quality of the work overall, the natural maple doorjambs and stairs and cabinetry—not with any bravado— he just wanted to know if he'd been treated fairly. I never told him anything. Perhaps he's still waiting, though it did seem strange, the master negotiator, asking me for reassurance. What could I say to him now? I've stolen his change and watched his building fall.

I take the money and go out. I have a twenty in my pocket, too, but I don't want to break it—not on coffee. Breaking it begins its slow decline to nothing.

I've forgotten that people go out, even on weeknights. Smith Street, which used to be made up of bodegas and check-cashing stores, looks more like SoHo. It's lined with bars and bar hoppers, restaurants and diners. Many of them are the same age I was when I got sober. There was a time when people spoke Farsi and Spanish on the streets and in the shops, but now there's white people mostly, all speaking English, tipsy and emboldened with magazine-like style. They peer into the windows of the closed knickknack emporiums that have replaced the religious artifact stores and social clubs.

It's hot but not muggy. I walk north with the traffic, trying to stay curbside so as to avoid getting trapped by meandering groups and hand-holding couples. I hop the curb and walk in the gutter to get around the outpouring from a shop. There's a party going on or breaking up. Inside there are paintings hanging on the wasabi green walls. There are small halogen track lights on the ceiling. Their beams wash out the paintings. Nobody's looking at the work.

"Hey!"

I can tell whoever is calling is calling for me. It's a woman's voice—full of wine and cigarettes. A bus approaches. I have to step up on the sidewalk toward the voice. She's standing in front of me.

"Hey," she says again in a cutesy, little girl way. Her hair's in pig-tails. Her face is as hot as the lights. "I know you."

Her name is Judy or Janet or something close to that. Her daughter was once in a tumbling class with X.

"Hello," I answer. I'm a foot taller than she is. I can't help but look down at her. She looks up at me, still smiling.

"Jeez, I never realized you were so tall. Now I know where that boy of yours gets it."

"Actually," I say, looking over her into the crowd of partygoers—I don't recognize anyone—"I was a small kid. I grew after high school." She's still smiling, but her face has lost some of the heat it held. She doesn't seem to care about the info.

"Whose show?"

She looks surprised. She touches her chest lightly with both hands. The bus rolls behind me, hot with diesel funk. My first job in New York was as a bike messenger. I once watched a guy skid on an oil slick and go down on Madison Avenue in front of the M1. It ran over his head—popped it open. Everyone watching threw up. She leans against the bus stop sign, flattening a breast against it.

"It's mine," she says.

I look over her into the glare of the makeshift gallery. It looks as if a flashbulb got stuck in midshot. I think it will hurt my head if I go into all that light.

"Come on. I'll give you a personal tour." She turns, expecting me to follow, which I do. She doesn't seem at all concerned with the light. Perhaps I have nothing to worry about, or perhaps she's become inured over time. The crowd parts for her, some smile and check me out. Now I recognize some of them, from the gym, from the coffee shop. They range in age from twenty-five to forty. Most of them appear to be single or dating. I can tell they're all childless; they're too wrapped up in what it is they believe Jane or Judy and I appear to be doing. I'm sure some of them will query her as to *what is going on* as soon as I leave.

Claire was still a dancer when we started dating. She'd had a show at the Joyce and a party afterward at her apartment. When I arrived, she was busy introducing Edith to her friends. The loft was full of admirers—new and old. There were prep school and college mates, other dancers, East Village divas both male and female. I watched Claire take Edith around. Her mother, as always, was unruffled by the chaos of new faces and personalities—gay boys and bi-girls and art freaks and the loud pumping disco on the stereo. Cigarettes and magnums of cheap Chilean wine. Edith was in full support of her daughter. Then she saw me. Perhaps Claire had described me to her mother and Edith was trying to determine if I was me. She looked at me too long. Claire noticed her mother's attention had shifted and looked to where she was looking. She smiled and made sure that Edith saw it. The dancers she'd been talking to looked as well. There was a nudge, a whisper, then Claire led Edith by the waist over to me. I met them in the middle of the room. Claire took each of us by the forearm and placed her mother's hand in mine. She made it clear to everyone there that she was mine and that our budding romance was mine to fuck up.

YOUNG
ADULT FICTION

FEATHERS

Jacqueline Woodson

Chapter 4

On the second day after the Jesus Boy got to our school, Trevor was absent and Rayray said it was because he broke his arm. Then everybody wanted to know how, crowding around Rayray to be the first ones to get the information.

"He missed the fence," Rayray said. "He was tryna jump from the big swings to this high fence that's like three feet away and he wasn't swinging high enough. I *told* that jive turkey before he even jumped that he needed to be swinging higher than that because even a fool knows you gotta get some height to fly over to the fence! When his mama was taking him to the emergency room, she said, 'If your arm isn't broken, *I'm* gonna break it because I told you about jumping out of those swings like that.'"

Everybody laughed, but it was hard for me not to imagine Trevor falling through the air—how scared he must have been, reaching and grabbing at nothing. I turned and looked at Samantha. She was shaking her head but maybe she was thinking the same thing.

In the summertime, Trevor's skin turned the prettiest copper brown. Once, when he was standing next to me at the park, I saw his bare arms up close, just hanging all quiet along his sides—and the skin, the way it had so many beautiful colors in it, the way it looked all golden somehow, stopped me. I stared at his arms and saw the Trevor that was maybe inside of the Evil Trevor—just a regular boy with beautiful skin. I saw that, even though he was mean all the time, the sun still stopped and colored him and warmed him—like it did to everybody else.

When I got to my desk, I looked up and saw the Jesus Boy looking at me. I couldn't tell what his face was trying to say—it was just blank and open and strange. I cut my eyes at him and opened my notebook even though I didn't have to yet.

Maribel's seat was right behind mine.

"That Jesus Boy is always *looking* at you," she whispered.

"Only way you'd know is if you're always looking at *him*," I whispered back. I felt her poke me in the back, but ignored it.

I wrote my name at the top of the page. Beneath it, I wrote the date. Beneath that, I drew a picture of a kid on a swing. Kids said it felt like flying to jump through the air, catch onto that fence, then let yourself climb down. They said something about being up that high let you see all over the place in a way that felt different than looking at the world from a window. I thought back to the day before when me and Sean were talking about those bridges he wanted built. Seems kids on this side of the highway were always trying to figure out ways to fly and run and cross over things and... get free or something.

Maribel was wearing a green sweater with THE CASEY SCHOOL written across the front in white letters. The sweater was too small and there were tiny lint balls on it. Everybody always seemed to be thinking about some other place.

I snuck another look at the Boy. He was still staring at me. I stuck out my tongue at him and turned to a clean page.

Ms. Johnson came in, took attendance and then she said, "Did everyone get a chance to personally introduce themselves to..." And then she said the new boy's name again—like she'd done the day before.

But I don't remember it now because the minute she called it, he stood up and said, "Everybody calls me Jesus, Ms. Johnson." Some of the kids laughed. Most of us just looked at him.

Ms. Johnson looked around at all of us and all of us found other stuff besides her to look at.

"I like Jesus," the boy said and sat back down.

I don't know if he meant he liked Jesus the person or Jesus the name, but I guess Ms. Johnson thought it was Jesus the name because she said, "Okay...Jesus." Her face just stayed calm so we couldn't tell what she was thinking.

"There's only two things wrong with that," Rayray said. He was sitting way in the back of the classroom and everybody turned around real fast to look at him. For a minute, the only sound was chair legs scraping against the floor.

"What's that?" Ms. Johnson said. She was frowning now. Ms. Johnson's a good teacher in a lot of ways. She laughs and I like teachers who laugh. And once a week she brings some kinda snack for us all—like doughnuts or mini candy bars or cinnamon graham crackers or really sweet cherries. And she always seems to bring the snacks on a day when I'm the hungriest, which is usually a day when school lunch is the worst—like on goulash day when they pour this stewy stuff that has things like green peppers and eggplant in it all over perfectly good rice and completely ruin it. Whenever they have that, I ask if I could just have the rice and Miss Costa always says *No* like it's against some kind of school-lunch law to serve goulash and rice separately. So on those days I'm really hungry and that's usually when Ms. Johnson decides to pull out her snacks.

The other nice thing about Ms. Johnson is she wants you to understand stuff. I mean, she doesn't just teach us and if we don't get it, she keeps on moving. She really cares about us understanding things and she'll take a real long time explaining something until she's sure everybody's got it. Sometimes that's a little bit boring if you already understand it and she's still explaining it. But that doesn't happen with me because I'm usually the last one to get it. The things I don't understand the most are science, math, grammar and geography. I understand independent reading and journal time and I understand the story part of writing but not things like diagramming a sentence or semicolons. Anyway, that's why when Rayray said what he said, Ms. Johnson stopped taking attendance to ask him about it. She wanted herself and all of us to understand.

"What are the two things wrong with it, Rayray?" And that's

another thing I like about Ms. Johnson—Rayray's name is really Raymond Raysen, but he decided he wanted everyone to call him Rayray. When he told Ms. Johnson that, she jumped right into calling him the name he wanted. Everybody calls me Frannie and so does Ms. Johnson, but even if I would've said, "Call me Floyjoy McCoy from now on, Ms. Johnson," my name would be Floyjoy McCoy. I guess it's strange that nobody ever calls me by my first name— Abigail or even Abby. I guess it's because Sean can almost say Frannie—it sounds kind of crooked, like somebody saying it under-water, but we know what he's saying. And maybe that's why it stuck—because of him.

Rayray leaned back in his chair. He was wearing this big shirt that said BLACK IS BEAUTIFUL with a black hand making a Black Power fist underneath the words. The shirt was too big for Rayray. He's real skinny, so when he wears big clothes, mostly you see the clothes, not Rayray. He slouched down in his seat and just about disappeared into that big shirt.

"Well, first of all," he said, "Jesus wasn't a boy, he was like God's son but not a man either—like a *Thing*-type person. Like a spirit guy."

Ms. Johnson and the rest of us just looked at him.

"And second of all, he wasn't white. He was like spirit-colored or something."

"What's spirit-colored?" his friend Chris asked. "I never heard of no spirit color."

I could see Rayray's little head inside his big shirt. He was frowning. "Like the color of air, brother-man. You know, like no color."

"When those cats put nails in him, he bled, though," somebody else said. "What color was his blood?"

Rayray shrugged. "Right on, my brother-man, I feel what you're saying. Blood is red no matter who it's coming out of. But that ain't where I'm going, you see? That kid ain't Jesus is all *I'm* saying."

"Say, brother," the kid said, which was jive talk for *I agree with you.*

Say, brother, I signed underneath my desk, then looked down at my hands. I had a pockmark on the center of each palm left over from the time I had the chicken pox. The marks were small and reddish brown. Sometimes when I was thinking about something real hard, they started itching. Maybe in another world, somebody would've thought they were nail holes, I don't know.

Mama lost one baby before I was born. Her name was Lila and she died when she was a month old. Something about her lungs. Something about her blood. We don't talk about her much. But there are pictures. Sometimes Mama kisses my palms and calls me God's gift.

I wondered what the inside of the Jesus Boy's hands looked like. I wondered if his mama kissed them and called him silly names. Of course when I looked up, he was staring at me again. Old Big Eyes.

"He's not saying he's Jesus-Jesus, right?" Rayray asked. "He's saying that's—like some nickname. I know this Spanish guy named Jesus but it's pronounced the Spanish way—not like the real guy. This kid ain't saying he's the real guy, right? I mean, how's he gonna be God's son and be in Ms. Johnson's class? No offense, Ms. Johnson, but even if that Jesus Boy was spirit-colored, he wouldn't be coming to Price. If he was really God's son, he'd probably go to a private school."

"Like where?" Maribel said. "The Casey School closed. There's not any private schools on this side of the highway. If there was one, I'd be going to it."

"Or like Catholic school," somebody else said. "Someplace with some religion, right?"

I saw Ms. Johnson smile a little bit. "I don't think that's what Jesus is saying about himself, everyone, are you?"

Ms. Johnson and everybody else looked at the Jesus Boy. He didn't move or shake his head or anything, just sat there, staring off.

"Are *you*?" Rayray asked him. "You aren't saying you're like God's son, are you?"

"I don't think it matters," Ms. Johnson said. "What matters is—"

"Aren't we all God's children?" Samantha said quietly. She looked around the room, taking us all in. "Each of you," she said, "is a true child of God." She turned to the Jesus Boy. "Maybe some are truer than others."

Rayray just looked at her and shrugged. "Jesus don't belong in this room is all I'm saying. And that cat's saying he's Je—" He stopped talking and stared at the Jesus Boy and frowned. Then we all looked at him.

He had his hands on his desk and was looking down at them. I saw a tear fall onto his pale hand and then another one, but he wiped them away real quick.

I heard myself saying, "He's crying, Ms. Johnson. The Jesus Boy is crying."

"Dag," Rayray said. "I didn't mean to make him cry. I swear, Ms. Johnson. I wasn't trying to be mean. I was just saying—"

"I'm not *crying*," Jesus Boy said real fast, shooting me a look that was so evil, I couldn't believe it came from his face.

"Are you all right?" Ms. Johnson said, her hand on his shoulder.

"Yeah. I'm okay," the Jesus Boy said, his voice soft again, so soft that maybe some of the kids didn't hear him.

"I lived on the other side of the highway already," the Jesus Boy said softly. He kept looking down at his hands, like he was talking to them, like he was talking to himself. "We...my family didn't belong there." He looked up and around at each one of us. It felt like everything stopped. There weren't tears in his eyes, but they were sad. "My daddy said it would be better here," he said, almost whispering it. "He said people would be...he said people would be... you know, nice to me." He looked down at his hands again. After a minute, he put his head down on his desk and sighed.

We all stared at him, and Ms. Johnson bent down and whispered something in his ear. He nodded and she put her hand on his back and led him out of the room. As he walked out the door, I could see that his face was all squinched up but his hands were just flat and calm, hanging down at his sides. Then he sniffed and his face just sort of sagged. I put my head down on my desk and closed my eyes.

"Is he some kind of crybaby or something?" I heard someone ask.

"Nah," I heard Rayray say softly. "You heard the brother-man. He's just like a little bit lost. It be's like that sometimes."

"Right on," I heard somebody else say. "It be's like that."

Usually, when Ms. Johnson left the room, we lost our minds with talking and jumping around and throwing things at each other. Rayray always acted the craziest. He could do standing backflips and usually did them in the aisle. But that day, he just sat quietly in his seat, rolling his pencil slowly back and forth across his desk. That day, the room was completely quiet. It was like we were all glued to our seats. It was like somebody had come into the room and gently lifted our tongues right on out of our mouths.

PART TWO

Chapter 14

When Trevor came back to school on Monday, he'd written NY KNICKS all over his cast and wouldn't let anybody write anything else.

"You ain't messing up the Knicks!" he said, standing in the school yard like he was the king of it with his broken-up arm all crossed and all.

"Knicks already messed up," Chris said. "Even the Cavaliers beat them."

"Yeah—for the first time in history," Trevor said.

"Still got their butts beat. I'm trading all my Knicks cards for Cavaliers. You got any?" Chris took a stack of basketball cards out of his pocket and held them out to Trevor.

Trevor scowled down at the cards and said, "Man, you better get out of my face."

Lots of people had been mad when the Knicks got beat by the Cavaliers. Even though it was the first time in the history of basketball, people lost their minds. Sean read every single sports page he could get his hands on.

Everything is changing, he'd said, looking a little lost.

It had snowed all weekend and the school yard looked like something out of a picture. Over where the little kids played, the jungle gym and slide and everything was all covered in white. Later on, they'd come outside and their tiny little feet would leave dirty prints everywhere. But now, it was just beautiful, the sky so bright over everything you had to shield your eyes. I stood there looking up at the sky, thinking about what Sean had said that morning. When we got to the place where he turned off to go to Daffodil, he punched me gently on the shoulder and signed, *I don't care about those dumb old girls.*

But he was lying and we both knew it. I watched him walk away, all dressed like a Black Panther but looking a little bit smaller than when we'd left the house that morning.

I didn't see the Jesus Boy come into the school yard until he was standing right near us, his hands in his pockets, his pale face turned up toward the sky, his long hair hanging all curly down his back. He saw me looking and waved. Samantha waved back.

The pocks on my palms itched. Whenever I scratched them, I thought about the sign for Jesus—the middle finger of one hand brushing over the palm of the other.

Maribel came over to us and stood next to Samantha. I rolled my eyes. She was wearing a new pair of platform boots—the shiny leather kind with the buckle. When I'd asked Mama if I could get them, she'd given me a look and said, *You can't even walk right in flat shoes!*

"A penny for your thoughts, Jesus Boy," Maribel said.

When me and Samantha didn't laugh, she said, "Well, that's all that boy seems to have. He came in with some more on Saturday. They must have a penny garden in their yard or something."

"Copper's supposed to be good for dirt," I said.

Maribel made a face but Samantha smiled.

Jesus Boy walked slowly, his head still kind of lifted a bit. He went and stood by the fence. After a few minutes, Trevor and all of them went over to him.

"You still here?" Trevor said.

The Jesus Boy looked down at his boots. He was wearing a new-looking blue peacoat that was a little too big for him.

"You hear a brother talking to you?" Trevor said.

The Jesus Boy looked up again and sort of shrugged.

"Rayray, you think this white cat's—"

"Leave him alone, Trev," Rayray said, his voice trembling a bit. "He ain't messing with us."

"Rayray's talking back to Trevor?" Maribel whispered. "You know it must be snowing."

But Samantha smiled. "He's taking up for Jesus Boy. Bible says when Jesus Christ came back, there were miracles everywhere."

"Nah," I said. "I think he just lost his mind. He was always a little bit crazy, so it's not some miracle or anything."

Trevor turned to Rayray. "I know you ain't trying to tell me what to do now." He tapped his ear with his good hand. "I just know that ain't what I'm hearing."

"Why you gotta be so . . . so mad all the time, Trev," Rayray said, taking a step back.

Trevor was quiet for a moment; he looked a little bit confused. Then he shook his head, laughed and turned back to the Jesus Boy.

Me and Samantha and Maribel stood shivering across from them. For some reason, I knew something was coming that I didn't want to see. I saw the way Trevor's face got angry again when he talked to the Jesus Boy. I saw the way the other kids were starting to move in closer.

"Well, it's just a bit too cold out here for me," I said to Samantha. "I'm heading inside." But just as I started walking away from them, I heard Trevor curse the Jesus Boy and tell him to throw up his hands. I turned back then.

The one fight I'd ever had was back in second grade. A boy whose name I didn't remember anymore had tried to take the money Mama had given me for an after-school snack. The boy didn't get the money—he'd knocked me down and I'd kicked him hard in the knee. I didn't like fighting. Not seeing them. Not having them. After I'd had that fight, even though nothing really hurt and I still had my money, I cried and cried and cried.

Jesus Boy stood there. He had a long red string of licorice wrapped around his finger. "Why do you want to fight me, Trevor?" he said, then put the licorice in his mouth and chewed slowly, not taking his eyes off of him. "Is it because I have a daddy? And you don't?"

I stopped dead. Nobody talked about Trevor's daddy. The whole school yard seemed to get quiet. Some of the kids said, "Oooh."

"I know this cat ain't say what I thought he said." Trevor took a step closer to the Jesus Boy.

"You heard me right," the Jesus Boy said quietly, but there was a hardness inside the quiet that made me shiver even more. I watched the Jesus Boy's face. It seemed so calm, like it knew some next thing was coming and was more than ready for it.

"White boy, you must—"

"I ain't your white boy," the Jesus Boy said. "You colorblind?"

He stepped away from the fence. A step closer to Trevor. Trevor didn't back up, though.

I took a deep breath. I couldn't believe he was standing up there, trying to tell them he wasn't white. Even if he did have a brown daddy, there wasn't anything about him that looked Not White.

"Yeah," Chris said. "He's spirit-colored. Ain't that right, Rayray?"

Rayray just stared at the Jesus Boy like the rest of us—trying to find the Not White part of him.

Standing there in the snow, with all those kids standing around, it came to me—his calmness, his hair, the paleness of his skin—he'd always had to walk through the world this way, push through. Maybe he'd met a whole bunch of Trevors in his life. Maybe he'd go on meeting them.

"My mama isn't white and my daddy isn't white and as far as I know it, you're the one with the white daddy living across the highway." He took another step toward Trevor, but even as he said those words, his voice stayed quiet. But then I looked at his hand, watched it close into a fist.

"I saw his daddy on Saturday," I whispered to Samantha. "He's brown like us brown. Not even light-skinned."

Samantha's eyes went wide, then she frowned, trying to figure it out.

"I bet that isn't his real father," she said after a while. "The way Joseph wasn't really Jesus' father."

"Girl," Maribel said. "This world is just too many things."

"Okay, Miss Parrot," I said. "Did you hear your mama or your grandma say that?"

"I heard *your* mama say it."

"Don't talk about my mama," I said.

"Shush, y'all," Samantha said. "Enough fights in this school yard already." She closed her eyes a moment and I knew it was to pray silently. When she opened them again, the Jesus Boy's hand was still in a fist, opening and closing. Opening and closing.

I looked at Trevor standing there, his face looking like it was trying to figure out what to do next. I looked at his broken arm. At the cast climbing all the way up to his shoulder, at the way his too-small coat couldn't quite cover it. The fence in the park faced the highway.

Maybe he'd hoped he could jump and keep on jumping—through the sky and across the highway, on and on until he landed right back in his daddy's arms.

And maybe because Trevor didn't have anything to say back to the Jesus Boy, maybe that's why he took a swing at him with that one good arm, missing and stumbling, then falling. And maybe because Trevor had always been on the evil side, maybe that's why kids started laughing when he fell, instead of running to him and helping him up out of the snow.

"You *crying*, man?" Rayray said. He looked confused and surprised. He was standing just a few feet away from his friend. But he didn't move toward Trevor. Didn't try to lift him up out of the snow. "I can't believe you're *crying*," he said.

"I ain't crying!"

I went to Trevor. The minute I saw him falling, I went toward him. It was automatic. Something inside me just said, "Go!" And I did. Because Trevor was falling and then he was in the snow. And in the snow he looked smaller and weaker and more human than any of us. When I looked up, the Jesus Boy was on the other side of me. And we were both lifting Trevor even as he tried to shake us off him and keep from crying.

Then Trevor was standing again. Standing but cursing both of us. But his curse words sounded strange—hollow and faraway. Like he was just learning them. Like he was practicing at being some kind of tough kid. Instead of truly being one.

Then he just stopped cursing and stood there, his head hanging down, his one good hand in his pocket. He didn't look like Trevor anymore. Standing there all pale and sad and shivering, he looked like he was somebody else.

Harlem Summer

Walter Dean Myers

ME AND HENRY TAKE A RIDE DOWNTOWN
AND A TRIP ACROSS THE HUDSON
TO FORTUNE AND HIGH ADVENTURE

We can't just jump up and ask Fats if we can play with him," Henry said as we stood outside of the Apollo Theater. "I think we should just say that we'd like to play at the Apollo. That way he'll know that we play and then he'll ask what we play. I'll tell him you blow sax and I wail on guitar, then we can just ease on into us playing together later."

"Yeah, but I want to play with him now," I said. "So maybe we should tell him that we were thinking about making a record."

"You think we're ready to make a record?"

"I've heard some of the Black Swan records and they're pretty good," I said. "You know what might be better is to ask him if we can get together in September."

"Whoa—and then we can practice over the summer!"

That sounded good to me. My dad had met Mr. Pace, the guy who owned Black Swan Records. I didn't want to tell Henry just yet, but I was sure we were on our way.

"Hey, is that it?" Henry pointed to a big green truck that had stopped on the other side of the street.

The crosstown trolley rolled slowly by and I tried to look through the windows to see if anyone was getting out of the truck. When the trolley had passed I saw Fats standing on the sidewalk looking over toward the Apollo.

Fats was wearing a suit jacket and a tie that was loose around his neck. When he saw me coming toward him he grinned that big grin of his and I smiled back.

"On time!" Fats pointed a big finger at me and made a face. I was so happy and excited I could have peed root beer.

"Hi, Fats." I shook his hand. "This is my friend Henry."

Fats beckoned to the guy who was driving and he got out of the big Mack and came up to us.

"Crab Cakes, these are my good friends Henry and Mark," Fats said. "Mark here is a little sweet on my sister, Edie, and maybe there's a song there somewhere."

I extended my hand toward Crab Cakes and he grabbed it and pumped it and then reached for Henry's hand and did more of the same. "You got a dog?" he asked.

"No, I don't have a dog," I said.

"You like dogs, huh?" Henry asked, giving me a look.

"I like my dog, Abby," Crab Cakes said. "I raised her from when she was firstest born. She couldn't even keep her eyes open."

"That happens sometimes," I said.

"We all ready to roll?" Fats pointed to the truck.

Henry and I both said yes. Crab Cakes got into the driver's seat, and Fats squeezed into the cab with him. Fats said there was plenty of room in the rear.

Two minutes later me and Henry were sitting on the floor of the truck bumping along 125th Street. Henry didn't say anything but I knew he was mad. The ride was breaking us up. We were bouncing off the truck floor like two black-eyed peas on a hot griddle and nowhere near enough to Fats to talk to him.

We rode fifteen minutes or so and then we heard the engine cut off. I could smell the river and when Fats hollered into the back of the truck that we had a while to wait before the ferry came we got out.

"I'm going to get something to eat," Fats said. "You guys stay with the truck."

Henry didn't say anything but I could tell he was still mad by the way his lips stuck out. We were at the 48th Street ferry terminal. It had grown cool and I felt a few drops of rain. I was having second thoughts about the whole job. I wiped the sweat from inside my collar as Crab Cakes came to the back of the truck and started talking about his dog again.

"I got her when she was about one day old," Crab Cakes said. "First thing she saw when she could see real good was me."

"That's good," Henry said. "She's home waiting for you now, right?"

"Naw, she's down home in Baltimore." Crab Cakes snorted twice, hunched his shoulders up and down twice, too. He was a small dude, maybe nineteen or twenty, and a little bug-eyed. "Down on North Central Avenue. You know where that is?"

"No."

"I live there all my life," Crab Cakes said.

"Go-o-o-d," Henry said, giving me a poke with his elbow.

Crab Cakes was a little weird. It wasn't just that he was talking about the dog, it was the way he kept hunching his shoulders when he talked and glancing around as if he was looking for somebody.

"You play an instrument?" Henry asked Crab Cakes.

"No, I got a dog," was the answer.

"Go-o-o-d," Henry said again.

It was 9:00 and we just sat there waiting and sweating, mostly sweating, until a little past 9:30 when we saw Fats coming back. He brought a bag of doughnuts and passed them around. Then he told us to get back into the truck and soon we were moving onto the ferry.

I had crossed the river on the ferry before, but never inside a truck. I think it would have been all right if I was in the cab. The smell of the water was good and the ride on the ferry was easy. A seagull landed on the tailgate and looked in at me and Henry with its head cocked to one side.

"This is not exactly the way to fame and fortune," Henry said.

"It's the way to five dollars and getting in with Fats," I said.

"Yeah," Henry said, wiping the sweat off his face with his shirt-tail, "him and this dude's dog."

Crab Cakes didn't seem to be as bright as me and Henry so I figured that Fats must have hired him because he could drive, or maybe because he was strong. Either way, he was getting in the way of us talking to Fats.

The ferry didn't take long and soon we were riding in New Jersey.

The roads in New Jersey were even worse than the ones in New York. When we heard the engines cut off I was sore and mad. We got out and I saw we were in an alley somewhere. A short white man came out and spoke to Fats. Then he came over to me and Henry and gave us the once-over. He looked like a tough guy.

"Bob Auerbach," he announced, looking us over.

"Henry Brown." Henry stuck his hand out but the white guy didn't shake it.

"You boys get the crates on the truck as fast as you can," he said. "I don't want to be here all night."

There was a loading platform and me and Henry went into the warehouse where there was a mountain of crates. Mr. Auerbach stood by the door and counted the wooden crates as we took them out to the loading platform where Fats and Crab Cakes were putting them on the truck. There was another white guy sitting in a corner with a shotgun across his lap. Henry took one quick look at the guy and rolled his eyes.

I was flat-out scared of guns and I kept my head down and didn't look around too much. What I was thinking was that maybe the crates that we were taking out of the warehouse had been stolen. Maybe *we* were even stealing them. The crates were marked WILDROOT HAIR TONIC and they weren't too heavy but there were a lot of them.

Henry and I were dripping with sweat when we got the last crates loaded. There was just enough room for us to squeeze into the back. Mr. Auerbach came and looked inside the truck.

"Don't let them shift around too much," he said in a gravelly voice.

Either Fats or Crab Cakes closed the back flap and in a moment, hot, tired, and with almost no air to breathe, we were bumping along again.

"Yo, Mark, we stealing?" Henry's voice came out of the darkness.

"If we don't know what the deal is we can't be stealing," I said. "If the police stop us we'll say we were just hired to load the truck."

"What you think Fats knows?"

"I don't want to know what Fats knows because then I'll know more than I want to know," I said. "And when I saw that guy sitting in the corner with that shotgun I knew right then that I didn't want to know anything."

The ride back took exactly forever. I could tell when we drove onto the ferry because I could smell the water. When we were rolling again I didn't hear much traffic and wondered where we were headed. I was getting nervous and Henry had moved right into his whiny voice so I knew he was nervous, too. When the truck finally stopped and the back opened, it was Fats. At first I didn't know where we were but then I saw that we were on 126th Street and St. Nicholas Avenue.

"What time is it?" I asked.

"Quarter past two," Fats answered, pulling one of the cases down.

"We going to unload the truck?" I asked, knowing I was already going to catch it when I got home.

"I don't know," Fats said. "Right now we just got to wait here a while. How you doing?"

"I'm roasted through," Henry said.

"I'm going to sit in the cab and look out for our connection," Fats said.

"Hey, Fats." I was talking funny because my mouth was so dry. "You know me and Henry play with a band. You ever hear of The Fabulous Three?"

"No, I haven't," Fats said. "Maybe one day you'll invite me to one of your sessions."

"Yeah, sure," I said.

Fats went up toward the front of the truck and leaned against the front fender. When he was leaning against the truck that way you could see just how big he was, which was enormous.

We waited for another fifteen minutes and then a dark car pulled up behind us. Two white guys got out and came over to us. Fats came to the back and told us to hand down a crate. They opened the crate right there on the street and pulled out two bottles of liquor. One of the guys, a small dude with a pinched face, took the top off one of the bottles, sniffed it, and handed it back to Fats.

"Just drive it up to the garage and leave it there," he said.

"Will do," Fats said.

"Ain't your crew kind of young?" Pinch-face asked.

"Yeah." Fats nodded and rolled his eyes. "And they ain't lost their wonderfulness yet!"

"I'm Henry Brown," Henry said, offering his hand.

The guy ignored Henry's hand but peered closely at him before turning and starting back toward his car.

The car moved around us slowly, and Fats was already stuffing some of the bottles into his coat pockets.

"When are we getting paid?" Henry asked.

Fats pulled some money out of his shirt pocket and paid us each the five dollars we had been promised. He pulled the tarp closed at the back of the truck and told Crab Cakes to take it up to 138th Street.

"The same place we picked it up," he said.

Me and Henry were both glad to see that truck roll off.

"So when we going to get together?" I asked Fats.

"Sooner than that!" he said. "I got to hear you boys blow!"

Fats walked with a side-to-side swing. He was so big he looked funny waddling down the street.

"You think he's really going to come hear us play?" Henry asked. ,

"We practice steady and by Christmas we're going to have a record starring Fats Waller and The Fabulous Three," I said.

I HAVE TROUBLE GETTING UP IN THE MORNING
TO GO TO WORK. I HAVE TROUBLE ON THE JOB.
I HAVE TROUBLE GETTING BACK UP TO HARLEM.
AND THE REAL TROUBLE BEGINS.

When I got home Mama was up and started in yelling at me about how she had carried me in the womb for nine months and how I wasn't even grateful. Then she woke Daddy up and told him that his worthless son had finally come home. Then she started yelling at him for not saying nothing and how he didn't care if I turned out to be nothing but trash.

"Why don't you ask him where he's been?" Mama yelled at Daddy.

"Where you been?" Daddy asked.

"Ask him if he was with his hoodlum friends," Mama said.

"You been with your hoodlum friends?"

"Why you asking him that, because you know if he was out doing dirt he ain't going to tell the truth!"

Daddy said something about there wasn't no use asking me if I was going to lie anyway and Mama got all over him about that. When I went to bed they were still arguing but it was better than Mama yelling at me.

Mama woke me up in the morning by shaking me and screaming in my ear that it was the third time she had called me.

"Now you don't have time for breakfast!" she said when I got my feet over the side of the bed. "Do you have money for a sandwich?"

I remembered the five dollars and nodded. She gave me a mean look and left with a *humph!* I looked at myself in the mirror and it was not a pretty sight. Eyes half closed. Pajamas buttoned wrong. A little dried something on my cheek. I rinsed my face with cold water and looked again. No better.

By the time I had finished washing up and getting dressed, Mama had made toast and handed me a piece as I headed toward the door. The Third Avenue elevated train rocked and shook its way slowly downtown and I decided that any work that started this early could not be right for me.

Exactly one hundred and three billion people seemed to work around 14th Street and they were all jammed up coming out of the station. A clock in a store window showed that I still had three minutes to go before I was late.

I met Miss Fauset in the lobby and we took the elevator upstairs. The staff of *The Crisis* was just finishing up the July issue and I watched as Miss Fauset pasted up copies of the stories on what she called a dummy board. Everything was checked twice.

"Dr. DuBois does not tolerate mistakes," she said.

I found out that Dr. W. E. Burghardt DuBois was the head of the magazine staff, and it soon was clear to me that nobody messed with him. Miss Fauset was the literary editor, and a woman named Effie Lee Newsome ran the children's section. I asked Miss Fauset if I would be doing pasting and she said probably not. I would be running errands, taking material to the printer, and checking the ads.

She wanted me to take several back issues of the magazine home and read them carefully. She also gave me another magazine, *The Survey Graphic*, to read. I wondered if I was going to be paid to do all of this reading.

Miss Fauset told me to start looking through the magazines and to find the works of people like Langston Hughes, Arna Bontemps, and Countee Cullen.

"These are *very* young and *very* talented writers," she said.

"They the New Negroes?" I asked.

"Yes, they are." Miss Fauset's eyebrows went up. "And they're very exciting."

She went over to her desk, pulled out a photograph, and then came back and laid it in front of me.

"Langston Hughes!" She said it like I was supposed to fall out or something.

I looked at the dude and saw that he had two eyes, a nose, and a mouth like everybody else, so there didn't seem to be anything new about him. I could only see one ear but I figured he had the other one so I didn't ask about it. I liked Miss Fauset though, so I didn't want to look as if I wasn't knocked out.

"He does look a little new," I said.

That gave her a little smile and I was glad I had lied.

My first official job at *The Crisis* was to go through the advertising section and compare it to the invoices from the previous month, to make sure we had not left anybody out. It certainly wasn't hard work but it was boring and it was hot.

The fans in each corner of the large office did two things: First, they pushed the hot air in your face. Then they made a little whirring noise as they turned slowly back and forth like they were trying to hypnotize you. Every time the fan pushed another little hot breeze into my face, my eyes started closing. I had to stand up just so I wouldn't fall asleep.

I looked around at all the other people in the office. They looked busy and interested in whatever thing they were doing. Miss Fauset said I was to go to lunch at twelve o'clock and I kept looking at the clock. The red hand went around and around but the others barely moved. I had to work to look away as long as I could and guess how much time had passed. Working was definitely not all it was cracked up to be.

For lunch I went to a diner on 15th Street that the office boy, Aussie Farrell, told me about. Me and Aussie had to go to lunch at different times in case someone wanted one of us to run an errand. I bought a pastrami on rye and an RC Cola. That was twenty-three cents. In Harlem you could have got the same pastrami and same RC Cola for fifteen cents.

The afternoon went by as slowly as the morning and I found out that I could actually fall asleep standing up. Everything in the office moved in the same rhythm as the fans except, of course, for the clocks, which moved slower and slower and slower.... ·

"It isn't going anywhere," Miss Fauset said when she saw me looking at the clock. "You don't have to watch it."

"Yes, ma'am."

By the time I was ready to go home I had a whole bag of books and magazines I had to read. Miss Fauset said I was going to love reading them and discovering what was going on in the black world, but it didn't seem that exciting to me. I lived in Harlem and I figured that was about as black as you could get without being in Africa.

The ride uptown was terrible. There were more people on the train and they were stinkier. I got home and started reading right after supper. I got through five pages of *The Souls of Black Folk* and started falling asleep. It was all about this heavy-duty drama stuff that sounded like school stuff except that it was black people. Then I had a great idea. I was going to tell Henry we should call ourselves The Hot Three instead of The Fabulous Three because that would make people think of The Hot Five, Louis Armstrong's group. I could practically hear us, with me playing sax like my man Buster Bailey sitting on a two-burner stove on a hot night, and Henry tearing up the strings, and Randy playing the ivories like Jelly Roll Morton—with our own business cards and everything. Or if I could get Randy to switch to clarinet, then Fats could play piano. That would be Groo with a capital V. Grooo-vy!

My brother was going out with this girl named Lavinia and they came tip-tipping in and soon they had parked themselves in the parlor, and Matt got his nerves swoll up enough to ask me to get her a glass of water. I told Matt that he was not a doctor yet and sure didn't have any servants running around and if Miss Lavinia wanted a glass of water I would point her toward the kitchen. Matt called me a plebeian. I told him to spell that out and when I look it up it had *better* not be anything bad.

Mr. Reece came by after supper, looking for Daddy, who had already taken off his shoes for the evening. When Daddy took his shoes off and "freed his bunions," he usually didn't put them back on again, not even for an extra job.

A lot of the jobs in Harlem were pickup jobs, just for the day. If you wanted to work for a moving company, you lined up on 126th Street and St. Nicholas Avenue. But if you wanted a pickup job at any of the clubs or cabarets, you had to see Mr. Reece. He and Daddy were good friends and when anything came along he let Daddy know. He came by after supper and said that two of the busboys were going to be out sick at Connie's Inn. Daddy asked Matt if he wanted to earn some extra money and he said no. Matt already had a summer job in an office on 136th Street and said that he had a lot of things to do for his boss in the morning. Mama was fixing to go out, putting on some face powder, but she stopped long enough to tell Daddy she didn't want Matt working in any club, anyway.

"Honey, we are black folks," Daddy said. "When we get a knock on the door it ain't no job, it's somebody looking for the rent. Folks in Harlem who want to eat can't be that particular."

"A doctor is particular!" Mama said, ending the discussion.

Mama left and Daddy was taking the jar of lemonade out of the icebox for Mr. Reece when I told him that I could use some extra money and would help clean the club.

"I see you waited until your mama left before saying anything," Daddy said. "But you can still go."

All the best musicians played at Connie's Inn. Me and Daddy and Mr. Reece started off together down to 131st where the club was located. It didn't take us very long and we got up there just as they were setting up the tables for dinner.

What they wanted me to do was to go around between the

nightclub acts and pick up the dirty dishes. They had black waiter suits in the back, and I tried a couple on before I found one with a waistline small enough and the legs long enough to fit me.

The crowd started drifting in around eight o'clock and then really picked up at nine. That's when the entertainment started, too.

The first act was a chorus line, dancing to a tune called "I'm Just Wild About Harry." The girls wore short skirts that stuck out from their waists and black ribbons on their arms. They were looking mighty good and moving those big legs right on the beat.

"You ain't here to check out the girls," said Pete, the head of the busboys. "You clean tables eleven to twenty and if you get any dirt on a customer the cleaning bill is coming out of your pay."

I should have punched him in his face but since he was about six inches bigger than me and uglier than a baboon's butt on Monday morning, I let him slide.

Around midnight, Daddy came over to me and told me that a famous white piano player named Jimmy Durante had just come in. I looked around for him and saw him sitting with another white man and two women. The guy had a nose big enough to play a tune on.

I worked for four hours, until 1:30, and made almost two dollars in tips. All the time I was working I watched the saxophone players and listened to them carefully. What I liked was the way they made everything look so easy. They never squeaked or missed a note. That's the way I wanted to play. I could imagine myself playing as good as them and even better. Maybe I would play something really fast, something jumping and have everybody standing up clapping, or maybe I would play something slow, like "Always" and have people in love holding hands or looking into each other's eyes. Then when I saw I was getting to them, I would look over at Fats and he would nod and roll his eyes. Yeah.

Me and Daddy got to our house, and Edie was sitting on the front steps.

"What are you doing out this late, girl?" Daddy asked.

"I had to see Mark," Edie said softly, her head down.

"Mark, you didn't do nothing to be ashamed of, did you?" Dad looked at me out of the corners of his eyes.

"No," I said.

"Well, you walk Miss Edie home and get right back here."

Soon as Daddy went inside I asked Edie what was wrong.

"Fats told me to tell you that Crab Cakes is gone," she said.

"So?"

"So? What you mean *so*?"

"What do you mean?"

"I mean that crazy fool drove off with Dutch Schultz's truck, and all the liquor y'all got from Jersey," Edie said.

"That truck belonged to Dutch Schultz?" I asked, hoping I had heard wrong. Dutch Schultz was only the most notorious gangster in New York City.

"Yes, it did," Edie said. "And he's talking about all of you owing him a thousand dollars and how he's going to have one of my brother's fingers cut off for every hundred dollars he ain't got."

"I don't have his liquor, Edie," I said. "And I don't even know Crab Cakes. I just met him the night we got the stuff from New Jersey."

"You also met Dutch Schultz that night when y'all came back." Edie squinted her eyes up. I remembered the pinch-faced dude. "And he met you. So you better start looking for Crab Cakes, that truck, and that whiskey or all of you are going to be in big trouble. You hear me?"

"That don't make no sense because I don't have any money to give anybody," I said.

"You got fingers and things he can cut off, ain't you?" Edie asked.

That's not what I wanted to hear.

ELIJAH OF BUXTON

Christopher Paul Curtis

Chapter 7

MR. LEROY SHOWS HOW TO *REALLY* MAKE A LESSON STICK

The on-again-and-off-again clouds got to be always on and they ended up blacking out the moon two nights later. Since it's dangerous to work with a axe when there ain't no light atall, Mr. Leroy figured he had to lay off his work early. It ain't our usual custom. Most nights he kept on working till long after I was home and sleeping, but this night we started walking together out of Mrs. Holton's field.

I don't work nowhere near as hard as Mr. Leroy, but that don't matter, I was good and tuckered out. Betwixt schooling and studying and choring 'round the Settlement and working till past dark with him for most of the last couple weeks, I'll own up that I was lagging that night and my mind might not've been quite right. That ain't to make no excuses 'bout what happened, it's just telling the truth.

Most times me and Mr. Leroy don't say much whilst we work,

not only 'cause it's hard to talk to someone that's knocking away at trees and swinging a heavy axe, but also 'cause Mr. Leroy don't seem partial to running his mouth nohow. To my way of thinking, that meant us walking home together was a good time to get a whole lot of the conversating done that we'd been missing out on.

Most every other night I gotta walk home by myself, and I ain't complaining, but sometimes it does seem like the walking would be a lot easier if I had someone to do it with.

It ain't no sign of being a fra-gile boy, but if you have to walk home on a night where the moon's got blacked out, you just might get surprised and find yourself jumping at noises coming from the side of the road or from out the woods and then running all the way home screaming.

Anybody that has some sense would be a little afeared that one of those bears or snakes or wolfs might've wandered out of their regular area and come over here, so maybe twixt the being real tired from all my work, and the being real happy 'bout having some company, my mind didn't have no chance at being right that night when the moon was covered and Mr. Leroy and me walked home together.

Since he waren't much of a talker, I figured he had plenty of practice on being a listener, and I was jawing at him pretty regular and fast. Even though it happened two whole days ago, I was still mighty worked up 'bout Mr. Travis near snatching Cooter's ear off and not teaching us 'bout family breeding contests. So after I talked for a while 'bout fishing and animals in the woods and Ma's scratchy sweaters and how many first-place ribbons Champion and Jingle Boy got at the fair, I started in on what happened when I got all those lines forced at me.

Whilst we were walking for the first mile or so, Mr. Leroy would grunt and nod his head every once in a while, like he was paying some mind to what I was saying. But by the time I started in on talking 'bout Mr. Travis, we'd covered us two miles easy and Mr. Leroy waren't showing no kind of interest in nothing I was having to say. He just tromped on ahead looking like he was wishing I'd be quiet. But like I already owned up to, lots of things were coming together to make me want to talk and not pay too much mind to who it was I was talking to.

I said, "And Mr. Travis went berserk and afore you can blink he jumps clean 'cross the room and I cain't say how he did it but he must've been flying 'cause to get at Cooter Bixby he had to go over three rows of children and didn't one n'em desks get knocked aside nor toppled over nor didn't one n'em children have no footprints on 'em nor bruises from where he must've stepped..."

I could tell Mr. Leroy didn't particular want to hear all this. He didn't tell me to be still, but he did pick up the pace of his walking like he was rushing to get home. I warent 'bout to miss the chance to get this off my chest so I started halfway running and halfway walking to keep up with him.

I told him, "So Mr. Travis has got Cooter's ear wound up so tight that it's starting to look like somebody's finger 'stead of somebody's ear and it's 'bout the most awful thing you ever seen in all your days...."

Then I said 'em, I said those words that made it so the lesson 'bout familiarity and contempt'll be fixed in my mind for's long as I live, even if that's to fifty. I said, "And me and all 'em other little nigg—"

I knowed better. Ma and Pa didn't tolerate no one saying that word 'round 'em. They say it's a sign of hatred when a white person says it and a sign of bad upbringing and ignorance when one our own calls it out, so there ain't no good excuses.

I knowed better.

I didn't think Mr. Leroy was paying me no mind. I didn't even get the chance to get the whole word out. I never even saw it coming.

It felt like whatever rope it was that was holding up the moon gave out all the sudden and the moon slipped free and busted through the clouds and came crashing down to earth afore it exploded square on top of me!

All I saw at first was a bright light. Which I figured was Mr. Leroy backhanding me 'cross my mouth. Then I felt my senses flying away. Which must've been me falling toward the ground. Then I felt like I'd been chunked by the moon. Which would've been me knocking my head 'gainst the ground.

I don't think I was out for more'n a second, but when I came to, I wished I'd been out for a whole lot longer 'cause Mr. Leroy was standing over top of me with his hand drawn back, fixing to crack me all over again.

He made up for all the not talking he'd been doing whilst we walked. Now he commenced jawing at me just as hard as I'd been jawing at him.

He shouted, "Is you out your mind?"

I was 'bout to say, "No, sir," but I figured this was one n'em questions people ask just for the sake of asking it, they don't really want no answer. I probably couldn't've said nothing no way, my tongue was too busy roaming 'round my mouth, checking to see if any of my teeth had got set a-loose by Mr. Leroy's slap.

He said, "What you think they call me whilst they was doing this?"

He opened the front of his shirt and showed me where a big square with a letter T in the middle of it was branded into him. The scar was raised up and shiny and was real plain to see even if there waren't no moonlight atall.

"What you think they call me?"

Mr. Leroy was screaming like it was *him* that lost his mind.

"What you think they call my girl when they sold her? What kind of baby they call her from up on the block?"

Mr. Leroy was spitting and looking mad as a hatter. I sure was glad he'd gone and dropped his axe when he'd first busted me 'cross the mouth.

I said, "Mr. Leroy, sir, I'm sorry..."

"What name you think they call my wife when they take her to another man for his own? What?"

"I'm sorry, sir, I'm sorry..."

"How you gunn call them children in that school and you'self that name them white folks down home calls us? Has you lost your natural mind? You wants to be like one n'em? You wants to be keeping they hate alive?"

I saw that Mr. Leroy really *was* out of his mind! He must've thought I was a white person that said that word.

I begged him, "Mr. Leroy, sir, please! I ain't white! Please don't hit me no more!"

He raised his left hand and I closed my eyes and tried to mash myself down into the dirt.

He said, "White person? You thinking this here's 'bout some white person? Look at this. Look!"

I opened my eyes and saw he waren't gonna slap me again. He was showing me where his littlest finger on his left hand use to be. He was pointing at all that was left there, a little stump.

He said, "Who you think it was cut my finger off? Who?"

I didn't know if I should answer him or just keep quiet and let him have his say. I shrugged my shoulders.

He said, "A slave, that's who. And the whole time he slashing and stabbing at me trying to cut my throat, what name he calling me? What name?"

I said, "I know, sir, but I ain't gonna say it no more."

He said, "You thinks just 'cause that word come out from twixt your black lips it mean anything different? You think it ain't choke up with the same kind of hate and disrespect it has when *they* say it? You caint see it be even worst when *you* call it out?"

I told him, "Sir, I only said it 'cause I hear lots of children say it."

"What difference it make who you hear say it? I can understand a little if one of y'all freeborn use it, y'all's ignorant in a whole slew of ways. Y'all ain't been told your whole life that's what you is. But someone what was a slave, or someone whose ma and pa was a slave and raised them good like your'n done, that just shows you believing that what we be. That just shows you done swallowed they poison. And swallowed it whole."

There waren't gonna be no more hitting, I could tell Mr. Leroy was calming down. He commenced rubbing on his left arm then reached his hand down to help me up.

Once I got up I quick wiped away the tears that were trying to get in my eyes. It ain't being fra-gile, but don't nothing in the world make you want to bawl more than getting a good backhand slap when you ain't expecting it.

Mr. Leroy said, "Now belting you like that probably waren't the right thing to do, 'Lijah, but I ain't sorry I done it. If my boy, 'Zekial, was to call someone out they name like that, I prays to God someone would bust him up too. Y'all young folks gotta understand that's a name what ain't never called with nothing but hate. That ain't nothing but a word them slavers done chained us with and if God's just, like I know he is, one day it gunn be buried right 'long with the last one of 'em. That ain't one the things we need to be carrying to Canada with us.

"Now if you and me's gunn do any more working together, you know what you gotta say."

I did. I told him, "I'm sorry, Mr. Leroy, I ain't never gonna use that word again."

He said, "You got to always keep in mind, Elijah, that I'm growned and you ain't. You got to always 'member that we gets 'long just fine but I ain't your friend. I cares 'bout you like you's my own boy, but you always got to give me my respect. You saying that word ain't showing no respect for me, it ain't showing no respect for your folks, it ain't showing no respect for you'self, and it ain't showing no respect for no one what's had that word spit on 'em whilst they's getting beat on like a animal."

Mr. Leroy used his hat to brush the back of my shirt and pants off and reached his hand out for me to shake it, then said, "Elijah, it's my hope that there ain't no hard feelings twixt you and me. I likes the way you owned up to what you done."

I shooked his hand and said, "No, sir, ain't no hard feelings atall."

Some of the time when a growned person asks you a question, you're smart to tell 'em what it is they want to hear, but that waren't what I was doing.

I said there waren't no hard feelings 'cause I meant it.

Pa's always telling me that people that use to be slaves are toting things 'round with 'em that caint be seen with your regular eyes. He says once someone was a slave there's always gonna be a something in 'em that knows parts 'bout life that freeborn folks caint never know, mostly horrorific parts.

He tells me that's why I got to be sharp on my guard when I'm talking with anyone that got free. They've seen people acting in ways that caint help but leave scars and peculiarities. Things that I might not think mean nothing, but things that can cut 'em to the quick. So I waren't doing nothing but telling Mr. Leroy the truth when I told him I waren't holding no grudges and that I waren't gonna use that word again.

He said, "Good, son. 'Cause I really want you to know what I'm trying to say and sometimes I ain't too good with my words."

I said, "I know what you're trying to say, Mr. Leroy. It boils down to familiarity breeds contempt."

Mr. Leroy picked up his axe and swung it 'cross his left shoulder then put his right hand on my head. I'll always remember Mr. Leroy's hand on my head and the words he told me. I'll always remember that night when there waren't no moon and me and Mr. Leroy walked home together.

Chapter 8

THE MOST EXCITING NIGHT
OF MY LIFE SO FAR

The next day after school, I was in the stable shoveling manure when Old Flapjack gave a snort. I looked up and the Preacher was standing in the doorway.

"Evening, Elijah."

"Evening, sir."

"Do you remember when I asked if you'd be willing to do something to help the Settlement?"

"Yes, sir."

"Have you changed your mind?"

"'Bout what, sir?"

"Helping the Settlement."

"Why, no, sir, but what was it that..."

The Preacher unfolded a piece of paper and handed it to me.

COMING TO CHATHAM,
THREE NIGHTS ONLY

Sir Charles M. Vaughn and his world-renowned CARNIVAL OF ODDITIES will be traversing through Canada West on their way from Chicago, Illinois, to Buffalo, New York, and points east. Sir Charles has graciously agreed to allow the citizens of Chatham, Buxton, and nearby environs to witness for themselves what they have only read about in the nation's finest newspapers. Hear the Calliope!!! Taste the Sugared Treats!!! See the Most Unusual Freaks of Nature You Can Imagine!!! Witness the World's Greatest Hypnotist!!! Rare Patent Medicines Available. Games of Chance!!! Members of All Races Welcome. Wednesday, Thursday, and Friday Only!!!!

Cooter'd already told me about this carnival, but he'd made the mistake of asking his ma if he could go. She'd asked him if he was daft then said she was gonna make sure he didn't sneak out by having him sleep at the foot of her bed on Wednesday, Thursday, and Friday.

I told the Preacher, "All the growned folks said we gotta stay away from this. They said there's gambling and all sorts of horrible things going on there."

He said, "So what do *you* think about it? I've thought of a way we can use your God-given gift to help get some money for the Settlement, but if you're having second thoughts..."

"But Ma and Pa wouldn't never let me go to something like this."

"Elijah, there are lots of things that you do that I'm sure your mother and father would be shocked about. I'm positive they have no idea how much time you and Cooter spend wandering about in the forest late at night, do they? This wouldn't be much different than that. It would simply be a matter of meeting me later tomorrow night and then the two of us going to the carnival. I'd be there to make certain nothing bad happened to you. But, if you've changed your mind about helping the Settlement, I understand. It's easy to talk about being helpful, but actually doing what one has promised can be a lot more difficult."

I saw what the Preacher was doing, I saw how he was using growned-folks talk to paint me in a corner. But the way I look at things, there's accidentally getting painted in a corner and there's not minding getting painted in a corner. And, truth told, I didn't mind getting painted into this one. What could be more exciting than going to a carnival to see freaks of nature and watch someone get hypnotized? Plus, the Preacher had figured out a way for me to help the Settlement too, what could be better?

"But I ain't got no money to get in, sir."

"Elijah, your money is no good when I'm around. Besides, if you insist on paying me back you can always double up on your tithing when you go fishing."

It weren't for myself exactly, it was for the good of the Settlement, so I said, "When should I meet you, sir?"

"That's my boy! We'll meet tomorrow night. Bring a sack full of your stones."

As interesting as this was starting to sound, there waren't no way I was gonna miss going to this carnival!

—————

On Friday night, me and the Preacher first came to a clearing that was a bit off from the main set of noise and excitement. In the middle of the clearing was a tent that had a big fresh-painted sign out front that said:

See Madame Sabbar,
the Royal Huntress from Sweden!
She Has Slain 541 Swedish Moth Lions
with No Weapon Other Than
Her Slingshot!!!!

A white man with a walking stick and a straw hat stood on a box shouting to people to pay a dime to come see this hunting woman. He yelled, "Marvel at the deadly accuracy of Madame Sabbar's slingshot! Come one, come all! You will be amazed at the things she can do with a simple stone. You will want to come back again and again. Your friends and neighbours won't believe you when you tell them about the power that Madame Sabbar's simple weapon possesses! Witness for yourself the astounding little lady who has killed five hundred and forty-one of the fiercest beasts in all of Europe, the dreaded Swedish moth lion!"

One of the white farmers called out, "That's a load of hogwash! There ain't no lions in Sweden!"

The white man pointed his walking stick at the farmer and said, "You're absolutely right, sir! Which is further proof of Madame Sabbar's skill; it shows she's wiped out the entire lot of them! Now, you'll have to hurry. Our next-to-last show begins in two minutes. Who's going to pay the ridiculously small sum of one thin dime to see this amazing woman?"

I couldn't believe it! The Preacher pulled me into the line and we waited to go in and see this woman! I started shaking right off. I hadn't never seen no one who'd killed a lion afore! I hadn't never seen no one that's ever *seen* a lion afore!

When we got to the front of the line the Preacher put down two American dimes and we went into the tent. We sat on a row of benches right up near the front of the stage. On one end of the stage there were five bull's-eye targets. Next to the targets was a big board that had a thick, dark green forest painted on it.

You could tell it waren't no forest from 'round here 'cause these woods had monkeys hanging in the trees. There were also six holes the size of supper plates cut into the board so's it 'peared to be a big knothole in each one of the trees. Under each one of the holes was a fancy writ number going from one to six. 'Cross the top of the board, spaced the same distance one from the 'nother, were ten lit candles and under the candles it looked like someone had throwed a sheet over the very top of the board. The sheet said, THE JUNGLES OF SWEDEN!!!

We didn't wait but a minute afore the white man with the walking stick and straw hat came out on stage and told some jokes that didn't no one think were funny. After he saw he waren't gonna encourage nothing but hisses from the crowd, he introduced us to the slingshot lady, and fierce-looking as she was, it was easy to tell she really had killed five hundred lions!

The man said, "Please, ladies and gentlemen, boys and girls, help me welcome Madame Sabbar, and perhaps she will show us her dexterity with these deadly slingshots."

The man pointed at a table that had on top of it three fancy slingshots. Next to the slingshots were little piles of things I figured the woman was gonna shoot. There were some grapes and some peculiar-looking stones with holes in 'em and some real pretty marbles and some rocks that looked a little too light to be proper chunking stones.

A tiny amount of clapping came out the crowd and Madame Sabbar picked up one of the slingshots and one of the marbles. She aimed at the first bull's-eye target and shot off a marble. It hit dead centre and busted through some paper and runged a bell. She did the same thing with the next four targets, ringing a bell every time.

Folks didn't think this was such a big ruckus, 'specially not one worth paying no whole American dime for! Only one or two people clapped, but there was a lot more grumbling and hissing going on too.

The man said, "Astonishing! Astounding! But it doesn't end there, ladies and gentlemen. Once she has prepared herself, she moves on to a more challenging task. It is a well-known fact that the Swedish moth lion is drawn to candlelight, so once the roar of one of these fierce Scandinavian cats is heard, Madame Sabbar's first duty is to extinguish all of the candles as quickly as she possibly can!"

The man put his hand on his ear and said, "Hark! What was that?"

All the sudden it looked like we were gonna get our dime's worth after all!

Somewhere from behind the stage came a roar that sounded like Mr. Brown clearing flum outta his throat, but a lot louder, and Madame Sabbar sprunged to work! She picked up a different sling-shot and all sorts of who-struck-John busted loose!

First thing she did was aim at the ten candles sitting atop of the board with the six holes. She was using the odd-looking stones with holes in 'em and when they flewed 'cross the tent they made a sound like one n'em fat lazy Buxton bumblebees. Once the buzzing stones got to the candles, they put the flame out quiet as a whisper. Waren't a *one* n'em candles disturbed neither! The only thing that moved on each one was the wick. Why, with the tent getting fulled up with the buzzing of ten stones and the flames getting snuffed out one after the 'nother, 'twas a sight I'd've paid one of my *own* dimes to see!

But what she did next topped even that. She turned the slingshot out at all of us in the crowd and commenced firing over our heads, putting out all the candles that runged 'round the tent!

Seems like thinking you're 'bout to get busted in the head with a buzzing stone and not having it happen makes you want to give a good old whoop. Folks that'd ducked down or throwed their arms atop their heads came right back up cheering and clapping!

Madame Sabbar gave one n'em lady curtsies.

The man said, "Did I mislead you? Did I not tell you you'd be amazed? But, oh, ye of little faith, the story is not even half told!"

The man pointed his walking stick at the board with the jungle and the six knotholes.

"For not only must Madame Sabbar be on the lookout for the

dreaded Swedish moth lion, she must also keep a sharp watch for the lion's allies, the savage members of the Swedish Mobongo tribe, and especially the young chief of the tribe, MaWee!"

From behind the holey board came a set of screams and yelps and jibber-jabber, then a little white boy hanging on to a spear and sporting a big old soup bone on top of his head marched onto the stage. The only clothes he was wearing was the bottom half of a woman's dress that looked like it waren't nothing but a bunch of long leafs sewed together. On his cheeks were painted black stripes. He was hopping from one foot to the 'nother whilst someone banged on a drum. If he'd have done it any faster and with any kind of rhythm, it would have come pretty close to being dancing.

"Beware, Madame Sabbar," the man shouted. "Young MaWee is very angry because he knows of your reputation."

The boy shooked his spear at the slingshot lady, but 'stead of being angry, the look on his face made it seem he was afeared.

"But, what is this? Oh, no! MaWee has used some of his conjuring powers on Madame Sabbar and has rendered her blind!"

The little boy reached in a bag on his waist and throwed something all sparkling and flashing at the woman. The white man with the walking stick tied a blindfold 'round Madame Sabbar's face then pulled a cloth sack over that so's we could tell she waren't seeing a thing.

"And now that he has blinded her, MaWee will hide behind one of the trees in the Swedish jungle and most foully lie in wait for an ambush!"

The man turned the slingshot lady so's she was facing the board with the holes in it di-rect. MaWee walked behind it. But afore he went I got a good look at him. This waren't no Swedish jungle chief atall! This was Jimmy Blassingame, one of the white children from Chatham that studied at our school!

The man said, "Madame Sabbar, what can you see?"

The woman raised the sack so her mouth waren't covered and said, "Alas, I see nothing. The heathen's magic has left me completely sightless."

The man said, "Oh, woe! And look at the cowardly savage! He's preparing to attack! What shall we do? How shall we save this innocent white woman? I can give her a weapon, but in her state how shall she use it?"

The man reached onto the table next to Madame Sabbar and put a different slingshot in her left hand. In her right hand, he put a bunch of the purple grapes. She plucked one of 'em and set it in the sling.

All the sudden Jimmy Blassingame's face popped out of the hole that had the fancy THREE writ underneath it, the last hole on the right in the top row.

The man screamed, "Madame Sabbar! The coward is attacking! Fire your weapon!"

Madame Sabbar lifted the slingshot and let one n'em fat purple grapes fly. It splashed on the side of the tent five feet above Jimmy's head.

"Oh, no! She *is* blinded! And look! The savage is moving to another spot from which to waylay this innocent white maiden!"

Jimmy's head came outta hole number five, which was on the bottom row in the middle of the board.

"I've got it!" the walking stick man yelled. "You good citizens of Chatham can help by calling out the number of the hole in which that black...uh...that black-*hearted* barbarian is hiding!"

Jimmy's face showed up in the last hole on the right in the bottom row and 'bout half the crowd shouted, "Six!"

Why, that hunting lady couldn't see a thing but she shot one n'em grapes so fast and true that it caught Jimmy square in the middle of his forehead! He'd ducked his head so that was all that was poking out of the hole.

Everybody laughed so hard that the tent shooked!

Jimmy went to hole number five, hole number four, hole number one, and hole number three, and every time his forehead popped out, the crowd snitched on him and Madame Sabbar gave him the same treatment.

After 'while, all the grapes that got smashed on Jimmy's forehead started leaking down into his eyes so he bended over to wipe at 'em. But when he did this he was right in front of the fifth hole and the crowd shouted, "Five!"

Madame Sabbar raised the slingshot and fired the next grape so straight that it catched Jimmy, who hadn't had no chance atall to bend his face down, right twixt his eyes.

And waren't a person more shocked by this than Jimmy Blassingame! His mouth came wide open, he stood up, his face was now in front of the second hole and, doggone-it-all, some of the rotten folks in the crowd hollered out, "Two!"

Madame Sabbar quick shot another grape and it disappeared down Jimmy's throat, making a sound like a soap bubble getting busted!

Jimmy's hands came up to his neck and he staggered out from behind the board with the jungle and the holes and started flopping 'round on stage like a fish tossed out of water.

The man with the walking stick commenced cursing and saying words I ain't never heard afore. He picked Jimmy up and gave him a squeeze 'round the middle. The grape popped outta Jimmy's mouth and rolled out into the crowd.

You'd have thought 'twaren't a funnier thing in the world had ever happened.

Even the Preacher, who most times is a pretty serious man, took to throwing his head back and howling.

Jimmy Blassingame didn't even have sense enough to get off the stage. He sat plumb up there where the man had dropped him and cried so hard that purple and black streaks ran down his cheeks and splashed onto his chest.

It sure was a good thing for Jimmy that I was the only one from school who saw this. Sitting there with purple and black streaks running down his chest and bawling whilst wearing half a woman's leaf dress was the kind of thing that no one wouldn't let him forget about for years. It would have got tied up with his name same way mine's tied up with Mr. Frederick Douglass!

The man with the straw hat and walking stick pointed at Madame Sabbar and said, "Please, give yourselves a hand for saving the purity of this poor white damsel, and let us show our appreciation for the most accurate hunter to ever roam the jungles of Sweden!"

Everybody 'cept for me, the Preacher, and Jimmy Blassingame clapped and hollered and whistled hard as they could.

The Preacher leaned down and yelled, "There's one more person I have to talk to," and pulled me out of the tent.

Chapter 9

THE MESMERIST AND SAMMY

Me and the Preacher walked through a patch of woods toward the sounds that were cutting through the night air. When we stepped into the Atlas Clearing it was like we'd fell off a cliff right into a whole 'nother world. What I saw was so shocking that at first everything on me acted like it wanted to draw up and squeeze together, the same way your body does if you're walking 'cross some ice that gives way and dumps you into frozed-up winter water. It was like it was too much coming at you all at once, like it would steal your breathing away from you. But I think that's what the carnival folks were trying to do.

Everything in the Atlas Clearing was set up to get your head started whirling and keep it going that way, and there waren't no hiding from none of it! Every part of my body was trying to grab attention away from the next part. My ears were steady picking up sounds that I hadn't never heard nowhere else. There were hoops and hollers from children and growned folks both, screams that had you thinking someone was looking death right in the throat but that quick turned to laughs that were kind of 'shamed-sounding.

There was a powerful hissing music whistling from a wagon that was throwing fog and songs out of a row of pipes, sounding so hot and hard and pointy that you'd've thought you'd took a knife and were scratching at something deep inside your ear.

But soon's it felt like the *sounds* were gonna cause your head to bust open, your eyes started taking over and noticing separate things out of what at first didn't appear to be nothing but a blur of colour and torches.

There were more of the walking stick–holding, straw hat–wearing white men singing out for you to come see what they had hid up in their tents. They kept calling out the same words over and over, sounding like the choir on Sunday but without no real feeling of happiness in the words.

There were bright red and blue and green and yellow banners strung up 'longside dull brown, high-reaching tents. On the banners were pictures of things that you had to pay a whole nickel to go in and get a look at. Why, terrible as those pictures were, I'd have paid a nickel to *not* go in and see 'em!

There was a painting of a white man that appeared to be half a human and half an alligator, joined up so's you couldn't tell if what you were seeing was the rear half of a alligator swallowing up the top half of a man, or if it was a man that had been born without no legs who had sewed the back half of a lizard onto hisself to see if maybe he could do some walking that way!

There was a picture of a white woman that looked like she had some child's arms and legs poking out of the side of her neck! And another white man that was picking up a full-growned elephant and holding it over his head like he was 'bout to toss it into the next county! Another banner showed a white man that was wide as a barn holding hands with a white woman that waren't much more than a stick with a hank of yellow hair on top. They were standing under a big red heart that said, BIZARRE LOVE!!!!

But the drawing that I knowed would keep *me* awake nights and discourage me from wandering 'round in the woods for a good long time was the one of a white man who had to be a conjurer! He didn't have no animal parts stuck on him, nor no parts of other people growing out of him that would invite staring, he had something worst. Something that I tried hard to look away from but waren't no way I could do it.

He had sharp, yellow, jaggedy-looking bolts of lightning shooting di-rect out of his eyes! The bolts were making the normal-looking white man in the picture with him float off his feet and scramble and scratch at the air like he was 'bout to drift up to the clouds! It would cost you a whole quarter of a American dollar to go in the tent and see the conjurer do this! I'd've gave *two* quarters of a dollar not to!

But sure as shooting, this was the other person the Preacher said we were gonna have to go see. He pointed at the drawing of the man with the lightning-bolt eyes and said, "He's the owner of the carnival. I want to get a look at what kind of rigmarole he's got going before I talk to him."

Another straw hat–wearing, walking stick–waving white man was out front of the tent calling, "Last show of the evening, last show of the year, last time in Canada, last chance of your lifetime to

see the fantastic Vaughn-O working his powers of mental prestidig-
itation!"

The Preacher slapped two whole American quarters on a table
and told the white woman sitting there, "Me and my boy want to see
the mesmerist."

I spoke right up and said, "No, sir! You go on in and see him. I'll
wait over yon by that tree."

The Preacher grabbed hold of my collar and pulled me into the
tent. This one didn't have no benches in it to sit down on, so we were
standing shoulder to shoulder with a bunch of folks from Chatham.
Soon's we were inside and worked our way up to the front, I clamped
my hand 'cross my eyes.

The Preacher put his mouth near my ear and said, "No-siree-
bob. I paid a whole twenty-five cents for you to watch this and that's
just what you're going to do." He jerked my hand away from cover-
ing my face.

The first thing I did was look straight up, partly so's I wouldn't
have to see the stage, but mostly 'cause if the Preacher was gonna
force me to watch and get floated off by lightning coming outta some
white man's eyes, I wanted to see if there was something I could latch
ahold on to afore I ended up in the clouds.

If I was gonna get lifted away, this was a good place to do it
'cause I couldn't've got no higher than the roof of the tent. There
were torches high up on the walls that I'd have to be careful of whilst
I was floating, but I figured if I kept a keen eye and kicked at 'em, I
could get by without burning nothing 'sides my brogans and maybe
the cuffs of my trousers.

I looked all 'cross the top of the tent and my heart started slowing
down. It was a true relief to see that there waren't no one from the
earlier shows still stuck up there. Maybe that meant the conjuring
wore off after while and you'd come a-crashing back down.

If I'd've knowed this was gonna happen I'd have brung me a
length of rope and tied it 'round my ankle. That way if I started floating, the Preacher could have pulled me 'long home like a kite. I'd
have felt a lot better 'bout waiting for the conjuring to wear off back
in Buxton than here 'mongst a bunch of strangers.

Afore I could do any more worrying, a curtain on the stage got
whipped aside and a tall, round white man in a long black cape was

standing right in front of us. His eyes looked a whole lot more like a dead person's eyes than a live person's. They were blank and blue and they 'peared to be looking square at you, but you could tell they waren't really seeing a thing.

A bevy of laughs and moans and screams came out of everyone that was jammed up in the tent. It ain't being fragile when I say that I was 'mongst the screamers.

I grabbed hold of the Preacher's shirtsleeve and mashed my face into it. He just as quick snatched it away and said, "I told you you were going to watch this. You can learn about how a flimflam works."

I noticed my own arm was being held on to tight and looked to see who'd grabbed me. A little white stranger boy, near 'bout as old as me, was laughing and carrying on something wild.

He swore, "Blang it all! This here's the fourth time I seen him and I still near 'bout jump out my skin when he first come on stage!" He talked like he was from America.

I said, "You saw him four times! Ain't you afeared of getting floated off?"

He laughed and said, "Pshaw! He just a old humbug! He can't float naught nowhere."

The boy had a head of thick curly red hair and a nose that looked a whole lot like a bird's beak. His eyes were a scary gray and blue colour, 'bout the same as the sky afore a storm. He waren't nothing but a child but the smell of cigar smoke came outta his mouth strong!

I said, "He really caint float nothing away?"

"Naw! Watch what happens. What's your name?"

"I'm Elijah."

The boy looked like I cursed at him. *"Elijah?* You sure?"

"Course I'm sure."

"You live down in Buxton?"

"Yes."

"Well, I'm-a tell you something, Elijah. You'd best not tell no one from Chatham that that's your name."

"Why not?"

"'Cause there's a rapscallion in Chatham what's already laid claim to that name, and he ain't the kind to be sharing nothing with no one! There was a boy up here whose name was Edward, and Elijah from Chatham didn't want no one else having their name even *start*

with the same first letter as his, so he made the boy change his name
to Odward! And Odward's own ma and pa calls him that now 'cause
they didn't want no trouble with the real Elijah. If I's you I'd find me
another name 'cause Elijah from Chatham ain't gonna be real happy
'bout meeting you, particular not with you being a slave boy from
Buxton."

"I waren't never a slave. I was freeborn."

"Don't matter. Just you be mindful of who you say that name to.
Elijah from Chatham ain't to be trifled with. He already killed a full-
growed Indian man! And didn't kill him with no knife or gun or
sword, killed him with one hand! His left one! And he ain't but twelve
years old!"

Those words hadn't had no chance to sink in good when the conjurer on stage came to life. He flunged his arms to the sides and
showed that under his black cape he was wearing a something blue
that looked a powerful lot like a dress with all sorts of shiny, sparkling, silvered stars and crescent moons. Why, it was pasted with as
many moons as stars! And that don't make no sense, that don't make
no sense atall.

All the folks that were screaming and laughing a minute ago set
up a mess of oohs and aahs that would have you believing they were
seeing the real heavens 'stead of a dress with sham stars and way too
many moons stuck all over it.

The little white boy dugged his elbow into my ribs and said,
"Keep a watch on his eyes!"

The most amazing thing happened! The conjurer's eyes rolled
back in his head and their place was took right away by *another* set of
eyes! Only difference twixt 'em was that these two eyes were brown,
and whilst the other ones seemed staring and empty, these eyes were
looking dead at you! And worst, waren't no doubt that *they were seeing you!*

I felt my legs commence shaking and grabbed ahold of the white
boy so's I wouldn't fall.

He said, "Them first eyes is painted on his lids, I was out back
smoking a see-gar with him and seent it myself. He ain't real atall!"

The conjurer was slow as anything peering hard at everyone in
the crowd. When his eyes hit 'em, some folks screamed, some folks

laughed, some folks cried, and some folks 'peared to be dumbstruck. I ain't sure which group I was 'mongst 'cause the fearing in me was too strong.

The white boy said, "Watch this. I'm-a have me some fun here!"

When the man's eyes struck him the boy stood bolt upright and his face frozed stiff as a stone! I quick unloosed his arm so's the conjurization wouldn't have the chance to jump off of him and onto me.

The man pointed spot-on at the boy and called out, "You!"

The boy's eyes near bucked right out of his head!

The conjurer-man's finger commenced crooking and bending in a way that got more screams and confusion to rise up from the crowd.

The boy looked at me, his face unfrozen for a second, and one of his gray eyes winked. Then quick as anything his face frozed up again, looking all stupid-fied, and he started pushing his way through people and heading to the steps on the side of the stage. You'd've thought the conjurer's finger was a magnet and the boy was made outta iron filings! When folks saw the spell he was under they stepped aside like he was toting a bucket that was overflowing with the plague!

He got up on the stage and the conjurer waved his cape over the boy's head twice. He said, "Boy! Do you know me?"

The boy said, "No, sir, you's a perfect stranger."

"Then we've never spoken?"

"No, sir, and I ain't never smoked no see-gar with you behind the tent neither."

Some folks that didn't know how frightsome this was laughed and the conjurer screamed out, "Silence! Do you not see that this boy is already under a spell and talking nonsense? Why, if I were to misdirect my attention away from him for merely one moment he'd be in danger of remaining a babbling idiot like this for the rest of his life!" The conjurer-man talked like he came from England.

Most folks got quiet like they were in church.

The conjurer waved his cape over the boy's head again and said, "Look into my eyes! Look deeply into my eyes!"

The boy couldn't help hisself, he looked and the conjurer started blinking first one eye then the other so's on one side of his face you were seeing a live brown eye, and on the other side you were seeing a dead blue one. Then he opened both dead eyes at once then both live ones till by and by your head was back to whirling and you knowed this boy had been wrong, this conjurer was real!

I snatched back ahold of the Preacher's coat sleeve.

The conjurer said, "Look even more deeply into my eyes!"

The boy's head started going back and forth fast like a pendulum in a clock that the weight's fell off. Then his chin dropped down on his chest and it 'peared he was out cold, 'cepting he didn't fall in a heap!

The man said, "You are entering a realm of velvet sleep, golden slumbers, and dappled dreams. Once I snap my fingers, you will lose yourself in my voice. Upon the sound of my fingers snapping, my simplest wish will become your irresistible command!"

He slow raised his right hand over his head, waited for what felt like was a hour, then snapped his fingers. At the same exact time someone banged a drum one terrible boom, and a flash of red and yellow powder exploded and popped and hissed all 'long the front of the stage. Screams and smoke from the powder rised up to the top of the tent, and, truth told, my scream was 'mongst the loudest and longest lasting!

The conjurer said, "When I count to three you will open your eyes and hear no voice other than mine! One...two...three!"

He snapped his fingers again and the boy's eyes came open and were staring di-rect at the conjurer! I knowed the poor boy was under the man's spell 'cause one of his eyeballs started looking right whilst the other one was looking left, then they commenced going in circles and rolling back in his head! My blood ran cold thinking 'bout how this boy thought this was all a flimflam, and now he'd gone and let this horrible-looking man snatch ahold of his soul! I knowed it waren't gonna be long afore this poor white boy would be scratching and clawing at the roof of the tent!

The conjurer said, "What is your name, boy?"

The boy started talking slow, having a hard time getting the words out, "My...ma named...me Samuel...but most...folks... calls me...Sammy."

"Samuel, who is the only person in the entire world whom you can trust?"

"You, master."

"That's right! And do you believe everything I say?"

"Like your mouth's a prayer book, master."

"Then why are you speaking to me in English? You are not a little boy, you are a chicken! And unless the chickens in Canada are very much brighter than American chickens, they do not speak English!"

'Twas the most amazing thing! The little boy started clucking and pecking 'round on the stage then he commenced scratching at the floor with his bare feet and you'd have swored he was digging up worms!

Near everybody in the tent acted like this was something funny! None of 'em thought to worry what Sammy's ma was gonna say when the son she sent to the carnival as a little boy came home as a giant bird! And even worst, a giant chicken!

The conjurer waved his cape again and called out, "You are no longer a chicken, you are a boy again! But wait, the weather has changed! It's positively freezing in here!"

Why, the boy took to shivering and teeth-chattering and knee-knocking so doggone much that I felt a chill of coldness run down *my* back! And this waren't no flimflam neither, 'cause Sammy started turning blue the way they say white people do when they're dead or just 'bout ready to die!

The mesmerist yelled, "Egads! This Canadian weather! One second it's freezing and the next it's like the fires of Hades! This heat is enough to kill!"

Sammy quit shivering and commenced wiping his brow and pulling at the collar of his shirt and saying "Whew!" so's you'd have thought he'd just got done plowing fifty acres in the middle of July with a mouse for a mule harnessed to a knife for a plow!

Folks laughed and screamed so much that you could see why this cost a whole quarter of a American dollar to come in and see.

The mesmerist said, "And what's that I see right in front of you, young Samuel? It appears to be the waters of Lake Erie, cool and deep and inviting!"

Sammy started brushing at the stage like it was covered with sand and he was clearing a spot to spread a blanket. But afore he could set hisself down, the mesmerist said with a voice that was fulled up with disappointment, "Sam-u-well, Sam-u-well, Sam-u-well."

Sammy frozed up and the man told him, "How can you even

think of relaxing at the seashore when you are just a very few feet away from bathing in this great lake's waters? You should jump right in!"

Sammy slapped his own forehead like he was thinking, "How come I didn't think of that?" and stuck one of his toes out to test the water. He let out a long "Ahhh!" and got ready to put his whole foot in this lake that couldn't no one but him and the conjurer-man see.

Afore even his ankles got wet the mesmerist said, "Sam-u-well, Sam-u-well, Sam-u-well."

Sammy didn't step no farther into the water and the conjurer looked at all of us who were watching and said, "Have any of you here ever heard of a boy going to bathe fully clothed?"

The crowd shouted outta one throat, "No!"

I kept my eye on Sammy and for a second the dumbstruck look flew off his face and his brow wrinkled, but just as quick he went back to looking stupid-fied.

The mesmerist said, "Of course not, particularly not when you are wearing the finest silk shirt that the most talented tailor in Toronto has to offer! Samuel, your mother would be appalled if you were to get that beautiful, expensive, and rather stylish shirt wet!"

Sammy slapped his forehead again and started pulling the shirt over his head. Once he had it off he waren't wearing nothing but a raggedy undershirt and commenced tiptoeing back into the lake. But afore the water could cover even his knees the mesmerist said it again, "Sam-u-well, Sam-u-well, Sam-u-well."

Sammy stopped with one foot in the air and looked back at the conjurer.

"My word! Ladies and gentlemen, would you look at this young man! He is a stubborn and ungrateful lad! Not only has his dear, beloved mother seen fit to clothe him in a fine silken shirt, she's also given him a silk undershirt! Please, Samuel, off with it before it's ruined by the waters of Lake Erie."

This time Sammy cut a look at the mesmerist that waren't the least bit dumbstruck, it was kind of edging on being worried.

He pulled his undershirt over his head and a bale of laughs echoed 'round the tent. Laughing is a peculiar thing 'cause there're lots of different kinds. There's the laughing you do at the end of a good story, the laugh you give when you're scared then find out you didn't have no cause to be, and the laughing that was bouncing 'round in this tent. It waren't a happy kind of sound atall. It mostly reminded me of the cutting sounds that a pack of hounds makes once they commence to ripping a possum to shreds. It was more like the sound you'd think the Devil would make if he had a good sense of humour and you'd told him a joke.

I waren't doing none of the kinds of laughing. I could see that if this started out being fun for Sammy, it sure was turning into something else.

Ma and Pa must be right 'bout what smoking does to a child, 'cause once his undershirt was off, we could see Sammy was right skinny and sickly-looking, and though standing in front of all these people without no kind of shirt on atall would have shamed me near to death, the conjurization was on him so strong that Sammy kept on doing it. But it *did* seem like his enthusiasm for the whole show was getting littler and littler.

He hugged his arms 'round hisself and started back to tiptoeing into Lake Erie. But Sammy gave a long pulled-out groan when the mesmerist and most the folks in the crowd moaned out, "Sam-u-well, Sam-u-well, Sam-u-well!"

A hoop and a holler came out of the crowd 'cause we were all pretty sure that even though Sammy's trousers looked like old and worned-out dungarees to us, to the mesmerist they were gonna be some more of that fine Toronto silk that caint stand getting wet.

"Egads, boy! I've never seen such a privileged yet undeserving child. Your mother's love for you knows no bounds! Silken trousers as well, can you believe it?"

This time the stupid-fied look left Sammy and afearedness and shaming took over. The red from his hair started leaking down onto the rest of his face. His ears started up glowing like hot pokers.

But he turned his back to the crowd and started unbuttoning those trousers!

He held up once they're all unbuttoned, but the mesmerist had no mercy in him atall. He waved his cape and said, "Off with the silken trousers!"

Sammy gave a gulp so loud everyone in the tent heard it, then he let loose of his pants and they dropped right 'round his ankles.

The crowd sucked in air then got real quiet 'cept for one man who hollered out, "Shucks, if his dern ma loved him so dern much, you'd think she'd have bought the boy *some* kind of underdrawers, silk or not!"

The laughs and howls and hoots must have raised the roof of the tent five feet, all 'cause Sammy was naked as the day he was born. And he turned red as any cardinal I'd ever seen. I'd druther have got floated into the ceiling for two hours than to stand there like that for two seconds.

The mesmerist's mouth flew open and he quick clopped Sammy in the head then pulled his cape 'round him and said, "The spell's over, pull your pants up, you little chowderhead. Have you lost your blasted mind?"

After they rough-handed Sammy and booted him out of the tent, the conjurer mesmerized two or three other folks but waren't a one of 'em nowhere near as interesting as Sammy.

It must've been getting near midnight when me and the Preacher left the tent and he said, "When we get to this next place just go along with everything I say, and fight that urge of yours to talk so much. Don't open your mouth unless you're spoken to."

"Yes, sir."

We walked a little ways into the woods and sat on a couple of stumps whilst folks cleared out of the carnival. Finally the Preacher said, "Let's go. And remember, the less you say the better."

Chapter 10

MEETING THE *REAL* MAWEE!

Me and the Preacher wandered 'round the carnival for 'bout another hour. Then we walked back into the Atlas Clearing and headed for a tent where most of the carnival workers were sitting. A big, rough-looking white man with bright red hair stood up and put his hand on the Preacher's chest and said, "Show's over, boy. We's pulling up stakes tonight and don't need no more workers."

The Preacher slapped the man's hand off his chest and stood so his jacket was open and that mystery pistol was showing. He said, "I look like a boy to you? I'm not here about work. I'm looking for the owner. And if you put another hand on me you'll be pulling back a bloody stump."

The tall conjurer-man with the two sets of eyes jumped up and said, "Hold on a moment, Red. I own this carnival, sir. How may I help you?"

The Preacher pushed past the red-hair white man and said, "Sir, I just want to start by telling you what a wonderful carnival you have here."

The conjurer reached his hand to the Preacher and said, "Why, thank you, sir. Whom do I have the honour of addressing?"

"I'm the Right Reverend Deacon Doctor Zephariah Connerly the Third. A pleasure to meet you, sir."

"Reverend Connerly, I am humbled to be in your presence. I am the lowly Charles Mondial Vaughn the *Fourth*, Knight Commander of the Most Honourable Order of the Bath. Knighted a mere fourteen years ago."

The Preacher said, "I'm the one who's humbled, sir. I've been to many such carnivals and have never seen anything that matches this one. You must be very proud."

"Indeed, indeed. I've worked years to assemble this family."

The Preacher said, "Which is why I wanted to speak with you."

The conjurer took a long pull on his cigar and blowed the smoke to the side, then said, "And what may I do for you, sir?"

"It's more what I can do for you."

"I'm intrigued. Do tell."

The Preacher pulled me from behind him and said, "Sir Charles, allow me to introduce the most amazing child ever to have lived in Buxton. Although he was born and reared in Africa, he has lived with me for these past four years. Maybe in your travels you've heard of the tribe he's from, the Chochotes?"

Sir Charles said, "Can't say that I have."

"There's a good reason you haven't. Sad to say, little Ahbo here is the last surviving member."

"Well, Reverend, that is indeed sad, but what does that have to do with my carnival?"

The Preacher commenced waving his arms, really warming into this tale he's 'bout to spin. "The Chochotes were fierce warriors who hunted and even fished with nothing but stones. Stone throwing was a skill passed from generation to generation, and little Ahbo's father, who was the king of the Chochotes, passed on the secrets of stone hunting and fishing to his son just before he was tragically murdered."

The Preacher sounded so heart-busted about this that even I was getting sad for little Ahbo, and I knowed that he was me and that there waren't probably gonna be a lick of truth in the whole story.

The conjurer said, "Pity that. But wait, do I understand you to be saying that this boy can catch a fish underwater? By throwing a stone?"

The Preacher said, "If only we were at a lake so he could show you."

The conjurer winked at the big, rough, red-hair white man and said, "If he can do that, he must have an unusually keen eye. Could he, mayhap, demonstrate his skill some other way?"

"Of course he can. I watched your Madame Sabbar earlier tonight, and while she was most impressive, I didn't see her doing anything little Ahbo couldn't match."

"No?"

"No. Perhaps we could go to her tent and show you."

"Well, sir, we were actually preparing to break things down, but I think little Ahbo might provide an interesting, but brief, diversion."

The Preacher, Sir Charles, and the other white man started walking toward the slingshot lady's tent with me trailing behind.

The conjurer looked back at me and said loud and slow, "Do... you...speak...any...English?"

It was kind of hard to look at him with his two sets of eyes, but I said, "Why, yes, sir, and some Latin, and I can understand a little Greek."

Oops! That must've been too much talking. The Preacher gave me a hard look then told the conjurer, "Plus, of course, he's fluent in Chochote."

One of the conjurer's eyebrows raised up and he said, "Indeed? To my ear it sounds as if the boy is very Canadian."

"That's because not only is he the best stone flinger since David, he's also uncommonly bright. He's lived with me for only four years and he's picked up the language and customs of Canada West so quickly it's truly astounding."

All the sudden a stranger boy came up 'longside of me and gave me some unpleasant looks. His hair was all matted up like a bird's nest and his clothes were so dirty that not even Cooter would've been caught dead in 'em.

He said, "Who you?"

I just 'bout said my name then remembered what Sammy had told me 'bout saying "Elijah" 'round here. I knowed the boy waren't from Buxton and I was pretty sure he waren't from Chatham but I couldn't be total for certain. I thought it'd be best if I didn't take no chances. He was littler than me so I said, "Why you want to know?"

He said, "Where y'all going?" He sounded American.

"Over to the slingshot lady's tent."

The boy spit, kicked his bare foot at the dirt, and said, "I knowed it!"

I could tell he was sizing me up to see if he could lick me. I puffed my chest up some whilst we walked.

The boy said quiet, "I's the *real* MaWee! But you's fixing to take my place, ain't you?"

"*What?*"

"That white boy waren't no good, I seent it, so now Massa Charles looking for *you* to take my place."

He tilted his head toward the conjurer and said, "He done tolt me it was just for whilst we's in Canada, but I knowed he was a-lying."

"Lying 'bout what?"

"You's trying to be the next MaWee, ain't you?"

"*What?*"

"But I'm-a tell you right now that you ain't gunn like it. You ain't gunn like roaming 'bout with 'em one bit. They ain't gunn say nothing at first but you gunn have to clean all them animal cages and fetch for 'em all times of the day or night, and the 'gator man gunn beat you every chance he get and you gunn be cleaning all they clothes, and they stingy with what they feed you, and it even ain't no fun after 'while getting hit in the face with them grapes neither."

I said, "I'm not taking no one's place. The Preacher's just bragging on me so's that man with all those eyes can see how good I chunk stones."

The boy gave me another rough look.

I said, "You travel 'round with these people?"

"Course I do, I tolt you, I'm the *real* MaWee."

"Your ma and pa travel with you too?"

"I ain't got no ma nor pa."

"You a orphan?"

"You best watch what you's calling me. What's a orphan?"

I said, "How old are you?"

"I ain't sure."

"You ain't had no schooling atall?"

"What I need schooling for? You ax too much questions."

"Who takes care of you?"

"Massa Charles do. He look after me good. He done paid more'n a hunnert dollars for me down in Loos-ee-anna."

"*Paid?* You're a *slave?*"

"Naw! I seent how slaves get treated. I ain't no slave."

"You ain't never tried to escape?"

"What you mean? If Massa cut me a-loose, what's I gunn eat? Where's I gunn sleep?"

"But this is Canada! You ain't but three miles from Buxton! You ain't never heard of *Buxton?*"

"Massa Charles say Buxton why he have to get a white boy to pretend he MaWee. He say y'all up here ain't gunn think it funny to see *me* get pelt with no grapes. Now he seent that white boy ain't no good and he gunn try you next."

I told him, "My ma and pa ain't 'bout to let me travel with no circus. Buxton's my home."

The inside of Madame Sabbar's tent looked a whole lot smaller without all the people piled up in it. Madame Sabbar herself was sitting on the stage smoking a cigar.

MaWee pointed at the white cloth atop the jungle board and whispered, "Can y'all read? What that say?"

I told him, "It says, 'The Jungles of Sweden.'"

"It don't say nothing 'bout MaWee?"

"No."

"That what I thought. He lie!"

The Preacher and the conjurer stopped talking and Sir Charles told MaWee, "Go light the candles as if it's a show."

"Yes, sir!"

MaWee struck a match and set all the candles on the board burning.

"Them other ones too, boss?"

"Yes, everything."

MaWee grabbed a lighting pole and went 'round the tent lighting the candles up high. When he was done he came back and said, "That all, boss?"

"Yes, MaWee, but don't leave. We're getting started in a moment."

"Yes, sir, boss."

"Now, Reverend Connerly, perhaps little Ahbo can demonstrate his skill."

The Preacher waved for me to come up on the stage.

He whispered to me, "First time through, just use your right hand."

This waren't gonna be nothing! It waren't even twenty paces twixt me and the candles that were sitting atop the Swedish jungle board. I reached in my tote sack and pulled out ten of the chunking stones and set them on the table next to me.

I looked at the Preacher and he ducked his head at me. I held on to my breathing and chunked with my right hand and passed stones into it with my left.

When I was done, all the candles had been put out just as smooth as the slingshot lady had done it.

The conjurer and the other white man looked at each other. Madame Sabbar blowed a long cloud of smoke out of her nose holes. The Preacher winked his eye at me.

MaWee called out, "Woo-ooo-ooo-wee! He good, Massa Charles! Y'all caint use him for nothing but tossing stones, he that good!"

The conjurer said, "You're right, MaWee, that was most remarkable! Now how 'bout the others?" He pointed at the higher-up candles.

This waren't gonna be as easy. The farthest candles appeared to be 'bout thirty, thirty-five paces away, and it was dark up that high.

The Preacher saw I was fretting and came up on the stage.

"What's wrong?"

"I don't know if I can put out the flames on the two at the back, sir."

"Just aim to knock them down, then."

"Yes, sir. Just my right hand again?"

"Yes."

I held on to my breathing and threw at the twelve candles runged 'round the tent. When I was done, one of 'em at the back had got knocked over and I'd clean missed on the one over the doorway.

Sir Charles and the other white man brung their heads together and started talking.

MaWee said, "Massa Charles, Massa Charles! You got to have that boy take over from Missy Sabbar! He good 'nough to take her place!"

The Preacher said, "And that's not half the story, Sir Charles. No disrespect intended, madame, but while you are without doubt a deadly accurate slingshotist, little Ahbo's skills include something else."

The Preacher's hands started unfolding and waving right along with the story. He said, "One of the reasons the Chochote tribe is now nearly wiped from the face of the earth is that they shared their land with an insect so vile that it is called the horrible giant Bama bee. Bees so large that they've been known to carry away a full-grown man as easily as a hawk carries a mouse. And they attack in swarms of ten, which forced the Chochote to learn to throw not only with accuracy but with speed as well. Might I propose, if she is not too tired, that Madame Sabbar and little Ahbo have a side-by-side demonstration that includes speed?"

Sir Charles said, "A race? Why, that might prove to be quite interesting. Madame?"

The slingshot lady didn't look too happy 'bout doing this but she chomped her teeth on her cigar and stood next to me.

The Preacher said, "If the young boy could light the ten candles on the board again, we can get this started."

MaWee waited till Sir Charles nodded at him then lit up all the candles.

The Preacher said, "Why doesn't the madame pick one side of the board and put out candles toward the middle and little Ahbo will do the same with the other side. We'll see who puts out the most the quickest."

The woman chomped her cigar harder and said, "Left." She raised her slingshot.

The Preacher whispered to me, "Use both hands. Beat her good."

He told Sir Charles, "You start them."

The conjurer-man said, "Both of you start on the count of three. One...two..."

Folks from Sweden must not be real good at counting. The conjurer hadn't even finished saying "two" afore Madame Sabbar put out the first candle on the left.

"...three!"

I throwed left, right, left, right, left, right.

I'd got six of 'em in the time she got four.

She spit her cigar out on the stage and said, "Light them candles up again, you little fool."

MaWee waited on the conjurer to nod then lit 'em all up.

This time I got seven and she got three. She knocked one of 'em over too.

She dropped her slingshot and walked out of the tent.

MaWee shouted, "Ooo-ooo-wee! He done run her off! He way better than her, you gunn let him take her place?"

The conjurer said, "My word, Reverend, you didn't exaggerate in the least. I think little Ahbo will fit very nicely into our family."

MaWee said, "He gunn take *her* place, boss? I ain't never seent no one what throwed so good! Lots of folks pay to see that boy throw! It be a waste of time having him get pelt with grapes."

The conjurer said, "Start breaking things down in here, boy. I want to leave by noon tomorrow. Red, go see if Madame Sabbar is all right. Reverend, we need to talk."

Him and the Preacher stood next to the stage.

Sir Charles said, "I assume you've had some expenses in raising little Ahbo. I'm willing to give you some consideration for that. You say the poor lad is an orphan?"

"Yes, I'm the only one he has."

"How much are you looking for, sir?"

The Preacher said, "Hold on here, you've misjudged me. I don't deal in human beings."

"Then what is it you're proposing?"

"The boy and I would be willing to travel with you for a while if you're willing to make certain guarantees."

"Such as?"

"Such as how much we would be paid. Such as what it is we would do in your family. Such as what it is we *wouldn't* do."

Sir Charles blowed out another long puff of cigar smoke at the roof of the tent and said, "Ahh, well, Reverend, what is it *you* propose doing? I can see that little Ahbo would be able to carry his weight and contribute to the family with his stone throwing, augmented, of course, by several other chores, but I really do not have a need for anyone else. I *would*, however, handsomely reward you for your transference of guardianship of the boy."

MaWee'd pulled all the candles off the top of the Sweden jungle board. He said, "Pardon me, boss, you wants me to take this sign 'bout that white boy off of here? We gunn put it back saying this here's the real MaWee's jungle, ain't we?"

The conjurer-man kept his eyes on the Preacher but nodded his head at MaWee.

MaWee pulled off the white sheet that said THE JUNGLES OF SWEDEN!!!

Writ out underneath the sheet in letters di-rect on the board was:

The Jungles of Darkest Africa!!!
Help Madame Sabbar Capture MaWee,
the Chief of the Pickaninnys!!!

All the sudden the Preacher was done talking. He grabbed hold of my collar and we marched out the front of the tent. Afore you could blink we're walking down the road back to Buxton.

Things happened so quick that I had to ask the Preacher, "Why'd we leave without saying good-bye to no one?"

He said, "It wasn't what I thought it was."

"What'd you think it was? Waren't it just a carnival?"

"Forget this happened. It was a bad idea from the start."

"What was?"

"Nothing, Elijah. I was simply looking for a way to help the Settlement."

I tried a couple more times but I waren't getting no more explaining from the Preacher. It 'peared he didn't want to talk no more, which I look at as he wanted to do some listening, so I told him all 'bout Sammy and how scared I was 'bout getting floated away and 'bout how Sir Charles paid a hundred American dollars for MaWee. I kept on talking all the way to Buxton but the only subject the Preacher seemed to take any kind of interest in atall was MaWee. He had me tell him 'bout it three times. I asked the Preacher if you were still a slave if you didn't mind working for someone and didn't have nowhere else to go.

Only thing he said was, "Yes, you're still a slave. But you're worse than a slave. You're an ignorant slave."

When we got home, the Preacher waited whilst I climbed in through my bedroom window. Once I got in I waved at him and he waved back and walked away. It waren't till I was in bed thinking 'bout the most exciting day I'd ever had in my life that it came to me that the Preacher'd headed back down the road to Chatham 'stead of toward his own home. That was just as peculiar as a whole lot of the things the Preacher did that night. I just chalked it up to some more of that growned-up behaviour that don't make no sense, it don't make no sense atall.

———————

On Monday morning, me and Cooter joined up in front of the schoolhouse. I was 'bout to explode wanting to tell him some more 'bout the carnival, but afore I could open my mouth he said, "Don't it seem odd ain't no one else here? Doggone-it-all, Elijah, the same thing happened to me last month when I lost track of the days and sat out here for a half a hour on Sunday morning wondering where everyone was at. Today *is* Monday, ain't it?"

"Yes, don't you 'member sitting in church all day yesterday?"

"So where's every..."

We both heard someone say, "Oooh!" and walked 'round back of the school. All the other children were crowded up in a big circle way out in the field. Wouldn't no one dare fight this close to the school so me and Cooter ran over to see what the commotion was.

I said, "I bet they found another dead body!"

Cooter said, "Uh-uh, Emma Collins is standing there and she'd have run off and told someone first thing. I bet one n'em moth lions from that circus you was telling me 'bout busted loose and they's holding him down till someone come to get it."

I looked at Cooter and couldn't help hoping that thickheadedness ain't something you can catch like a cold.

When we busted into the circle it waren't neither a dead body nor a lion. 'Twas a little stranger boy standing there looking like he's 'bout to cry.

I knowed this boy, but I couldn't get ahold on from where.

Then it hit me. 'Twas MaWee! Somebody had cut all his wild hair off and put him in some proper clothes.

I said, "You escaped! You're free!"

'Twaren't odd for folks that just got freed to look and act confused, but I hadn't never saw no one that looked and acted like they were mad 'bout coming to live in Buxton afore. And MaWee was good and mad. Why, he was pouting and looking like he had rocks in his jaws and was grumbling so's everyone was wondering if he was crazy.

Emma Collins asked him, "What? You're wishing you hadn't escaped? You're wishing you were still a slave?"

MaWee rubbed his hand over the top of his head like he was still wondering where all his hair was at.

"I done tolt you I waren't no slave. And I didn't do no escaping neither. I gots snatched off by *his* friend!"

He pointed spot-on at me.

I said, *"What?"*

"After y'all left, your friend come back and stoled me from Massa Charles."

I couldn't help myself, I knowed I should've kept my mouth shut, but I said, "The Preacher?"

MaWee said, *"Preacher?* He sure don't act like no preacher I ever seen."

Cooter said, "What happened?"

"Soon's we got done breaking everything down, that friend of his bust in holding on to two guns and set to pistol-whipping Massa Red. Then he grab Massa Charles' hair like he 'bout to scalp him. He shoves one n'em guns right in Massa Charles' nose.

"We all thinking it gunn be another stickup and boss is sure afeared of this man and say, 'Ain't no need to hurt no one, just take the money.' But that there boy's friend..." MaWee pointed right at me. "... say he ain't looking to rob us and then he point the gun what ain't jammed up Massa Charles' nose dead at me! He tell the 'gator man he gots one minute to tie my hands up. All the time he got that pistol up in Massa Charles' nose so deep, blood running down his face."

Tears were pouring out of MaWee's eyes. "Once the 'gator man got me roped good, that preacher tell 'em this here's Canada and folks is free and he taking me to Buxton and he gunn kill anyone what try to stop him. Then he tell Massa Charles that once we gets to Buxton, y'all's army gunn make sure don't no one come and try to get me back. He say he got him the fastest horse in Canada tied out in the woods but it waren't gonna be no different if he had a old broke-down mule 'cause he ain't gunn gallop him nor trot him nor rush him atall. He say he ain't 'bout to run from no one, 'specially not in his own country. Then he tell Massa Charles the way to come if he want to find where y'all live. He tell 'em that the road to Buxton branch off to the right 'bout half a mile down and if they daft 'nough to follow him and wants to meet the Lord that bad, then that the way they gots to turn."

Everybody was looking shocked at MaWee's story.

He wiped his nose on his shirtsleeve and said, "Then he pull me outta the tent and tug me off into the woods and put me on top that pretty horse and tie me to the saddle and tie them reins 'round his waist and put one n'em pistols in each his hands and we starts walking right down the middle of the road.

"I just knowed Massa Charles and them gunn come rescue me and I'm hoping when they kill that man they aims good and they don't shoot me by mistake."

MaWee kicked at the ground and said, "Only thing I can figure is they took the wrong branch once they come to where the road split up at. But don't none y'all be surprise if they come busting in that there schoolhouse and take me back with 'em."

Emma Collins said, "Why're you wishing for that? You're free now."

MaWee said, "How's I free when they tolt me I ain't got no

choice but to go to school? How's I free when they got that Johnny boy and his momma watching over me like a sheriff?"

The bell runged and it came to me that I was gonna have to be careful with MaWee. If Emma Collins or one n'em other girls got wind that I was wandering 'bout past midnight at the carnival they'd get me stewed up in a world of trouble.

As we walked up the steps into the schoolhouse, Mr. Travis said, "Good morning, scholars, strivers, and questers for a better future! Are you ready to learn, are you ready to grow?"

He saw MaWee and said, "Well! Congratulations! They told me you'd be joining us today. Welcome, young man."

I could tell being free was gonna be a hard row to hoe for MaWee. 'Stead of answering Mr. Travis in the proper way he, bold as anything, said to him, "How many people in y'all's army anyway?"

Children jumped to the side and cleared out of the way so's not to interfere with Mr. Travis getting a proper snatch at MaWee. But Mr. Travis surprised us. He didn't cane MaWee nor scold him nor 'buke him in the least. He gentle laid his hand on MaWee's head and, without no sting in his voice atall, said, "My name is Mr. Travis. When I call on you to speak you will address me as that or as 'sir.' I have a feeling you and I are going to be spending a great deal of time together. Once again, welcome and congratulations."

MaWee said, "Thank you, sir." Both me and him kept peeking out the window all through the day waiting for Sir Charles and the rough, red-hair white man to come. But they never did show.

Up for It: A Tale of the Underground

Written and Annotated by L. F. Haines

3.

RESPIRATION: NEW YEAR'S EVE NIGHT, 1992

Someone is on your side
—Stephen Sondeim's "No One Is Alone"

In the darkness and the wet, he slipped to his knees in the mud. His hands, breaking his fall, sank up to the wrist in the oozy soil. He would have, otherwise, fallen flat on his face. He felt *that* weak. He had been running very hard. He was breathing heavily but he could not understand why, for he had not been running very long or very far. He had only started yet he felt that he had been running for a long time, the whole evening. But he knew he had not because he could hear over the bang and bark of the thunder the voices of the others, the boys coming after him, shouting. He shifted the burden inside his shirt. He was trying very hard to make sure that the objects would not be damaged. They had to be as fragile as the regular ones, he assumed, the ones people bought in stores. Damn, why am I running with these things, he thought.

A web of lightning, like wild lines of growth in the sky, like the roots of some giant plant in heaven, lit up the earth and then he could see that he was on his hands and knees in the grassy knoll in front of something, a building, a house of something. He could see the sign clearly in the brief brilliance of the lightning, swinging wildly in the wind, battered by the sheeting rain. The house of what? He couldn't tell despite the fact that he saw it clearly. What building was that? I don't know where I am, he thought. Above the sign had been a blue light. He had been running toward that light, then it sputtered and went out. He waited for it for as long as he could. But after a moment, he began to run again.

As he ran all he could think of was that he could not be caught. He had to get away, from those boys, from the police and security guards who were chasing him. "Get the power back on!" he heard someone shout. "Get the back-ups going!"

"They're going this way!" someone shouted. He realized now that the voices were growing more distant. He was running the wrong way. The other boys were headed toward the turnstiles and so were their pursuers but he was now at the picnic pavilion. He huddled underneath a picnic table to catch his breath. He moved his burden carefully, cradling them almost like precious jewels, against his belly as he crouched beneath his wooden sanctuary. They weren't pursuing him anymore. They had lost him or he had lost them. He could rest a moment, somewhat protected from the rain and the wind. He knew how to get out now, where he was: cut across the field by the monorail tracks, climb over the chain-link fence there and follow the interstate a short way to Bishop Road. He could walk home from there, a long walk in the driving rain but he could do it. Besides, he had to get home. He bumped his head against one of the rough wooden planks and he shivered deeply. It was getting colder, a lot colder very quickly. Damn, he thought, ain't I got enough trouble without having to get pneumonia, too. He peered from underneath the table for a moment in every direction. He could no longer even hear the voices. He took a deep breath and shot out, hurtled another table in one bound, tore down the field and made straight for the fence. He pushed his burden gingerly around in his shirt to his back, so he could climb the fence freely, pressing against it with his chest and stomach. He clawed it like an animal trying to get free of a trap. Just beyond, in a sudden flash of light, one

could see a sculpture of animals and on its base were the words: WEST-
MORELAND CITY ZOO SOUTH GATE.

He looked in a doorway covered by an awning, just beneath a street-
lamp, and saw, leaning against the frame, drunk, high, or asleep, the
man called Gentleman Brown, a joint hanging from his lips that he
sucked on, without holding it in his fingers, with a vigorous virtuosity.*
One eye shut, the other covered by his patch. A tight shirt opened at
the throat, a gold choker, his black leather trench coat, a broad-
brimmed slouch hat underneath which the boy could detect the black
outlines of a scarf wrapped around his ears. Two Dobermans sat on
either side of the door and a particularly baleful pit bull was on the
front step. Maybe he's been celebrating the New Years too hard. That
asshole! That goddam asshole! The boy remembered at that moment,
against his will, when Brown slapped him hard across the face, after
they had played together impromptu, at Shere Khan's studio last year.

"Don't ever play like that again," Brown spoke smoothly, in such

---

*I know for a fact that when The Gentleman first came out of prison in 1987, he was clean. He had gone in to-
tally messed up. But he came out, surprisingly, clean. He had even converted to Islam while he was in prison,
which surprised a lot of people who never thought The Gentleman had much use for religion, and would never
completely renounce Catholicism, the religion in which he had been reared. The other thing that was different
about him when he got out of prison was that he started wearing an eye patch more, and he didn't wear the
glass eye as much. I helped him get a job playing piano with saxophonist Charles Lloyd's band for their Europe
tour. By the time The Gentleman got back to America (Lloyd had fired him after four weeks), he was a pot-
head, had VD (it is amazing that The Gentleman is not HIV-positive), and the Islam had gone by the way side.
He was smoking joints the size of Havana cigars and then eating three Big Macs after with buttermilk. "This is
healthier than cocaine," he said. "I didn't have any appetite then. All I do now is eat when I smoke joints." I
guess he just wanted needed to be a Muslim while he was in prison. He never talked much about prison, not
with me or with anybody else I know that knows him. Perhaps he talked about it with Justin Arion. The person that knows the most about The Gentleman in prison was Agnes Arion. And at this point in the proceed-
ings, she is in no position to tell anyone anything. The only good thing about The Gentleman after he got out
of prison was that he stopped taking cocaine. He said that was one drug he couldn't conquer, by which he
meant control. It controlled him. I never tried to get him any jazz jobs after the Lloyd thing blew up. He joined
pianist McCoy Tyner's band several months after the Lloyd thing. This time he was playing alto and tenor sax.
(The Gentleman is a beautiful sax player.) But he was fired after three weeks and that pretty much ended his career as a regular working jazz player. He went back to producing records for Shere Khan and becoming, once
again, Khan's musical right hand man. I thought he was wasting his time and talent doing that and told him so.
He told me to go do something unmentionable to myself and I decided I wasn't dealing with that childishness
anymore. He does spot pickup jobs and sits in sometimes. But he really doesn't work in the jazz trade anymore.
He said he was glad about that because jazz was boring anyway and he didn't understand how anybody other
than musicians who were hung up on technique ever listened to it. "Jazz is dead," he said to me. "Zombies play
it, people who are dead and don't know it." "You're wrong, Gentleman," I told him. "You're describing vampires. Zombies are people who are alive but don't know it." "Same difference," The Gentleman said. "No, it's
not," I said. "Besides, you're just tired." He nodded to that. "Empty velocity," he said. "That's all it is now."
"Don't you mean 'empty virtuosity'?" I asked. "Same difference," he said. "Maybe you're right," I agreed.
                                                                                              —L. F. Haines

a bizarre contrast to his rage. "Don't ever disrespect any musician you're accompanying by playing against him on the bandstand. No matter how much you hate the person you're playing with, on the bandstand, that's all you got, is the people you're playing with. Don't come up here being a kid, a wise-ass punk who thinks he can play. Grow up or get off the bandstand. If you ever pull a stunt like that again, I'll do worse than slap your face. I'll kick your ass."

The boy had wanted to cry and he had wanted to run away, humiliated as he was. But he did neither. He wanted to speak, to condemn Brown, to threaten him. But his throat was so tight, he could not bring himself to speak without fear of losing complete control of himself. And what could he say, really? Brown was right. He *was* trying to screw up the piece, to throw Brown off. What made matters worse was that Brown was so good a musician that he was never fazed by the boy's misplaced accents, odd flams and drags, strange triplets, abandonment of the bass drum, abandonment of the hi-hat, or overbearing volume. Brown adjusted instantaneously to anything he heard and continued to pour out chorus after chorus of invention.* He

---

*"Hey, Brown, don't be going around hitting the boy like that!" Shere Khan said when he saw what Brown did. Even I was irritated with Brown about that and I have more patience with him than most. "Don't act so damn thuggish," Shere Khan continued. "Why don't you act like you've got some class? Do you want the world to think you are a total shithead?" "Like you?" Brown asked sarcastically. "I'm initiating him for the Society of Ear Lords." Brown laughed. "The kid passed the test. He knew the tune well enough to screw it up. He knew how to screw it up. It was subtle at first, clever. It didn't get sloppy until the end. It was good. I just taught him about respiration. You gotta know how to breathe to be a good player, to be an Ear Lord." "What are you talkin' about? I ain't no horn player! What do you mean respiration? You ain't got to breathe special to play drums!" Prince shouted. Shere Khan said impatiently, "Cut the bullshit, will you, Brown? You're just upsetting my boy. Teach my future star, don't brutalize him. There ain't no Society of Ear Lords." Brown just went about his business, tying his shoelaces, spitting on the floor and walking out of the door.

When I talked to Prince later he was still upset about the incident. "He said I disrespected him and maybe he was right but he disrespected me. He picked that ii-V-I tune and put it at that tempo just to jack me up. He wanted to force me to play the tune his way. You know, he just thought I wouldn't know the tune, couldn't deal with it, all like that, 'cause I was a dumb kid from the hood. But I knew it was the chord changes to Coltrane's 'Giant Steps.' I know who John Coltrane is. I mean, I heard that kind of music. I can run with that. I can roll that way. I don't need to get my head rubbed by that asshole. I know the tune but I hate it because it just sounds like you're practicin'. I hate a lot of Coltrane's tunes because when I'm playing for real I don't want to sound like I'm practicin'. I want to sound like I'm performin'." "I thought you were practicing," I said. "I thought this was just a rehearsal, a jam." "No, it wasn't nothing practice about it," he said, surprised and annoyed at my ignorance that I would think so. "Did it sound like he was practicin' to you? He wanted to know if I could perform with him, not if I could mess around with him. He knew I would hate that piece." "That's funny," I said. "Brown told me he hated the tune, too, for the same reason." "Then, why did he pick it for us to play? I don't mind being tested. I know Brown is a great musician. He got a rep. I know he was playin' professional before I was born, when he was a kid. But why he want to test me with that?" Prince asked, caught between anger and anguish. "If I know Brown, he just wanted to find out if you hated it, too." "Say, Ms. Haines, is there any such thing as an Ear Lord?" Prince asked suddenly, "You know, what Brown was talkin' about." I told him not anymore and left it at that. "Just some old-time musicians, huh?" he continued. "Something like that," I said. He never asked about them again. It was funny that this was the first time he called me Ms. Haines. He never called me that before.   —L. F. Haines

ain't human, the boy thought. He can't play through what I'm doin', like I'm not even doin' it.

"What the hell are you doing out here?" came a voice from the doorway. The boy noticed that the man's eyes or eye, in this case, never opened. How did he know someone was walking by him? How did he know it was me, thought the boy. Does he know it's me? He'll know if I answer. The boy wanted to get in from the rain. This fool doesn't even have sense to get in out of the rain, he thought, looking at Brown.

"Nothing. I'm going home," said the boy.

"What you got there?" Gentleman Brown asked, still not moving, but opening his eye. The boy had moved closer, unconsciously, because the man's voice was quieter than his face would make you think. The boy saw that Brown spoke through clenched teeth. The Gentleman stepped forward, into the rain. The boy could see him more clearly. Brown's jaw was wired shut. It's true, the boy thought. Somebody really jacked Brown up. That's what happens being around Shere Khan. That's what happens to people around that goddam Shere Khan, even Brown, except nothing don't ever happen to Shere Khan himself.

"I ain't got nothing," the boy said, slightly belligerently. "I'm just goin' home. I was lookin' for my Mom and now I'm goin' home. What's it to you, anyway, what I'm doin'? You ain't my father."

"Thank goodness for that," The Gentleman hissed. "That's all I need to add to everything else that's on me, bringing misbegotten, smart-assed, ignorant-assed brats like you into the world."

Brown turned to look at the dogs, his dogs, then turned back to the boy. "I heard the Blood Warriors were out tonight. I hope you didn't run into them. They don't like the friends of Shere Khan much," said Brown, moving still closer to the boy and pushing back the scarf from the side of his face. The rain rolled down the side of Brown's face, dripped from the brim of his hat. The strange tattoo on Brown's cheek quivered in the wet.

The boy shivered at the sight. They did do it, he thought, as he looked at the raw red gash where the rest of an ear should have been. Wow, they really did it. Damn, how can he hear anything? Maybe he can't play anymore.

"As you can see, they damn sure don't like me, Horton," Brown rasped quietly.

And with that, Brown suddenly spun away, grabbed three leashes the boy had never noticed, jerked his silent dogs, and walked roughly by the boy, who thought that he would lose his fragile burden.

A flash of lightning at the instance of the near-collision revealed the savage, ravaged face of Brown with the clarity of a close-up. His face had the texture of plastic, even the thick mustache. His skin did not seem like skin but rather merely like a surface. His face might as well have been made of porcelain. He had never seen Brown look so sick and strange, the dreadlocks flying under his hat. The sudden, bright illumination, the fearsome animals, made the boy recoil in fear and shock. The man never slackened his pace, never turned to see what or whom he nearly hit; he simply jerked the strange animals that pulled taut their leashes with their muscular, angry shoulders. I'm lucky he didn't walk through me, the boy thought. What the hell was that about? With that stupid asshole, it could be anything. All I know is he's gonna mess up that leather coat walking in the rain like that. He shrugged at the thought. Brown could buy a thousand leather coats, custom-made, if he wanted. The boy was surprised to see Brown in the neighborhood at this time of night, surprised to see him alone. What the hell is he doing standing in a doorway in the rain on New Year's Eve night? Maybe he's looking for Shere Khan and them, the boy thought. Well, he can have 'em. I hope whoever jacked him up cuts his whole face off next time, that asshole.

Then, he ran the rest of the way to his building as if he wanted to avoid, for now at least, being on the same block as Gentleman Brown. He couldn't help thinking that maybe it was an omen that he ran into Gentleman Brown; after all, no one had seen him around the last few weeks. Everyone had heard about what happened to him, that the Warriors had carved him up as a warning or somebody did. Brown was into too much shit just like all them guys at Felony/Art. Why can't people just make music? Why does it have to be all this other stuff? When he turned, Brown and his animals had already disappeared, as if they were a vapor dissolved in the air. What struck the boy as funny, odd, was that Brown seemed almost to have been waiting for him. But why would Brown be waiting for him? Why would Brown even know he was out? And what did Brown know about the Blood Warriors being out tonight? Did he know what happened at the zoo? Why did he call me Horton? Who the hell is Horton? For the boy, the night continued to unfold much like a nightmare being drawn out of a narrow glass tube. "I hate you, Ivanhoe Brown!" the boy screamed into the night, the cry sounding flat and dead in the rain. The loneliness of it frightened him.

The boy didn't realize he had lost his key until he was leaning against the door of his apartment, wet, cold, tired. He had walked all the way from the zoo and he had to walk up fifteen flights of stairs because the elevator wasn't working, again. That damn thing never works, he thought. The water dripped from his clothes and body. He felt his burden and it was still safe, still undamaged. He knew a way to get in. The apartment next door was vacant and the lock had been broken sometime ago. He could get into his apartment by climbing from that apartment's terrace to his own. He had done it before. It wasn't very dangerous, not if he was careful.

There were people around, more than usual. But no one paid much attention to him or thought it strange that he was out so late. He thought that he might be stopped. After all, he was only fifteen, and so he was violating curfew. It didn't matter much. He knew that the sort of people who would wonder what a drenched boy was doing out past midnight were not out themselves. He was worried that he might be stopped by a cop and asked what he was carrying and he knew then that it would all be over for him because he could not come up with an explanation for what was in his shirt that could convince himself, let alone someone else. There were some party revelers around. The people on the floor below were having a party; their door was probably open and people were out in the hall. The music blasted up to him as if the sound had exploded from a shotgun. He could hear it two floors below as he was walking up all those flights.

He tried the door of the apartment next door and it opened. He knew it would. He walked through the darkened room. It was still raining heavily. The thunder rolled and the lightning still buzzed and blitzed the sky. The boy had no idea what time it was but he knew it was very late now. The rain must have washed out some of the celebrations, for, as warm as it had been, the streets would have been crowded with people. It was pitch black in the apartment, except the small rings of yellowish red light of cigarettes and little burners of blue flame. It looked almost pretty in its eeriness. A bolt of lightning cut through the room for a moment and the boy could see the bodies

there. He held his breath for a moment for fear of recognizing someone. But it was dark again. He did not see the person he feared he
might. He could hear people moaning, cursing; most were unconscious; he stepped over one or two. He could hardly stand the odor,
the body funk, the stench of burning spoons, the acrid odor of drugs,
the sickening bitter sweetness of alcohol wafting in the air like an
elixir. He wanted to run through the room for fear he would get high
just from the fetid air, high or sick. He tried not to look either to his
right or his left but to walk straight ahead as if he were on a
tightrope. No one said anything to him. He finally reached the sliding
glass door of the terrace, the rain blowing fiercely through it. He
opened it and was glad to step outside in the fresh air, in the wind and
rain. He no longer felt wet; he had been wet for so long. He stared
down, fifteen stories to the street, and could see some police cars,
some people milling around. Others were running to get out of the
rain. He felt someone behind him and turned, as lightning streaked,
to see a bedraggled man with burning red eyes, wearing a long dirty
coat, grinning with three dirty teeth in his face. The man staggered a
little but the boy was so close to him that he jumped, startled by the
nearness of the derelict. He could smell the derelict's breath.

"Happy New Years, my man," the derelict said, sloppy with happiness. He knew who the derelict was. He used to be one of the best high
school basketball players in the country. He was thirty but he looked as
if he was nearly fifty. Another guy in the room had won two Golden
Gloves championships and was a shoo-in for the Olympics. There was
a well-known minister there as well as an elementary school principal.
A fly girl he knew from elementary school. A Sunday School superintendent. The boy was disgusted and ashamed. The rain splashed
against the derelict. The wind blew against them. A sudden crack of
booming thunder, violent and deep as an earthquake, made the boy
jump as a frightened rabbit in a quarry.

"Get away from me, you stinkin' junkie!" he shouted, pushing
the derelict as hard as he could back into the apartment and slamming
the sliding glass door together as if it mattered, because there was no
glass in the door. He then climbed up on the edge of the terrace, the
rain blowing hard against him. Ten feet separated that terrace from
his apartment. He did not look down because he knew if he did he
would be too afraid to jump. He pushed his burden around to the nar-

row of his back and hoped that the jolt would not damage it. Suppose they're alive, he thought. Damn, that would be bad if they broke.

He jumped just as another flash of lightning lit the air. It startled him, for some reason he thought for a moment that it had struck him, and he fell heavily against the rail of his terrace, slippery with rain. He could feel his burden hit his back, the buckle of his belt hard against his navel, and he could actually feel his shirt balloon from his trousers. They were on the verge of falling out. He grabbed hold with his arms as his feet slipped and his weight pulled against the rail and he felt it loosen a bit. In a panic, fearing he was about to plummet fifteen stories to his death, he grabbed the rail savagely and pulled himself over it. Once on his terrace, he scrambled to his feet, pushed against the sliding door and realized it was locked. He gritted his teeth, punched against the frame of the door several times to loosen the unreliable lock, pushed the door and entered his darkened apartment.

He stood stock still for a moment and then in the darkness called out, "Mom?" And again, "Mom? Mom, you here?" All he heard was the rain, the thunder, the noise of the party down the hall. He crept across the living room in the darkness, opened a door and slipped quietly in.

"Where you been?" asked a little girl's voice in the darkness. The boy jumped again. He did not turn on the light but went straight across the room to a small cot where a little girl was sitting. Her face could not be seen clearly in the darkness.

"Jesus, girl, you scared the daylights out of me! What you doing up?" the boy said.

"You all wet!" the girl said, her shoulder brushing against his shirt. He felt cold again and was beginning to shiver. "You been out there with Zulu and Shere Khan and them, ain't you?"

"Where's Mom?" he asked, ignoring her question. He shifted his burden to his stomach again. They felt cool now. They had felt warm when he had grabbed them at first. He thought it could not be good for them to cool off.

"She went out looking for you," said the little girl. "She knew you was in trouble with Shere Khan and Zulu and them and she went out to find you," she said.

"You sure?" he asked. He kneeled down beside the cot and was close to the little girl now.

"Did you see her next door?" the little girl asked anxiously.

"No," he said sarcastically. "Just people over there having a wonderful time living in the wonderful world of S4." Damn, I wish she hadn't gone out. It'd be a real bad time for her to be goin' back with her being pregnant and all. Damn, why she always getting pregnant so much anyway?

"That's good. That means she went looking for you, like she said."

"You cold?" he asked, changing the subject. "It's startin' to get cold again. Maybe I better turn on the heat."

"I ain't cold. I'm all right," she said, "What you carryin' in your shirt?"

He laughed out loud, almost bitterly. Then, he carefully took out three objects. They didn't smell very good. He hadn't noticed that before; perhaps in the excitement, he hadn't realized fully how much everything stank. And he felt his nostrils were filled with that odor. It made his stomach heave a little.

"Whew, you smell bad. What is that? I can't see," the little girl said.

She turned around, arched her leg deftly and turned on a little night-light with her toe, something for a kid who might still be afraid of the dark. But she wasn't afraid of the dark anymore. She just wanted to see the boy and what he had been carrying. He wanted to tell her to put it out because he was afraid of the light at times like this. But he did not want her to know he was afraid. The small pool of light dimly lit the room. Her face seemed oddly young and gnomish in the light as if she were both a child and an imp. But her gestures and voice gave her away as nothing more than a little girl, younger than the boy. She gasped when she saw the boy's face.

"You got blood on you!" she said. "You get shot or something?! You hurt, Prince?" She was starting to get hysterical.

He looked down, touching his chest, which he saw was stained with watery blood. Damn, what is that? he thought.

"Calm down! That ain't my blood," he said. "That's bird blood. I was at the zoo. That's where Zulu and them went. To the zoo. Shere Khan wasn't there. He ain't gonna be out there in something like that. He ain't no gangbanger. Just like he says, he's an artist and a businessman. He's a credit to the community, like he says, you know, all that crap. I'm out there with Zulu, Bad Archie, Ping Pong, Master Jay, Burnt, and them other crazy fools that hang out at Felony/Art. What Shere Khan call them—His Bodyguards." He fell back on his haunches. His sneakers squished. He was getting the carpet in the room wet but he didn't care. He felt he should have cared but he was too tired. He held his head down. He placed the three objects on the edge of the little girl's bed.

"It's eggs," she said, completely surprised. "What you doin' with them eggs?" Then she added, disappointed: "I thought it was gonna be a pet or somethin' like that."

On her cot were three dirty brown eggs, somewhat larger than chicken eggs. The boy knew now why the eggs smelled bad. He could see chalky streaks of feces on them. Damn, I been carryin' these stinkin' bird eggs and they was covered with bird shit! I can't believe that!

"They bird eggs," he said, moving them off the little girl's bed before they stained her blanket. I gotta clean them, he thought. I heard this stuff carries diseases. "I don't know, some kind of bird eggs, herons or swans, or cranes or something. I don't know. There was a lot of birds around. We was at the Bird House. Them boys was goin' around smashin' all those eggs that were there. And then the birds went crazy and started smashing 'em, too, almost like they'd rather see their children dead by they own hand than see us kill 'em. I couldn't stand it. I just couldn't stand it. You know, they animals and all but they was killin' their own children. I knew it was really wrong to be doin' something so bad that it make some animals want to kill their own children. So, I grabbed these before the birds could get 'em." He shook his head as if he still could not believe what had happened or what he had done. "It was all crazy. Them birds tried to rip our heads off, too. I guess they had a right to, with those boys smashing them and all. But birds are nasty. Don't let anybody tell you different."

"Why they go to the zoo? What you do at the zoo with them boys? Did you go there to kill birds?" the little girl asked, absentmindedly rubbing her feet together.

The scene flashed through the boy's mind again. The rain, the thunder, the lightning, the terror, the screaming boys like mad ghouls, like the possessed, the birds running or attacking, the blood. He saw Zulu take out his automatic and blow one bird's head apart and just laugh. One boy hit a bird with a brick so hard that the bird's blood shot out as if sprouting from a hose and splattered against him. But one bird savagely bit a boy's face. Another boy was clawed across the chest. Then, the Blood Warriors—Grinder, 7th Speed, Gears, Chaos, Rudolph Matthews, MoonMan, Cowboy, and the rest, with their leader, Glorious Gilpin the First (his legal name)— showed up and starting shooting with sawed-offs and assault rifles. Gilpin, yelling, his yellow, contorted face drenched with rain, his cape billowing in the wind, the lightning flashing off the darkness of his weapon: "Where's the goddam egg? Where's the goddam egg? Where the goddam kilos? I want our m—f—ing kilos!" And Zulu and them shooting back but running because they were clearly out-gunned and were surprised. Then, it came to him that he did notice at the time how much he thought the birds stank, how much like children they seemed in their panic, how sticky and sickening the blood. This don't make no kinda sense, he thought of that moment of savagery. A boy was shot. He remembered that. He saw that, the boy, falling. He didn't know which one, from which side. A zoo person was shot, too. He saw that. He did not lift his head as he spoke to the little girl.

"I don't wanna talk about it," he said. He picked up the eggs, rose to his feet awkwardly, and turned to leave the room. "Just go to sleep. I'll go out and find Mom."

"But what happened, Prince? What y'all do at the zoo? Are you in trouble?" she persisted.

He turned fully to face her again.

"I told you," he said angrily. "I don't want to talk about it. We just, I mean, they just killed some birds at the zoo. Then, the Warriors came. A boy got shot. A person who works at the zoo got shot. Maybe more than one. That's all. That's all I know. It was crazy. If you want to know why, ask them. Don't ask me. It wasn't my idea. Why don't you just go to sleep and keep your damn mouth shut? You always want to be askin' things with your nosy ass! Just go to sleep!"

The room was silent. Prince noticed for the first time that the world itself seemed silent. The party down the hall had stopped. The rain had stopped or at least slowed down. There was no thunder or lightning now. He could hear the little girl sigh deeply. She's gonna cry, he thought. She's gonna cry now, cry herself to sleep. He walked over to the cot again and fell to his knees, putting the eggs on the floor again. A trickle of water ran down the back of his neck.

"Don't talk to me like that, Prince, and be hurtin' me," she said, sobbingly. "I was just scared. I was scared them boys was gonna kill you or something." Damn, she can hear people around here cursing like maniacs, calling her and everybody else everything but a child of God and it don't do nothing to her and as soon as I get mad she starts to cry. He was quiet for a few seconds.

"I'm sorry, Miss Glory," he said, soothingly. "I didn't mean to get mad at you. I'm just mad at myself, that's all. I can't afford to get in no more trouble, with Zulu and them or with the cops. I'm trying to stay in good with them so I don't lose my drums, or go back to Youth Detention, or lose my life, although I think them drums is worth more. Then, I don't know if Mom is backslidin' or what. 'Specially since they made the apartment next door a junkie hangout with a lot of juiceheads, too. What you gonna do? Man, like, what *are* you gonna do, like, really?" He spoke very softly.

"I can help you, Prince. Let me help you," she said eagerly.

He gently pushed her down in the bed and covered her with the blankets.

"Just go to sleep, girl. You can help me in the morning."

"It's already morning," she said. "Prince, don't go back out. Stay here with me. I'm scared bein' alone."

"What you lyin' for? You ain't scared of bein' alone. You been left alone before." A shaft of guilt shot through Prince when he said that. Hadn't he learned from what happened to his other sisters? Hadn't his mother learned, not to ever do that again? Man, she ain't even learned to stop having babies, he laughed to himself.* He thought he could only learn from his mistakes in music. And he did and had corrected them all. He could understand nothing else, nothing greater. And his mother did not even have music from which to master the art of correction.

"I'll be right back," he said. "I'm just gonna go 'round the block

---

*Prince's mother had seven children at this time, expecting her eighth. The fate of the other five will be told in its proper place. Suffice it to say that there were several different men involved and Gloria was Prince's half-sister. "How can she be my half-sister?" he said to me. "Either you got a sister or you don't. Can you have half-a dog or half-a cat? If I got a half-sister, where's the other half?"   —L. F. Haines

and see if I see Mom, that's all. I swear. I ain't goin' far." He grinned at her and winked. He started feeling around the floor around her cot.

"Where's that xylophone? I'll play you something to go to sleep to," he said. He slid his hand under her bed but felt nothing. He scurried to his feet and went to his own room, thinking he knew where it might be. He started rummaging through a carton in the corner, near his bed. He did not move much of the stuff in the box as the xylophone was on top of everything else. Under it were several hand puppets. It all belonged to the Susan Arion Children's Theater, puppets he used for his music presentations for elementary school students that were sponsored and put together at the theater. Damn, I totally forgot about the jazz babies, thought Prince. Man, I had this crap for weeks. I got to get this stuff back to the theater. I wonder why they haven't asked for it. I wonder why Mr. Gerron didn't ask for this. Well, Mr. Gerron kinda strange, anyway. He don't seem all there.

He noticed something in the corner of the carton that he had seen before but he had never paid attention to, and he felt something like a revelation descend. Half-hidden under some puppets and other props, he saw it. He pushed the other objects away and pulled it from the box, an oval wooden object, very dirty, beaten and chipped, an egg covered with markings. He knew that tonight was not simply a random act of violence. The boys went there looking for something. This! Prince thought, they were looking for this! That's why we were looking among those bird eggs. They thought somebody hid this in the zoo. He shook it and heard something rattle in it. But why would they want this piece of junk? Must be something valuable inside or something, he thought. It sure ain't no five kilos, if that's what they want. It's too light for that.

As he held it, he felt it vibrate a little, then more, shaking his body. Suddenly, he felt something electric pulse through him hard and quickly. The shock threw him backwards and as he flew back, he threw the egg back in the box. He lay on his back for a moment, then sat up. What the hell was that? he thought. What is that thing? He was breathing hard, as if he were running hard again. He wanted to cry out but refrained himself, fearing his sister would shout out in concern. He didn't want her to know what had happened. He hoped she hadn't heard anything. He looked at his hands, as if he half-expected them to be burned. Seeing his palms unharmed, it occurred to him that the sensation he felt was not entirely unpleasant, just unexpected. But it wasn't entirely pleasing either. The strange surge made him feel odd, more aware but more aware of what? Something. Sound? The breathing that filled his head was not his own merely; he could hear clearly his sister breathing in the other room. The faint buzzing of the night-light in her room. The ticking of the watch on his wrist. The faint creaking of the dirty dishes in the sink. Was he not able to hear these same sounds before? A musician with a good ear can hear things like that, he thought. But he could not recall having heard them before or being aware of it. The noise was not cacophonous. Indeed, it wasn't noise at all that he heard. It didn't sound like noise to him. For a moment, despite all the sound entering his ears, he could control it, tame it, make sense of it, hear it as music, utter music. He crawled back over to the box, peered in at the egg. He touched it gingerly at first, jerking his hand back as if he expected it to be hot. The wood was, to the contrary, cool. He touched it again, feeling nothing unusual. He picked it up again, holding it. Nothing happened. Maybe it was just some kind of static or somethin', the boy thought. Maybe from being out in that storm or being wet and on this rug or something like that. But I thought wood didn't carry electricity. Maybe there is some kind of thing in it, a generator, maybe, like that. All I know is that was pretty damn weird. Maybe that's why they want it. Maybe it's some kind of hook up to something. Maybe it's something you got to know how to use. If it is, the boy thought, Shere Khan would sure know. Maybe it's gonna lead them to five kilos or something. Maybe it can *make* five kilos.

He shook his head, and the sounds that he heard faded away. If only Shere Khan and them knew he had had it in this carton in his bedroom for the last week or more. If only he had known, he could have given it to them and that would have been that. But how did it get here? I mean, who put it in this box? The last person who had it was Mr. Gerron. I wonder if he put it in here. But why would he do that? In fact, Prince was completely puzzled. What was it? He could clearly make out words, LED ROAR. He thought about it a bit more and realized that he couldn't give it to Shere Khan. They'd want to know how I got it. Maybe somebody at the theater might get trouble. But didn't he owe Shere Khan something for all that

Shere Khan had done for him? Getting him a great drum kit, good musicians for a band, paying his scholarship for N_____ Latin School, helping him with his sister and mother,* giving him a spotlight feature in "The Hip Hop Nation of S4" that showed him playing a ferocious drum solo and talking about how important music was to him. This made him famous for a while when the film turned out to be success. Why shouldn't he be loyal to Shere Khan who had, after all, treated him well. But then he thought he didn't want to get tied with Shere Khan any more than he had to. If he gave Shere Khan the egg, it might just pull him in deeper into all of this. He didn't want Shere Khan to be grateful to him for anything. He thought that would be worse than his being grateful to Shere Khan. I give him the egg and that'd just be a lot more bullshit with him and me. And maybe the cops would want to know about the egg. Maybe it is some kind of dope in this thing. Don't feel like it but it might be. Something stolen, maybe, that's worth a lot of money. Then, if the cops get in it, I'm really messed up, with some dope or some other crap. I could go to prison behind something like that, not to

---

*Shere Khan served as a benefactor for a good many people in the neighborhood called S4. In fact, he once complained to me that he gave away so much money that he was surprised that he had any left for himself. "I am the personification of largesse, the lord of the largesse," he said. "And I still live in S4. I'm not like these other Hip Hop stars who can't wait to move to some upscale neighborhood in lily-white land when they get some dough. And, look, I own businesses in this neighborhood, like the black newspaper, barbershops, a couple of gas stations, two McDonalds, a dry cleaning business, a Laundromat, five apartment buildings. I got a major grocery chain to locate here. I own businesses outside the neighborhood like a pottery shop that makes pots for plants, a company in Pennsylvania that makes pulp for apple juice, a minor league basketball team, a car dealership, two radio stations, a film production company. I employ people from the neighborhood. I create jobs." Khan had gotten into trouble with the NAACP for not allowing union organizing at some of his places of employment. He said angrily, "I'm not like these so-called activists, these chickenshit, left-wing militants begging the white man for jobs. What the hell do my employees need unions for? I'm taking care of them better than any union. Did the union get 'em a job? Did these left-wing organizers bring any businesses down here? Have they created one free-market job in their lives? I have. Any jobs they created were made by government funds they got. I made jobs from running businesses. I love America. It is the greatest country on earth. I really mean that. Where else could a guy like me have my chances? But I hate those complainers, f—ing whiners, the goddam protesters! Any of them looking out for a boy like Prince Timmons? He'd be in jail right now, his sister in some institution, his mom back on the street selling her ass and doing crack if it wasn't for me. I put him in a goddam movie and got his talent out there for people to see all over the country. I'm better than the church, the NAACP, and all the rest of them combined. I have done nothing but good for people in S4. With the movie, S4 has got to be the most famous black neighborhood in America next to Harlem." When I asked him, since he thought so much of Prince Timmons, why didn't he adopt the boy and his sister, indeed, the entire family. He looked at me thoughtfully for a minute, then said, "You can't make things too easy for people. They won't appreciate how they got what they got. If I started doing stuff like adopting people, I wouldn't be doing anything but taking care of people. I'm too much of a padrone as it is. I'm trying to teach his family how to take care of themselves." What Khan was really upset about was that the NAACP, black ministers, and others had severely criticized his company for putting out records full of profanity, advocating violence, and nearly pornographic in their sexual references. "I know you're not going to tell me that you are giving the people what they want," I said to him. "What the hell else am I going to tell you?" he shot back. "That as a businessman I want to give the people what they don't want." "Don't you have a responsibility to the public for the art you produce?" I asked. "Yes, I do," he said soberly. "I have

Youth Detention but to prison. Goddamit, they hook me up with all that stuff that went down tonight, I'll be in all kinds of trouble. I got to get rid of this thing because I sure don't want Zulu and them to find it here. I'm lucky they didn't already. I don't know what this thing is and I don't want to know. I just got to get rid of it. He placed it back in the carton, noticing that despite the fact it was so dirty, there wasn't a trace of dirt on his hands. It didn't give the strange sensation it had when he first touched it. He had no curiosity about it anymore. He simply wanted it out of his life. He thought of giving it to Gentleman Brown but quickly rejected the idea. He couldn't tell which way the wind blew with Brown, although he had an urge to tell Brown he had found it and ask for his help. Maybe he should just give it back to Mr. Gerron. It was his stuff, his puppets. He made them. If he took the egg out, wouldn't Mr. Gerron want to know what happened to it. Or maybe Mr. Gerron didn't know it was even in the box. Lots of people hung around the children's theater and he remembered that Mr. Gerron didn't even hand him the box of puppets. He just pointed indiffer-

a responsibility to make the art as good as I can for the sake of the artists who record for Felony/Art and for the sake of the young people who buy the records. I do that. My production standards are the highest in the business. My artists are among the most innovative in Hip Hop. Not just anyone can record for my label. If the people who criticize me for debasing art had any real ability beyond their bourgeois brainwashing to truly appreciate art and the talents that my artists have, I might listen to what they have to say. But they don't know anything about art. Everybody thinks Bessie Smith and Louis Armstrong and Jelly Roll Morton and Bennie Moten are all great artists but they weren't considered that back in the day. They were considered filthy, debasing black people and all like that. These people think Charlie Parker is such a great artist now but that's because somebody told them to think that way. It's not because they were able to think that on their own. On their own, they only thought that Charlie Parker was a noisy saxophonist who took drugs, ran around with white women, and debased the race. Just like they think about Gentleman Brown, who is even more a genius than Parker ever was. And you want me to take what people like that think seriously?! After all, those people who don't like me and Felony/Art, they're the gatekeepers. They're the ones that set the standards. Everything they don't like becomes the gatecrasher. You have to be a gatecrasher. But if they don't like it, they have no one to blame but themselves. Because this is the goddam world that they created, that they engineered. It's not my world. It's their f—ing world. I'm only the progeny. It's me who recognized the possibilities in a boy like Prince Timmons, not the gatekeepers, who only saw some boy in S4 who banged on the drums and who ran around the streets. They would only stifle his creativity. They don't know how to develop it because they keep thinking that what he is needs to be changed. But he really needs to be nurtured in his natural environment that produced his creative spark." I detected a note of The Gentleman in the speech but not pure Ivanhoe Brown; they were truly Shere Khan's sentiments. I must add that, to finish off an earlier point about how Shere Khan lived that it is true that Shere Khan had a house, two, in fact, in Prince's neighborhood. But he also owned homes in the wealthier parts of town including a mansion in Chelsea Hills, not far from where Justin Arion lived. But to his credit, one tended to find him quite often in his offices located just a few blocks from the Absalom Jones Housing Projects. But he clearly did not continue to live in S4 where he was reared. Some said he kept his connection with S4 because he intended to run for mayor. "Are you going to run for mayor?" I asked him. "You're only twenty-six. You're a little young, aren't you?" "Hell, I can run for it legally. I'm thinking about it. I'd be one f—ing strong candidate, don't you think, Haines? My life story offers the people real hope, no more sob stories. I'm a success story." "If you do, you'd better clean up your language a little more," I said. "That's no problem. I can talk the King's English, when I need to," he grinned.   —L. F. Haines

ently to a corner and told him to take them. That old geezer didn't
even offer me a ride home and had me hauling that shit on the bus.
At least Mr. Arion would have given me a lift. Prince was supposed
to bring them back in a week, but it wasn't unusual for Prince to be
late and, besides, they had extra puppets. They got tons of puppets,
he thought. And what about the Blood Warriors? They were looking for the egg now, too, probably because they just wanted the
Assassins and Shere Khan not to get it. What if *they* found out he
had it? My ass wouldn't be worth a penny. But why did Zulu and
them take me to the zoo tonight, asking me about the egg? It's like
they thought I knew something special, that I had seen the egg or
that I knew it was in the zoo just like they did. Man, I ain't never
heard of any egg until tonight.

Finally, Prince decided he'd take the egg somewhere, hide it, and
then let Shere Khan know where he might find it by calling him
anonymously or sending him an unsigned note. Then, he would be
out of it. No one could know he possessed the egg or ever had it. If
Mr. Gerron wanted the egg back, that was his lookout. He shouldn't
have put it in the box, if he did. I'd rather have old man Gerron
pissed at me than Shere Khan.

"What you doin', Prince? What's taking you so long? You sick
or something? Sound like stuff is fallin' in there? You all right?"
Gloria's voice sounded shrill and nervous.

"I'm comin', Miss Glory," he said. He grabbed the toy xylophone, two small sticks and two of the puppets and went back to her
room. He shifted to sit Indian-style on the floor with the little instrument on his lap. He began to play a soft lullaby and even though it
was a toy, he played it very well and the instrument sounded, not like
a toy, but like something that could play real music. The little girl, lying on her side, shut her eyes and smiled. He played the lullaby for a
few minutes. The song evolved into something truly beautiful, yet it
remained simple. He tapped out an intricate but smooth rhythm but
added little arpeggios and made dreamy taps on the side of the xylophone with the opposite end of the stick. It was plain to hear instantly
that Prince was an accomplished musician. The music he played for
the little girl was lovely, its gentle poignancy an odd counterpoint to
the evening that the boy named Prince had experienced. He tried to

remember the words, to hum them, so he could play the melody better but he couldn't remember them all:

In the starry night so still
Listen to the Whippoorwill
Forest shades repeat his song
Dreamily it floats along

Hark, the whippoorwill
Listen to the whippoorwill

All he could remember was something about whippoorwill. He remembered that when he first heard it, he felt stupid because he did not know what a whippoorwill was until Kid Ryder told him, sensing that he didn't know that it was a bird, a nightjar, not a sprite or a fairy or a wood nymph. "Everybody sings about whippoorwills," she said, "like Hank Williams." And she sang:

Hear the lonesome whippoorwill
He sounds too blue to cry

"My aunt taught me that," she chimed but he ignored her. I must have been wearin' my ignorance on my face like a goddam rash, like Cain or something. She just could look at me and say, "That's a dumb guy." Naw, I bet she thought, "That's a dumb nigger." I didn't even know it was a bird. He just walked away from her. The song grew more complex as he played, until one was startled by how much music he was getting from a toy instrument, and how casually he did it. I need a smoke, he was thinking as he played. I wonder if Mom's got any smokes around here. He stopped when he thought for sure that the little girl was asleep. He put the xylophone on the floor, stood up, and started toward the door.

"Where'd you learn that tune? I never heard you play that before."

He turned around, startled by her voice. She's always playing possum. Maybe she don't ever sleep, he thought.

"I heard it somewhere," he said.

"Where'd you hear it?" she persisted.

He groaned a little. "If you gotta know, I heard that Kid Ryder sing it a few weeks ago in the band room."

"I knew Kid Ryder had something to do with it," she said, bouncing up in bed again. "It sure is pretty." Ever since the boy had met Kid Ryder at the start of the school year and mentioned her at home on occasion, the little girl couldn't get enough of hearing about her. He couldn't understand why his sister was so taken with some silly white girl she had never met and was not likely to meet. "So, she taught you the tune, huh?"

"Kid Ryder ain't teach me squat!" the boy spat out. "There ain't nothing that smart-ass, stuck-up Kid Ryder can teach me about no music, her and her corny accordion. I forgot more about music than she ever gonna know. I heard it and for some dumb reason it stuck in my head." But he had to admit to himself that she showed him the chords for it. He was usually showing her things and this stuck in his mind because it was one of the few times she showed him something. It was on the accordion she showed me that song, he said to himself. She ain't never showed me nothing on the drums. He corrected himself.

"You said her brother can play," the little girl said softly.

"Yeah, her brother can play his ass off. But she's just a stuck-up little brat. And she sure can't play no drums," he said, vehemently.

"You said once she was pretty good," she continued softly.

"I ain't never said that or nothing like it," he said. "I probably said she was better than anything else Mr. Ellison had. I never said she was good. She's too shaky. Now, go on back to sleep." He walked across the room and tucked her in again. The Drumbabe, as he derisively called Kid Ryder, was a whitebread little freshman, trying to be different with her dumb pilot's helmet with the goggles, and playing that accordion, some cornball instrument for old white folks into polkas and square dancing. He wondered why Mr. Ellison put her in the advanced jazz band. Maybe because of her brother, to make him happy. Kid Ryder is just a dumb white girl.

"It's a pretty song," she said again.

"Yeah, it's pretty," he relented.

"You shouldn't talk bad about Kid Ryder 'cause her Daddy died and Mom said you shouldn't talk bad about people when somebody in they family pass," said Gloria.

A pang of guilt seized the boy so strongly and suddenly that it nearly took his breath away. Maybe Kid Ryder can't play. Maybe she was just a dumb white girl. But Prince knew it was wrong to speak ill of her with her father so recently and tragically killed. Besides, he knew Mr. Arion, had met him at the children's theater, knew that Mr. Arion wanted to help him, if he could, but was unsure because, at least as Prince saw it, Mr. Arion must have felt reluctant because he thought Prince was tied up with Shere Khan. Prince thought that Mr. Arion was going to buy Felony/Art. It was the word for a long time. That would have been sweet for me, maybe, to get out from under Shere Khan and them but Shere Khan messed that up. Mr. Arion liked his playing, liked it a lot. And he liked Mr. Arion's playing, making it a point to listen to several of his records.

Prince remembered going into the band room at school late one afternoon a few weeks ago, no one expecting him, secretly like the thief that he was, and saw Kid Ryder there, alone, her back to the door, singing. She didn't know anyone was there. Prince could tell she had been crying. He saw balled-up tissues on the floor. Her voice was quiet, private in its grief, yet it had a richness and feeling he never noticed before, a trueness of pitch and power, that Prince admired. She's a pretty good singer, he thought, more charitably than usual when thinking about her musical abilities. She could sing with a band. She's pretty solid. She's got technique. It was a hymn. He didn't know it, had never heard it before, but he could only stand to hear so much of it before he felt her grief and his own.

For all are one in thee, for all are thine
Alleluia! Alleluia!

She stopped abruptly and hung her head. Prince was afraid that perhaps she sensed he was there. But she was so enclosed in her sorrow that she was hardly aware of where she herself was, let alone that anyone was around. She had removed her pilot's hat, holding it in her hand. She looked strange to Prince without it. She began to sing again, another song, more rhythmic:

A stick, a stone
It's the end of the road
It's the rest of the stump
It's a little alone

Prince listened for a while, for the song enchanted him and he could not tell quite if the song was happy or sad. Was the song about life or death?

And the riverbank talks
Of the waters of March

Before she could turn around, before the song could dredge up within him oceans of grief and whatever comes after, he quietly slipped out of the band room. He had heard that song before but could not remember where. He looked at his sister in the bed, at that moment, and clenched his teeth. When he remembered seeing Kid Ryder in that room, hearing her sing, he felt he might cry. He didn't feel sorry for her. He had been taught it was not a good idea to feel sorry for anyone, ever. It won't do her any good or me either. It actually surprised him for a moment that he was surprised that people like Kid Ryder felt pain and loss. They don't have everything, he thought. Not even bein' white and havin' money. They don't have everything.

"You right," he said, thoughtfully. "You can't speak bad of people when they have a loss. And I wasn't speakin' bad of her. She just can't play the drums, that's all. She's tryin', I guess. I know, I mean," he stammered, "I know, you know, it's hard for her, too." There was a moment of silence.

"You gonna do the puppets for me?" she asked, suddenly.

He sighed, looked at her, then grinned.

"Okay, for like a quick minute. Then, you go to sleep." He knew he would have to do the puppets. She wouldn't go to sleep otherwise.

He crouched down on the floor below the level of her mattress. There was silence for about a minute. Suddenly, a figure peered over her mattress, looked around, and slowly rose up. It was Wally Wallaby, a bright-eyed, apple-jack-wearing youngster who studied the piano but was not a good student.

"Hmmm," said Wally Wallaby, in his high, soft voice, "The coast is clear. I can cut out of here and old man Monk won't ever know I was here and gone. 'Cause old man Monk, all that dog be thinkin' about is music, music, music. And some old-time music from way back when, at that. Man, I can go play some ball and don't have to be bothered with all these dumb lessons. Let me hat on up and ride on out of here."

Gloria knew her part. She and her brother had done this many times.

"But Wally," she said, "You know what Mr. Monk said. If you don't know your lesson, you might get caught out there on the street by Misterioso. He always hunts down kids that don't know their music. You know the only way to stop him is by becoming a player."

Wally looked up, surprised.

"Oh, I didn't know the squirt, Miss Glory, was here. Well, it ain't no sweat off you if I don't do my lesson, is it? And I got Misterioso's number figured out. Ain't no Misterioso gonna get a hold of me. I know enough music to keep that guy away."

But suddenly, up over the landscape of the bed was a huge shadow. Wings arched out, his long red face and burning eyes looking down at Wally Wallaby, the huge ram horns jutting from his forehead, it was Misterioso, the grand master of all chaos, confusion, and corruption, the magician of the night, the Dark Prince of All Disorder, he who would banish jazz and its minions from the world. In his stentorian tone, he bellowed:

"Dare you challenge me, o weak, pathetic one?"

Trembling, Wally Wallaby did not dare to look up. What would he do? How would he escape the wrath of Misterioso? Could he tame the savage beast with song? Could he soothe the fiend with tones, make it obey his will through music? O, Wally Wallaby's skills were so modest and Misterioso was so powerful. But Wally Wallaby peered around Misterioso, looked at Gloria, and seemed to smile and wink. She could swear he did. That Wally Wallaby's got some trick up his sleeve yet.

"He's just a magician," said Wally Wallaby, "But I'm an Ear Lord. Always put your money on the Ear Lord."

"Tune in again to find out what will become of Wally Wallaby!" said Prince, in his own voice, as the puppets disappeared and he rose from beneath the bed. He couldn't go on. His mind was occupied with other things.

"Prince, finish it now!" Gloria shouted.

"Can't. I told you just a quick minute. Now, you go to sleep before I bust you one," he laughed.

He picked up the eggs and the puppets and walked across the room again and stood with his face to the door. He waited nearly a minute in silence.

"Happy New Years, Miss Glory," he said at last.

"Happy New Years, Prince," she said. Several seconds of silence and Prince stood still at the door as if he were waiting for something.

She had asked him once, when he added this new element to the story line a few months ago, what's an Ear Lord?

"They, they, like, special musicians," he said, trying to think of something, wondering why he had even thrown the term into the story. "They not only play well," he said, beginning to get an imaginative flow, "but they try to do right things with the music they play, you know, inspire the people, make the people want to do right. People are lazy when they listen to music. The Ear Lords try to play music so that the people can wake up to themselves, not hypnotize them, the way people want with music, but to wake them up to what they can be, what they should be. Something like that, I guess.

"You know, it's like them Greek myths I read about. That guy named Orpheus. He was like an Ear Lord, except he didn't make it. He went to hell and played music and almost got his girlfriend out. But you know Ear Lords try to do something brave with music like that, something so that people think playin' music is important, more than just some noise you like." He rubbed his lower lip with his finger. That sounds pretty good, he thought, better than saying it was just a group of some old-time musicians. He thought she was going to ask him if he was an Ear Lord but she didn't.

"Is Kid Ryder an Ear Lord?" she nearly whispered, as if in awe of the thought of it.

"What?!" He was incredulous. "The Drumbabe an Ear Lord?! First, you got to be good on your instrument. Real good and she ain't even close. Her brother might be one day. Maybe me too. But you got to be more than good on your instrument. You got to do something worthy on it. I ain't quite there yet but I expect to be there." He grinned a little, but was disappointed that his sister did not immediately think of him. But she too was disappointed.

"I thought you already were one, like Kid Ryder," she said.

The boy stood at the door and waited. He didn't know whether he felt happy or sad. It all seemed mixed up and he felt some of both. "Now go to sleep for real."

"They ain't gonna kill you, are they, you know, Zulu and Shere Khan and them or them Warriors," she never turned her face to him. She buried it in the pillow as if not only afraid of the answer but afraid of the question itself.

"Ain't nobody killin' me, Miss Glory. Especially no dumb niggas from around this way. God ain't gonna let me die behind some dumb stuff like this. He ain't even gonna let me get sick." He spoke with a confidence he did not honestly feel but he wished he could.

Before he shut the bedroom door he heard her say in a fierce whisper, "Kid Ryder can too play and so can Wally Wallaby 'cause he's an Ear Lord and he'll show that Misterioso tomorrow!" He grinned as he pulled the door behind him. Kid Ryder really got somebody on her side and she don't even know it, he shrugged.

He went to the kitchen and placed the eggs gently in the kitchen sink, filled it with water, and, with a sponge and dishwashing liquid, carefully cleaned them. He frowned the whole time, hating the filth. If I had known they was this nasty, I wouldn't have taken 'em. Shere Khan and them could have wiped out the whole lot of 'em. What's that to me? I ain't no bird-lover. I hate pets, animals, whatever. The only times he had ever been to the zoo before tonight was on class field trips. It would never have occurred to him to go unless made to do so. After he finished with the eggs, he thoroughly washed the sink with scouring powder, and, then, dried the eggs on paper towels, leaving them on the drain board. I coulda just let 'em dry by themselves on this drain board and not use any paper towels. That was a waste, he thought. He had to get rid of the eggs but he did not know how.

He took some clothes from a dresser, went to the bathroom and had a long, hot shower. He was still feeling cold and it was only after the shower that he felt better. Wearing fresh, dry clothes, he felt renewed and less tired. In the refrigerator, he found some cold chicken and potato salad that he wolfed down because for the first time he realized that he was very hungry and had been for some time. He still thought he could smell the eggs, although they did not smell anymore. He drank some water and then he drank a can of beer. He found a package of cigarettes on top of the television and smoked one. It made him feel good. He drew the smoke deeply into his lungs and blew it out with mellow pleasure. He hadn't smoked one in a long time, a few days, because he had been trying to give up the habit. Mr. Ellison had been on him forever about smoking. The hell with that, he thought. You gotta die of something. One thing's as good as another. At the rate things are going, I ain't likely to live long enough for these things to kill me. He stuck another cigarette behind his ear, as was his habit, for later. When he thought of Mr. Ellison, something in him went soft and he almost felt like crying. I ain't been much good to Mr. Ellison. And I've disappointed him again with this. That ain't much of way to thank somebody trying to help me and my family as much as he did. It was Mr. Ellison who got Shere Khan to be my sponsor. Maybe that wasn't so good, after all. I don't think Old JAS understood exactly what Shere Khan was all about. Old Shere Khan really did throw a guy out of a ten-story window. That ain't no lie no matter how much Shere Khan denies it. Shere Khan has killed people and that's a fact that everybody 'round this way knows, even if they go 'round actin' like they don't. He put on a dry pair of shoes and found a spare key. He rifled in his drawer until he found a pair of sunglasses. He put them on and grinned to himself. He grabbed his gray fedora off a hat rack. He went back to his bedroom and stood over the carton of puppets for a moment. After deliberating, he pulled the wooden egg from the carton, put it under his arm. I know where I can leave this right now, he thought, and I'm gettin' rid of it right now. He went to his sister's room to check her again. She seemed asleep. He began to sing in a low voice:

When the moon is new
I always make a little wish or two
And when I want someone to tell them to, what do I do?
I page Miss Glory

She shifted a little on her side, breathing through the small circle shaped by her mouth. Good, she really is asleep, he thought. She'd be jumpin' otherwise because she really likes that dumb song. Where'd I learn that old-assed tune?

He crept to the door of the apartment and looked around the

room for a moment, as if he were trying to remember something. She'll be all right, he thought. I'll get back in an hour. He realized as he stood there that he never turned on a single light in the house during the whole time he was there. He had simply raised the shades to open the night into the living room and the kitchen. He never even turned on the bathroom light. He had washed the eggs in darkness but did not think that it was dark. Why did he walk around in the darkness? He would have said that he was afraid of the lightning. He had always been afraid of the lightning and his mother, when she was around, always turned out all the lights in the house and sat huddled with him and Gloria in darkness whenever they had thunderstorms. She taught him that fear. And he always remained afraid for a while after the storm ended. Is it safe to turn on the lights again, Mom? he would ask. Is it safe? The storms might come back. She would always tell him when it was safe again. He adjusted the egg under his arm, turned and slipped out the door, locking it behind him.

He ran down the endless flights of stairs, renewed with a mission, and out the front door of his building at the Absalom Jones Community Housing Projects. He turned to look behind. No one was there, only a wall covered in graffiti, an elaborate code of drug-dealing and gang warfare. Looking at the wall made him aware that he had been afraid for a long time, so long that he had forgotten that he had been afraid, had lived so uninterruptedly with fear; he felt for a moment unnerved. He wanted to go back into the apartment. The outside world was too much for him, overwhelming in its brutality. He swallowed and pushed the egg under his arm. It wasn't very big but it was awkward, almost as if it were making itself bigger and more difficult to hold than it should be. There was something about it that made it seem almost alive, more alive than the real eggs he had been hauling about for what felt like half the night.

It had stopped raining completely. The sky was beginning, in fact, cleared. The full moon was hazy through the clouds. There were still faint rumbles but the weather had calmed to such an extent that it was almost now a beautiful night. Just as he was walking across the basketball courts, which were well lit for a change, toward the street he heard someone call him from behind.

"PT, you shouldn't be keeping sleaze hours. I know nothing good happens before sunset, but it's gale force winds after five, and not everybody knows how to ride out the storms," a soft, slurred voice said, from near the front door, "Where's your mother?"

Prince turned only partly toward the speaker, shifting his body so that the person who spoke could see him only in profile.

"I'm lookin' for her, Mr. President," Prince recognized the voice, a bit relieved it wasn't someone else, "I mean, she was out lookin' for me and now I got to find her. You know how my mom is. I don't want her to get into any trouble." He started to say, "Especially with her expectin' and all," but he held fire. Everybody knew she was pregnant but it wasn't necessary for him to mention it to people as if it were a topic he wanted to discuss with them.

"The fuzz will want to freeze you. They do not serve youth but to be a chill on everything. Bad weather for outdoor mothers. Can't leave a handicapped girl like your sister in a crib with no crutches. Got to have some crutches for her." The voice was growing louder and a bit more slurred as if mysteriously energized.

Prince frowned. Shit, the old winehead wants to start giving lectures. Why don't he just take himself and that portable oxygen on up to his crib and mind his business. Like he really gives a good goddam about me or my mom or Gloria. Why don't he go play his tired old shit on the tenor saxophone or get a bottle of bourbon and leave me alone. What can he be playin' on an oxygen tank, anyway? How can that old fart even breathe? Prince was especially upset about the remark that he should know better than leaving Gloria alone. How would he know about anything? What's he talkin' about crutches for? She don't need no crutches. How the hell could she use crutches? Why don't he look after his own kids, if he got any?

"I'm sorry, Mr. President, but I got to be going. I don't have time to talk to you right now. Maybe tomorrow we can talk about some of those tunes you wanted to get together with me about. You know, 'I Surrender, Dear' and 'Honeysuckle Rose' and them blues tunes." Prince started walking away. He was thinking at the moment how he hated talking about music with Mr. President, how much he hated those old tunes, how much he hated blues. He's as bad as Mr. Mingus about that memory lane stuff, like music died when they got old. Those guys think their chord changes were the greatest ever made or something. Like there's something wrong with us for thinking their shit is old and tired now. Why can't them old guys just say they had their day and go shuffle off to the old folks' home with their portable oxygen? "Don't get tuberculosis," Brown once told him, "You know that kills more musicians than anything, tuberculosis. You can't breathe for shit and then you just finished playing music." He thought at the time that Brown was just talking crazy as he always does. I ain't heard of no musician dyin' of tuberculosis, not any more than anybody else. But he looked at Mr. President just then and thought, Maybe he got TB. Maybe that's why he needs the oxygen. Don't want that TB around me.

At just that moment, the egg slipped from his arm and crashed to the pavement. The noise startled Prince who was not even aware that the egg was slipping from his grasp. The fall was thunderous, a much louder noise than he expected it to make. He expected it to be smashed because it sounded, when it landed, as if it had splintered apart. It sounded, not as if it were hollow, but as if it were solid and extremely heavy. But when Prince looked down he saw the egg was unharmed. He picked it up, bracing himself for Mr. President asking him about it. How could you explain that he was out in the middle of night to get rid of this ridiculous thing? When he stooped to pick it up, fleetingly, an image passed before his eyes of Mr. President, of how he must have looked many years ago, as a young man, dressed in a strange yet dapper suit with a huge gold watch chain, his hair slicked back with pomade and gas and lye, a brown, handsome face, the golden tenor tilted sideways. Prince heard twelve bars exactly of Mr. President playing a song called "I Can't Get Started With You." Prince did not know how he even knew the title of the song but it seemed suddenly as if he simply knew, although he had never heard the song before or even heard of the song. It was as if, for a moment, Prince could hear and hear and hear, all the music that Mr. President had played, had wanted to play, had needed to play. Then, the image of the young Mr. President slipped the horn from his mouth, abruptly ending the tune, looked at Prince and said: "Time has come. Help us help you." And the image was gone. Prince shook his head for a moment, removed his sunglasses, and rubbed his eyes. He looked over to Mr. President, who simply stood there, staring at him.

"You getting ill?" Mr. President said, completely uninterested in the wooden egg, "You look cramped in a small space."

Prince was terrified almost beyond control of himself, when he

saw, through his sunglasses, across the basketball courts, the face of
the old drunken man carrying a battered saxophone case, slovenly in
his cheap, worn suit, a portable oxygen unit strapped around his
waist, his face cupped by the air hose. He had just come from playing
somewhere, for New Year's, for the dancers, probably in some strip
joint or something like that. Some old people who wanted to hear old
music or some drunks who weren't even paying attention to what he
was playing, Prince thought with bitterness. He's worse than
Gentleman Brown. At least Brown's got money and is making hip
records.* How can that old coot help me or how can I help him?
What had Prince seen or thought he had seen? Why did he have that
hallucination? He had never thought of Mr. President before, never
dreamed about him, never gave a thought to how Mr. President
might have looked as a young man. It frightened him to think that he
would now, that he even could, for he felt as if he were not in control
of his mind. What made it all the more frightening for Prince was the
idea that perhaps he was being told by someone or something to think
about what Mr. President had seen and he hardly wanted to entertain
the idea that the old man had seen anything but what someone like him
would be expected to have seen. And even more important was that
something or someone wanted him to think about what Mr. President
had *heard*. He looked at the egg curiously. Had it made him think about
Mr. President? Had it given him the vision, the unsettling image.

"I gotta go, Mr. President, I really do," Prince said in a voice that
sounded strange to him, jittery and high-pitched. He took off the
sunglasses and looked again at Mr. President. "I gotta go. I'll talk to
you later." He stuffed the sunglasses in his pocket and started running down the street.

"You young cats too much into being cool. Too much refrigera-
tion in this life. That's when that happened. When people got refrig-
erators and forgot how hard it is to keep something cold, except the
fuzz, them authority figures, ya dig? They know all the tricks for
freezing all the pipes," Mr. President called after him.

*Everyone should remember that Brown had written and produced a big hit last year for an adolescent girl with a
so-so voice named Gable entitled "What Would Billie Say?" with the refrain, "Have you ever wondered if things
really are any different today/Like, if she were at the mike, what would Billie Holiday say?" It was clever with a
nice beat and made Gable an overnight sensation who even got a movie deal. I told Brown he had a knack. "It's
bullshit," he growled. "But it's better than most of the other bullshit that's passing itself off for music these days."
—L. F. Haines

He's talkin' like the total loon he is, Prince thought, zigzagging across the street and up the block. He looked behind for a moment and saw no one. He began to walk down the street, past a barbershop, a small grocery store, a bar that had just closed. There were some people about, two men walking toward him, passing without noticing him at all, some people leaving the bar, but no one paid him any attention. He saw a sleeping man on a broken-down sofa as he passed a litter-strewn lot. The man had made a small roof of plastic and cardboard over the sofa, propped up by some crates, to keep the rain off but with little success. He and the sofa were soaked but the man slept on, peacefully. Prince crossed the street again, was walking toward a small storefront church next to a curio store.

He had not taken a half-dozen paces away from Dr. Ahmed's Shop of Curio Objects when, just as he was about to turn because he felt someone behind him, someone pushed him violently to the ground, and as he was falling, deftly snatched the egg from his arm. Prince scraped his face against the wet pavement, hit his head so hard that for a moment he was dizzy. But everything cleared quickly. He had used his arms to slow his fall and both his wrists hurt. His hat fell and drifted in a small puddle. He gathered himself on all fours, pushed himself back and squatted on his heels for a moment. His clothes had been dampened by the wet ground. He felt in his pocket for his sunglasses and realized they had broken in the fall. Damn, those shades cost good money, too, he thought disgustedly. Then, he exhaled deeply, got to his feet and retrieved his fedora. He turned, seeing nothing but a deserted street, empty. He was not surprised that whoever took the egg had disappeared so quickly, that the robbery had, in fact, happened so quickly. People sense you got something of value in two seconds and they're on you before you turn a corner, he thought. It's like getting struck by lightning when you think you got a clear day. There was no point in looking for someone. There were a lot of nooks and crannies in the neighborhood through which one could hide from sight. Besides, Prince had no desire to follow his assailant. I'm not getting jacked up over that thing. Let whoever took it, have it. They didn't kill me and I'm not gonna push my luck. As long as Shere Khan don't know I ever had it, then I'm cool. And even if he does find out, I'll just say I was bringing the egg to him when I got rolled. Maybe whoever took it knew what they were looking for, was looking for it. I don't know how they could have known I had it or would be out with it now, but information in this neighborhood travels fast and odd, and in totally messed-up versions or versions that get people messed up or messed over. Probably some dumb junkie took it thinking it had some dope in it. He shook his head, brushed off his fedora. The brim was wet but he adjusted it on his head. He wiped his bruised palms on his water-stained trousers. He began to walk down the street, the opposite way of his assailant, looking for his mother. As he walked, he rained pieces of his broken sunglasses like dark sprinkles on the pavement, like Hansel dropping pebbles in the moonlight. He was trembling.

PERMISSIONS AND CREDITS

NOVEL EXCERPTS

From *Dark Reflections* by Samuel R. Delany. Published by Carroll & Graf, 2007. Copyright © 2007 by Samuel R. Delany. Excerpt reprinted with permission of Running Press/Carroll & Graf, a member of Perseus Books Group.

From *The Great Negro Plot* by Mat Johnson. Published by Bloomsbury, 2007. Copyright © 2007 by Mat Johnson. Excerpt used with permission of the author.

"GhettoNerd at the End of the World 1974–1987" from *The Brief Wondrous Life of Oscar Wao* by Junot Díaz. Copyright © 2007 by Junot Díaz. Used by permission of Riverhead Books, an imprint of Penguin Group (USA) Inc.

From *Man Gone Down* by Michael Thomas. Published by Black Cat, New York, 2007. Copyright © 2007 by Michael Thomas. Excerpt reprinted by permission of Grove/Atlantic, Inc.

YOUNG ADULT FICTION

Excerpt from *Feathers* by Jacqueline Woodson. Copyright © 2007 by Jacqueline Woodson. Used with permission of G. P. Putnam's Sons, a division of Penguin Young Readers Group, a member of Penguin Group (USA) Inc., 345 Hudson St., New York, NY 10014. All rights reserved.

Excerpt from *Harlem Summer* by Walter Dean Myers. Published by Scholastic Inc./Scholastic Press, 2007. Copyright © 2007 by Walter Dean Myers. Excerpt reprinted by permission of Scholastic Inc.

Excerpt from *Elijah of Buxton* by Christopher Paul Curtis. Published by Scholastic Inc./Scholastic Press, 2007. Copyright © 2007 by Christopher Paul Curtis. Excerpt reprinted by permission of Scholastic Inc.

Excerpt from *Up for It: A Tale of the Underground* by L. F. Haines. Copyright © 2009 by L. F. Haines. Printed with permission of the author.

ABOUT THE EDITORS

GERALD EARLY is a noted essayist and American culture critic. A professor of English, African and African American Studies, and American Culture Studies at Washington University in St. Louis, Early is the author of several books, including *The Culture of Bruising: Essays on Prizefighting, Literature, and Modern American Culture*, which won the 1994 National Book Critics Circle Award for criticism, and *This Is Where I Came In: Black America in the 1960s*. He is also editor of numerous volumes, including *The Muhammad Ali Reader* and *The Sammy Davis, Jr. Reader*. He served as a consultant on four of Ken Burns's documentary films, *Baseball, Jazz, Unforgivable Blackness: The Rise and Fall of Jack Johnson*, and *The War*, and appeared in the first three as an on-air analyst.

E. LYNN HARRIS is a nine-time *New York Times* bestselling author. His work includes the memoir *What Becomes of the Brokenhearted* and the novels *A Love of My Own, Just as I Am, Any Way the Wind Blows* (all three of which were named Novel of the Year by the BlackBoard African-American Bestsellers), *I Say a Little Prayer, If This World Were Mine* (which won the James Baldwin Award for Literary Excellence), and the classic *Invisible Life*. His latest book is *Just Too Good to Be True*.

To view the contributors' bios, visit www.bantamdell.com.

ALSO IN BOOKSTORES

Best african american 2009 essays

GERALD EARLY, SERIES EDITOR

DEBRA J. DICKERSON, GUEST EDITOR